FALL FROM THE MOON

A BÁNALFAR NOVEL

C.S. HALE

FALL FROM THE MOON
By C.S. Hale

Edited by C.J. Redwine at manuscriptcritiques.com
Jody Wallace at www.jodywallace.com
And Jessica Nelson at Indie Books Gone Wild www.ibgw.net
Interior design by Gaynor Smith also of Indie Books Gone Wild
Cover design by Melissa Stevens at www.theillustratedauthor.net

Published in the United States of America

ACKNOWLEDGEMENTS

It takes a village to create a book.

To my family who for years has had to put up with my disappearing to play with my imaginary friends — Thank you for your patience and understanding.

To Bethany — I don't know what I would have done without all your encouragement over the years. I've loved watching you grow and am so thankful that I now have you to help guide me. Thank you!

To Maureen, Megan, and Laurie — Thank you for being my springboard and wading through the infant versions.

To C.J. — Thank you for all of your support and encouragement over the years. You have made me a better writer and kept me writing.

To the gals at Eastside RWA — Thank you for providing me with a circle of fellow writers. You provide me with a much needed refuge.

To my Nashville writing tribe — Writing is usually a solitary endeavor. Even though we are miles away, all of you are just an internet connection away. You support me in more ways than you can know.

For my Dad and the Ostby Clan

With storytellers on both sides of my family,
how could I end up anything else?

CHAPTER 1

My hand weighed heavy on the door frame. Clouds of steam filled the air in front of me as my breath condensed in the chilled air of the compartment. I bit my lip, tasting blood as I willed the tears filling my eyes not to fall. My gaze traced the rise and fall of the sheets that covered what remained of the *Cove*'s crew. Was it better or worse that I had needed to be the undertaker for only the last five? Well, that Bari and I had.

"Goodbye, Bari," I whispered and hit the switch. The storage bay grew dark as the compartment's lights went out and the door slid shut with a hiss.

My white protective suit rustled as I made my way back to the rack. I hung it up next to the other four and forced my feet down the passageways, away from all the death. Every step snipped at the ties of community that had bound us together until my feet felt as though they walked on glass.

I entered the bridge and took a seat at the control panel. Lights still flashed, alerting all observers that the ship had "malfunctioned." That was an understatement for the massive explosion that had taken out the engines.

It was supposed to have been a standard run to Miseruha. Pick up the load of Rovar silk and return to Earth. Until the hyperdrive developed some problem that I never understood, but then I'm the protocol specialist, not the engineer. I'm just supposed to make sure negotiations are successful, not actually get us there. Which we didn't.

Zhou pulled us out of hyperspeed so the whole engine wouldn't blow. Dave got to work on fixing the plasma mechanism that fuels the hyperdrive. But that was when things went from bad to worse.

I was in my quarters studying up on the customs of the Addunka for our next trip. Dave had some problem. Zhou went to help with the repairs. The mechanism sprang a leak. Mass panic ensued that didn't include me because I am the nemesis of anything mechanical. Other than a tablet, anything that needs to be turned or tightened or adjusted breaks if I'm involved. Dave had even broadcast over the intercom, "Hey, Astrid! Have you been messing with the compressors?" Yeah, I'm not that insane.

So, there I was, safely tucked up in my cabin, when plasma flooded three-quarters of the ship. You do not want to see what happens to flesh after it's been exposed to plasma. There wasn't much left of Dave and Zhou. Doc rushed in to try and patch up the rest of the crew who had been exposed. Too soon, it turned out, for the leftover vapor ate his lungs over the course of three days. One by one they slowly died. Katrina, Addison, Jerra, and the rest of my companions. One by one they were covered with shrouds and placed in the storage bay that Bari had set to "cool." One by one, until it was just me and Bari in the protective suits, transferring our friends to their temporary grave.

And then it was just me. For Bari had also tried to help — they all had — and exposed himself to the plasma while I spent the first twenty-four hours in my room eating from the replicator and researching. I now knew more than I wanted to about plasma exposure and the local star system. And enough about the big blue planet we were currently orbiting to add weight to my fervent prayers that rescue would come. Medieval Earth level of development according to the first line of the scant file — if anyone bothered to read beyond the *Do Not Contact!* that scrolled across the screen in flashing red letters.

The letters had pulsed with the same ominous rhythm as the engine warning light on the panel now before me. I took off my jacket and tossed it, hiding the sensor from view. Putting my feet on the edge of the control panel, I rested my chin on my knees and willed the comm panel to spring to life. After eight days of distress calls, someone should have come to our rescue. When my feet fell asleep and I could no longer stand the tingly sensation, I transferred the comm link to my room. How many more days would I be forced to remain in this dying ship full of my dead friends?

Beep. Beep. Beep. Beep.

I jerked awake. But it wasn't the comm panel making the noise. Dave had silenced the dulcet voice that broadcast warnings throughout the ship shortly after the mechanism had sprung a leak, but an alert tone sounded every time a new light came on. I jogged down to the bridge and shoved my jacket off the panel. It had been two days since I'd covered the flashing light.

My heart did a free fall before slamming back into my chest. I had just ripped off the ship's own shroud — *System failure detected. 20 hours of power before total failure.*

I stared at the words, and my lips began a new prayer. My hands shook as I checked the comm panel. Then checked it again. Fingers

slipping on the keys, I sent out yet another distress call. Not that it would do any good. My time had run out.

While the *Palmas Cove* had several escape pods, they wouldn't get me very far. An escape pod couldn't fly me out of the system. People who haven't been to space assume that escape pods are miniature ships, but they're not. They're for intra-system travel only. An escape pod will get you to whatever planet you're circling above because the number one rule in space travel, as the Shororato like to remind us at every opportunity, is that you only travel to approved systems. Oh sure, there's always some numbskull that likes to buzz developing planets, like the UFO boys back in Earth's history, but the Shororato always track you down and then it's a lifetime in a stark white cell where you begin to curse the fact that they've outlawed the death penalty. Zhao had pulled us out of hyperspeed into the nearest star system without checking the system's status. He hadn't cared at the time.

I went to the window and stared down at the planet. Not unlike so many others in the galaxy, including my home planet of Earth, Teridun Four was a patchwork of white clouds, blue oceans, and greeny-brown continents, all clues to the life that it teemed with. I chewed on my lip. I also couldn't leave the *Palmas Cove* here in orbit. Agçay Enterprises would be responsible if someone from the planet spotted the floating crypt the ship had become. The Shororato might even come after my family, since the ship's log would show that, as the last remaining crew member, I had become responsible for its fate.

I tore myself away from the view, my speed increasing with every step, as if I could somehow outrun the truth. The bottle of Nilheim whiskey sat on the galley table where Bari and I had left it. I pulled the stopper and swigged back a large mouthful. The

cheeriness of the bright, herbaceous liquid was in stark contrast to the prickly feeling of Death standing behind me complete with black cloak and scythe.

Which death do you want, Astrid?

There was only one way to ensure that no one from the surface spotted the *Cove*. I would need to send it into the sun. I sucked back another mouthful. My throat tightened, rebelling against the burn.

I slowly made my way back to the bridge, the bottle still clenched in my hand. I stared at the planet, weighing my options.

Which death, Astrid? the voice in my head asked again.

Finish the bottle, take a tranquilizer, and burn with the ship? A slow, maddening death in a Shororato prison if I broke the law and landed on a forbidden planet? A more painful death if the inhabitants decided I was a sorceress and disposed of me in a bonfire?

But the inhabitants could also be welcoming. The Maya on Earth had been.

Until the Shororato had discovered the visitors.

I used another swallow to force back the bile that rose as the memory of the "informational" video replayed in my head — the wild eyes that were somehow haunted and vacant at the same time, the ravings of the now lunatic prisoners as they beat their heads against the stark white walls. Required viewing for everyone over the age of fourteen the first time they left their home planet.

I went to the computer and pulled up the file on Teridun Four again but, of course, there was nothing new — just the warning and the development level. My mental file flicked open and offered me a wealth of information I didn't really want. I've always been a history buff, which made my foray into customs and then interstellar customs a no-brainer, and I know the medieval history of more than one planet. During that time period on Jimal Four, women

were viewed almost like gods. On Lykka, we were equal partners. But medieval times were not good for women on Earth. They were property. And even smart, extraordinary women like Eleanor of Aquitaine had it rough. Which, in my opinion, made her even more extraordinary that she was able to become extraordinary. But it was bad because I knew, I KNEW, how careful women had to be during that time, and all the things that could happen to them, and I really didn't want to go there, in so many ways.

I'm good, I'm *really* good, at customs and protocol and knowing the right thing to do or say. My mother used to say that I became a protocol specialist because a career as an actress would have been too confining. But I'm good at my job because when it's all over, I get to be me — a wise-cracking, somewhat klutzy, smartass — and I knew that if I set foot on that planet, I'd never get to be me again.

CHAPTER 2

Merchant Vessel Palmas Cove *— Final Transmission. Crew dead. Have contracted plasma poisoning. Distress calls have gone unanswered. Since Teridun 4 is a 'no contact' world, am setting autopilot and plotting coordinates for the sun.*

Protocol Specialist Astrid Carr

I touched "send" and sat back, pressing the heels of my hands against my eyes. The message was a load of crap. After having spent a full day drinking and wandering the ship, wrestling with the decision, my desire to survive overcame my sense of duty. I had no intention of turning myself into ash. The transmission was a safety measure in case the Shororato finally came looking.

I scrounged through Zhou's luxurious — by freighter standards — captain's cabin until I found the bottle of Aurielian wine I knew was stashed there (forty-thousand Earth credits a bottle). I put on my favorite outfit, tried not to think about it being the last time anyone would wear it, and dragged myself to the bridge.

I gave myself a funeral. I figured it was fitting since a) everyone was going to think I'd contracted plasma poisoning and had burned up in the sun as a final act of heroism, and b) I wouldn't be me anymore. Though I'd created more personas than I can count in my nine years as a protocol specialist, at the end of the day, at the end of the trip, I got to take the mask off and just be me. The Astrid Carr who had grown up on Earth and traveled the stars would be dead. I couldn't even imagine the persona I'd need to create to survive on the planet. I'd have to take my cue from the inhabitants.

The stars stretched out like a carpet of diamonds before the windows. Teridun Four was a large, blue, and white marble to my right, its strange, red moon a glowing orb off to my left. Somewhere out there in that sprinkling of tiny lights was my sun. On the third planet were my parents, my brother Finn, his wife Amy, my nephew Henry, and my niece Iris. At some point, they'd repeat this with many more tears and much less alcohol. It was not the way I'd want to go out, and I counted myself lucky that I was at least still around to do it right.

I broke the seal on the bottle of wine, chugged back about a quarter of it, and lifted it in toast.

"We are gathered here to remember Astrid Gabriella Carr …"

When I was done, I left the remaining wine tucked up on Zhou's seat along with the origami cranes that I'd made for each of the crew. It was the most I could do to give them the funeral I'd just given myself. There were too many things that still needed to be finished before my journey to the surface and being blinded by tears wouldn't help the process. I looked around one last time. I had already prepared them for their journey to the afterlife. They each had a crane to carry their soul to paradise, and they were getting the funeral my Viking ancestors would have had — taking their ship and setting it aflame. A king couldn't have asked for a better funeral, so I tried to ignore the tiny voice that whispered it was all such a waste.

A strange thing happened when the people on Earth learned that we were not, in fact, alone in the universe. Besides the conflicting emotions of horror that there were others who were more technologically advanced than us and joy that, once again, whole new worlds were available for us to explore, another response, a psychological one, occurred that no one saw coming. Being human — Earth human — was no longer enough. Even being Chinese or Russian or American wasn't enough. As the ability to leave the solar system finally became possible, humanity clung to our planet. Oh, there were some who couldn't wait to shake the dust of Earth and our system colonies off and leave, but most people dug in to our world, curling their hearts and minds into the soil, and began searching for just how long they'd been there.

It was a genealogist's dream. Fortunes were made as eleven billion people began to research where they had come from. Two hundred years later, the practice hadn't died out though the fervor had, for the most part, abated. It did result in my parents being proud of our heritage and in my brother Finn wanting to recapture the glory of the past, for which I was now grateful. Finn had moved to Edinburgh, found a lovely Scottish lass, and been married in a full Gaelic ceremony. I'd skipped the plaid and had commissioned a green dress that was fitted all the way to my hips where it flared out into full, long skirts. The sleeves, likewise, were long and bell-shaped. It didn't scream "Highlands" and currently hung in the closet in my quarters. While I would have looked ridiculous in it on Earth, there were places in the galaxy where formal dress was expected. And so, I would not be putting down on the planet clad in a skin-tight pair of pants and a form-hugging shirt.

There was only one other thing I'd be taking with me, not that anyone would know. The syringe was eight-inches long, the needle an inch and a half, and it hurt like hell when I jabbed it into my thigh. The extra dose of repbots that flowed in from it, finding their way into my bloodstream, would protect me from the alien viruses that I had no immunity to and would be vigilant to any sign that I was developing allergies to substances in the air, water, or food.

Counting to ten was difficult, but it wasn't the searing pain in my leg that distracted me from my task of "One … two … three …" It was the ghost of Doc. And Zhou. And Bari. And the twenty other members of our contingent. Katrina, whose face had melted off because she couldn't keep from embracing Dave's corpse when it was finally recovered. Addison, whose lungs eventually brought up blood because she stayed to help Doc, even though she knew what the end would be.

"Seven … eight …" And here I was — the lone survivor — because I'd stayed tucked up, nice and safe, until the danger had passed. I might have been named after the daughter of a Viking king, but sitting there, injecting the microscopic robots that could save my life into my leg, I had to confront the fact that the only reason I'd survived was because I was a coward. Yes, it was better that I wasn't accompanying my comrades on their journey to the sun. They deserved glory. I deserved everything that awaited me below.

I programmed the coordinates of a wide, open plain that reminded me of the Mongolian steppes as the landing site. Away from civilization, but not too far. The computer had told me there were towns in the foothills to the east and more in the wooded area to the west. I supposed that someone would see the falling "star"

and come investigate. I would have. But I doubted my reception would be what I would have given myself. Maybe it was lucky the escape pod had no self-destruct mechanism. The technology would be proof I wasn't a witch or something, but it would announce that I was an alien.

The *Palmas Cove* had already begun its course toward the sun when I pushed the button that detached the tiny, two-seat pod from the ship. I watched the *Cove* glide away between me and Teridun's blood-red moon, the color a reminder of the enormous price paid, before it headed toward the furnace of the sun.

Below me, Teridun Four was not so different in appearance from Earth — clouds, seas, continents — but I knew enough about the galaxy to understand that anything could await me.

It was ironic. I was still gazing at my grave. No one would know I was there. Whatever else happened, the planet before me would be my last. Cremated, buried, left above to be torn apart by animals, I was looking at my final resting place.

A loud, insistent beeping from the control panel cut through my macabre thoughts. The pod began to shake violently. Everything I looked at was nothing but a blur. I reached out a hand, desperately trying to pull the scrolling message into focus, but my hand kept closing around nothing. Or worse, slamming into the panel.

Wham!

My ears rang from the impact. Something had hit the pod, but then the shaking became spinning and the ground rushed up, filling the window. I closed my eyes, held onto the seat, and prayed.

Don't let me die. Don't let me die. Don't —

CHAPTER 3

The world still spun. A roaring like the ocean, only magnified, filled my ears. But instead of white and blue, the world was now green and blue. The kaleidoscope of images shifted until they became something that looked like hills, but I couldn't make them stay still. My head pounded, vibrated with a roar I could feel even in my tear ducts. I turned, searching for the walls that should have enclosed me, and fell to my knees. Long grass tickled my hands.

Time became a wash of blurred forms, heat, foreign yet familiar smells, and swirling grass. Almost like a night in Tokyo where I'd walked into a club and the rest of the evening dissolved into nothing more than lights and disjointed images.

But there was no traffic here. Just grass. And a pressure on my upper arm. I tore my gaze away from the wavy, green blur and stared at my arm, willing my eyes to focus on whatever was causing the discomfort.

"Tay! Tay! Mood nee do lait." A baritone voice wormed its way through the roaring.

The shifting images began to settle. Long blond hair swung around a thin, handsome face that was not that foreign, though something seemed off. Blue eyes stared back at me. *Humanoid.*

The man gently pulled on my arm again. A flash of silver caused my eyes to water. Armor. He was wearing armor. *"Mood nee do lait!"* His voice was more insistent this time.

I could practically feel the thrum in my head as my language chip started its decoding program. It had ninety-thousand languages stored on it, but this one was new. Not surprising, since the planet was off limits. It would only take a few hours, if the people around me continued speaking, and I would not only begin to understand their language but speak it. A necessity for a customs specialist and essential for my survival here.

The analyst part of my brain finally kicked in. I knew that I'd hit my head — hard — at some point during the crash. The blurred vision and ringing in my ears were proof of that. And a mental whirring began as my ingrained protocol process kicked in. *Assess.*

A cluster of men behind Blondie possessed similar hair and green robes over articulated armor, though they were wearing helmets. Some were astride, others standing and holding reins to creatures that looked like a cross between horses and deer. *Knights. Security.*

I looked again from the hand around my arm to its owner's face. *Concern. Urgency.* I blinked as a wave of pain accompanied the analysis.

"Cortan!" one of the other men shouted. Blondie turned his attention to something behind me. His hand tightened on my arm.

I followed his gaze. A line of men on horseback appeared over the ridge of one of the rolling hills in the grassy sea and drew to a standstill. They were darker, more wiry than the ones now with me.

Appearances can be deceiving. It's one of the tenets of customs and diplomacy. A stabbing pain shot between my eyes. It was too

soon to do this. The repbots needed more time to work on whatever damage had occurred to my brain.

"Mood nee do lait."

Just because someone finds you first doesn't mean you should go with them. Sometimes "the first" can be the death of you.

Blondie sighed heavily. Panic crept through my belly. Would he throw me over his shoulder and carry me off? The sound of scraping metal filled the air as I hesitated.

"Cortan!"

A horse on the hill stamped impatiently. The cloak of its rider flared around him with the motion. My stomach pitched. Something wasn't right with the men on the hill. My brain scrambled to process the information but a wave of pain shut it down. I took a step toward Blondie.

He scooped me up and tossed me on the back of one of the strange horses before swinging up behind me. One arm clamped me against his chest, the other grabbed the reins. Blondie clucked to the horse and we thundered off, his men moving to protect a cart I now noticed next to my escape pod. Other men with ropes were attempting to hoist it onto the cart.

"Cosul, mo banorisa. Drea nigh dull," he said in my ear. The whir in my head caused my eyes to water. Of course, that also could have been the wind streaming by my face as the horse covered the grassy sea in massive strides.

I'm going to be sick, I thought, just before I passed out.

A gentle rocking motion matched the throb that pulsed through my head with every heartbeat, the pain somewhat mitigated by the cool air that brushed my face.

"Are you sure she's alive, Heymond?"

Rescued. We'd finally been rescued. I lifted my head.

"Welcome back, princess."

My breath caught. I opened my eyes then gulped back a scream. I wasn't in my bunk on the *Palmas Cove* fighting off the mother of all hangovers. Our distress call hadn't been answered. The nightmare had been real. The rocking motion was the stupid horse, and I was still in Blondie's arms.

Only now he'd been joined by a company of men. And I understood them. I must have been out for hours, long enough that the chip had decoded whatever language Blondie and the others spoke.

"Where are we going?" I asked.

"To the castle. Valemar is expecting you."

Expecting. That didn't sound good.

I kept silent and took in my surroundings. The road wound through a wood of tall, ancient trees. At least, I took them to be ancient from the girth of their trunks and the open space around them. They had long since crowded out any competition except for some kind of bracken that dotted the forest floor wherever sunlight reached through the leaves. The air had the unmistakable scent of chlorophyll, and the horses' hooves made a dull clomping on the earth.

And what strange horses they were. The shape of their heads was like the deer on Earth, with bumps that made me wonder if someone had cut off their horns. But they were bulky, with tails and manes like horses, and solid, not cloven, hooves.

The men were not that strange, though all of them looked like their hair had never seen a barber even if their faces had. Not a whisker among them, and all had long, straight hair like Blondie.

Which I needed to stop calling him. Rule number two: *Always get their names.*

I'd developed a list of rules for myself when I first began at Agçay Enterprises. Customs, protocol, and politics can throw you into the deep end, as I quickly learned. Hence rule number one: *Things are never what they seem.* When you learn things the hard way, you want to remember them. Especially if it's not *you* who had to learn that lesson.

I mentally pulled up my work persona and put it on. For the foreseeable future, there would be no Astrid Carr, only Protocol Specialist Carr. A piece of armor to match the ones the men wore. Even if mine was weak. The pounding in my head kept drumming out my thoughts.

"Who is Valemar?" I asked.

There was a chuckle. "Our king, my princess."

I tried very hard to keep my body from tensing. It was either a good thing that I was on my way to the highest authority or it was very bad. And it was the second time that Blondie had called me "princess."

Banorisa — princess, the chip supplied. So third time. It was a puzzle I was willing to let slide for the moment. "And you are?"

"Heymond, captain of the King's Guard."

There were a million questions I wanted to ask, but rule number seven — *Don't ask about what you should already know* — tied my tongue. *How far have we come? What are you doing with my ship? Why is your king expecting me?*

The last one was the most troubling. The answer could have been simple. Someone had ridden ahead and notified the castle of today's strange events and, hence, I was expected. But the hairs on my arms and the back of my neck had lifted, and rule number

thirteen was *Don't ignore your gut*, and I was pretty sure my gut and my hair were connected.

I tamped down the thought as my stomach rolled and pain stabbed between my eyes. I was in no condition to do this. I'd keep my mouth shut and my ears open and just try to survive the next twenty-four hours. Or however long their day was.

The road meandered through stretches of woodland and farms. The place reminded me of Nottinghamshire in England. The area had a lushness to it. Farms were tidy, full of crops and healthy-looking livestock. The woods were wild but inviting.

Heymond skirted around the small towns that we encountered, so I was not surprised when he took us around a larger one. We forded a river within sight of the town then followed the river on the bank opposite it. The castle that came into view was magnificent, with towers and ramparts. Stained glass glittered in many of the windows.

The flag waving in the breeze was quartered blue and green. A crowned, bearded, blue creature with a tail like a fish sat in one green field with a green, stag-like animal in a rampart, upright fighting position, on the blue beneath.

Heymond halted his horse-like creature near a small boat tied up on the bank of the river. The hairs on my arms rose again. The Tower of London has a watergate. Known as the Traitor's Gate, it was the entrance used by prisoners in the castle's ancient past. The passageway had the benefit of forcing new arrivals to view the piked heads of recently executed prisoners as they passed under London Bridge. A decoration I was glad to find missing here. They were, however, taking me in the backdoor, and the significance of the gesture was not lost on me.

Heymond dismounted and helped me slide off. He led me to the waiting boat. I hesitated before I took the boatman's hand.

"And you're bringing me in the back way, why?" I asked, trying for the regal tone of a princess.

"Too many eyes, my princess. There are those who won't be happy you're here." Heymond bowed slightly and extended his hand. I gave him a hard look but said nothing. That didn't keep me from cursing the truth of rule number five: *There's always intrigue.*

I took the hands offered me as I stepped into the boat, then held back a gasp as the boatman's hair swung forward and revealed his ears, something that had been hidden beneath the helmets of the others. They were curved ears, something between an elf and a wolf. The erect ears of a predator.

I allowed myself a gulp as I stepped toward the seat, my back to the others. The pounding in my head renewed as my heart kicked into readiness to fight or flee. Neither of which was an option. I balanced myself on the seat, thinking of a question I could ask, just to get a chance to see their teeth. Heymond and his men had talked off and on for hours, but I hadn't cared. Hadn't paid attention. Not that the chances were great that they'd actually eat me. Still, I'd had a close call once on Peryglis Seven, and it was best to be prepared. Even if it was being prepared to die.

"Do I need to worry about the eyes *inside* the castle?" I asked imperiously.

Heymond chuckled. His teeth were flat like mine. "No, my princess. We'll have eyes on them."

There were few eyes to see me as we made our way from the watergate. The passageways twisted back and forth upon themselves. We went up a few sets of stairs, and then we were in a grand hallway

that I knew would lead to the throne room. Glances lingered on me and heads turned to whisper, but there were no shocked looks on the faces we passed.

The throne room, however, was surprisingly empty. The man who rose from the throne as we entered was tall, even taller than Heymond. His long hair was white-blond, a perfect backdrop to his crown of leafy gold branches interlaced with rolling silver waves and studded with blue and green stones. His long green robes glittered with an iridescence. The king's expression briefly showed surprise before it was covered by a mask of graciousness. I'd met his type before. Handsome. Proud. Lethal.

His eyes flicked toward a woman lingering by a side door. Deep red hair flowed to her waist, the darkest red I'd ever seen that didn't come out of a bottle, almost matching her robes. She gave him a barely perceptible nod. I swallowed dryly as every warning bell in my system went off.

Heymond bowed his head. "Raislos is aware."

"And the craft?" A voice like a polished stone flowed from the king's perfect lips. It was smooth yet ungiving and nestled against me like the heated stones of an Altraxan massage. I wanted more.

"On its way."

Heymond's words broke through my distraction, and I realized they were talking about the escape pod. How long had I been out there, wandering incoherently? If they'd seen my fall to earth, it still would have taken hours to mount the retrieval.

The king gave a nod, and Heymond turned to leave. The look he shot me was inscrutable. The king made a tiny gesture of dismissal, and the red-haired woman melted away through the door leaving the two of us alone.

"Astrid Carr at your service," I said.

The king's mouth curled into a thin smile. "I hope to be of yours, my princess, for I fear we have a problem."

"Oh?" I asked, pasting my "curious" smile on my face.

The king wandered over to a small table and poured a glass of what looked to be wine. "The steppe where you landed is … disputed territory, and the Cordair are not as accommodating as we are." My mind flashed back to the appearance of the men on the ridge. I blinked back a shooting pain. There was something about them I should know. "And as you have chosen to seek refuge with us," the king continued, "I thought I should make you aware of what you're facing."

He extended the glass of wine to me which I declined with a shake of my head. A true smile crossed his face with a huff of laughter then he brought the glass to his lips and drank. "There. It's not doctored in any way. You're welcome to this one, or I could pour you another. No way to guarantee there's nothing in the other glass, though." An eyebrow arched. He'd taken my measure surprisingly quick.

"Maybe later. And since I've introduced myself, perhaps you'd be willing to let me know whom I'm addressing. Your Majesty," I added.

"No?" he said, referring to the wine and drank before replying. "I'm Valemar Dönal Carbrev, King of Bánalfar and the Lian Isles." He poured wine into another glass and held it out to me. "You're going to need this." I hesitated then took it from him. The glass was paper-thin and filled with a yellow wine that looked and smelled like a bright summer day. "I don't think you're the fainting sort, but still …"

"No," I said, and drew up the invisible armor I'd forged from nine years of dealing with nearly every type of intrigue imaginable. I flashed him an inscrutable smile. "I'm not the fainting type."

"Hmm." His lips turned up in amusement before he continued. "Tomorrow Raislos of the Cordair will appear on my doorstep and claim you and your ship as his property."

I was barely conscious of bringing the wine to my lips before I swallowed. Valemar's eyes danced with amusement. He picked up the carafe and brought it forward. "There's only one thing that will stop him from claiming you."

I kept my gaze on the wine flowing into my half-empty glass. "And that is?"

"If you're my wife."

CHAPTER 4

The sound of breaking glass filled my ears. Strong fingers closed over mine. "I think I need to sit down," I said weakly. My knees shook and threatened to collapse beneath me. As the only seat in the room was the throne, I allowed Valemar to steer me through the side door. It swung shut with a heavy thud, closing us in.

He pulled out one of the chairs from around the large table. *Council chambers,* my brain automatically supplied, clued in by the dispatch box, writing paraphernalia, and maps scattered across the table. The red-haired woman had thankfully vanished.

I squinched my eyes closed and tried to wade through the military tattoo of pain drumming in my skull. "I must have hit my head harder than I thought." The words were out before I could stop them.

Valemar's hand settled on my head. "May I?" I opened my eyes to find concern in his and gave a small nod. His fingers were gentle in their probing and soon settled over a knot high above my left ear. He curled a finger under my chin, gently raised it, and searched my eyes.

Blue. His eyes were the blue of a Caribbean sea and, for a moment, my soul swam in them.

"Your pupils look fine but that is a nasty knot on your head. Have you lost track of time?"

"Yes," I answered, having no clue just how much. I caught a flash of panic on his face. His lips pursed. "Don't worry," I said before he could speak. "If I haven't already lapsed into a coma, it's not likely to kill me." Another twenty-four hours and the repbots should have finished their repairs.

One eyebrow rose. "Medical training?" he asked.

"Not really." I didn't want to have to explain my invisible helpers. I smiled. "I'm just made of sterner stuff."

He walked to the other end of the table. *Smart,* I thought. *Giving me his back so I can't read his face.*

He placed a hand on the dispatch box. "That should help you make your decision then." There was a wry smile on his face when he turned back around. "If death ... or a coma isn't in your future, then you'll need to decide if you want to become Cordair property or my wife."

I swallowed heavily. "Hopefully, there's option three — let me leave this place."

Valemar moved to stand behind the ornately carved chair at the head of the table. "I'm afraid not. We have a treaty that technically places your arrival here within Cordair lands. Raislos would be well within his rights to claim you. I'd risk open warfare if I didn't return you. I'm not willing to put the lives of my people in jeopardy for a stranger. But for my wife ..."

There were rare times when I wished I'd had the ocular sensor implanted when I'd had the language chip done. Lies flash orange. Helpful, unless the sensor fails and burns out the retina. I had thought it unnecessary as I usually I read faces very well. I knew Valemar was not telling me something. The sensor would have let me know which part was a lie.

"You are the king. Why would you want a stranger for a wife?"

His eyebrows raised a fraction of an inch before the mask of graciousness returned. "But you are a princess, are you not?"

"Am I?"

His eyes turned cold, and again I got the sense of lethal. "You are the king's daughter, are you not?"

Despite the fact my gut was telling me this wasn't good, or maybe because of it, three hundred years of Viking kings rose up in me. I might not be the Astrid Trygvesdtr I was named for, but I chose that moment to claim my heritage.

"I am."

The danger faded from his eyes. The trace of a laugh played on his lips. "And whom do kings' daughters marry?"

"Whomever they chose?" I asked, feigning innocence. A deep laugh burst from Valemar. "What?" I asked, keeping up the charade.

"I was afraid you'd be lacking in fire. Though, of course, being from the moon how could you not?"

One piece clicked into place. He thought I'd fallen from the moon, their blood-red moon. I bit back an exclamation as another piece clicked into place. The red-haired woman. She had to be a priestess of some sort. Valemar had sought confirmation from her that I was what he thought I was. Clearly, I was not what he had expected.

The humor faded from his eyes. "Raislos will not respect you. The Cordair have spent too many millennia down in their mines. They've left behind the light and worship the dark things that lurk there. Mother Moon has become nothing more than the source of

blood to feed it." The hairs on my arms rose. Valemar's next words confirmed my fears. "Should he think that Oluendi requires the blood of the moon, I'm sure he'd hand over his property."

A cold chill settled around my heart. Option one was now off the table. There was, apparently, no option three. Which only left option two.

Valemar fell silent as I deliberated — the mark of a skilled negotiator. I certainly wasn't going to choose possible death.

But that wasn't why you chose to go with Heymond.

Though Valemar didn't know it, that first impression I'd had was important — to him, to me. I just wished I could wade through the discord and figure out why.

"What concerns you?" he asked. My thoughts must have shown on my face.

"Something I've forgotten," I said, honestly. "But no matter. I'm sure it will come." I gave my head a small shake. "So you've provided me reasons why I should marry you. Why should you marry me?"

For the first time, I saw gentleness fill his proud face. "For it is my duty, my princess."

In the end, I gave my consent. What choice did I have, really? Two good reasons to marry. The only reason not to — that I'd met my husband-to-be only moments before. If I'd had any doubt about the planet's development level that was the kicker. Earth and other places, you'll still find arranged marriages. But most people want to choose whom to love, not hope it will come. But then, arranged marriages aren't for love. They are for the creation of families and the tying together of similar interests. Or business dynasties. Of which the ruling of people could be considered one. I was sure, despite his claim of duty, that was Valemar's reason now — hoping the King of the Moon would look well on the man who'd married his daughter.

In any case, shortly after I'd agreed to marry him that evening, Valemar summoned a host of people to begin preparations. It might have been a hasty marriage, but it was still the marriage of a king.

I was bathed then laced into a long, red dress. The sharp glances of the women sent to attend me were more disapproval than curiosity. I couldn't stop my shudder of relief when one of them, a younger woman just a few inches taller than me with light brown hair, offered to finish the preparations on her own.

"It's your dark eyes and hair," she said, giving me a sweet smile, and picked up the brush. "You look too much like the Cordair."

I closed my eyes as she swept the brush in gentle, soothing strokes. "You fear them?"

The brush stilled. I opened my eyes to see her face fall in the mirror. "The Cordair have spent thousands of years under the earth, digging. Releasing things that were best left alone. It has turned their eyes, their hair, and their hearts dark." The brushstrokes began again. "Or so it is said … Your hair is so dark. With curls." She smiled at me again. "The others may find it disturbing, but I think it's pretty."

I murmured a "thank you" and watched her turn my mahogany-colored tresses into near ringlets. It was strange to see it down and yet be so formally dressed. I usually twisted it up when I worked. The protocol specialist is there to facilitate, not be admired. Usually. And I would be working tonight. Probably one of my most important jobs yet — negotiating for my life.

I stopped the train of thought before it could go further. There'd be plenty of time later to think about how I was paying for it.

The girl's gentle strokes lulled me into a half-sleep, a few moments away from the thoughts and troubles of not only the last day but, truth be told, the last two weeks. Ever since the engine had suffered the leak. I was sad when she put the brush down.

"Thank you," I said. She gave me an awkward smile and straightened up the items on the dressing table. "Can I ask your name?"

"Daria," she said, looking down. A light blush appeared on her cheeks.

"What now?" I asked.

Daria packed away the few cosmetics they'd used to highlight my eyes and darken my lips. "They should be here shortly."

"And then?" I tried hard not to bite my lip.

Daria looked up with surprise. "They'll take you down to the Cair."

Which I could only guess meant "church." New words didn't always translate at first. And if I learned to associate the new word before the chip figured out a translation, then the new word would be absorbed into the language I heard. Just as "kindergarten" and "angst" had been absorbed into English without translation from the original German. The process by which we learn language to begin with, and why all languages are fluid.

But that still didn't answer my original question. "I mean once they take me to the Cair." I managed a weak smile. "I've been to weddings in many cultures. They're all different." Daria took my hands and raised me to my feet. "What can I expect here?" I asked her as she knelt.

Daria stopped arranging my skirts and looked up. "Did no one tell you?" I gave a small shake of my head. She looked down again and continued her arranging. "You'll state before the Möd that you freely choose to join. You'll offer each other food and wine to show that you'll feed each other. You'll place a belt around each other to show that you will clothe and protect the other. The Möd will cut your fingers which you will then join and offer your blood to the Father and Mother."

My fingers curled inward. Blood-letting wasn't unheard of in wedding ceremonies, but the pads on my fingertips wanted no part of it. I, on the other hand, hoped that would be the only blood shed.

"Thank you," I said, and tried to shake off my fear of what would happen out of public view. Hopefully. The Scadasi did consummate their marriages in front of their guests. "And after?"

Daria stopped shaking my skirts. She slowly rose. "Have you not been with a man before?"

I scrambled to think of how to answer that. Her surprised question gave me the courage to tell the truth. "I have. It's just … it won't be at the church? Or the feast?"

Her eyes widened then she frowned. "Church? No. Do a husband and wife lie together at the feast where you come from?"

I fought back the blush that came to my cheeks. "No. But some places they do."

Daria hummed. "People are more open during the Blood Moon." She smiled. "But, no. We'll prepare you for bed and Valemar will join you. After the feast."

"Just one more question." My face flamed. "Will Raislos demand proof? That Valemar and I are really husband and wife?" I hoped she'd get the picture without my having to explain it. There were places in the galaxy, as well as time periods on Earth, when a witness was required to make sure the marriage was indeed valid.

"There will be crowds enough in the Cair for the Cordair to know you are truly wed." Daria opened a box on the dressing table

and lifted out a gold crown studded with cabochon rubies. She was tall enough that I didn't need to dip for her to place it on me. The crown was heavy and sat on the lump on my head. She stepped back and surveyed me. "I think that will do, my princess. If you will follow me."

I was placed on a bay horse — as I still thought of the creature — sidesaddle, so that my long skirts draped down its side. Valemar rode next to me on a white steed, wearing robes the brilliant blue of a tropical sea. The gold and silver crown had been replaced with one of silver, studded with blue-green opals. The lump on my head ached from the weight of mine.

Heymond led the cluster of guards that escorted us out of the castle gates and into the throng lining the streets of the city. The hairs on the back of my neck prickled, making me certain that someone was watching. Someone other than the well-wishers lining the streets. I was glad for the protection of the guards, but still felt vulnerable, exposed — waiting for an arrow to find its mark. Sneaking me in through the watergate now made sense. Someone didn't want me here.

I tried to lift the practiced, gracious smile I'd fashioned through years of being in the most boring to the most frightening of meetings but it wouldn't stay on my face. I turned my focus inward and recited the planets in order from Earth to Sexta. The muscles of my face slowly relaxed but a silent scream lingered at the back of my throat.

The cathedral, or Cair as they called it, was placed on the highest point in town. Valemar dismounted at the steps then helped me slide off my horse. He took the tips of the fingers of my left hand with his right and led me inside.

Like the great cathedrals of Europe or Hentetti Five, there were no seats. People parted to let us pass. The windows were filled with stained glass in various shades of red, but my eyes found it easier to trace the pattern of the stones beneath my feet.

Valemar came to a stop. He released my hand, bowed, and moved to my right. Red robes stood before me. My gaze traveled from their hem until it came to the face of the priest. Bald, his erect, pointed ears gave him an appearance almost bat-like. Behind him stood five women also in red robes, all of them with hair in various shades of red. The woman with the darkest, reddest hair was the woman who had been with Valemar when I arrived.

"Valemar Dönal Carbrev and Astrid Gabriella Carr, you come today to be joined as husband and wife. To survive this life, we must be fed." One of the red-haired women brought forward a plate of bread. "Repeat after me — I will share my bread with you though it be my last."

Valemar tore a piece off and brought it to my mouth, repeating the Möd's words. When I'd chewed and swallowed, I did the same for him. His lips gently closed over my fingers. His eyes held a smolder that hadn't been there before. I dipped my gaze as the Möd began again.

"My wine and water are yours. You shall never go thirsty."

The next woman brought forward a cup. Valemar held it for me to drink from. There was wine in it, strong, rich, and red that burned its way past my heart. I took the cup and held it out for him. His hands closed over mine as he tipped the cup toward him. Skitters of energy raced up and down my arms.

"I shall shield your body from cold and sun and harm."

Two women came forward. The belt Valemar took to tie around me was of green leather, fashioned to look like the leaves in his first

crown. I stared at his robes as Valemar said the words and tightened the belt around me. I couldn't shake the feeling that it was a noose. His hands briefly rested on my waist before he took a step back and the women handed me his. Of blue leather, it had been tooled in a pattern that resembled waves.

I repeated the words and Valemar lifted his arms so that I could circle mine around his waist and place the belt. My nose came against his robes, filling my nostrils with a clean, spicy scent. I became aware that I now held him in an embrace, even with the belt in my hands. I ran my fingers down the length of the leather, slipped the loose end through the buckle, and tightened it to the top of his hips.

The dark red woman stepped forward and offered the Möd a knife. A look of triumph lit her eyes. I clenched my teeth together to keep them from chattering. I'd had more than enough pain to last me a while.

The Möd took my right hand and squeezed the pad on my index finger. In a flash of steel or silver, he cut my finger so quickly that I didn't initially feel it. I sucked air through my nose and clenched my jaw as the pain registered. The cut was deep. My blood dripped, splashing like rubies onto the floor. I blinked back tears as the knife flashed again, making the cut on Valemar's finger. Then Valemar joined his left hand to my right and gently pulled me forward to the altar behind the Möd.

"Our gift to the Father," Valemar whispered in my ear then spoke aloud. I rushed to catch up as he held our entwined hands, cuts pressed together, blood mingling, over a bowl of water. "From whence we came." I could smell brine as our blood dripped in, turning the water red. "Our gift to the Mother —" He moved our hands above a small cup of oil. "— who makes all life possible."

The Möd stepped forward and wrapped a small cloth smeared with pitch, or something else that was thick and tacky, around each of our fingers as a bandage. Valemar whispered in my ear again. "Pick up the cup." I added my hand to it. "And say with me: We join the two —" The words caught in my throat. "— and create life in the holy dance of blood and sea, earth and moonlight." Valemar set the cup down and guided my hand to a taper that sat burning behind the basin.

No other words were spoken. Valemar tipped our hands, bringing the candle to the bowl, igniting the oil. Then he bent toward me with the flame and blew it out as I added my breath. A cheer rose up from those watching.

Valemar handed the candle back to the Möd and took my hand to lead me out, a smile lighting up his face. I added one of my own but it wasn't real. The Alfari might fear the Cordair and their worship of the dark. I couldn't help but worry about this culture and why it would require a blood sacrifice at a wedding.

Valemar took my hand as we rode back to the castle side-by-side. What started off as simple pageantry became a lifeline as we progressed through the streets. The crown pressed on the lump on my head, adding to the ache. Forms became blurs again. By the time we rode through the gates, I clutched his hand in a death grip, afraid I'd fall from my horse.

"What is it?" he asked as I slipped down. My head came to rest on his chest.

"The crown. Do I need to keep it on?"

Valemar's fingers ran through the locks of hair hanging down my back. "Once we're inside," he murmured and took my hand to lead me in.

Day had begun to slip into night while we'd said our vows. Torches now guttered in the darkening hallways of the castle. "Send for Ferrick," he said to someone as we walked down the hall. I could

hear musicians, but Valemar drew me into an antechamber and sat me down in a chair.

I groaned with relief when he removed the crown from my head. His fingers gently probed the bump, and he hummed with displeasure. "It's grown," he said, raising my chin. "And your eyes are glassy." I heard the door open and close. "It's her head," Valemar said to a brown-robed figure.

The man who stepped in front of me was the oldest person I'd yet seen here. Bald to his ears, the remaining dark blond and gray hair had been gathered into a braid which fell over his shoulder and hung nearly to his waist. He looked in my eyes then extended his hand toward my head. "May I?"

I nodded.

"It's larger than it was this afternoon," Valemar said as the man probed my bump.

His eyes fell to the crown on the table. He harrumphed. "You just *had* to marry her today."

"I did," Valemar said, his voice indignant. "Raislos will be here in the morning. It was marry her or turn her over." The man hummed an acknowledgement. "Can you give her something?"

"And what about the feast?"

"She needs to be there. It needs to be public."

The man made a noise of disapproval. "She should be in bed." He threw Valemar a pointed look. "Sleeping." Then he sighed. "But I suppose that's not going to happen."

"I don't want any medicine," I told him. The repbots had enough to do. I didn't want them dealing with any more foreign substances than necessary. Not when even I was beginning to worry about my head injury. "The food's all foreign as it is. I don't want to increase the risk of allergic reaction."

"You've got a smart one there," the doctor said to Valemar. Then he sighed again. "Very well. Water — no wine. A little bland food. Try to keep activity to a minimum." He stood and turned to go. "Or you may just be able to give Raislos a corpse in the morning." The man dipped a small bow at the door. "My king."

No sooner had the door closed behind him than one behind me clicked open. I turned my head and stifled a groan. The red-haired woman slipped in.

"Is it really that serious?" Valemar asked her.

She bent down and ran her hand along my face. Her fingers traced their way back through my hair and caressed the bump above my ear. She closed her eyes and muttered something, almost a chant. They went wide when she opened them, and she took my chin. Her gaze passed right through me.

"She has help, but it will take time." A shiver ran down my spine. She blinked then glanced over her shoulder at Valemar. "Do what you need to do. She will survive."

The woman gathered her shawl around her and melted out the door. Her words left me frozen to the spot. My eyes were wide as Valemar took my hands and raised me from my seat. Just what did he have planned?

A hot tear spilled down my cheek, something that never would have happened without the stupid head injury. Professional, studied Astrid slipped from my grasp. I had the inexorable feeling that I was falling. Had I even left the escape pod? Maybe this was a crazy dream.

But the hand that brushed the tear away was real. Valemar bent his head and whispered in my ear, his voice warm and gentle. "I shall shield you from cold and sun and harm."

In the Cair, to me, they had been just words — a script to recite. But here, in this room, as Valemar spoke them again, they sounded like a promise.

Once seated at our place of honor, I managed to pull up and keep a smile pasted on my face. The banquet room was loud and hot and crowded but at least I didn't need to stand. I sipped water, nibbled on some fruit and bread, and watched the people around me. Change the faces, change the clothes, and it could have been a party nearly anywhere in the galaxy.

After a while, I became aware of the death glares that a woman with strawberry blond hair kept shooting in my direction. At first, I'd thought they were aimed at Valemar. Then I noticed her eyes soften as she gazed at him, only to have the fire reignited when they flicked back to me.

If looks could kill…

I filed her away for further investigation. Looks can't kill, but they can definitely hatch plots. Hence rule number four: *Always know whom you're dealing with.* My money was on a spurned lover — I'd taken her place — which could make her dangerous and not just merely annoying. It could be that she hated seeing her king take an outsider as a wife (there were several in the crowd who showed a similar reluctance to the women who had been sent to dress me), but I couldn't afford to be careless. My life depended on it.

I hadn't been going to ask Valemar about her, but he caught my glances at her and leaned in. "Zhanet, my moon mate," Valemar said. "They don't often end up as wives, but …" His mouth moved up and down in a shrug.

Which answered one question but raised so many others. And added a new tempo to the rhythm pounding away in my head as my inner protocol specialist suffered culture shock and mentally kicked me for being unprepared.

Whether to comfort me or irritate her, Valemar's hand came to rest on my back. His fingers traced some unseen pattern. The motion was so like that of my mother's soothing touch when I was sick that I found myself leaning into his embrace. Zhanet colored and looked away.

I must have dozed for the next thing I was aware of was Valemar's voice in my ear. "They're ready for you."

I opened my eyes. Women were rising from the tables, singing. I scanned the room, but Zhanet had vanished, which relieved me. I didn't want her tucking me into my wedding bed. How many other of Valemar's former lovers were among the women, I didn't know. Would I be the last of his lovers or just one of many? How could I find out without causing any more ripples that I already had?

Down the corridors, up the stairs, the women drew me, singing. Torches flickered along the walls, making the shadows dance. The women excused two guards who stood outside a door and led me inside what turned out to be a fairly modest bedroom. I'd been in larger, grander bedrooms in hotels all over the galaxy. It was by no means spartan, but it was not what I'd expected of the bedroom of a king. There was an average sized bed covered in ordinary textiles. A small table with two chairs held a few bottles and glasses. There were two doors leading off to other spaces, but those the women left alone.

They unlaced the heavy red dress and stripped me bare before raising my arms and settling a sheer gown over me. Sleeveless and long, it covered my body but left nothing to the imagination. At least they hadn't left me naked. Daria threw back the covers and, once I'd climbed in, tucked me into bed. She gave me a reassuring smile and filed out behind the others, still singing, before closing the door behind her.

I hugged my arms around my knees and waited. I was in no way a virgin, but other than a couple of times when I'd had *way*

too much to drink, I'd never slept with a stranger. I didn't know how women had done it throughout the ages — bed someone they'd barely met. At least I had the advantage of knowing what was coming. Or thought I did. Occasionally you got surprises. All life forms aren't built the same way, as I found out on Betel Five when I took a Derthryn banker I'd worked with for years up on his offer to see the stars from the hotel roof.

I eyed the bottles on the table and scrambled back out of bed. The reason there are so many drunken one night stands is that alcohol turns off the thinking part of the brain. You're left staring at someone hopefully attractive and your instinctual brain takes over with its messages to reproduce. That was what I needed now.

I poured myself a large glass from the bottle that looked like wine. I swigged back a sizeable gulp and then bent over, exhaling in shock, when it turned out to be much stronger. After fanning away the burn, I braced myself and downed the rest of the glass. I was just refilling it when a creak in the hallway alerted me that someone was there. The door opened and Valemar came in. An eyebrow rose and an amused smile lit his face.

"I thought Ferrick said no wine."

"It's not wine," I said and picked up the cup. "It's much stronger than that, and I'm going to need it if I'm going to do this."

Valemar held back a smile and watched me drain it. His eyes traveled over me then he took the cup from my hands and placed it on the table. His hands came up and caressed my face. I closed my eyes, trying to hold back the tears that were rising. There was no love here. I was handing over my body in exchange for safety. Sanctioned prostitution. Trading sex for something else. At least I knew what I was doing, what was coming. I couldn't imagine the terror of all the brides who hadn't known just what would be done to them.

Valemar slowly closed the distance between us. I could feel the heat of his body through the nothingness of my nightgown, smell the spicy scent from before. His every exhale was deep and husky. His fingers curled along my jaw, raising my face. His lips came down on mine, brushing me softly, and I could taste wine.

I decided I should do this properly and kissed him back. I ran my hands up his chest and found firm, chiseled muscles under his robe. There was a warrior's body there. The instinct part of my brain kicked in, moving me closer against him.

Valemar's hands traveled down my back, across the tops of my buttocks, and came to rest on my hips. His movements were slow, precise. And reminded me of something.

My conscious brain chased after the memory and found it. A camping trip in the Scottish Highlands when I was ten. My father and I had been eating apples by a stream when we heard movement through the bracken. A deer emerged and then stared at us. Its nose quivered as it took in the scent of the fruit. My father turned his hand flat and extended the apple. Slowly, impossibly slowly, he edged in the deer's direction. The deer twitched her ears and flipped her tail, but she allowed my father to approach. She cautiously took the apple when he came close enough, chewing it up in loud crunches as my father stayed still.

I was the deer in this scenario. Valemar was moving slow, letting me get used to him. Letting me see that he meant me no harm. Seduction works for a reason.

I did my best to turn off the thinking part of my brain, allowed myself to get lost in the feeling his lips and hands were creating. The nightgown fell from my shoulders shortly before he picked me up. His lips stopped as he carried me to the bed but began again when he'd placed me on it, pausing only to shuck off his robe.

I shivered, all too conscious that we were both naked, and Valemar pulled the covers up over us. He stroked me from shoulder to hip while he kissed me, gradually easing himself on top of me and then between my legs. My body responded and was ready for him when he entered me.

There was a reverence to his lovemaking. I had been desired in the past. Even loved. But Valemar made love to me as if I were a miracle. He swept away the shame I'd been feeling. I began to think that this could actually work and lost myself in the pleasure, crying aloud as I climaxed.

A creak outside the door froze us both. Valemar's hand snaked under the pillow next to me. We didn't even breathe, just listened. The sound of footsteps faded down the hall.

I felt more violated at that moment than I did with Valemar inside me. I blinked. Tears slipped down my face, into my ears. Valemar brushed them away with his hand. His lips traced the tracks they'd taken then he began to move again. But the moment had been spoiled. This was a business arrangement, and someone had just made sure that I'd paid.

CHAPTER 5

It took me ages to fall asleep. Valemar curled around me and nuzzled my hair before he nodded off while I lay there, listening to his even breathing. In a stranger's arms, in a stranger land, with no hope of return to anything I held dear, the loneliness was crushing.

I forced myself to assess the situation, starting with the person who'd been listening outside the door. Uninvited, apparently. Though expected enough for Valemar to have placed a weapon under his pillow. There is always intrigue, but it's one thing to try to decipher the players and the details from the outside. It's another when the intrigue involves you. I was a juicy fly caught in a spider web. Whether I was dinner or bait, I couldn't tell.

I didn't get much beyond that before the alcohol and the head injury finally combined to push me into the sleep the doctor had recommended. I awoke in the morning with Valemar gone. Whatever had been under his pillow was gone as well.

While I waited for someone to come and fetch me for the morning's confrontation with the Cordair, I clambered out of bed and checked out the two doors that, as far as I knew, didn't lead out of the room. Behind them were two separate dressing rooms with bathrooms. One meant for a man. One for a woman.

A long rack of dresses ran along one wall on the woman's side, shoes tucked underneath them. The opposite wall had drawers and shelves. I pulled open one drawer and found underthings. The boxes on the shelves contained pieces of jewelry. My hands shook as I placed a box containing a brooch shaped like an insect back in its place. The bedroom might be modest but the gowns were extravagant. They were fit for a queen. So why were they already here?

I found the toilet, finished my business, and sorted through the dresses. They all laced up the back. There was no way I was getting into them without help.

I pulled on a green robe with swirling patterns that reminded me of paisley and crawled back into bed. My headache had subsided, but my brain felt damaged. The same thought kept playing over and over like a defective recording. I remained stuck in the loop until the floor squeaked. A short knock tapped against the door and Daria entered.

"I tried to get dressed myself but I couldn't do the laces," I apologized.

"That's my job," Daria said. "You're not expected to get dressed on your own."

I had wondered at the practice of ladies maids in centuries past. Why couldn't a person just dress themselves? Because there weren't any zippers. It was a maid or loose-fitting clothing.

I got out of bed and joined her in the dressing room. Daria took a gown that was almost the same blue as the robes Valemar had worn for the wedding from its hanger and threaded her arms through the neck. I dropped the robe and raised my arms so she could slip the dress over my head. As Daria began to thread the laces through the holes, I closed my eyes to block out of the vision of all those dresses behind me, and asked the easiest of my many questions. "Why the green and blue?"

Daria tugged on the strings. "The blue is for the Lian Isles and the Aelon Sea to the north."

I looked over my shoulder when she paused. Her eyes and smile showed her thoughts to be somewhere else. She met my gaze and returned to her task, smile still in place. "The air is warm and scented with fruit. The waters are bright blues and vivid greens, though the green on our flag represents the green of the fields and forests of Bánalfar. The two lands have been joined for more than two thousand years — on the flag, on the crown. In our hearts."

She tied off the laces and picked up a box. Inside sat a smaller version of the crown Valemar had been wearing when I met him, the interwoven leaves and waves. A queen's crown.

I stared at it and swallowed. "Daria … why are there gowns already in here?" I bit off the possibilities so as not to give her the idea of an answer that I might find acceptable.

Surprise colored Daria's face. Her eyes widened, and her cheeks flushed. She set down the crown, picked up a brush, and came to stand behind me again.

"This is the queen's chambers," she said.

I gave her marks for her quick maneuvering then asked the question I didn't really want to know the answer to. At least, my heart didn't want to know, while my head said it was the lesser to two evils (though not the only option). "So Valemar has had other queens?"

Daria's hands stilled. "No, my queen."

My ribs relaxed and I inhaled, only then realizing that I'd been holding my breath. So that was one minefield I wouldn't have to walk. Which would mean …

Don't ask questions you don't want to know the answers to.

It had been drilled into my head by my family for as long as I could remember. Part of the reason I was so good at my job. I did my research and ran every scenario so I knew what the answers were likely to be before I asked the questions. The evidence was mounting for an answer I didn't like. An answer that shook me to my core and frightened me in a way I'd never been frightened. Not when the mechanism had exploded and the plasma leaked and the crew slowly died. Not when the pod malfunctioned and I ended up crash landing. Not even when separatists had broken into our negotiations and taken us hostage for ten hours on Regen Four. If my guess was right, I was in way over my head, and I didn't want it confirmed until I felt like I could remain upright upon hearing it.

"Well, at least the wardrobe is proving useful," I said, and pulled at the fabric of the sleeves skimming my wrists.

Daria put the brush down and lifted the crown onto my head. It looked awkward there. Not because I didn't think it belonged, but on Valemar's head the colors had shone. My dark hair covered them in shadow.

"The green stones bring out the green in your eyes," Daria said. That was true, and I murmured my thanks, all the while thinking about how out of place it looked. "They're waiting for you in the throne room," Daria said, and I followed her out, steeling myself for the confrontation with the Cordair.

Daria took me in through a door behind the dais. Heads bent toward each other as hushed murmurs were exchanged between the thirty or forty people assembled there. Valemar's eyes flicked toward me and he rose, coming forward to meet me.

"What do I need to do?" I asked him.

"Just stand beside me," he said and took my hand. We walked over to the throne. Valemar sat, leaving me standing on his right. I wondered if there was a queen's throne or if queens even got to sit in his presence. He nodded to the guards at the main doors. The other guards lining the walls stood a little straighter as the doors were opened. Outward, I noticed. Harder to break into. The remaining people stepped aside, forming an aisleway. A band of about twenty marched in, and my brain finally recognized what was wrong with the scene.

I grabbed at the arm of the throne. Valemar's eyes flicked to me, and he assumed a lazy pose. I struggled to breathe, struggled to keep my face neutral and not break rule twenty. It was all I could do not to scream.

Awrakian armor. There were men before me clad in Awrakian armor.

"You've got something of mine, Valemar," their leader, a grizzled man of late middle age, drawled.

I heard myself laugh. *Good.* My protocol specialist was taking over. "Yours? Do you know who I am?"

"The Moon Princess is my wife, Raislos," Valemar said. He raised his hand, the bandage on his finger like a wedding band.

"And even if that weren't true," I continued. "I am no man's possession."

An amused smile lit up Raislos's face, and he glanced over his shoulder. I followed his eyes. *Oh, fuck!* This time I did better hiding my surprise, but my stomach fell until it was somewhere around my shoes. The man he exchanged a look with was a Hormani black market trader. The Hormani's eyes met mine. His eyebrows raised, daring me to say something.

Raislos turned his attention back to Valemar. "Fine. Have her. But hand over her ship."

I laughed again. "My ship. My possession." I paused just long enough for Raislos to open his mouth. "My wedding present to my husband."

Valemar chuckled lightly beside me. "Seems you've traveled a long way for nothing, Raislos. I'd offer you hospitality, but I'm sure you are in a hurry to return to Rock Dorach."

Raislos's eyes filled with loathing. "You may believe your ridiculous prophecy, Valemar, but don't pin your hopes on it."

My eyes narrowed. *Prophecy?*

"There are things in play here of which you have no understanding." Raislos flashed Valemar a dangerously smug smile. "The Alfari may have kept my people trapped in the mountains for hundreds of years, but that will change."

The crowd gasped but Valemar didn't even flinch. "You can try." The ice in his voice would have made me abandon any plans I'd had, but Raislos simply turned and walked out the door.

The Hormani trader's mouth curled up in amusement. His eyes lingered on me for a moment, a challenge of his own, before he followed the others out.

"Talk. *Now,*" I hissed at Valemar under my breath while maintaining my regal façade.

"Heymond," Valemar called. "Make sure they find their way back to their land. Undisturbed ... if possible."

Heymond gave a curt nod and melted away after them, while his men peeled off the walls and followed. Valemar rose and extended his hand to me. We adjourned through the same side door to the council chambers in which we'd had our first "talk." I paced the floor.

"The armor they are wearing ..." I gripped my hands so they didn't flutter and watched my feet and my swirling skirts as I moved. "It's not of this world."

Valemar hummed, a deep musical sound like a bassoon. A frown turned down the corners of his mouth. His hands came to rest on the back of a chair. "The stranger."

"Yes." I stopped my pacing and thought about how to word the next information. One thing had become clear with the audience. My position here was tenuous. I'd have to tread carefully. "Trading … here, on this planet, is forbidden." Valemar's scowl deepened. "They're not supposed to be here." *I'm not supposed to be here*, I added silently.

"And there are those who would stop it?"

"If they knew." My heart thudded. *You don't want them here.*

Valemar absorbed this new information. "Can you tell them?" His stare pinned me to my spot. I swallowed deeply.

"I have no way to contact them."

Valemar leaned against the chair, silently appraising me. It was a risk, having told him I was cut off from my people.

"Do you know what they are trading for?" I asked.

"The Cordair are miners. Gold, silver, iron, copper, gems. If it comes out of the ground and has value, they trade it."

I couldn't see the Hormani risking the wrath of the Shororato for mere gemstones. Then the image of a brassy-green ore sitting on a conference table came to mind. One of the most valuable contracts I'd ever helped negotiate, worth the entire GDP of Earth. Chalcopyrite. Used to fuel plasma thrusters. If they were trading that, nearly anything was worth the risk.

"There's a mineral, greenish yellow in color. Takes an almost crystalline form. Do the Cordair mine that?"

The door opened behind me and I was unpleasantly unsurprised when the red-haired woman slipped in the same door she had last time. This place had to be a warren of rooms and passageways, people passing unseen.

Valemar's eyes flicked from her back to me. "I do not know. I take it that it is valuable."

"For some," I said. "And they'd be willing to do anything to get it."

"You see now why she came, my king," the woman said.

Valemar stepped away. "But she can do nothing."

"She may not know what she can do." The woman looked at me. Her eyebrows rose. "In more ways than one." The woman returned her attention to Valemar. "But now you know. Now you can plan. *They're not supposed to be here.*"

"Can I ask who you are?" I said, unable to hold back a sigh of exasperation. I wanted a name to go with this red ghost who moved at the edge of things.

"Shale," Valemar said. "Our Mödatal."

"I think you would call me a seer," Shale said. I shivered as ripples of awareness ran down my spine.

I've been many places, seen many things. Unbelievable things. Things that could only be described as magic. And yet, every fiber of my body wanted to scream out at this woman. And she knew it, and it made her smile.

"Do I want to know the prophecy about me?" I asked them. "I assume there is one."

Valemar walked over to the small table that held glasses and a carafe of wine. "*As the darkness gathers,*" the Mödatal intoned, "*she will fall from the moon. The daughter of kings will drive back the outsiders and —*"

"*And she will save us all,*" Valemar said, his voice cutting across hers. They stared at each other for several heartbeats. Shale gave him a piercing look which Valemar returned, unblinking. She shrugged and dropped her gaze. "You may go," Valemar said to her.

"As you wish, my king." Shale glanced one more time at me before leaving. I got the feeling from their exchange that there was something Valemar didn't want me to know.

And I realized I couldn't tell him the truth. I couldn't tell him that I was not this Moon Princess he believed me to be. If he thought I had no value, especially since I'd let him know how precarious things were, I would become a mere bargaining chip. One he might be willing to hand over for the right price. One the Hormani would be all too willing to take and, no doubt, suggest to the Cordair that I indeed should be sacrificed to their god, thereby eliminating the potential problem of my exposing them for what they really were.

My best chance of survival was to be right where I was … as long as I could keep Valemar happy.

"So you think I can save you?"

Valemar poured a glass of wine. "That is the prophecy." He picked it up and faced me.

"I don't believe in prophecies." Since there would be so much else I would withhold, I felt I owed him this small truth.

"Many of my people would agree with you."

Religion and politics. The two minefields one found everywhere. Business was much more straightforward. "And you believe or you would not have thought me worth the risk," I said. Valemar sipped the wine. Seeds of doubt flickered his eyes. "A risk you now regret?"

He threw back the glass and drained it, took his time placing it on the table. I stood still, watching him. Valemar came over to me and stroked my cheek with the back of his fingers while his eyes searched my face. "How bad is it?" he asked.

I swallowed. The Hormani could do a lot of damage before the Shororato became aware. A Cordair army clad in the impenetrable armor could probably do what Raislos had promised. There was no

one around to stop them but me, and what could I do? "Potentially very bad," I said. No sense sugar-coating it.

Valemar's hand fell away. "Then you're our only hope."

Lord help us all.

CHAPTER 6

Valemar had his seneschal Orin give me a tour of the castle since Heymond was away escorting the Cordair. Well over six feet tall, as most of the Alfari seemed to be, I could have been a child, trailing in his wake. "How do you learn your way around this place?" I asked as we headed down yet another small, twisty staircase and through another narrow corridor. "It's a rabbit warren."

Orin turned toward me, his brows crinkled together in puzzlement. "Rabbit?"

I sighed. "Surely you have something similar here. Small animals that tunnel into the earth. Goes in one way, pops out another."

"Ah, *kinnin*." He chuckled. "Yes, very much like a *rabbit* warren. Trial and error, my queen. Go the wrong way often enough and you learn the right. Makes it harder for potential invaders to get far should they breach the gates."

That made sense. "And when was the last time you had trouble with invaders?"

"About a hundred and fifty years ago." There was a weight to Orin's voice that hadn't been there before. "They managed to cart off the throne before their convoy was overtaken, besieged, and the throne returned. They didn't last long in the castle. As you've noted, if you don't know where you're going, it's hard to get there. It can take years to learn your way around. A lifetime to learn its secrets."

"If you're allowed access to them."

Orin glanced over his shoulder. "A wise observation," he said with a smile.

"I'm not a beginner to intrigue," I said dryly, and tried to mark my surroundings.

"Then you should do well here."

My tour concluded at the stables. *They were really more like elk than horses.* Elk with manes and tails. Common riding animals had their horns cut off, as farmers had done with cattle in Earth's past until they'd developed the polled breeds. Why risk being gored?

The war horses, however, were different. The prongs on each antler had been drilled so they could be tipped with slicing blades in times of battle, able to cut great swaths through foot armies, Orin told me. I was beginning to see why the Cordair would want Awrakian armor. Few weapons could pierce the lightweight protection, let alone primitive knives. Even ones affixed to the horns of rampaging deer.

But nothing prepared me for the sight of Valemar's war horse. Large as a Clydesdale but much more nimble, its antlers were broad like a moose's but with pointed prongs around the edges. I had no trouble imagining it when Orin told me the beast was capable of scooping up and tossing full-grown men.

"His name is Muirbrook."

"Muirbrook?" I asked when the chip didn't translate.

"The large wave that comes after an earthquake."

"Tsunami," I said as the chip belatedly offered the translation.

"*Tsunami?* Tsunami," Orin said, trying the word on his tongue.

"That's what we call the wave. Able to wash away entire cities," I said, calling to mind the devastating one that had hit the eastern Pacific in the late twenty-second century.

"Ah, you have oceans, too, then? Our star gazers can't see through your red clouds."

I just smiled and didn't answer. Muirbrook hung his head over the stall door and snuffled me. "Hello there," I said and offered him the back of my hand. His breath was warm and wet. The short hairs around his nose tickled. Looking for a treat and finding nothing in my hand, he batted it with a snort and stomped his feet. They were larger than dinner plates, and the ground rumbled beneath us. "If I'd known I was meeting you, I would have brought something."

Muirbrook tossed his head and fixed me with a glare. I glanced at Orin whose eyebrows had lifted. "What?"

"He's not a pet," Orin said.

Muirbrook swung his massive head toward Orin. "I can tell that," I said. "He is, however, a noble creature deserving of respect." I smiled as Muirbrook snorted at Orin and turned back my way. "He expects to be waited on and assumed I would do so. Next time, my honored gentleman."

Muirbrook shook his mane. Having suitably impressed us, he began to munch on the hay in his stall.

"Do women ride to war on the moon?" Orin asked.

"Some," I answered. "But I haven't. I'm a sit at the table and help with negotiations type. What do your women do here?" I asked.

Orin gestured toward the doors at the end of the stables. "What women do — sew, sing, cook, raise the children."

I gave him a non-committal, "Hmm."

"And yours ride to war?"

"They do everything a man does." Orin's face twitched with amusement. I let the insult pass. "Or everything a woman does. Their choice. Just as a man gets to choose what he wants to do. Even raise the children." Orin's eyebrows shot up. "Have you children of your own?"

"I'm a child of the moon," Orin replied.

"Which is?"

Orin gave me a surprised look. When he saw I was in earnest, it fell from his face. "Does the moon not affect you? When it is full, we here on Crenfor are overcome with the urge to mate." A warning bell went off in my head, but I silenced it. "Children of such unions are given into service when they are born, if their parents are not married. Sons to defense, unless they are red of hair. Daughters as servants or as acolytes of the Cair."

"So, you have no children of your own?"

"If I do, they have entered service."

This was a caste society without the stigma, the bastards not being full members but viewed with respect. Daria, too, had to be a child of the moon. As were Heymond and every other soldier I encountered.

"Can you marry?" I asked.

"Soldiers cannot but others can."

No one to leave behind, I thought. "But you can still find … comfort when the moon is full?"

"As long as it's not a night of guard duty. Then we take a draught that counteracts the pull."

I nodded. "Makes sense. Don't want enemies taking advantage of you being … otherwise engaged."

Orin laughed. "You definitely do think like a man."

If I was going to find a way around the problem of the Hormani, I would need to.

Orin's tour had given me a glimpse of the political climate, but there was one big piece missing. I swallowed my distaste and asked Daria to arrange for the Mödatal to meet me for some afternoon refreshments.

The red-haired seer surprised me by knocking before she came through the door, but it didn't stop my hackles from rising at the sight of her. "My queen," she said and inclined her head.

"You may go," I told Daria. I gestured for the seer to take a seat. "Wine or tea?" I asked as Daria slipped away.

Shale adjusted her shawl. "Wine," she said, watching me.

I poured her a glass of the golden liquid and handed it to her. She took it from me without a word. I poured myself a cup of the tea. A faint jasmine-like scent rose from the amber brew. I curled my hands around the cup and sat back, withholding the urge to blow on it in case it was an insult. "Valemar told me the prophecy doesn't have … universal acceptance."

Shale gave me an enigmatic smile and sipped her wine. "That is true."

"And why is that?"

"Time dilutes most things."

"Then there is opposition to my being here? Other than the Cordair?" I clarified.

She waited until I began to squirm. "Yes," she answered simply.

"And what will they think now that I have arrived?"

The Mödatal stared into the depths of her wineglass. "Does it matter? You have arrived."

A disbelieving laugh rumbled through my throat. "Any opposition is worth noting. It has a way of breeding rebellion."

Shale ran her finger along the rim of the glass. "What they want does not matter. You —" She looked up and fixed me with eyes of dark blue. "— are the only thing that matters."

"But the risk they pose to me does matter."

Shale's finger fell away. "They will try to undermine your influence for you are not what they expected. They will not believe that you are the Moon Princess or that you can save them. They will believe that you serve the Cordair in secret and will only bring trouble to the region."

I sipped the tea, now wishing I'd chosen the wine. The price on my head kept mounting. "Will they actively seek my removal?"

One side of the Mödatal's mouth curled up in a smile. "Assassination of the queen would go against their self-preservation interests. No one would be willing to let them live." I blew out a breath I hadn't realized I'd been holding. "You have time, my queen. The path you walk is uneven. There will be times you stumble and fall, but this is the path you were meant to be on. You have power that you recognize not. It will be revealed to you. In time." She held my eyes and drank from her glass. Solid. Unmovable.

"How widely known is the prophecy?"

"Most people in the street could tell you the gist of it." She smiled. "You were last looked for when Aedenfal was overrun a hundred and fifty years ago. Dönal Carbrev and his brothers rode with the Red Army and drove the Cordair back. They took Fairfada, the steppe upon which you were found. Valemar's father gave it back, with some conditions, hoping to placate the Cordair." She gave a laugh full of irony. "A generation earlier and you would have had no need to rush to marriage. How the gods do laugh at us."

She drained her glass. "Any other questions for me?"

I played with my tea cup. "Valemar finished the prophecy for you. I had the feeling he added his own ending."

"The daughter of kings will save us all," Shale said.

"But that's not what I asked."

She sat impassive, as if I hadn't said a word, which was answer in itself. She would not be the one to tell me. "Anything else, my queen?" I shook my head. She put her glass back on the table and rose. "You have time. What you need to do will reveal itself." The Mödatal inclined her head and withdrew from the room in her ghost-like fashion.

I reached for the carafe and poured myself a glass of wine. The Cordair wanted me. The Hormani wanted me dead. The Alfari feared me.

I tipped my head back and gulped the wine without breathing, wiped away the rivulet that flowed around the glass and ran down my chin. The alcohol burned in my stomach.

Of all the scenarios that had played through my mind as I'd watched the planet turn beneath me, blue and green and covered in lacy clouds. So familiar, yet so foreign. Never in my wildest dreams could I have concocted one where I was queen, where I was valuable.

One step at a time.

I knew the political landscape. I knew what was expected of me. Now I just needed to figure out what to do.

There was another banquet. Long lines of important personages queued up before our table, Valemar introducing them as they appeared. I was met with looks of awe, some of curiosity, and some frank appraisals. Zhanet was not introduced to me. She stayed at her

table forty feet away and threw me looks of hatred. When her gaze wasn't resting on Valemar with longing.

I smiled and inclined my head. I wished I had a tablet or secretary to form a guest book for me to study because I'd never be able to match the faces with the names on my own. *Always be prepared, Astrid,* my protocol professor had drilled into me. I'd assembled and studied the photos in guest books for hours every trip. *Always get their names, Astrid.* Rules two and three. But here, I was a novice.

Begin at the beginning.

"You know I'll never remember them all," I whispered to Valemar as another couple returned to their seats.

"I wouldn't expect you to."

"Are you going to tell me who I *should* know?"

"And who do you think you should know?" Valemar asked.

I pulled off a small piece of the roasted meat on my plate. The meat was tender and flavorful like duck but the animal it had been sliced off of was built more like a small pig. "I suppose the traditional answer should be 'the wives,' but you and the Mödatal have other plans for me."

Valemar's eyes twinkled and one eyebrow hooked. "How was your luncheon with her?"

"It answered some questions and raised others."

Valemar chuckled. "She does have that effect on people. Coran Pöbid and his wife Blanid," he added in a louder voice.

I inclined my head to them. The lump on my head had gone down a little, but the crown I wore pressed down on it, renewing the ache. "How many of these people want me dead?" I whispered as they moved away.

Valemar's eyes moved to Zhanet, who still stared at me. She caught his gaze, colored, and looked down at her plate. "There may be one or two who wish it, but no one would move against you."

"Not even the ones who believe I'm not the Moon Princess, that I'm a Cordair plant meant to tempt you into further concessions?"

Valemar's eyes hardened and the smile dropped from his face. "I would kill them all if they harmed you," he breathed. "Their blood would flow in the streets." Valemar blinked as the next couple moved forward, and he lifted a smile back in place. "Felhim Stöon and Elja."

I inclined my head to them, but my eyes lingered on Valemar. Was it me who was so valuable to him? Or was it something else entirely?

I excused myself early. The weight of the crown had made my head pound again, and I sighed in relief when Daria lifted it from me. I sighed again, more of a moan, when her fingers ran through my hair and she began to massage my scalp.

"It's definitely smaller than before," she said, fingering the lump. "Would you like a pain draught tonight?"

I winced as she probed a tender place. "No, thank you. I'll be fine."

She picked up a brush and gently ran it through my curls, easing out the tangles. I stood when she finished. Daria untied the bow and began to whip the laces through the eyelets. The bedroom door opened. Valemar stepped through. He leaned against the open door of my dressing room.

Daria stopped her work and dipped a small bow, keeping her eyes downcast. "My king."

"You may go," Valemar said to her and moved behind me. "I'll finish your task."

Daria exited the room without looking up. I heard the bedroom door open and close as Valemar's hands took up the laces and began

pulling them through the loops. Goosebumps rose on my arms. I fought back a shiver.

The heavy silk fabric made a noise like a small scream as the lace whisked through the holes. Similar to the one I was choking back. How had they done it? All those women. Billions of them. How had they taken a man they hadn't chosen to bed? Night after night, allowing him to use their bodies. An unpleasant but necessary wifely duty.

Just lie there. At least you get children from it, they'd been told.

Their bodies weren't their own. And while last night hadn't been unpleasant, I couldn't imagine a lifetime of nights, being used to quench Valemar's lust, though no children would come from it.

The lace whipped free of the final eyelet. Valemar laid it over the back of the chair and eased the gown from my shoulders. It fell to the ground in a puff of silk. New goosebumps rose as he ran his hands down my bare arms before returning to untie the straps of my slip. This, too, fell to the floor, joining the dress. Valemar's hands caressed my shoulders. He leaned in and inhaled, his nose traveling from my neck to my ear. The hairs on my arms lifted, ready to push him away since my hands weren't. I blinked back tears, but they overflowed and ran down my cheeks.

Brush them away or let them fall? Draw attention to them or —

I dipped my head as Valemar turned me toward him. Then he froze. His hands fell away. "Being with me pains you?" Confusion filled his voice.

I choked back the sobs that filled my throat and kept my head down, refusing to meet his eyes. "I was raised to take a husband out of love, not duty."

There was no answer, no movement from him. I lifted my eyes. Everything about him was stunned. His gaze had turned inward,

unseeing. Not even a hair moved. His eyes widened. He blinked then looked at me.

"I'll not force you," he said, and turned his head away. His jaw clenched. "I'll not touch you again until you ask it of me." His lips curled into a snarl that trembled. Then he turned and walked out of my dressing room. The bedroom door closed behind him, echoing in the empty room, filling my ears as if Valemar had slammed it shut.

I crossed my arms against my chest and shivered, staring at the bedroom door. I'd gotten what I'd wanted. But now I was truly alone.

CHAPTER 7

It turned out to be a sleepless night. I found a nightgown and crawled into bed. Shortly thereafter, the floor outside my door creaked. My heart leapt, hoping it was Valemar; though I didn't want to give him my body, I did feel safer in this uncertain place when I was with him.

But the person settled themselves outside my door without entering. A guard.

My face flamed as I thought of the castle learning that Valemar did not share his new wife's bed. Driven out, for he had come and then left. I wondered if he'd be sleeping alone. Zhanet would be more than willing to comfort him. The precariousness of my position crashed down upon me.

Think! part of my brain shouted. *You always find some way through.*

Not always, I replied. Sometimes my advice was to simply walk away. There was always another deal to be had. Another planet.

But no more. Teridun Four would be where I remained for the rest of my very short or very long life.

I lay there and watched the sliver of the blood-red moon creep across the window, bathing the room in a soft red light, not unlike night or emergency mode onboard ship.

Where to begin? How do you find the beginning when you drop down in the middle?

The moon had traveled nearly the full length of my window before my brain asked, *So, what is the middle?*

Rule seventeen kicked in: *When all else fails, make a list.*

I was married. I was queen. I was the foretold savior of a prophecy. I was stuck here.

For the time being, my brain said.

"Permanently," I whispered back to it. "There's no way off this planet."

Yes, there is. The Hormani come and go.

I sucked in a breath. That was true, though not currently useful. I could envision no avenue of escape that didn't result in my being found and handed over to the Cordair as a gift. But it *was* true.

I have no allies, I thought, continuing the list.

Not true, my brain said. *You have Valemar. And Daria. And the Mödatal.*

I pondered that while the moon slipped beyond the window, the weak red light became shadow, and the bright, yellow-white spangle of the stars reappeared in the dark velvet emptiness that was their home. I was useful to Valemar and the Mödatal. Daria had never been anything but kind. Valemar and the Mödatal would be allies while I had value to them.

I rolled over and cradled the pillow under my head. I had to maintain my value.

It was this thought that circled around my brain the rest of the night, leading me to the conclusion that my greatest ally was the husband I currently wanted to avoid.

The guard outside my door departed when Daria arrived. "What would you like to wear today, my queen?"

Armor, I thought. I'd be going into battle. I had decided I would meet with Valemar. It was part of rule six — *Know when to put your cards on the table*. Only then could I begin to find a way to fit in between expectations and reality. I managed to pull up a smile. "Something cheerful, perhaps."

Understanding filled Daria's eyes. "Of course."

She cinched me into a gown that was green like the summer fields. Flowers had been embroidered along the boat-neck collar. Despite my initial protests, she added a small crown studded with peridot. "Never hurts to remind him that you are Queen," she said, placing it on my brow.

I swallowed heavily. "Does everyone know?" I whispered.

"That he has to earn your favor?" Daria said, giving me a sharp look. "Yes, they do." She finished adjusting my curls and stepped back. Her eyes met mine in the mirror. "You are the Moon Princess we've been waiting four hundred years for. Valemar may be a powerful king, but he is one of many. It is he who must please you."

My eyes widened. I'd spent so much time focused on me that I hadn't seen the bigger picture. Probably because I didn't believe. But they did. And if they believed it, then it had value. I just needed to claim my value, lie though it was. Wasn't that part of rule fourteen?

This was just another negotiation. I had something they wanted. They had something I wanted. I simply needed to figure out how to align the two.

A guard led me through the snaking passageways to the room Valemar was in. I waited outside while Heymond finished giving his

report. He dipped a bow to me as he left, then walked down the hallway, his green cloak billowing out behind him.

You are the queen. You are the princess, I chanted inside my head, then drew myself up. It was with head lifted high that I entered the room.

Valemar's eyes flashed with the same hurt as the previous night. A blush colored my cheeks. "You wished to see me?" he said.

"While I don't believe in prophecies," I said, "and I don't know what I can do, the Mödatal does believe I can help. What had you been hoping for from me?"

Valemar huffed. "An army." He threw himself from his chair, walked to the window, crossed his arms, and scowled at the view.

I swallowed deeply. "An army *would* drive away the outsiders. And there is one." Valemar froze. "But even if I could contact them, you wouldn't want them here. They're ... not forgiving." Valemar turned to face me. "Trust me. They are the last help you would want. Your world would never be the same."

"You do not command them?"

I shook my head. "No. They are an authority unto themselves."

"And the outsiders who now trade with the Cordair?"

I gave a gentle laugh. "They are smugglers. The only danger from them is what they would do to keep the Shororato from discovering their activities."

"The Shororato?"

"The army I spoke of." A simplistic description for the galactic police based on Karjiny Five, its forces drawn from the entire mobile galaxy.

Valemar began to pace. Even his hands took up the movement, his thumbs traveling along his fingertips. It had to be painful, the pressure against his wedding wound, but his face merely reflected his preoccupation.

Valemar stopped and turned to me. "Yesterday, you told me the risk from the outsiders was bad."

"Yes." My mouth went dry, and my throat constricted. "The armor the outsiders have given the Cordair. Though lightweight, it is impenetrable."

"There are no weaknesses?"

"None."

The blue of Valemar's eyes nearly disappeared, replaced by black as his pupils dilated. All the more visible as his eyes widened. This strong, proud man was now afraid. I thought back to the group that had greeted us. There had been, what? Five of the group with the armor? "How much of it do they have?"

"I do not know."

The words passed silently between us. A few suits wouldn't shift the balance if war were to come. But an entire army clad in it …

"And the outsiders would do anything to protect the supply of this ore?" Valemar asked.

"They need to be careful since trade with this planet is forbidden. But yes, they would."

Valemar nodded. I could see thoughts pass through his eyes, plans beginning to form. His lips moved silently, but I could read them. *She may not know what she can do.*

Further discussion was interrupted by a knock on the door. It opened before Valemar could reply. A blond head appeared (they all seemed to be blond), head bent, hair trailing on the floor, eyes averted.

"I am sorry for the intrusion, my king, but the karawack are hatching."

"Thank you," Valemar said. The door swung shut again.

"Karawack?" I asked.

"Messenger birds. Do you not have them on the moon?"

"We had carrier pigeons several centuries ago, but now we can send messages with … a form of light."

"Light?" Valemar's brow furrowed. "I had assumed that your birds had died or escaped when your ship fell." His eyes crinkled further, deepening the crease on his brow. "How do you send messages with light?"

"It's complicated," I said. "More complicated than I can explain. But I could eventually show you how we started out, with wires and sound."

"Wires? How would that work over long distances?"

I smiled. "We actually ran wires over our entire planet and the sound traveled down them."

Valemar frowned. "But the time, the cost … How did you keep them from being cut? You'd lose the message."

I laughed. "That did happen."

"I think I'll keep the karawack," Valemar said. "Now come. I must hurry. They imprint as soon as they hatch."

Valemar led the way out the door and down the hall. The passageway twisted and turned and I soon became hopelessly lost. Learning my way around needed to be my number one priority. After self-preservation.

"How do the karawack work?" I asked. Carrier pigeons didn't imprint. Or if they did, not in the way that was urgent enough to pull a king from a meeting.

"Work? They carry messages."

"But the imprinting part. Our pigeons returned to the place they lived."

Valemar led the way down a twisting staircase. "Ah." He turned his smiled at me over his shoulder. "The karawack imprint on a

person. They always return to that person."

The stairs ended. Valemar pushed open the door at the end. I could see stacks of cages containing both brown and white birds with crests on their heads and long, trailing tail feathers. They looked like pigeon-sized peacocks but without the brilliant colors.

"My king." A man dressed in a brown tunic and pants bowed deeply and backed away from a low table. A nest sat in the center, containing several brown and white, heavily speckled eggs. The eggs clicked and bumped against each other.

"Stay here," Valemar said to me, and took a seat on the stool next to the table. He began to stroke the eggs, running his hands over them and crooning to them in a low voice. The caged birds took up Valemar's spoken song, adding their own thrum. The dungeon-like room vibrated from the sound.

There was a crack and one egg split into several thick shards. The chick inside gave a mighty shake and emerged, naked and pink, its head searching for Valemar's voice.

Valemar picked it up and brought it close to his mouth. He sang to it and gently stroked the chick with one finger. The chick raised its head and squawked at him, reveling in the attention. Valemar placed the chick back in the nest when the next egg cracked open and repeated the process with all six eggs.

It was the strangest birthing I'd ever seen. A king, sitting on a stool in a dark, closed room filled with the scent of burning lanterns, hay, and dung, singing to one ugly baby after another, for they were ugly without their feathers and their eyes still closed. But they were his children. Each was treated with such love and tenderness that I looked at Valemar with new eyes.

When all six had hatched and been handled and sung to by Valemar, the attendant stepped back to the nest and picked up a

chick. He brought it to one of the cages and slipped it inside. The buff brown mother clucked to it and settled it under her wings. The bulbous head of the chick, however, poked back out, searching for Valemar.

He followed the attendant over to the cage with the last chick. "Tomorrow," Valemar said, and six small heads squawked at him. "I'll see you again tomorrow."

"We'll have you down for the next hatching," Valemar said to me as we made our way back up the stairs. "You'll need your own birds."

"You said they always return to a person. How does that work if you're not at home?"

"No matter where you travel," Valemar said. "They always find you."

"And you asked me how we sent messages with light?" I said incredulously.

Valemar opened his mouth but closed it again before he spoke. "I guess both our planets have mysteries."

"My mystery is how you ever learn your way around this place," I said as we headed down yet another hall. Had we come this way the first time? All the castle needed was changing staircases and it could have been a wizards' school.

Valemar laughed. "One piece at a time."

But it did lead, with a couple of twistings and turnings, back to the room we'd started in. And back to the conversation that had been interrupted.

"I asked you yesterday if you regretted your decision to marry me," I said. "I have no army for you."

Valemar's eyes reminded me that was not the only thing he wasn't getting from me. "And do you regret your decision?" he asked.

I dropped my gaze. "No," I whispered. "I am sure you saved my life." Valemar crossed to the table. "Where do we go from here?"

"You are my wife," he said. "My queen. You take up your role."

I swallowed heavily. What would he do with a wife who brought no army, did not share his bed, and had no idea how to be queen? I picked at my nails. "I'm not sure what that entails. I did not rule ... on the moon."

Valemar's eyebrows shot up. "Oh? What do princesses do on the moon?"

"Well, this one had a job."

Valemar's eyebrow hooked in question. "Explain."

"I worked as a protocol specialist. I am familiar with the customs of more cultures than I can count."

Valemar laughed. "A fitting ... job ... for a princess."

"But, obviously, I know nothing of your culture. Or even of what cultures there are on your planet."

"Why not?" Valemar asked.

"Contact with your planet was forbidden."

It was not the first time I'd said it, but this time it made him angry. "Why? Surely you can see us as we can see you. You had said that trading was forbidden. But contact!?" He spit the word.

I backed up a couple of steps and twisted my fingers. "We're not supposed to interfere. The traders. Even —" But the word dried up in my throat. He had no idea why I was here. No idea who I really was. He believed I was the answer to hundreds of years of prayers. I couldn't shatter that.

I turned my eyes to the floor. I could still frighten him with my answer. He worried about the Cordair. Now he worried about the Hormani traders and their impregnable armor. But he hadn't yet connected the dots. If an army could descend from the moon but the Alfari couldn't travel there, where could they go if that army was hostile?

Even with two hundred years of science fiction and with colonies on the moon and Mars under its belt, Earth had still freaked out when first contact was made. Entire segments of the population committed suicide. Iran and Korea launched attacks against the visitors that quickly came to nothing when the missiles were destroyed long before they reached their targets. China kept a tight leash on the United States, but mistrust had been rampant. Would Earth be conquered and subjugated?

But the Shororato offered technology. We'd thought ourselves alone in the woods, living in a cabin, and then a mighty and mostly benevolent society appeared from the other side of the mountain. Valemar, though, couldn't even imagine the technology that existed. The opportunity for annihilation. I couldn't let him know he was an ant in a land of giants.

But I could hint.

"Imagine a world where Awrakian armor is the norm." I raised my eyes and watched the color drain from Valemar's face. "Would you want them inserting themselves into your business? The traders have chosen the Cordair. Should those traders have interfered in your world?"

"No," Valemar whispered.

"Has the balanced shifted?" I asked. His eyes again filled with fear. "Contact is forbidden for your protection."

"You said I would not want your army here. That they are not forgiving. Are they the reason behind the order?"

"It is their order," I said. "They are the ones who enforce the rules."

If he asked the next question, I wasn't sure I would answer it. I waited for him to make the connection, for him to figure out that *I* wasn't supposed to be here.

I saw it enter his eyes, a flash of understanding. Then it was shoved aside by four hundred years of expectations. And I was grateful for the prophecy. It bought me time.

"To be queen, I need a teacher," I said. "I am familiar with the role of queens in many places, but I do not know what your culture expects. And my skills don't match with most of those I do know."

"I should send you to my mother," Valemar said, dismissing the idea with a laugh. "More than a seven day ride north of here at Vanerife, our stronghold at the edge of the Aelon Sea. She prefers the sun, blue waters, and gentle breezes. And the cross of cultures that meet there."

"And Aedenfal?" I asked, for that was what I'd heard this place called.

"Our easternmost stronghold. It has stood poised between the grass and woodlands for thousands of years. Longer than the Alfari have been here."

Which still left south and west. Valemar's kingdom was large, I realized.

"One day you shall see it all," Valemar said. "But back to your problem. Daria served my mother. She can help you quite a lot."

"But her position ..." I was grateful he'd offered someone I was already comfortable with, but servants were usually meant to be invisible. That wouldn't help me if I was meeting with groups of wives.

Valemar frowned. "She is your right hand. What about her position?"

"Oh." I fought back a blush that rose. "Many cultures view servants with disdain. They deal with the dirt that you don't want on you. They're not worthy of so many things."

The furrow between Valemar's eyes deepened. "But you need them. They are a gift from the Mother and the Father. Without them there is no protection. Without them, nothing gets done. Do other cultures not value these things?"

"Not in the way you do," I said with a smile. "They are too important for those things. The servants too replaceable."

"I do not think I like your other cultures," Valemar said, still frowning.

"And I think I will like yours very much."

CHAPTER 8

Though princesses are now rare, Earth is a place where fairy tales are still loved. We still watch the Disney movies from four hundred years ago. They are as timeless as Shakespeare's plays, only much more beloved. We want the escape, the happily ever after, rather than the end of a Shakespearean tragedy: a stage littered with characters who strove to live their dreams only to receive death in the end. Adults know that dreams and people die, and so we watch the fairy tales and hope.

As much as I'd wanted to be Belle — for Belle, to me, was the smartest princess — I'd never thought about what came next for all those Disney princesses. Their stories ended in triumph. Witches vanquished, beasts transformed. Princes met and married.

I had married a king, but I wasn't like those princesses. I hadn't actually triumphed. I had succeeded in not dying. I had managed to find a place to build a life. But it was all founded on a lie and a role I wasn't sure I could do. Not even Eleanor of Aquitaine could help me. While I admired her smarts and daring, truth be told, she had ended up imprisoned in a castle in England while her second husband, Henry Plantagenet, carried on with their son Richard's betrothed. Not a future I wanted.

I stood at the window, watching the river flow below me, my mind drifting with the water. It didn't seem possible that I'd crossed the river and entered the castle just two days earlier ... that it had been only two days since I'd strapped myself into the escape pod and prayed to live.

A knock sounded at the door. I turned from the window as Daria entered with the luncheon — fruits and sliced meats, a hunk of bread, and some sweets arranged on a tray. "I thought you might be hungry," she said as she placed it on the buffet table against the wall.

"Thank you." I crossed the room and took the plate that Daria offered. I've eaten more foods on more planets than I can count. Every culture has their bizarre foods, some more palatable than others. I learned early on not to ask where the food came from, to go by taste. After all, who would eat honey if you told them it was really bee barf?

I'd been pleasantly relieved to find the food here was more familiar than foreign. I stacked things on my plate and accepted a glass of wine from Daria.

"The table or the window, my queen?" Daria asked.

"Table," I said. While it would have been pleasant to lounge on the sofas by the view, this was a working lunch, and business is best done at a table. *Reminds the parties of their responsibilities.* A deal done on a sofa or in a nightclub doesn't carry the same weight. Play is play, and business is business. Things get murky when the two are mixed.

We crossed to the table in the center of the room. Daria took the seat to my right. "Valemar said you needed my help."

"I am Queen —" The word still sounded foreign on my tongue. "— but I'm not sure what to do. What my role is."

"Did they not train you as princess?"

"I was expected to have a life away from court. I spent my time traveling, working with traders —" Daria blanched at the word. "— as assistant of sorts. I worked as a protocol specialist."

Daria turned her eyes to the table, though they darted over the surface. Her breathing staggered as she fought for control. I could tell she was trying to reconcile this vision of me working with the outsiders now trading with the Cordair and the vision she'd had of me as savior.

"As a protocol specialist, you helped your employers navigate the customs of whomever they traded with?"

"Yes." I was glad she'd made the connection so quickly.

"And your employers traded widely?"

"Yes, they did." I smiled, thinking she'd never imagine just how widely that was.

The tension passed but a frown remained. "Why did you not do this for your family?"

Because they were ordinary, not royal. "That was what was required of me."

"And when you married, would you still travel?"

I'd never really thought about it, but my constant travel had been what caused the end of my last relationship. Though Dmitri and I had met on Xiros Six — *We had to cross half a galaxy to find each other,* he'd said to me — the fact that we were rarely on the same planet (translation — that *I* was rarely on Earth when he was) had spurred him into giving me "back to the stars."

I tried to picture what it would have looked like: marriage, children. That would have necessitated putting down roots. And while home was basically my room at Finn's house in Edinburgh, it was merely a stopover. A place to visit family and connect before the next journey to the far-flung places of the galaxy.

"I don't know that I would have married," I said to Daria. "I wasn't obliged to do so."

Her eyebrows hit her hairline as her eyes widened. "But you did," she whispered. "You chose to marry."

"I did," I said. "But then, I didn't really have a choice. And now, here I am … not knowing what to do. Outside the bedroom," I clarified, in case she concluded that I had sent Valemar away for that reason.

Daria sipped at her wine, and I took the opportunity to pick at my lunch.

"So you were wondering about how a queen functions in our land?"

"Yes."

"Well —" Daria picked up one of the smaller fruits and popped it in her mouth. She chewed slowly. "Reina — Valemar's mother — rules the north when he is not there. She meets with emissaries from other lands, receives reports regarding the welfare of the city and outlying areas, judges major complaints, approves plans for the running of the High — staffing, menus, guard details. I would expect that Valemar wants you to take up those roles for his other residences." She gave me a sly smile. "It sounds similar to being a protocol specialist."

Pieces of it did. But the rest? What did I know about how a household, let alone a large household, ran? And acting as judge?

But I could start with the smaller pieces. I could meet with emissaries and other groups, preferably along with Valemar. I would need to become an apprentice, to learn as princes do.

A voice in my head reminded me that wives learned because they were their husband's relief from the day. *Tell me your troubles.* So many secrets spilled on the pillow. So much counsel given.

I ran my thumb over the bandage on my finger. At some point, I'd have to wrap my head around that reality. I *was* married. I could, however, pull on my work persona and begin the job in front of me.

"That is true," I said to Daria. "But I am going to need some teachers. I know nothing about Bánalfar or the lands around it. I know nothing of your history or customs or religion." I closed my eyes. *Crap!* The Mödatal would likely become my tutor. I sucked in a breath and continued. "Even your plants and animals are foreign. If I am going to become what you have described, I am going to need to learn it all."

The advantage of having Reina as a role model was that she didn't spend a lot of time in sewing or gossip. I've never been good with a needle, not that there's much call for one. My mother did try to teach me to sew on a button once, "just in case." I bled all over the shirt and have picked out clothing without that particular device ever since.

I'm not averse to gossip, it can be informative. But business gossip doesn't do the damage that personal gossip can (unless you want it to), and women/girls in groups still give me hives after the torturous school days of my teenage years. I couldn't imagine they were much better all grown up with nothing else to do but talk. In my experience, they reined in their claws better when they were in mixed groups.

Instead, I began to spend my afternoons in the company of Padrid, an old, gray-haired man with a wizened face but sharp blue eyes. They danced with delight when we were introduced.

"I didn't think I'd live to see the day," he said, bowing low. The rolled-up scroll under his arm reached toward the sky. "And yet,

you've come." He straightened and took my hands. "And you've a curious mind, they've told me."

"I need instruction on Bánalfar," I said. "There are so many things I don't know."

He squeezed my hands and took the scroll from under his arm. "I've just the thing." Padrid turned to the table and placed the scroll upon it. He tacked down the corner of one side with a glass and the other with the edge of a book. Then, with a wave of his hand, he unrolled the curl of paper to reveal a map. I moved around the table to get a better look as he set items on the last two corners.

Painted in brilliant colors, the top of the map showed a coastline dotted with islands. The waters were done in turquoise blue and the islands and lands along the coast a soft green. The color deepened the farther south it went. Forests were dark green and brown. Deep blue rivers cut through the forests and rich green farmland, the rivers growing wider as they neared the sea. The grassy steppe where I'd crashed took up most of the right-hand side of the map. To its east were the hills and mountains of the Cordair, shown in deep brown and gray. Gray and white mountains marked the south. The west had gentle hills running off the edge of the paper. Just left of the center, a cluster of large trees had been drawn.

"Bánalfar as it has been for two thousand years," Padrid said. His voice was laced with pride and awe.

"That is quite a feat," I said.

His eyes widened in surprise. "Is it not that way on the moon?"

"No," I said, a smile softening my words. "Ambition has a way of making men want to change both the land and its people."

Padrid grunted. "Sounds like the Cordair." He stretched out a finger over the map then looked back over his shoulder at me. "Can you read our words?"

"I can," I said.

"And you speak our language. How is it you can do both of these things yet you have no knowledge of us?"

"I have a gift for language, both written and spoken."

Padrid's bottom lip pooched out as he bobbed his head in thought. "As it should be." A smile lit up his face. "Well, let's get you up to speed on the rest.

"Valemar's people have always lived in the north, among the Lian Isles and Vanerife," Padrid said, pointing. "It's said they have been there since we first left Father Sea for the land." Padrid's finger traced down to the center. "Gladama — the Glade of Time. These ancient trees have sheltered us for thousands of years. The Lagofinn, Valemar's ancestors, traveled down here more than two thousand years ago when the trees were first threatened."

Padrid's eyes smoldered with anger. "The Dorchior, ancestors of the Cordair, did not value the trees. Or the land. Even then they dug, chopping down the trees to fuel their furnaces." His finger traced its way to the east, to the dark hills of the Cordair. "They chopped down the trees that struggled on the hills. Few grow there today, even though they now use black rock to fuel their furnaces. And the people are dark as well."

Padrid's eyes flicked over me, taking in my dark hair and flat, round ears. "They are dark in their hearts, dark in their looks, and dark in their practices. Even their homes are buried in the rock they spend their lives in." His finger traced its way back to the steppe. "Fairfada, the Sea of Grass. Enartin, Valemar's father, gave it back to the Cordair. Hoped it would keep them from pillaging the farms and towns along the western edge. They're to let our anapali graze unmolested in return for twenty percent of the wool harvest. But our animals go missing."

"Twenty percent?" I asked, all too familiar with those who skimmed off more of a portion than was contracted.

Padrid barked with laughter. "You are a wise one. Yes, and still we keep our part of the bargain. But Aedenfal —" His finger moved to the city we were now in. One of five large cities marked on the map, and perhaps the largest after Vanerife. "Aedenfal stays ready. Stays armed."

And soon faced soldiers clad in Awrakian armor. Change was brewing, and even I could feel it.

CHAPTER 9

I might have been the fulfillment of a prophecy, but I was still an outsider. It was there in the looks that most of the inhabitants of the castle gave me. There weren't many that I spent time with as I slowly settled into a pattern. Daria brought me breakfast, laced me into my dress for the day, then watched, occasionally giggling as I tried to learn my way around the warren of rooms and passageways that made up the High, as the castle was known (the town was known as the Low), ready to help me find a way back to familiar ground. Afternoons rotated — Padrid with his history lessons and Valemar for trade or politics.

I spent no time in the company of women other than Daria, which was fine by me. I hated their whisperings and looks of distrust. Padrid grew to overlook my dark brown hair and strange ears, but generations of viewing the Cordair as dangerous beings meant many of the people were wont to lump me there as well. And it probably didn't help that it was widely known that Valemar didn't share my bed.

He'd made no overtures toward me since the second night of our marriage. The first few afternoons had started awkward, though my questions transformed him into the statesman, eager to talk about the lands and people he loved. He was cordial at dinner but either oblivious to the whispers around the banqueting room or indifferent to stopping them. From the looks of hatred Zhanet still threw me, I didn't think Valemar was sharing her bed, either.

I put off instruction with the Mödatal as long as possible, but after seven days, I knew I really needed to include her. For my visit, Daria and I donned long, red veils and walked to the Cair in the company of Heymond and one of the castle guards. I could have had her come to me, but I thought it best to be seen trying to fit in.

The inhabitants of the Low surely knew who we were for there weren't any other women from the High who went about with armed guards. It was my first chance to see the town properly, without the crowds lining the streets and a star chart fixed in my mind.

I'd studied medieval and tech-young Earth one year as a prep for my customs course. Aedenfal reminded me of those early maps I'd studied, before the ease of transportation and communication turned the cities inside out — the wealthy abandoning the centers of town to the poor. The homes and businesses closest to the High were large and well maintained. Both were adorned with flowers and displays meant to catch the eye and please the nose. The size of the buildings as shrank we traveled farther away. The homes and businesses became modest, but still clean. There were no homeless inside Aedenfal.

"There are always those who don't want to work," Daria explained when I asked. "You'll usually find them loitering around the taverns. But there is plenty in Bánalfar. There is always something to do, some way to earn coin."

"And those who can't work?" I asked.

Her head jerked toward me, a flash of red veil. "But everyone can work," she said. "Unless they're ill, everyone *can* work."

"So only those who are in hospital don't work."

"Hospital?" Daria asked.

"A place for the ill. When you're so sick you need constant medical care."

"Why wouldn't they be at home?" She sounded incredulous.

"When you're very ill and you need constant nursing care and attention from the doctors."

"But surely your family or servants could nurse you best." Her head shook from side to side. "Sounds awful."

"On the moon, doctors and nurses get specialized training in how to treat and cure illnesses. They're much better prepared to help the ill than the sick person's family members." And they had tools, such as the repbots currently flowing through my blood, but I didn't share that with her.

"Like Ferrick."

"Yes, like Ferrick. But you'd go to him so he could watch over several ill people at the same time."

"Hmm. I guess that would be more efficient." She still sounded doubtful, and by this time we'd come up the rise that the Cair stood on and to the great doors that marked its entrance. Heymond had the other soldier stay outside while he followed us in.

Again, I was struck by the height inside the cathedral and fascinated by the patterns the stained glass windows cast on the walls and floor. Daria led me into an alcove where we lit small red tapers and added them to the nearly hundred already burning in tiers of sand-filled trays.

We walked past a side chapel where a few people, both men and veiled women, knelt in prayer. The gasps that issued as we passed

told me that not all of them were focused on their devotions. Daria opened a wooden door halfway down the sanctuary toward the altar.

"I'll wait for you here," Heymond said, inclining his head, and took up a post against the wall by the door.

We went down a hall lined with wooden doors. A tall candelabra sat at the bend, thick yellow candles guttering in the drafts. Daria went three doors down beyond the corner and knocked on the door to the right.

"Enter."

"I'll leave you here," Daria said with a bow. "Come find me in the sanctuary when you're ready to leave." She backed away then turned and disappeared around the corner. I sucked my breath in and made myself turn the knob.

The Mödatal sat on a low sofa arranged at a right angle to a fireplace in which a fire blazed even though the weather was warm. "My queen," she said, and dipped her head. She gestured to the matching sofa across from her. "Tea?" she asked as I took my seat.

"Yes, thank you."

It was warm by the fire, but goosebumps crawled across my arms, making me wish I'd brought a shawl. I clasped my hands in my lap to keep from trying to rub away the signs of my unease.

The Mödatal handed me a steaming cup. The aroma that wafted up was woodsy. It had a smoky flavor, unsweetened, but not unpleasant. She gave me a cat-like smile and curled her bare feet up next to her. "So you've come for religious instruction?"

I blew on the tea to cool it, having learned that such an action was not an insult. "I'm not sure what your religious beliefs are here."

"We worship Father Sea and Mother Moon." The Mödatal picked up her own cup, an action I found reassuring for I had wondered with that smile of hers if she'd doctored the tea. "All life comes from the sea, but without the Mother who creates the tides and pulls us toward her, there would be no procreation. The sea would never change and would stagnate. There would be no rhythm and no life. But you know this, for it is true on your world, too."

The hairs on my arms stood up, adding to the prickly feeling that crawled over me. "For some species," I said.

"And what do you worship?" she asked. There was a challenging glint in her eye.

Religion wasn't a daily part of my life though I had grown up going to church. I'd been so many places and seen so many things that I found the effort to define God somewhat limiting. Each culture sought to put the idea in a box they could understand. But it was bigger than that. When one spent so much time out in the stars, in the utter vastness and void of space, you came to realize that there was something about the universe itself that wanted life. Within the emptiness, it was created over and over again. Life that was more familiar than foreign. Something, someone craved relationship, and even I could feel it.

"Connection," I said.

"Yet you also fear it."

I blushed, thinking she was speaking of my empty bed.

"That as well," the Mödatal added, as if she'd read my mind. "We worship life and the forces that create it. Are in awe of the forces that create it. It has a power here that you have lost on your world … for you have too much light." My eyes widened.

The Mödatal sipped her tea. "Our moonlight is half-light. So much dimmer than the day," she continued. "Not a white stone in the sky, but a ruby. And its blood pulls on our blood more than yours does." Her eyes met mine, and I knew that she did not believe I was from the moon.

"You told Valemar I was the Moon Princess."

"You are the Moon Princess." Her eyes held nothing but certainty. "You are the daughter of kings, are you not?"

My heart fell into my stomach. This woman knew things about me she shouldn't. "Yes," I whispered. The hairs on my arms became like porcupine quills. What was she that she could divine these things?

The Mödatal laughed, a light, tinkling laugh. "I'm no outsider like you. You know what I am." It had barely begun in the back of my mind, the wondering that maybe she too was from the stars. And somehow, she knew perceived even that. "I am a seer."

"But the prophecy is four hundred years old."

"Yet I saw you coming. How else would Heymond have known where to be? If not for me, you'd be with the Cordair right now." I shivered. "Yes, you would have gotten a much different reception from them."

"But I can't do what you or Valemar want me to do."

The Mödatal sipped her tea again. "And what is that?"

"An army! Valemar wants an army."

She met my gaze over her cup. "You have an army. But the time isn't right."

I fought back the urge to scream. "And I suppose you know when that time is?"

"Um." She swallowed her latest sip. "No. But it's out there." She fixed me with a hard stare. "You weren't out there until nineteen days ago. Mind the tea," she added as my hands went slack and the cup nearly slipped from my grasp. The *Palmas Cove* had entered the system nineteen days ago.

I lifted my cup and gulped, wanting to fill myself with something other than the sensation that things were wildly out of control.

"People come to the Cair on their own most of the month. For sanctuary. To light a candle," the Mödatal went on as if most of our conversation hadn't happened. "The Cair will be crowded the morning of the resting moon with people seeking the Möd's blessing and to offer prayers that the Blood Moon has created life." A wistful expression settled on her face. "They come to be part of a community. Your role as queen is to be part of that community."

"They don't trust me," I said, and stared into my now-empty cup.

"You are not what they expected."

"I am dark."

"They fear the darkness of the Cordair, but you are dark like the moon."

"The moon is red," I said.

"Yes, ours is no pearl. Or diamond light in the sky. Pale, as Valemar and his ancestors are sun-washed pale. Like yours were. But you are dark like our moon, for our resting moon is dark. And from the moon you have come." She offered me her first real smile. "They will see that in time."

Despite the Mödatal's scarily accurate information and insistence that I was supposed to be here, it was hard to wrap my brain around the idea. I thought about it on the mile or more walk back to the High. I was no savior. I'd survived the plasma leak simply because I was holed up in my cabin going over another file.

Think, Astrid! If this wasn't a 'no contact' planet, what would you be doing?

Daria walked silently next to me, allowing me to be lost in my reflection.

Finding a way to call for help. Not an option here.

Imagine you had been left behind on Reggi Five after the drinking game with the Nortani delegation. My head pounded in memory of the hangover. *What would you have done?*

Find a way to transmit a signal. Loneliness washed over me, digging its needle claws into my heart. I'd always been part of something. I'd never not had an out.

I bit my lip as the thought crossed my mind — I should have just drunk myself to oblivion and gone on the journey into the sun with the rest of the crew. I wasn't supposed to be here.

But you are here. You chose life.

I had. And I'd done it again when Valemar had offered his protection. But the expectations chafed. I'd anticipated having to struggle to blend in, butI hadn't considered that someone might hand me a role. Especially one that was so not who I was at my core.

You were practically a statesman, the voice in my head argued. *Isn't that what they're asking you to do?*

No. It was a whole lot more. But I could start there. Despite my misgivings, the Mödatal seemed to be an ally. She didn't have a timetable, had repeatedly told me to be patient.

I started my list of what to do next. One — ask Valemar for a task, something I could actually do. Despite all the changes in Europe and Asia over the last five hundred years, there were still kings and queens on thrones. The countries that didn't have them changed with every whim of the populace. Countries like England, Sweden, and Japan had changed, too, but there was pride in being rooted in something so ancient. Royals were important touchstones for their populaces. I needed to find a way to integrate myself into the Alfari.

Step number two I pushed away. It was one I wasn't ready to take. The rest of it would ultimately hinge upon it, but I wanted to claim the last bit of me while I still could.

And then I reviewed my list of allies. Valemar — who counted only because he believed I was the Moon Princess. The Mödatal — for the same reason.

I watched Heymond striding along in front of Daria and me, hand on the hilt of his sword, just in case. *Mo banorisa.* He, too, believed I was the Moon Princess. All of them did. I had allies only because of a lie.

I sighed. My life was a house of cards that one breath could collapse.

I had Daria lace me into a deep red gown that evening. The moon was growing fuller, bathing Bánalfar and all the lands of Teridun Four in a red glow similar to that used by militaries all around the galaxy to illuminate their ships at night. I'd once asked why and had been told that red has a longer wave length and less energy so it doesn't travel very far. It doesn't light up the sky. It also doesn't degrade your night vision like white light does. So Teridun's moon allowed its creatures better access to the dark. All of them but me.

The Mödatal was right about one thing. Laced into the blood-red dress with my dark hair flowing past my shoulders, I did look a lot like the nearly full moon in the sky.

Our visit to the Cair had not gone unnoticed. When I entered the dining hall that evening, I watched them take in my dress and my hair. I held myself like a queen, and when their eyes met mine, it was with grudging respect and a dip of their heads. Valemar tried to mask his longing, but I could feel his desire washing over me even when his attention was focused on his plate.

Zhanet followed our every move. There was no hatred in her eyes tonight, though she ground her teeth. Her gaze traveled from

an appraisal of me, to Valemar's suffering, and back again. When our eyes met, she smirked. *It's only a matter of time,* her smile seemed to say.

I ran my thumb along the scab on my index finger. How long could I keep Valemar from my bed before it turned out to be too long?

I wandered the next day, proud that I was finally beginning to learn the twisting passageways that made up the non-public halls of the High. I'd left Daria behind, determined to venture where I hadn't gone before, willing to become hopelessly lost.

I was about half an hour into my wanderings. These areas of the castle seemed little used. Empty. Quiet. So it was easy for me to hear the whisper of fabric, the quiet shuffle of feet in quick movements. The hiss of something cutting the air.

His back was to me when I crept down the short passageway that led to the room. But he froze, aware that he was no longer alone. Then the movements began again. The ballet of kata. His hands moved almost too fast to see — a curved sword in one hand and a wicked looking knife in the other. My impression of how lethal Valemar was was absolutely justified. I couldn't imagine anything standing against him and still live.

I backed away and left him to his practice. My hand trailed against the stone as I continued down the corridor for I found it hard to keep my balance. Valemar could slit my throat and I'd never see it coming. But instead, his blade was mine. I just needed to claim it.

CHAPTER 10

The full moon, or Blood Moon as the Alfari called it, arrived. I'd been on Teridun Four for thirteen days, in the star system for almost twice that. My mind was elsewhere, wondering what my family was going through, when Daria asked me to raise my arms and lowered the dress over my head. It was only when she set about pulling the fabric and arranging it that I realized she wasn't going to be lacing me into it. The dress was cut similar to the one she usually wore, but even hers was less fitted than usual.

"It's the traditional Blood Moon dress," Daria said when I asked. There was a strain to her voice, and her movements were quicker than usual. "If there's nothing else, my queen …"

"You may go," I said. She ducked out in a hurry.

As I watched her go, Orin's explanation of the full moon's effect on the Alfari rippled up from my memory. Tonight would be a night of couplings. *The Alfari are overcome with the urge to mate.*

I walked down to dinner, contemplating my safety as well as the chances I'd be greeted by an orgy. I wasn't. Dinner was nearly its normal affair. Platters were passed around, wine was poured, but everyone's focus was on the food. There was little conversation. I wondered if that was because the moon had not yet risen.

Valemar's movements were slightly drunken as I took my seat. His pupils were heavily dilated when he turned his gaze to me. On Earth, certain species only mate at the full moon, drawn to the surface of the water or into the sky by the light. Teridun's moon apparently had the same effect on its people.

I saw a brief flash of longing in Valemar's eyes before he blinked and looked away. Longing, not lust. When he picked up his wine, his gaze went across the room to Zhanet. Her eyes met his, and I remembered the look she'd given me a couple of nights before. She was his moon mate. She was who he'd have been with tonight if I hadn't been here.

And as I watched Valemar, I realized that she was who he'd be with tonight if I did nothing. The room seethed with clamped desire.

I'd wanted to marry for love, but I hadn't. And even if I had, half of all marriages failed. But what was love? *I love the way you make me feel.* Husbands and wives changed partners when that feeling changed.

But what if you picked a person to fulfill the role of husband or wife? The role didn't change, even if that person or your feelings did. And frequently love did come when a marriage was arranged. One only had to look at how devoted Edward I of England had been to his wife Eleanor. He'd had no affairs, taken no mistresses, during their marriage. And he'd been so devastated when she died that he had stone monuments erected at the places her body had rested overnight at on its journey to London for burial, twelve crosses in all. He'd continued their personal traditions and attended memorial services for her even after he married again to ensure the succession.

Love was possible where there was respect. And Valemar did respect me.

When the meal was nearly finished, I took Valemar's hand and stood. Other couples were already drifting away. We didn't speak as we walked back to my room, but once the door closed, Valemar leaned a trembling hand against it.

"Are you sure?" he asked between ragged breaths. His eyes blinked, and he struggled for focus. "I won't be able to stop."

"I know."

He stared at me clearly through the moon lust for just a moment then pulled me to him, bringing his mouth down on mine. His kisses were urgent, though his hands shook. He held me, breathed me in, pressed me against him. When I kissed him back, he took my dress in his hands and began to lift it over me, our mouths still connected. He drew the dress and my shift over my head in one smooth motion then pulled off his tunic. Then his mouth was against mine again, and he carried me to the bed.

His leggings were shucked off as he crawled onto the bed to join me. I shivered as his bare skin came against mine. His hands came to my face and he stared at me for a moment before losing himself again to the urge.

Even in the throes of moon lust, Valemar was a skilled lover. Something that made it easier to turn off the thinking part of my brain, the part that kept screaming that I was only property to be used. My body responded as before, and this time I didn't shy away when he looked down at me after, stroking the hair out of my face.

His dilated eyes slowly contracted. Then he placed his arm under me and turned onto his back, pulling me onto his chest. It was then that I noticed the tattoo of green leaves that circled his chest and shoulders like a permanent livery collar. I may have seen a flash of green on our wedding night, but I'd tried so hard not to look, to not make the experience any more real than I'd had to, that I had missed the striking set of linked leaves. The hand that reached up to run through my hair had a similar tattoo, a hand's width from the wrist.

"Why did you change your mind?" Valemar's voice rumbled in his chest and echoed in the ear I had pressed to it.

"You're my husband."

Valemar tucked the strand of hair lying across my cheek behind my ear. "I thought you wanted a marriage built on love."

"Love doesn't always last. But it needs to start somewhere. We might grow to love each other. But we can't if I don't try."

Valemar didn't answer. He just continued to run his fingers through my hair in long slow strokes, which was an answer in itself.

"What are these?" I asked, running my fingers along the tattoo on his chest.

"Barat leaves. Padrid told you about Gladama?" I nodded. "They're a symbol of protection given to warriors." He held up an arm. "So that our hands are quick and sure." His fingers touched the leaves on his chest. "So that the trees shelter us and our hearts, even in battle. They protect us as we protect them. It's the leaf in our crowns and your wedding belt."

"I just thought those were symbols of Bánalfar's woodlands."

Valemar chuckled, shaking me as his chest moved. "That is true, too." His arms came around me and he buried his lips in my hair. "Does this mean that I am welcome here, or do you still need more time?"

My brain wanted to scream, *More time!* But my heart ...

Valemar had offered me his protection from our very first meeting, and here, in his arms, I did feel safe. I trembled as I let go of the fear and held onto trust. Even so, I had trouble giving voice to the words.

"You are welcome," I said, and another little piece of Astrid Carr slipped away.

I awoke the next morning, still in Valemar's arms, my cheek stuck to his chest. "Good morning." His voice rumbled against my ear. His hand ruffled my hair. Gently. Softly. Slowly. I was still the deer.

"Morning," I said. But then a wave of pain surged up from my heart. My limbs began to shake. The box of emotions I'd been shoving things into ever since the *Palmas Cove* had entered the system heaved inside my heart. With a twist, the horror broke free. It pounded against my breastbone as it rushed out, and I gasped, trying to call it back.

Valemar raised my chin, held it until my eyes met his. I blinked, trying to see through the brine collecting on my lashes, and forced my chattering teeth to speak, to explain.

"There was an accident. I —"

But I clamped down, refusing to part with the rest of the information. Telling him I wasn't supposed to be here, telling him I'd called for help but no one came, telling him I was no princess but a peasant, would only harm me. It was the Moon Princess that Valemar held so tenderly, not me. So I hid, burrowing into his embrace as I tried to shove the lid back on.

Valemar sighed and continued to stroke my hair, offering the comfort he knew I'd accept. But the comfort made the pain more real. Each sweep of his hand brushed away a little bit of the wall I'd built up around myself.

"I thought I'd already mourned," I murmured into his chest.

"Grief is strange," Valemar said. "It hits you even when you think you've dealt with it and things are fine." He fell silent for a

moment then swallowed heavily. "Sometimes when I'm doing my jaldun, I hear my father's voice … remember his instructions, his touch shaping my movements. I remember, and I wish that he were still king and not me."

Both my parents lived. I had a brother and sister-in-law. And a niece and nephew. I had family. But they no longer had me.

"How long has your father been gone?" I asked. *How long will they mourn me?*

"Ten years," Valemar whispered.

"How?"

My head moved as he shrugged. "A wasting disease."

I could feel his pain then, roiling away beneath the surface, the intimacy of the marriage bed allowing me to see this man's suffering. And he mine. Even when I hadn't known that I still mourned.

I kissed him then. Not because I wanted him to wash my pain away. I kissed him so I could wash away his. Valemar kissed me back and rolled us over.

At some point, I was going to have to tell him the truth. And I wanted it to be his wife he was looking at when I did. Not an imposter.

"What would you like to do this morning?" Daria asked as she laced me into the dress for today. I'd chosen one in a sky-blue color. My insides were still raw. I ached for everything about my previous life, but I wanted the sadness inside me to turn the color of a summer day.

"I'm open to suggestion," I said. Crawling back under the covers for a good cry wasn't going to happen.

"Well, we could always go sew with the ladies." Daria giggled.

"Sew! I can't sew." The words were out of my mouth before I could stop them.

Daria's face appeared over my shoulder in the mirror. "You can't?"

"Not a skill I needed," I said.

"Hmm." Daria's eyes darted back and forth as she thought. She raised them to me. "Do you want to learn?"

I gave her a gentle smile. "Not today."

Daria tied off the laces and straightened the run. "I doubt she'll be there today."

"She?"

Her eyes sparkled with merriment. "Zhanet. I doubt she'll be there today. She won't want it rubbed in her face by the others."

"No, I'm sure she wouldn't," I murmured.

While I was glad to have removed that potential problem from my future, it rankled that everyone knew what I did. And what I didn't do.

Daria began tidying up. "She should have known he'd never marry her."

"Oh?"

"People don't usually marry their moon mates."

"Don't they?"

"Well, it's just sex. Anyone would do."

"I see." I held back a giggle. "So you weren't choosy last night?" Daria blushed furiously. "And does this 'anyone' have a name?"

"Yes," she said. "But he's part of the castle guard."

"Ah. No chance of marriage then."

Daria folded my dressing gown over her arm. "Do you ... on the moon?" she asked. "Do you marry your partners?"

"Sometimes," I said. "Sometimes it's just sex, but usually it's a trial run. You spend time together with someone you're interested

in. Enjoy each other. See how you work together in all things before marriage." Daria nodded.

I thought about her first question, what I wanted to do. In the fourteen days I'd been here, I'd only been outside the High twice. Both times to the Cair. "Something outside?" I suggested. "Shall we do something outside?"

"We should visit the shops on the high street," Daria said. Her eyes began to glow. "The queen should be seen supporting the local merchants."

"But I don't have any coin."

Daria waved her hand dismissively. "You're the queen. You don't need any coin. If the merchants wish to be reimbursed for anything you select, they'll send a bill to Andol, Aedenfal's treasurer."

I'd certainly purchased things with other people's money before, but there was at least some type of transaction that occurred. This was going to be an odd shopping trip indeed.

There was nothing that I actually needed. I had clothing, jewels, and cosmetics. My food was provided for me. I was curious, though, as to the kinds of goods to be found in the shops of Aedenfal. Daria took me to a clothing shop first.

"Ah! My queen!" The proprietor was the shortest Alfari male I'd yet seen, only a few inches taller than me. He bowed deep then looked up at me. "What can I show you today?" He straightened and tapped his fingers excitely. "I have a Fairfada grazed anapali in a new color." The man darted to the left where bolts of fabric sat stacked on white-painted shelves. He pulled down a purplely-red bolt, unwound it once, and held it out to me. "They're calling it Cordair Blush."

It did look about the color of Raislos's face when I'd laughed at him. I took the cloth between my fingers. "This isn't silk?" I asked, surprised at the softness.

"Silk?" A furrow appeared between the proprietor's eyes.

"A fiber insects create."

"Ah! You want the *gresánve*." He snapped his fingers and darted off to the other side of the shop.

"I thought most of my gowns were silk," I said to Daria. "I can tell some of them are wool."

Daria picked up a bolt and handed me the tail end of the cloth. "This is anapali grazed on Bánalfar grass." The fabric felt like cashmere. "Your dress, most of your dresses, are anapali grazed on Fairfada, the grassland to the east." She set the bolt down again. "With such a difference in the quality of the wool, you see the importance of the grazing rights. And the animals."

The proprietor bounced back with a bolt of sheer white fabric in his hands. "The finest gresánve. Just in. Perfect for some new nightdresses for you, my queen!" His cupped hand traced the air in front of me, illustrating how they'd cling.

Up close, there was a silver opalescence to the fabric and a slight stickiness that reminded me of spider web. I could well imagine what any nightdresses would look like on. "What gives the fabric its color?"

The man's eyes bulged in their sockets. "Well, the gresán itself," he said with surprise.

"So there's crushed gresán coating the fibers?"

"That's how we get the shine on many fabrics," Daria said.

The iridescent robes that Valemar had worn at our first meeting had glittered like some kind of beetle. Now I knew there probably was beetle in it.

Which wasn't that strange. The look, the feel of fabrics was what mattered throughout the galaxy. The protocol specialist in me kicked in. Perfect opportunity to do some research.

"I think I'll just look around a while," I said and inclined my head. I hoped he'd take the hint I was dismissing him.

His smile wavered before it was yanked up again. "Of course. Of course. Just let me know if you need any assistance."

"I really don't need anything," I said to Daria as the proprietor reluctantly slunk back behind the cutting counter. Daria picked up the end of the gresánve and draped it over the back of her hand. It clung to every curve just as I'd imagined it would.

"Oh, I don't know. You've nothing of this in your wardrobe." She gave me a saucy smile and waggled her eyebrows. "Might come in handy."

"Uh huh. And what is a gresán?"

"It's an insect that lives in the upper canopy of trees. Makes its home with these fibers."

"And what does it eat?" I asked

"Small creatures."

I bit my lips. *Of course it did.* "Let me think about it," I said. "Why don't we take the opportunity of being here and you can give me an education on the fabrics and the dyes used to color them."

We walked around the shop. Daria pulled down bolts of fabric, had me run them between my fingers. I could soon tell the difference between the ones made from the four most common wools and the three most common plant fibers. Some dyes, she knew, came from plants. Still others were secrets closely guarded by the weaver.

When I thought I'd gotten a good grasp on the textiles and the proprietor had nearly fainted from holding back both his enthusiasm at having the queen in his shop and his dismay at my not having

purchased anything (all the while Orin was keeping any other customers at bay), I picked up the bolt of gresánve and brought it to the cutting table.

"I'll take one nightdress in this," I said, and drew up my work persona to keep from blushing at his licentious appraisal of me.

The tape measure trembled in his hands. "Of course!" He all but squealed, delight lighting his eyes.

Daria whipped the tape measure out of his hands. "*I'll* measure her. Just tell me what you need."

The smile slipped down his face and never quite returned. He pulled a sheet of paper from the stack and gave Daria the first measurement he'd need. I raised my arms to the sides and stood still as Daria pinned down the end of it on my shoulder with one finger and marked a spot on my wrist with the other. She moved the tape measure to my collar bone and ran it down to the top of my bust, then under. Moved it from the top of my bust to my waist. Circled my hips.

It was not a nightgown I planned on wearing any time soon, but I wanted to have it tucked away. An elegant, sexy weapon waiting in my wardrobe. The time might come when I'd want Valemar to think with his lust.

It did make me think that I should get him a gift, something I could present him with when we were alone. Something that wasn't my body. Something that would communicate my thankfulness for his taking me into his life. He'd married me for his own agenda, but then I'd had one of my own as well. All business transactions were that way — the meeting of two people's self-interests for mutual benefit. The best understood how to sweeten the pot. And I'd worked for some of the best. I needed a gift that was personal, that showed I was paying attention to the man.

Daria handed the tape back to the proprietor and the two of them began to haggle over embellishments. I kept my mouth shut. Daria knew my tastes by now.

The gift also needed to reflect me. *Do you have oceans on the moon? Our star gazers can't see through the clouds.*

And then I had the answer. A gift that reflected both me — Astrid — and the Moon Princess.

The proprietor was just putting his pencil back behind his ear when my attention finally returned to my surroundings.

"And I'll take the entire bolt of fabric," I said. "Whatever you don't use, send up to the High with the dress."

"We'll just measure it up now," Daria said in a sweet tone that belied the steel underneath.

A flicker of annoyance crossed the man's face, and I knew I was right to have purchased the bolt. Moon Princess nightgowns were sure to become all the rage, commanding just about any price. My buying the bolt meant my dress would be the only one. At least, until he managed to secure another length of the cloth.

The bolt was unfolded, measured, and folded up again. I put on my best regal smile, thanked the man, and made my way outside where I erupted into giggles, startling Orin.

"I'm so glad you thought of that, my queen," Daria said. The bell on the door jingled as she closed it behind her.

"Yes, well I realized whatever I had made would soon be copied. And something like that, not seen in public, copied exactly —" I shivered. Images of Zhanet draped in the fabric came to mind. "Any chance of intercepting the next bolt of fabric, too?"

"I'll put out some feelers," Daria said. "Where to now?"

"I was thinking of getting Valemar a gift. A public gift," I clarified, since the nightgown could be considered one. "A telescope, perhaps?"

Daria hummed. Her eyebrows inched together as she thought. "Who would make such a thing?" she asked.

I frowned. "I'm not sure. It would have metal." But I couldn't see a blacksmith making something like that. "And glass." Maybe a jeweler?

"We could try the glass shop the next street over," Daria said.

The windows of the shop were filled with colorful vases, an array of wine glasses and water goblets in various styles and shapes, and, what were to me, fantastical creatures. Whether real or imaginary, I couldn't tell, not being familiar enough with Teridun's fauna to know the difference.

"My queen." The proprietor gave me a low bow. His long blond braid slid over his shoulder and down toward the floor. "To what do I owe the pleasure?"

"I'm looking for a gift for the king. I was thinking a telescope, perhaps, but I'm not sure where I'd find one."

He straightened up. A thoughtful smile spread across his face, and he inclined his head. "We have done such things." His arm swept toward the back counter. "If you'd like to describe to me what you're looking for, I'd be glad to write up an order. Though I must warn you, large lenses can be tricky."

We wound our way through the displays. Necklaces made from glass beads draped from wire stands like garlands on Christmas trees. On another table, several small freestanding and hand mirrors had been grouped in a tasteful arrangement. My eyes traced the curve of one, and a file flicked open in my brain.

"Do you use mercury in the backing on your mirrors?" I asked. The proprietor froze in his tracks. "My people first made mirrors using a silver mercury amalgam. Then they found that a tin and silver amalgam worked better. Some continued to use the mercury, until it

was found that mercury exposure could cause madness. Silver nitrate eventually became the most common backing."

A client from Tendorra Eight had insisted that I acquire some mirrors from Versailles for him before he'd agree to the deal Agçay had proposed. The request was an impossibility, of course, due to their heritage status, but I'd done so much research on the antique ones that were available, hoping to placate him, that my brain now went into analyze mode whenever I saw an old or foreign mirror.

"Trade secrets, I know," I said when he didn't respond. "I was just curious."

The proprietor shifted, turning so I got a side view and not the dishonor of his back. "Tin and mercury," he said when he'd recovered his voice. He stepped behind the counter and took out a sheet of paper, his eyes low, still hiding his gaze. "What were you looking for?" He dipped a pen into the ink and waited, his hand poised over the paper.

"Well —" I began, ready to rattle off what I remembered of my grandfather's telescope, when I caught sight of a spyglass on a shelf behind the counter. In that moment, I knew I hadn't been picturing Valemar staring through the small opening of a contraption as big as I was. However, a spyglass wasn't much good for stargazing. You could see the moon in greater detail with a spyglass, but it was most often used to get a closer look your enemies.

This time my mind filled with the memory of the Cordair and the Hormani trader walking out of the throne room in their Awrakian armor and the smug smiles they threw me as they left. "Actually, is the spyglass for sale?" I asked as my stomach twisted into knots.

The proprietor picked the spyglass up. And picked up my thoughts. The now serious expression on his face was softened by

the pride in his voice. "It is telescoping," he said, and demonstrated, sliding it to its narrowest length, opening it back up, then closing it again. "Can fit in a pocket." The proprietor brought the spyglass back to its full length and offered it to me, laid across his palms.

The metal was cool to the touch. *Brass*, I thought. It sat comfortably in my hands. I held it up to my eye and turned toward the display shelves in the windows. I could trace the variegated colors on the vases. I could see every petal on the flowers in the planter box across the street. I swallowed hard. War was coming. I didn't know how soon, but the undercurrent had been there since Heymond had first taken my arm. At some point, Valemar would ride to war. I couldn't stop it, but I could acknowledge that I knew the stakes.

I closed the spyglass back up and handed it to him. "I would be willing to sell it to you if it meets with your approval, my queen," he said.

"It does." I laced my fingers together to keep my hands from shaking. "Could I perhaps get it engraved?"

He flashed me a gracious smile. "Of course."

Daria and I browsed while he took it into the back room. He emerged about fifteen minutes later. The words I'd asked for scrolled across the center section of the spyglass, only visible when it was fully extended. He tucked it into a fabric lined box and held it out to me.

"I, too, hope for the words you've placed there," he said.

I thanked him, and Daria and I rejoined Orin outside. "You look like you could use a pick me up," Daria said. I hadn't been able to find my smile. "There's a sweetshop around the corner that serves the most wonderful lian tarts."

A bit of sunshine. That was certainly what I needed.

CHAPTER 11

I had the box waiting on the table in my room that night. I put on a nightgown, even though I was sure I wouldn't be wearing it for long, and covered it with a robe. I had told Valemar that he was welcome in my chambers and now expected that he'd join me nightly.

And he did. He didn't knock, but I heard the floor squeak outside my room. I slipped a bookmark into my book. Valemar opened the door and came in. His eyes moved from the empty bed to my chair by the lone, high window. The candle next to me flickered in the draft.

"Am I welcome tonight?" he asked.

"Of course. You are my husband." It had taken me awhile to get there, but I now accepted my role. I picked up the gift. "I got you something today. A belated wedding present." I held the box out to him.

Valemar crossed the room and took it from me. He opened the lid then set the box on the table.

"I'd been thinking telescope, since I come from the stars. But this is more portable."

Valemar lifted the spyglass from its cradle and extended it. He held it up to his eye and swung its focus out the window toward the blood-red moon, still nearly full though it was now waning.

"The clouds are much clearer." He lowered the spyglass.

"I had it engraved."

Valemar turned it. His fingers traced the inscription. "*May you use this for the sky and not the horizon,*" he said, reading it aloud. His hand stilled then slowly closed the instrument. He placed it back in the box and shut the lid.

Valemar reached out and stroked my cheek with the back of his hand. "Thank you," he breathed.

"You are welcome, my husband," I said. And then I brought his lips down on mine.

Daria had a box of her own when she came to dress me the next morning. "A gift from the Mödatal," she said. "Some of the tea you shared."

"Thank you," I said absently, curled up in bed, my chin resting on the book I'd attempted to read after Valemar had left.

"My queen?" Daria asked as I continued to frown.

"I'm to stay inside today," I said with a moan. I set the book aside and followed Daria into the dressing room.

"I see." Daria lifted the sky-blue dress out of the closet and threaded her arms through the neck. I lifted my arms as she placed the gown over my head. "And the problem is?"

"Padrid is with Valemar. I need to stay close for Master Ean." The clutch of karawack eggs had been Valemar's consolation when I'd asked to go riding.

"*We're too close to the frontier,*" he'd said. "*The Cordair frequently have*

scouts lurking nearby. It's not safe. They'd snatch you if the opportunity arose." I'd pouted but he'd just kissed my head and offered the eggs. *"Do something inside with Daria instead."*

"There's always the solar," Daria said as she began on the laces.

"I can't sew," I said. "And they all look at me funny."

"Well, you are kind of intimidating," she said with a teasing smile. "The dark, mysterious Moon Princess who's now their queen."

"They're never going to trust me, are they?" I asked, not bothering to filter my whine.

Daria tugged tightly on the strings, briefly cutting off my ability to breathe. "In time. But we need not join them in the solar. I could teach you in one of the smaller rooms that overlook the river."

"I'm dismal with anything mechanical," I warned her. A needle was metal, so that made sewing mechanical, right?

She just gave me a puzzled look. "I've tried," I said. "My hand doesn't know what to do."

Her eyes twinkled. "Will I need bandages?"

"Yes! Probably." An image of Dave doubled over with laughter filled my mind. He would have loved to watch me try.

"Then I'll come prepared."

Daria traced a pattern on a piece of fabric using a pencil. A barat leaf, I found when she handed me the embroidery frame. I'd lazily traced the outline of the ones on Valemar's chest this morning. My finger was certainly familiar with the shape.

My finger, however, was not familiar with the needle Daria handed me. A dark green, silken thread hung from its eye.

"Do I need to knot it for you?" Daria asked.

"You're so lucky I'm not the Red Queen," I muttered under my breath.

"Was that a yes?"

"No. I can tie a knot," I said, and looped the end over itself before pulling it tight.

"Just checking. You did say you hadn't sewn before."

"Oh, I've sewn. Or tried to sew. It didn't work out so well." I shuddered, thinking of my bloody fingers as well as the mass of tangles and knots that had my mother in fits of laughter the one dismal time she'd tried to teach me to sew on a button. *Did the cat get at it?* she'd asked me. She knew very well it hadn't. She'd sat next to me the whole time.

"Hold the frame in your left hand and poke the needle through the fabric from underneath at the stem of the leaf." My hand sought and sought the end of the stupid stem, finally finding it about my eighth try. "Poke it most of the way through then pull it tight from the front," Daria continued.

"Don't you dare tangle," I muttered to the thread as I did what she asked. The thread stopped. I hesitantly turned the frame over to check. No tangles. I blew out the breath I'd been holding.

"Go about a seed-length down and poke the needle back through, just like you did the first time." This time the thread snagged. "Use your middle and fourth fingers to smooth it while you pull," Daria said as I picked at the knot. "Here, watch me."

She held up her frame so that I could see the underside and started a new stitch. The middle finger on her left hand held the thread down and away from the work area while her right hand poked the needle through. Her right hand then switched to the top and she pulled. Her left fingers came together, smoothing the thread as it ran between them. "This way I can feel for tangles and

hopefully catch them before they can become knots. But sometimes that happens even to me."

Her ring and middle fingers went wide as she poked the needle through. Again she pulled. Again, they straightened the floss.

"Why don't you play with the thread and get used to the feel." Daria gave me a gentle smile and turned her attention to her own sewing.

I did as she suggested, tugging the thread, releasing it, pulling it through, and pinning it back with my finger. Slowly, I began to trace the outline. We worked in companionable silence, the quiet only broken by my occasional exclamations when I jabbed the needle into my finger. Whenever I did, Daria just bit her lips and closely inspected her own work.

We stopped when lunch was delivered.

"There's a pot of the tea you requested," the girl said to me. She placed the tray on the table and bowed out.

I set my sewing next to me on the bench and got up to inspect the tray. Breads, fruits, and meats had been arranged on two plates. I poured myself a cup of the smoky tea and brought a plate to the bench. I balanced the plate on my lap while Daria helped herself.

"Is this the Mödatal's tea?" she asked as she slowly lowered the pot.

"Yes. Why?"

"No reason," she said, but the strain in her voice told me there was. There was an odd expression on her face when she sat back down. She gave me a smile that didn't quite hide it.

"Should I not be drinking the tea?" I asked. The cup was warm in my hands but I hadn't brought it to my lips.

Daria blew on hers. "There's no reason not to." Her eyes avoided mine.

As I debated whether or not to probe any further, Daria gave me an awkward smile and took a sip. I finally brought my cup to my mouth and drank. *Honey was what it needed.*

Daria picked up my hoop and inspected the long, straight satin stitches she'd me taught me to fill in the leaf. "You're coming along nicely."

"Astrid Carr, seamstress. Who would have guessed?" I put a slice of meat on a slice of bread. My new-found skill should have made me happy, but it only confused me.

Daria fixed the last of the jeweled pins that held my hair in an elaborate updo. "Do you need anything else, my queen?"

"No," I said. "You may go." She gave me a smile and slipped from the room.

I turned back with a sigh and caught my reflection in the mirror. I didn't recognize the woman who stared back at me. She had the same eyes, the same curve to her jaw, but the rest of her was foreign. It was the Moon Princess who looked back at me. The Queen of Bánalfar.

I sucked in a bracing breath. A few hours was as much time as PS Carr had to play a role. A few hours and then Astrid Carr got her life back. Negotiations didn't go on twenty or more hours a day for weeks on end. Time was too precious a commodity.

I longed to strip off the gown, the jewels, and even the makeup. I had known that I wouldn't get to be Astrid once I had set down on the planet but the strain of playing this current role had settled into my bones. And I hadn't even done half the work I would need to do to truly become the woman in the mirror.

Make a list, the voice in my head whispered, reciting rule seventeen.

"I don't want to," I whispered back.

You need to study the file.

My future would be bound up in the connections I'd make here in Aedenfal but I was tired of trying to figure out how to stop the stares and the whispering.

You haven't really studied how this society works.

The voice was right, and Orin's description of a woman's role in this society meant that at some point, despite my reluctance, I would have to participate in the singing and dancing and sewing.

"Fine," I whispered to the image that stared back at me. "I'll join them tomorrow."

Somehow, I needed to find my place among them. My life might very well depend on it.

Daria found the front panel of a bodice that was to be embroidered in barat leaves and deemed my efforts the previous day sufficient to try working on it. Four women had already gathered to sew in the solar when we arrived. They jumped to their feet and dipped their chins down to their chests as we entered. "My queen," they all murmured.

One woman with corn-gold hair rose from her place by the window. I'd been introduced to her, to all of them, but I couldn't remember any of their names. They were a blur amongst the hundreds that had paraded by me at dinner that second night. I kicked myself. I should have found a way to have Padrid or Daria help me study who they all were, found some way to make a guest book. "The best light should be yours," she said to me.

Daria wavered behind me, but I took her arm and towed her with me to the vacated place. The other women shared a look then

shifted to make room for Daria. Without another word, they picked up their frames and continued their sewing.

Daria took the bodice from her sewing basket, threaded a deep green floss onto a needle, and handed it to me. The air was thick with tension as I knotted the thread and began to trace the leaf outline as I had done the day before. Daria had started on her own work when I broke the silence.

"I'm embarrassed to say, but I don't remember who all of you are."

Jaws clenched and several faces turned red. Not an embarrassed red.

The woman with the corn-gold hair put her work in her lap and held her head high. "I am Laera. Wife of Garris, Aedenfal's steward."

And there it was. In my sessions with Padrid and Valemar, I had learned that Garris oversaw Aedenfal, High and Low. Orin was the seneschal in charge of defense, but Garris was the steward, in charge of administration when Valemar was absent. In Vanerife, Reina, Valemar's mother, fulfilled that role. It was a role I might be expected to take here or at another of the large keeps in Bánalfar, potentially displacing Garris. And I'd slighted Laera by not remembering her.

"Of course." I smiled, hoping to erase my offense. "Everything's so new. There's so much to learn. So many people to get to know." Laera shot Daria a glance and gave me a too-thin smile before returning to her work.

The remaining three exchanged panicked looks. Two quickly returned to their work, leaving the last girl, for she seemed hardly more than a teen, alone with my attention.

"I am Niah," she said. "My father is Cheál Orie. Our flocks of anapali are the largest on Fairfada. He sent me to foster here with Vienne and her husband." She blushed and looked at the oldest

woman whose hair had once been blond but was now streaked with gray.

"My husband is the master of the weaving guild," Vienne said. "Niah and our son, Reez, have recently become engaged."

All the better to ensure your supply of Fairfada grazed anapali, I thought.

"Our last member is Cadalin," Vienne continued. "Her husband, Ehard, is away on business right now. He's the chief distributor of our cloth."

Cadalin was a younger woman with pale, strawberry blond hair. Beneath her sewing, I glimpsed a swelling belly. The four of them were working on what I now saw to be baby clothes. "You honor us with your presence, my queen," she said.

"I see you are all sewing baby clothes," I said, not willing to ask Cadalin about her condition in case the Alfari considered such a question rude.

"Cadalin is expecting," Vienne said.

Cadalin's hands folded around her belly. Her face became serene. "Sometime this fall."

"Your first?" I asked. Cadalin nodded. "How exciting," I said, unsure of what blessings or congratulations to offer. I would have to ask Daria.

"And what are you working on, my queen?" Laera asked.

I blushed. "I'm practicing new skills. I'm afraid I've spent more time with papers and books than a needle." A hiss rang in the air as Laera and Vienne inhaled sharply and looked at one another, eyes wide.

"Did your mother not teach you?" Laera asked.

"She tried. I was too clumsy then. It wasn't a skill I needed as much as reading or languages, so I never learned." The older women turned back to their sewing, eyebrows raised so high that deep furrows appeared on the little space left on their foreheads.

"Languages?" Niah asked. "Do you speak more than one?"

"Yes," I said, thinking of the thousands stored on the chip in my brain. "More than I can count. I have something of a gift for them. I didn't even speak yours when I first arrived."

"Really?" Cadalin's eyes lit up. "You speak something different on the moon?"

"It's very nice to meet you, Cadalin," I said in English.

"Mee … tyoo," Cadalin said. She laughed. "How strange that is on my tongue."

"Yes, my tongue often got twisted when learning unfamiliar phrases." I began to rattle off greetings. "*Hajimemashite. Goshorahane. Adjo foramayno.*" The younger girls began to giggle. "I spent my days translating and checking protocols." I held up my sewing. "This is new for me." My fingers tightened on the frame as another piece of Astrid Carr ripped away. "So many things are new for me. But I'm glad to learn."

I bowed my head and blinked, concentrating on the pattern before me, afraid of what they might say next. Or questions they could ask.

"And we're glad to have you," Laera said, though she sounded anything but glad.

I bit back a sarcastic response to her tone, though I should have said it. The Moon Princess surely would have. But I knew what was behind their behavior, and I feared their asking the questions that I couldn't answer. *What are you going to do about the outsiders? How are you going to save us all?*

So I concentrated on my sewing and held my tongue. It was a relief when Ean knocked on the door and announced that my birds were hatching.

CHAPTER 12

Daria followed me down to the aviary and stood off to the side as I took my place on the stool next to the nest. I ran my hands over the eggs as I'd seen Valemar do.

"Hello, little birds," I said. "It's time to hatch."

Valemar had sung to them but I knew no songs for birds.

Like a bird on the wing … The Scottish lullaby my mother had sung to Finn and me rose in my mind. "Onward the sailors cry," I softly sang, picking up the song. "Carry the lad that's born to be king." My fingers followed the rise and fall of the five speckled eggs. "Over to the sea to Skye."

The egg under my fingers cracked. I pulled my hand back and watched as the pieces were tossed away by the shake of the chick inside. It squawked. Its head bobbed, searching, and I brought it close.

"Loud the winds howl, loud the waves roar. Thunder clouds rend the a-air." Though I sang, my mother's voice was all I heard. I could almost feel the touch of her arms, folded around me. The chick squawked again, and I gently ran my finger over its naked, unseeing head. "Baffled our foes stand on the shore. Follow they will not dare."

My mother had sat in her nursery and held me like this, stroked me like this, softly singing the same tune. Now, she was gone. I was gone. And my only children would be these birds.

The chick pushed against my finger as I stroked it. Its squawks slowly changed to match the rise and fall of my voice. The adult karawack stopped their thrumming and fell silent, listening.

I held the chick until the next egg cracked. The chick screeched when I exchanged it for its sibling but soon fell back to chirping with me. I brought the new chick close and continued my song. Over and over I sang the haunting lullaby.

My body began to move in time with the tempo, to sway back and forth as though I were in a rocking chair. My mother had rocked me like this every night when I was little, curled up in the blue-striped chair, telling me stories of her own once the night's book had been read.

But I'd never feel her arms around me again. I'd never have a child of my own to tell stories to, or a soft, downy head to caress.

My voice caught in my throat. The chick in my hand gave a peeped a question: *Why had the music stopped?* I laughed, though it too caught in my throat and came out more as a sniffle.

The next egg cracked. *Five.* I'd have five downy chicks that would imprint on me. Five chicks that would grow up and follow me anywhere.

When I'd sung to the last and returned it to the nest, I slipped my hands under my legs, sitting on them, to keep from scooping the newly hatched karawack back up and holding them to my heart. They needed their real mother and her warmth. I pressed my thighs harder against the stool when Ean reached into the nest to retrieve the chicks. They squawked in panic as he lifted them away.

"I've never seen anything like it," Ean whispered to me as he picked up the last one. He gently stroked the chick. Its frantic peeping tore at my heart. "The birds respond and bond. But with you … five years is the most people get with them. Five years and then they look for a mate. But yours —" He looked up at me with something akin to awe. "Yours may have imprinted for life. Whatever you sang to them created a powerful link."

He placed the last one in under its cream-white mother. She met my eyes and bowed her head to me, then silently settled the last chick under her wings. Five heads poked out and searched for me.

"Tomorrow," I whispered to them. My throat had grown too tight for any other sound. "I'll see you tomorrow."

Ean walked with me to the door. "What was that song?" he asked.

"A lullaby my mother sang to me."

"Lul-la-by?"

It wasn't unusual for me not to know when the chip didn't translate and my native language emerged. "Songs that mothers sing to their children to calm them. Cradle songs?" I said, trying again.

"Ah." Ean's eyebrows lifted.

It had been a morning full of babies, and I was now weary from it. "Thank you, Ean. I'll be by tomorrow to see them."

I took Daria's arm and leaned on her the few steps to the base of the stairs. "Back to my room to rest, I think. And maybe some of the Mödatal's tea."

I sat on the floor at the foot of my bed, my back against the footboard, and cradled a cup of tea in my hands. There was no window seat to nestle in or I would have curled up there instead.

Pain flowed from my heart with every beat. I'd lost so much and the little I did have could be taken away at any moment. Even my birds.

I was the Moon Princess only because of a lie. Laera and Vienne had shown me this morning they didn't believe it. They would have treated me with respect if they had. Or awe, not that I wanted it. Even Valemar's acceptance of me was based on that lie. And while he treated me with respect and tenderness, what would he do when the mask of the Moon Princess fell away and he was left with only me?

I shuddered and let the steaming liquid slip down my throat. I pressed the cup to my chest where it warmed my heart. But brought no relief.

I gulped the last of the tea and got to my feet. In my wardrobe, I found the red lace veil and covered my head. I needed to confess my sins to the one person who would understand. The person who had gotten me into this mess.

I walked alone to the Cair. A guard peeled off from the line by the main gate of the High and followed me into the city, but he kept his distance. My veil spoke to my destination and, even covered, my height spoke to my identity.

Once I passed through the side door of the sanctuary, I turned the veil back and let it drape across my shoulders. I found the door that led to the Mödatal's rooms and knocked.

"Enter."

She wasn't surprised to see me. "My queen." She gestured to the chair in front of her. "To what do I owe the pleasure?"

But she knew. The look in her eyes and the smile on her face said she knew.

"I'm not who you think I am."

She laughed. "We've been through this before."

"I am not the Moon Princess."

"Did you fall from the sky?" Her eyes flashed with the challenge. "Are you the daughter of kings?"

I ground my teeth and answered. "Yes, I fell from the sky. But you can hardly call me 'the daughter of kings.' They lived and died nearly two thousand years ago."

"But you are a daughter, and they were your ancestors." Her eyes danced with glee. "Blood will tell."

I shivered. On Earth, we have the same saying. "That doesn't help me now! I'm no princess and they want a princess."

The Mödatal shrugged. "They expected a princess."

Every comment I'd held back, every sideways look and snide remark that I'd endured, found its voice as I shouted at the seer. "I'm not what they expected!"

"No. You're not," she said simply. "And this is not the life you expected." She let the words sink in. "The *place* you expected … Can you change that?"

"No," I whispered.

"So, you must change your expectations."

"But it's a lie. It's only a matter of time before they discover I'm a fraud." I sank back into my chair as the word echoed in the room.

The Mödatal sighed heavily, the sigh of a mother explaining something to a child for the hundredth time. "Did you fall from the sky?"

"Yes, but —"

"Are you descended from warrior kings?"

"Yes, but —"

"Then you are the Moon Princess, the fulfillment of the prophecy."

"I can't save anyone!" I wailed, drowning out her other words.

The Mödatal clenched her jaw. Anger lit up her deep blue eyes before she closed them and inhaled deeply. The hairs on my arms lifted as the energy in the room changed. "You could not save the others. But their job was to bring you here. You gave them a proper funeral."

Her lids opened. Nothing but white showed in the sockets before her eyes rolled back into place. She stared hard at me for a moment. "You are right. There are too many expectations on you." My jaw dropped. Now she was agreeing with me?

The Mödatal set her cup down, uncurled her legs, and walked over to the fire. "What do you want to do about it?" she asked, staring into the flames, her back to me.

"I —" But the words faded in my throat. *Confess to Valemar?* Not if I wanted to live.

I pressed the scar on my index finger, a butterfly of flesh and skin, red and flayed and still healing.

I had sought life when I'd hidden in my cabin after plasma flooded the ship. I could have gone out and tried to help. And died. But I'd stayed put. Out of the way. Safe.

I'd sought life when I broke the rules and took the escape pod. I'd sought life when I accepted Valemar's offer of safety.

I looked at the Mödatal, the light dancing across her red hair, causing it to glow like the embers in the grate. I'd keep my mouth shut to keep my life. And she knew it.

"You think you have me all figured out," I said, my voice hoarse with anger.

"I know you better than you know yourself." Her chin lifted as she continued to stare into the flickering flames. "It's what scares you. It's why you fear me."

"You're so certain of my future."

Her gaze moved from the fire to me. "Pieces. I see pieces."

"And you're willing to trust pieces?"

Her laugh echoed in the room. "That is the definition of faith. The assurance of things hoped for, the conviction of things not seen."

I'd heard that somewhere before but couldn't put my finger on it.

The Mödatal turned from the fire. "What do you put your faith in, Astrid?"

I tried to wet my tongue to answer. "That life has a purpose."

She smiled at my answer. "And what is your purpose?"

She'd backed me into a corner, backed me into the place where I had to face the voice that whispered, *This all happened for a reason.* She stayed silent, letting that whisper work its way into my head. Then she spoke again, as if she knew my heart wasn't yet ready to hear it.

"They expected someone like them. They expected a rescuer who'd drive back the Cordair. You have no army …" She paused. "And you look too much like the Cordair." I gritted my teeth, tired of hearing it. "Would you abandon them?"

"No." I'd abandoned enough already.

"You do not yet know who or what you are. You dropped — literally — into something beyond your imagining. Give yourself time. Give them time. Have faith that all will turn out right."

I walked back to the High glad for the veil, for it blocked the world from me. I'd stripped away the mask, bared myself to the Mödatal, and it hadn't fazed her. I couldn't bear to put the mask back on, and so it was me who walked under the veil — Astrid Gabriella Carr. Not the Moon Princess. Not the Queen of Bánalfar. And no one knew because of my shroud.

I didn't go down to dinner. I sent Daria with my regrets and hid away in my room.

Valemar came up as he did every evening. This time cautiously, peering around the door he never bothered to knock. "They said you were ill."

I went to him and put my arms around him. Listened to his strong, steady heartbeat under my ear. His arms came around me and he held me close.

What had I imagined when I'd fallen from the sky? Not this — that I would find comfort in the arms of a king.

Valemar stroked my hair and placed his lips on my head. "What is wrong, Astrid?" he murmured. When I didn't answer, he lifted my chin.

It was not the Moon Princess who looked into his eyes. Or even Protocol Specialist Carr. It was broken and bruised Astrid who had no idea in hell what she was supposed to do.

Valemar simply held my gaze and brushed the hair from my face, unafraid of what he saw.

What would I have wanted when I'd fallen from the sky?

This. Someone to hold me and comfort. Protect me.

I reached a hand up and stroked Valemar's face, then pulled his lips down to mine.

CHAPTER 13

I sang children's songs to my karawack the next morning, not lullabies. Songs I remembered from school: *Twinkle, Twinkle Little Star*, *On Top of Spaghetti*; and *How Many Toes Does a Thorian Have?* One by one I lifted the chicks from underneath the cream-colored mother, cradled them in my hand, and sang complete nonsense, comforted by the fact that Ean and the others didn't speak English and therefore wouldn't be alarmed by my loss of the meatball or its disturbing journey. Or by the fact that you could tell a Thorian's age by counting his or her toes. I spent half an hour being thoroughly and utterly me.

I ran my hand down the cream-white mama after I'd put the last chick back. She stretched, pushing herself against my hand as I stroked her.

"Sari may become yours, too," Ean said from behind me as I closed the door to the cage. "I don't know that such a thing has happened before. Not with an adult bird."

I clicked the latch into place. "Whose was she?"

"Adan's." Ean caught my puzzled look. "He was the steward at Snow Reach, Bánalfar's southernmost stronghold." Ean clucked to the mother bird. "We never did find out what killed him, but Sari here cried as soon as he died."

"They know when a person dies?"

"Aye. It's the bond that connects them to their person that allows the karawack to find them anywhere. When their person dies, a karawack shrieks from the loss of that bond."

I looked at the five small heads poking out from beneath Sari's feathers. How far would the bond reach? As far as Earth? If we had karawack on Earth, would my family know I was still alive? I suspected they wouldn't know what to think. I was alive, but where was I?

I had every reason to believe that none of the messages from the *Palmas Cove* had gotten through. I suspected the Hormani had blocked them. The *Cove* would have just vanished into the blackness of space. No message of our being in the Teridun system. No message of my supposed journey to the sun.

No Shororato to come looking.

I laid my hand on Ean's arm. "Thank you. I'll be down again tomorrow."

I'd thought about children the night before as I lay in Valemar's arms after our lovemaking. At some point, he'd begin to wonder. At some point, I'd need to explain genetics to him and how it was basically impossible for us to conceive. Humans and chimpanzees share about ninety-five percent of the same genes, but we can't crossbreed. Within the galaxy, there are species that can but it's rare. And frequently their children are infertile, as with mules on Earth.

Which would be harder to face — an empty cradle or no grandchildren? Either would mean the loss of Valemar's bloodline for he was the only child of an only child. I hadn't been able yet to ask Padrid about it. What would they do if Valemar had no heir? What would Valemar do to me when I told him?

I'd listened to Valemar's heart beat and envied Cadalin and her swelling belly. New life. Something creatures everywhere craved.

I determined at that moment to help Cadalin, if she'd let me. Sew clothes or provide resources. Anything. The karawack would be my only children, but I could help the Alfari welcome a new life.

And so, with that resolve, Daria and I made our way to the solar once I'd sung to the chicks. There was still the bodice of barat leaves to work on if Cadalin turned me down. Or if Laera and Vienne blocked my attempt. They'd been trying to freeze me out with their icy demeanor but it wasn't going to work today. I was the queen. They were my subjects. And Astrid Carbrev, Queen of the Alfari, planned to be useful.

They shared a glance when we entered. Laera and Vienne vacated the best seats by the window for us, eyes downcast as they took their new seats.

"Would you like help?" I asked the women. Daria opened up her sewing box. "You'll probably have to teach me, but I'm willing to learn."

Cadalin looked to Laera for an answer.

"Are you sure it's not beneath you, my queen?" Laera asked. Her wide eyes held Vienne's.

"Nothing should be beneath a queen. If she is not willing to do what needs to be done, of what use is she?" Even Daria gave me a stunned look. "If she is not willing to shelter, then why should she be sheltered? If she is not willing to serve, then why should she be served? If she is not willing to fight, then why should she be protected? If she is not willing to sew —" I paused and bit back a smile. "— however badly, then why is she in the solar?"

Silence hung in the room. The leaping animals on the cheery tapestries lining the walls offered the only hint of movement.

"I would understand if you would not wish your child to be clothed in my clumsy attempts, but I would at least like to try. I would like to be useful."

"No. Of course n-not," Cadalin stammered. "I mean, I would not be embarrassed to have my child clothed in something made by my queen."

I smiled kindly. "What would you like me to work on?"

"Perhaps we could teach you to hem," Daria said.

"I think we have something." Cadalin turned to the basket between her and Laera.

Laera sorted through the small garments in various stages of completion and pulled out a white square of fabric. Daria's cheeks reddened. Eyes firmly fixed on the floor, she rose so that Laera could take the place next to me. I prayed my face hadn't flushed as well. I had told them nothing was beneath me, so how could I now complain that I was now being asked to hem what was obviously a diaper?

Laera didn't meet my eyes. "Fold the edge over, then over again." She swiftly turned the fabric. Then using the fingers of just her left hand, she pinched the folded edge between them to keep it from coming undone and ran her thumb along it to smooth it down. Laera adjusted the pleat with her free hand until it was uniform. "Then sew down the edge."

Cadalin handed her a needle. It flashed in the sunlight as Laera moved the needle swiftly in and out of the fabric, leaving a neat row of stitches along the top. When she neared her index finger, Laera set the needle high in her lap and turned the next section. "Now you try."

It was fabric, not paper like my origami, but my fingers had no trouble creating the folds. "It's just like the outline stitch, only smaller," Daria said when I picked up the needle.

In and out. In and out. I concentrated on making my stitches small and even.

I ran my finger over the first completed section. "This isn't that different from the paper folding I've done."

"Paper folding?" Vienne asked.

"Yes. You take paper and, depending on where you make the folds, you can create all kinds of animals or even boxes." Mild curiosity appeared on their faces.

"What are they used for?" Niah asked.

"Decoration." Though the cranes weren't. They had a purpose. "Toys," I added, thinking of the jumping frogs.

Laera's eyebrows lifted. "You'll have to show us sometime," she said in that tone of voice that always meant the opposite.

"Well, not today." I folded the next section of white cloth. "I have plenty of work for today." I smiled at them and focused on the needle. They could try and intimidate me, but today not even diapers were going to get the best of me.

I hadn't thought about folding anything since I'd made the twenty-three cranes for the crew. But cranes are not just creatures that carry departed souls to the afterlife. They are also symbols of good fortune and long life. One tradition was to do a *Senbazuru* — a group of one-thousand cranes folded and strung together so that its creator could ask the venerable cranes to grant a wish.

That, I thought as I looked through the paraphernalia on Valemar's desk, *would be one thing I actually could do*. Make a thousand cranes and wish for the Cordair to be gone. But not today.

A hinged, wooden box contained the creamy sheets I was looking for. Thick but not stiff. I sat at the table and folded one

corner to the edge of the other side. I sharpened the crease with the back of my fingernail and turned down the remaining edge. That piece I folded back and forth then ran my tongue along the crease. The moisture softened the fibers and allowed me to make a neat tear.

With the excess gone, I had a square sheet of paper, and my fingers began their work, the steps so familiar that I didn't even need to think.

Valemar came in as I searched for something to distract my drifting mind from the last time I'd done this. His hair draped across my back as he peered over my shoulder. "What are you doing?"

"Origami," I said. "The ancient art of paper folding." My fingers continued. Fold … crease … turn … fold … crease … turn.

"I see. And why do you fold paper?"

I looked back at him and gave him a mysterious smile, my lips passing just inches from his. "Wait and see."

I opened my last three folds and flipped the paper over. Fold … crease … turn … fold … crease … turn.

"You keep undoing your work," Valemar said, soft in my ear, when I opened the folds on that side as well.

"Hush."

Fold … crease … turn. Following the creases I'd already made, I began to turn the diamond in upon itself. The ends of the paper began to point up like the wings they'd become. I folded down the wings, pinched them against the body while I made the head, then pulled. The body popped, filling out. I offered Valemar my crane.

"What is this?"

"*Tsuru*," I said. "The sacred crane. Legend says they live to be a thousand years old."

"Very possible," Valemar said, his eyebrow hooked, as he stared at the bird in his palm.

I gently shoved him with my shoulder. "Not the paper, silly. The real birds. They are white with black feathers on their inner wings. These droop and give the birds the illusion of a black tail when their wings are folded. Their throats are black, and the crest on their heads is red. And they stand nearly as tall as I."

"Do they?"

"They may not live a thousand years, but often to seventy. And once they find a mate, they stay with their chosen one as long as they both live."

Valemar brushed the hair back from my face and tucked it behind my ear. His finger traced the curve of my ear, flat against my head — so unlike his own. "Tell me more," he whispered.

"They're a symbol of luck and longevity." My mind filled with the image of my last cranes all lined up on the bridge of the *Palmas Cove*. I bit my lip and pushed it away, reached instead for the new life all around me. "I thought I'd give this one to Cadalin."

Valemar pulled a chair up next to me and sat down. He twirled the paper crane by its tail. "Who taught you?"

"One of my teachers at school." I smiled, thinking of my fourth grade year and Mr. Patterson who'd brought in the stack of origami paper. He'd been of the opinion that we spent too much time with our eyes glued to our tablets. And we still did, for the patterns were found there. But then our eyes would shift to the folds, and our hands flipped something other than an image on a screen. And soon we could do both.

But such a world was utterly foreign to Valemar.

"He wanted us to have a connection to the past," I said instead. "People on my world have been folding paper this way for over two thousand years."

"Not too long then," said the man whose family had been ruling Bánalfar for nearly that amount of time.

"It's still ancient."

"Are you calling me ancient?"

I smiled. "Only your bloodline." I sighed. The Shororato would occasionally intercede in Earth affairs so things didn't get "out of hand," but countries still rose and fell. "No one has held power that long on the moon."

"It *is* a moon of blood."

"It is a red moon, the color of fire." I took the crane from Valemar and spun it back and forth between my fingers, bringing it to life. "In the land of the crane, red is a lucky color. Red brings happiness. A bride wears red on her wedding day, and it is forbidden at funerals."

"The moon has brought me happiness," Valemar said.

My breath caught in my throat. "Has it?"

Valemar reached out and stroked my face. "Definitely."

CHAPTER 14

I spent the next several days singing to my birds, sewing more diapers for Cadalin, and studying with Valemar and Padrid. But I was never outside the walls of the Low. Other than the few hours I'd spent in the steppe and then on the back of Heymond's horse (mostly unconscious), I'd been cooped up one place or another since the *Palmas Cove* had set off from Earth weeks earlier. I could see the open fields and inviting woods on the other side of the Leisna from the windows of the High but I had not been allowed to visit them. The sound that drifted up to my window of boys playing in the river below sparked rebellion in me.

I sought out Valemar in his study. "What are my duties as queen?" I asked him, feigning innocence.

Valemar looked up from his papers. "Why do I get the feeling this is a trick question?"

"I just want to check that I'm working on all my skills."

Valemar pressed a fist to his mouth. "And what skill do you think you're lacking in?" he asked from behind his hand, his serious tone negated by the amusement dancing in his eyes.

"Well ..." I stepped to the front of the table. "I know that Aedenfal is only one of Bánalfar's strongholds." I traced a pattern on the table with my index finger, watched the oil from my finger create loops and swirls on the surface. "I would expect that you travel between them. Do you plan on leaving me here?"

Valemar frowned. "No."

"And how do you get from place to place?"

"Darana," he said, naming the animal I always thought of as a 'horse.' "Where are you going with this?"

"Ah." I dropped down into one of the chairs and tapped my fingers on the arms. "Then we have a problem."

"Spit it out, Astrid."

"I don't ride."

Valemar sat back in his chair as stunned as if I'd hit him. "You don't ride? What do you mean you don't ride? You rode here from Fairfada."

"In front of Heymond. Unconscious most of the time."

"You rode to and from the Cair on our wedding."

"Sidesaddle. At a walk. All I had to do was sit."

The information proved too much for Valemar. He flung himself out of his chair and paced the room. "How do you get from place to place on the moon?"

"Not on darana." I suppressed a sigh. Surely my metal ship was a clue that things were different 'on the moon.' "So, you can see that I am clearly lacking a skill I need," I said as Valemar continued pacing the room, now mute. "I am hoping you'll lift the restrictions that have kept me within Aedenfal's walls. Unless you intend me to ride clamped in someone's arms every time I need to travel."

Valemar gave me an icy glare.

"Then I should learn to ride. Someplace with soft ground in case I fall? The fields outside Aedenfal, perhaps?" His eyes narrowed even further. For a moment, I thought he was going to refuse.

"Is it really that dangerous outside the walls?" I asked. Fear made my voice tiny.

A breath he'd been holding rushed out with a whoosh. "No," Valemar said. He came to stand next to my chair. "The Cordair have been keeping their scouting parties to the eastern edges of Fairfada. It's just …"

And I knew from the look in his eyes what his fear was — that I'd appeared from nowhere and could just as easily vanish.

"Are the fields and woods surrounding Aedenfal safe?" I asked again.

"Yes."

"Do you want a wife who rides like the wind or one who needs to be carried?"

Valemar's eyes twinkled. "Like the wind?" He squatted down next to my chair.

"It could happen today," I said as butterflies collided in my chest. "Don't know how to stop. But eventually on purpose, leaving any pursuers in the dust."

Valemar brushed a strand of hair from my face and tucked it behind my ear. "Have you had to leave pursuers in the dust?"

"A few times, but then it boiled down to who had the fastest ship," I said, thinking of the time the Lesela had changed their minds on the price of the cell growth serum and how it was only Dave's special modifications to the *Cove* that had enabled us to escape the system.

"By ship." Valemar looked thoughtful. "So you sail everywhere?"

"I suppose you could say that." Large vehicles were sometimes called *land yachts*.

Valemar continued to play with my hair. "We've never really talked about the moon."

I swallowed heavily. "No." I hadn't brought it up. It was easier to keep the truth hidden if I let him believe what he wanted to believe. Easier to keep from shattering his world. Safer for me, not only for that reason, but the voice in the back of my brain thought it would be better if I broke the law as little as possible. Just in case the Shororato did show up. Things would go even worse for me if I altered the perceptions of this world, if I changed how they perceived the universe.

Valemar's eyes narrowed, catching the fear that appeared on my face. I could see questions flash by in his eyes. Questions he left unasked.

Valemar dropped his gaze. "Is it safe?" I asked again, my voice little more than a whisper.

He gave my hand a squeeze. "Yes."

Valemar stood up without looking at me. "I'll have Calan make the arrangements. You should be able to ride." He picked up several of the papers and began to study them. It was a subtle dismissal.

I rose from my chair. "Thank you."

Our conversation might have come to an end, but I had a feeling that the questions had just begun.

They took me out through the watergate. Calan, the darana master, waited on the far bank with four other riders and a mount for me. The boatman offered me the same gracious smile he had when I first arrived, and it was as if the clock had turned back on itself. I was glad that Heymond was not in the group. If time unwound, I would have to start at the beginning again.

The oars splashed, each stroke temporarily drowning out the hum of insects and the stamp of hooves, impatient to be off. The aroma of wet and dying grass filled my nose. Calan reached an arm in to help me from the boat when we reached the other side. "My queen."

I took his hand and scrambled onto the bank. A light breeze lifted the hair from my shoulders. I fought back the urge to climb onto the strange horse and kick its sides, send it running through the trees, the wind streaming back my hair, pulling the water from my eyes. I couldn't drive here. There were no cars to climb into. No convertibles to put the top down and let the speed take over my soul, to put distance between me and the things that chipped away at my life.

One day, maybe, I'd be able to climb on a darana and do that. Maybe one day soon. But not today. Today, I needed to learn to control the animal. Today, I needed to learn to control my body.

Today, I needed to be the queen.

I walked up to the mount Calan had selected for me. "Hello, pretty girl." She snuffled my outstretched palm. I reached up and scratched her cheek. "What's her name?"

"Loenir," Calan said. "Old Alfari for 'the light of the stars.'"

I suppressed a smile. Her coat was just darker than their hair, dusky yellow but still blond. "Do all Alfari come from the stars?" Loenir tossed her head.

"The old tales say it's so, that our blondness comes from the stars and our red hair comes from the moon," Calan said.

I looked at him over my shoulder. "And dark hair?"

Calan's eyes fell. The other men looked away. "It is said to be a mark of those touched by Oluendi."

"Ah. I see." So the general consensus was that I had been touched by evil. It explained a lot.

And their thoughts weren't so different from those held by Earthlings. There was still the idea that the good guys wore white and the bad guys wore black (though the Shororato uniforms were white, and they were something in between). I'd despaired of it myself after my mother had taken me to see the ballet *Swan Lake*, for Odette, the princess, was the white swan, and Odile, the evil enchantress, was the black.

We once feared the dark, my mother had said, drying my tears. *For we were vulnerable, unable to see what things lurked there.* She'd turned her gaze to the heavens, and I'd looked up, too. *But space is black and filled with so many things. Do we see the stars at noon?* she'd asked and looked back down at me.

No, I'd whispered.

They cannot be seen in the light. It is only the dark that allows us to see some things clearly. And gently wraps us as we sleep at night. She'd smiled and tucked her arm through mine.

"Darkness is the only way we see the sky's diamonds," I said aloud, echoing my mother's words. "*Loenir* is not possible without it."

The men shuffled their feet. "Very true, my queen," Calan said.

I gave Loenir a pat. "Now, what do I need to do?" I asked. "I'm familiar with the concept, but I've never really ridden on my own."

Calan held the stirrup for me. I put my foot into it, grabbed the front of the saddle as instructed, and heaved myself up. Calan's hand went out to catch me if I fell, but I was easily able to swing my leg over. I gave thanks for the long tunic and leggings Daria had dressed me in.

I looked to my right, searching for the other stirrup, but Calan said, "Not yet, miss … my queen. They're just there so your legs

don't get tired from dangling. You don't keep your seat by gripping a saddle. You stay on a darana through balance. Sit there awhile and find your balance."

I kicked my toe out of the left stirrup and did as he suggested, feeling for how my form matched Loenir's. Calan took up Loenir's reins and mounted his own animal. I laid my hands on my thighs and focused on finding my center as Loenir began to shift beneath me.

"If you were a child, we'd have put you up there bareback," Calan said and clucked to Loenir. The other men mounted up and took up positions around us.

We headed off toward the trees, my pelvis swinging in rhythm with Loenir's steps. The reason some cultures had women ride sidesaddle became clear. Battered and bruised and probably concussed, I'd not noticed the motion when I'd been squished in the saddle with Heymond. Then Loenir picked up a trot and slammed my lady parts against the saddle. *Ow.*

"Easy there," Calan said, calming her. "She's just excited," he said to me.

I fought the urge to grab my now painful crotch. "I can tell," I said, and hoped I wasn't wincing.

"You've got a nice center," Calan told me. "But we'll just walk for a while and let you get used to the rhythm."

I wasn't going to complain, despite the pain. I was outside in the fresh air, sky and trees and grass all around me. And thanks to years of yoga, my body was already searching for how to balance in this new, moving space.

When my dangling legs began to drift against Loenir's sides without squeezing, Calan stopped his mount and gave me the next set of instructions. "Your legs are how you control a darana, not the reins. Squeeze to go. Squeeze harder to go faster. Pressure right

to turn left. Pressure left to turn right. Unless you're using the reins."

"What?" How could it be right one way and wrong the other?

"A darana is going to move away from pressure. Press against it with your left foot and it's going to move right. If you press with your left leg and pull the reins to the left, its mouth turns left while its head moves away from the pressure of the reins on the right and the darana's hindquarters move right like a pendulum."

One of the other riders demonstrated, turning his animal in a circle, first one direction, then the other.

Calan clipped a rope to Loenir's halter and threw me the reins. "Remember, pressure equals 'go.' Lots of pressure — the 'hanging on for dear life' pressure — equals 'go very fast.' Don't do that if you can help it. I don't want to be chasing you all the way to Fairfada or Lendurig, rope or no rope."

I swallowed heavily and picked up the reins. "Right."

"Other way, my queen," Calan said, referring to my grip. He took his animal's reins between his thumb and index finger. "Find the middle, take them in your left hand, let the extra drop over your thumb. Leaves your other hand free. Should you need to, or want to, you could use both hands. Just hold the reins this way." He demonstrated the method. "Slack enough to give her her head, but if you tip your hand forward, you'll pull the reins back. Enough to slow her down."

"What do you say to stop?" I asked.

"Stöd."

"Stöd," I repeated, though I had a feeling I'd be yelling *Whoa!* if Loenir decided to take off.

Calan tied the rope to his saddle. A good fifteen feet trailed between us. Enough that Loenir was mine to control, but at least I

wouldn't end up miles away on my own. If I didn't fall off first.

"Squeeze and click your tongue," Calan said.

You wanted this, I told myself. *You need this*, my more practical side reiterated. I would not be a helpless woman being led from town to town at the mercy of others.

The image of the Cordair lined up along the ridge, the Hormani with them, came to mind. I'd had the chip implanted, I'd learned to hold my liquor, I'd learned to scroll through endless bits and pieces of information all to give me every advantage in my job. I could damn well learn to ride a horse — a darana — for this one. Even with all the confusing directions.

"Come along," I said to Loenir and clicked my tongue. Then I squeezed with my legs and held my breath as she sprang to life beneath me.

"Ooch!" Daria stifled her giggles as I bit back the rest of the expletives on my tongue and gently lowered myself into the tub of hot water.

"You're going to feel it tomorrow," she said.

"Not helping." The water came up over my breasts and I finally relaxed against the back. "How long do I have?"

"No more than half an hour."

I whimpered. Everything hurt, even though I'd managed to stay on the horse.

Daria gave the bed a sidelong glance. I managed to silence a new groan. I would not have had to worry about "riding" again tonight if I'd been sidesaddle. Daria shook out my towel, fluffing it up before she placed it on the stool by the tub. "Maybe he'll still be away tonight."

"Away?" The water sloshed as I sat up. "What do you mean 'away'?"

"The king left with Heymond and a few others shortly before you went out riding. Didn't you know?" I shook my head. Daria hummed. "He hasn't returned … that I've heard. Maybe you'll have a night off."

Maybe. But that left me alone at dinner with the court. For the first time ever. No confidant at the table. I sank back down until the water came up to my chin. If I could, I'd plant Daria at the table, right next to me. But I couldn't.

In the end, I chose Padrid for my dinner companion. I expanded my knowledge of Aedenfal's neighboring towns and villages. He didn't comment on where Valemar had gone or the empty seat to my left.

I probably should have placed Laera next to me instead. While I had become an expected member of the solar, there was still an element of mistrust that seethed there. My decision to choose Padrid wouldn't help that, but I was too sore and tired to walk the minefield of Laera's expectations and listen to her thinly veiled criticisms.

My bed was empty when I went to my room and remained empty until the wee hours of the morning. The faint light of early dawn had given form to the shadows making up the room when a pressure next to me woke me.

I could smell the darana on him before I rolled over. Valemar sat on the bed, his back against the headboard. There were a thousand questions in his eyes but he didn't ask any of them, just stared at me. There was one thing that would have changed how Valemar saw me. It had been loaded onto a cart and stored — I didn't know where, but far enough away for a full-day journey.

I tried to lift a smile, but it kept slipping from my face. He looked at me as if I were a stranger. My eyes began to sting, and still he stared, the guarded expression on his face creating a wall between us. I forced the words out, though they were little more than air. "I'm still me. I'm the same girl Heymond brought to you. The same woman you've lived with these last few weeks." Valemar reached out a hand and traced the shape of my face. "What you saw doesn't change that."

His face softened. "No, it doesn't." He pulled me onto his lap and began to stroke my hair.

What he'd seen, what he'd finally gone to see, didn't change who I was.

But it did change how he looked at me.

CHAPTER 15

Fourteen days later we rode out the gates of Aedenfal bound for Torfin and, from there, a pilgrimage to Gladama. It was a five day journey to Torfin, renowned for its wine. Valemar intended to inspect the crops and the wineries. Part of me wondered if he just wanted to put space between me and the Cordair.

I knew he'd gone to inspect my ship that day, knew it from the trace of fear I'd seen in his eyes. I'd seen the same look on the faces of people in the history files, pictures of people on Earth after they'd discovered they were not alone in the universe. Valemar had received the reports, knew my ship was made of metal and contained strange technology, but he'd fit the information in with his expectations of the Moon Princess. That had all changed when I said I didn't ride.

Part of him now knew that I was strange and terrible — though that didn't stop him from coming to my bed every night. And part of him now realized just how great a threat the "strangers" were that were trading with the Cordair. His world had been shaken. And so we left Aedenfal as soon as the young karawack were old enough to travel.

I was proud that I rode on my own, though the long skirts that allowed peeing alongside the road to be more private made climbing into the saddle more difficult.

It was a nice day for travel. The sun shone brightly and the morning air was cool. I'd pieced together from the maps I studied with Padrid that Aedenfal was situated about the same latitude as San Francisco or Athens on Earth but in Teridun's southern hemisphere. The Lian Isles to the north had weather similar to San Diego, and Snow Reach to the south to the mountains of the Sierra Nevadas. From the state of the harvest, I assumed we were in summer, though at this latitude Bánalfar wouldn't have a full four seasons. Vanerife, the capital city, had only one — a summer of varying degrees of hot and mild.

We were not a large party: Valemar, me, Daria, Padrid, the Mödatal, Heymond and a scant score of twenty knights, Ean and one of his assistants, and the drivers of two wagons. One wagon held trunks of our clothing, the other — cages of karawack.

Besides singing to them, we now let them out to fly for an hour every evening to build up their wing muscles. How the fully grown birds must hate their cages, for the instinct to connect with their imprint was so great that we often had to toss the birds aloft to get them to fly. It was quite the spectacle. The flock of young karawack circling around their imprint, alighting on them, bobbing their heads in curiosity, as if they couldn't figure out why their imprint wouldn't join them in flight.

I'd found it magical the first time mine had done so, being the still center in a blur of wings. It made me feel every bit a Cinderella — without the sleeping by the fire. And wasn't I? For I had crashed down a nobody and now I was a queen.

We spent the first day traveling at an easy walk and spent the night at a manor house. I was met with some stares, eyes that lingered on my hair, before smiles were hoisted and our hosts became the image of graciousness. We cantered some the next day, playful races to break up the monotony, lunched under the shade of a tall tree while we waited for the wagons to catch up. We could have been anybody on the road. Certainly not what I'd expected of a royal party passing through the countryside.

It was when a lone traveler passed by us, headed in the opposite direction, as we lunched under the tree, that I remembered something I'd read years before. The man greeted us with a simple "my king, my queen" and a dip of his head as he passed, recognizing Valemar and, by extension, me. I'd read that heavy security when kings traveled was only a necessity when there was mistrust between a king and his subjects. The article had compared the exploits of England's Plantagenet kings who'd ridden around the country with only a couple of trusted friends to the scores of knights necessary to ensure the safety of the Tudors. Security was tight at Aedenfal, but then it was only a hard day's ride from Rock Dorach, the Cordair stronghold in the Archjarn mountains, near the eastern edge of the steppe. We were headed west, into the heart of Bánalfar.

The farther west we traveled, the fewer looks my hair received. The Alfari I saw still had hair in various shades of blond, with the occasional variation of some degree of red, but the mistrust I was greeted with faded with the miles. The warm cheers that greeted us when we rode through Torfin were as much for me as for Valemar.

The steward of Torfin and his wife greeted us at the main door to the High when we dismounted. "We are so glad to welcome you, my king and my queen," Brinna, the steward's wife said. "Both of you."

Brinna was shorter than most of the Alfari I'd met, only an inch or two above my height. Her dark blond hair hung in a long braid

down her back, decorated with a jeweled clasp that tied off the end. Her smile was the most genuine I'd seen in a long time, and it made me glad that Aedenfal was days behind me.

Brinna herself showed me to the room I'd be sharing with Valemar and had our trunks brought up and water fetched so I could wash the dust off. Daria she placed in a room just down the hall.

The Mödatal had left us soon after we'd ridden through the gates of Torfin, opting to stay at the Cair rather than the High.

"Why is that?" I asked Daria when she dressed me for dinner. "She comes with us but she doesn't stay?"

Daria tied off my laces. "She's traveled with the king for the last year, advising him. Ever since she received the message that you were coming." A snort of disbelief escaped before I could stop it. "But you are here," Daria said, meeting my gaze in the mirror. "She wasn't wrong about that." Daria bit her lip, and her gaze dropped. "Do you think she was wrong?"

We'd never talked about it, how I wasn't the Moon Princess. Partially because I couldn't bear to break Daria's illusion of me. Partially because the things that Mödatal Shale knew about me were spookily true.

"What is the prophecy?" I asked Daria. I couldn't remember the details.

"That the Moon Princess —" Daria frowned. "No, that's not quite right."

Startled, I turned around. Daria chewed on her lip. Her eyes focused on the floor as she thought. "She will fall from the moon. She will be the daughter of kings. Drive back the outsiders. And something about life."

"I thought everyone knew the prophecy." At least, that was what I'd come to expect.

"Oh, we've known there was one. There've been many over the years. But the one about you —" Daria smiled up at me then lifted the necklace I would wear tonight from its box — gems representing clusters of the fruit used to make Torfin's famous wine. "When the strangers began appearing in Cordair lands, strangers no one on Crenfor had seen before, it began to be whispered. All of Bánalfar began to worry that the Cordair had finally found allies who would help them take back what they lost millennia ago." She clipped the necklace around my neck and adjusted it.

"Have they?" Daria asked. Fear shone in her eyes. "Have they finally found allies who could undo it all?"

I had to swallow for my mouth had gone dry. "Yes," I whispered.

"And you've come to stop them?"

It was the first time she'd asked. I'd told Valemar and the Mödatal that I didn't know what I could do, but I couldn't tell Daria that. She'd become my place of refuge in this crazy storm. I couldn't crush her belief in me.

"They're not from Crenfor —" as the Alfari called the planet, "— and neither am I. That will be their undoing," I assured her. I only wished I were as certain as the Mödatal.

At dinner, Brinna sat on my right and chatted away; told me stories, asked for mine. Laera had never joined me at the high table. But then Garris, her husband, hadn't joined Valemar, either. Here, in Torfin, Jaros sat on Valemar's left, discussing the state of the crops. It was a change I decided to ask Valemar about. I'd been a part of Valemar's circle at Aedenfal, but only his.

"Would you like to see the crops?" Brinna asked me. "The king and Jaros ride out tomorrow to inspect them. Would you like to go along?"

"I would," I told her. "Everything about Bánalfar, and, indeed, Crenfor, is still new. Wine is made from so many different fruits. I'd like to see what is used here."

"That settles it," Brinna said, lilt in her voice vaguely reminding me of Gaelic or Galetean. Her eyes sparkled. "We'll pack a picnic and join them."

Daria left Valemar to undo my dress since he'd followed me out after dinner. He nuzzled my neck from behind before he began pulling the ribbons from the lacings.

"You never had Garris at high table in Aedenfal," I said as the ribbons scritched their way free.

"No." Valemar stayed intent on his task.

I looked over my shoulder. "Why was that?"

His eyes briefly met mine then returned to his work. "There were no reports to give. I had all the knowledge I needed."

I turned and took his hands. "Is it an honor to sit next to you at meals?"

Valemar pressed his lips together. "It is."

"Then why —"

Valemar took my chin and pressed my mouth against his, silencing me. He broke off the kiss then stroked my cheek with his thumb.

"I know you found it hard to fit in at Aedenfal," he said. "You remind them too much of what they fear." He kissed me again. "Would you have wanted that every night? Laera at your side with a look on her face like you'd mucked out the stables and hadn't bothered to change?"

"No," I whispered.

"So I put others at the table who you would want to talk to."

"And quietly shamed the rest," I said.

"And quietly shamed the rest," he affirmed.

Valemar ran his fingers through my hair, then pulled me closer. He looked over my shoulder, down at the laces, and renewed his efforts to undress me. I giggled into his tunic.

"I have been on the road for five days without the opportunity to properly enjoy you," he said. I thought of the nightgown made of gresánve in one of the trunks Daria hadn't had a chance to completely unpack.

The ribbon came free in a rush. Valemar dropped it and slipped the gown from my shoulders where it fell to the floor with a soft whisper. His eyes ran hungrily over me and lingered on the swell of my breasts beneath the thin, nearly sheer fabric of my slip.

He brought my face closer for another kiss while his free hand began to gather up and raise the fabric of my slip. "How did I get so lucky?" His lips brushed against my cheek as he spoke.

"You had a seer to guide you," I said, nearly as breathless as him.

"You could have said 'no.'" His voice caught.

"I could have." I brushed back his long hair and swallowed. I still thought him lethal. Having watched him at jaldun, I knew just how deadly he could be.

But his blades were mine. He'd meant every word of his marriage vows.

He'd offered me everything, and I could give him nothing. I couldn't save his people. I couldn't even give him a child. Here he stood, about to try again, hoping that soon he'd see my belly swell, and there'd be nothing.

"Astrid. What is it?"

I dipped my head. *I should have said 'no,'* I thought. *He's pinned all his hopes on me and it will all come to ruin.*

Valemar lifted my chin. "What if I'm not the savior?" I whispered. "What if I can't save you?"

"Do you trust?" he gently asked me.

I couldn't answer. I couldn't say "yes" when all I thought was "no."

Valemar wrapped his arms around me and tucked my head under his chin. "Then I'll just have to do that for the both of us."

CHAPTER 16

I'd taken part in several negotiations of wine sales and, out of curiosity, had read up on what was involved in making it. I'd had a general idea of how to make wine on Earth. Take a bunch of grapes, squish them, let them ferment, bottle the wine. But what about strawberry wine? Or dandelion? What was involved in the process?

It turned out there was a reason that grapes were the main source of wine on Earth. They had the perfect balance of sugar, acid, tannin, salt, and yeast. Most other fruits and herbs needed a boost, be it from sugar or yeast.

On Zigbar Three, a melon-like fruit, known as the cambari, made the most heavenly wine I'd come across — sunset orange, sweet yet tangy. Earth wine had been a little hard to get used to again after that perfection. Sietti Nine produced tiny currant-like fruits with a high carbon-dioxide output when fermented. Its wine is ruby-red, sparkling, almost like a Lambrusco, but with a richness that Lambrusco doesn't have. I was curious what was used here on Teridun Four. Or Crenfor, as I supposed I would now know it as.

Brinna and I joined Jaros and Valemar on darana to inspect the closest field. The men would ride farther every day while we were here, but they began with a field within the shadow of Torfin's walls.

The fruits were walnut-sized, about the shape and color of plums. Valemar jumped off his mount and picked one for me. "We call them pilva," he said, and handed it to me. It had a sparkling flavor, sweet yet acid. The seeds were small, and I plucked them from my tongue.

"Have I had the wine?"

Valemar laughed. "Frequently."

"Then I'm sure I enjoyed it."

Valemar swung back into the saddle and moved his animal forward with just a leg command. He and Jaros began to talk about expected yields and harvest dates.

"So you'll be back for the harvest," Brinna said to me.

"Will we? Valemar helps with the harvest?" It didn't seem like a thing a king would do.

"Do you not know?" Brinna's eyes grew gleeful. "No one's told you?"

"Told me what?"

"About the king's wine."

"What about it?" I definitely was missing something.

"For the last … oh, hundreds of years, the king presses wine."

If Brinna got any more joyful, she'd explode. "With a press?" Brinna bit her lips but the corners of her mouth still curled up. She shook her head. My eyebrows flew up. "Not … surely not …" Brinna nodded tightly, her lips still clenched between her teeth. "… with his feet?"

Her smile widened even further and pulled her lips from her mouth. "Umm hmm."

I sat back hard enough that Loenir shied. "Easy." I gave her neck a pat as I blinked. Somehow I couldn't quite picture Valemar barefoot and bare-legged, stomping fruit.

"Does the queen stomp grapes — I mean pilva — too?" I asked. That would definitely be a first for me.

Brinna laughed, and it trilled, just like her voice. "Reina? No."

"Would I be expected to?"

"If you wanted to join the sale."

My forehead wrinkled. "Valemar presses his own wine to sell?"

"Oh!" Brinna's eyes lost their glee and softened. "You don't know. The story is that several hundred years ago, Bánalfar, indeed all of Crenfor, had a very cold year. Crops suffered. People began to starve. The Cordair raided along Fairfada more than they had since they'd been pushed out of our lands.

"The pilva didn't mind the cold weather. The fruit wasn't as sweet without the warmth, but it did grow. King Haldan saw how his people were suffering, and yet how good the harvest of pilva was. He came to Torfin to oversee the harvest and pressing, which was done by foot then.

"The juice was tart but drinkable. Haldan told his people it was just like the year — not sweet, but survivable. He shucked off his hose, tied up his tunic, and joined them in the press.

"The wine was distributed throughout the land." Brinna's eyes began to twinkle again. "Some bottles were sweeter than others. It was said that those were bottles made from the juice pressed by Haldan's feet, that the touch of the king had transformed the pilva. A demand grew for them and prices rose.

"Haldan saw all this and came back the next year for the harvest. Again, he pressed the pilva, alone this time. But these bottles he claimed as the King's Wine." This time I heard the capitals in the

name. "Haldan sold the wine and used the money to buy food to distribute to those who had worked yet were still suffering. His descendants still carry on the tradition."

I began to see how Valemar's house had endured for two thousand years. "Do you have the poor, then?" I asked. I'd seen them everywhere in the galaxy. There were a couple of places that didn't, but those cultures had a policy of executing anyone, other than children and the elderly, who was a "drain on society." Every planet, every society, had people who struggled to make ends meet. And on every planet there were also people who didn't want to work, if they could help it. Sometimes the two were connected. Sometimes not.

"Aye," Brinna said. "Life is hard for some poor souls." She frowned. "And life can be too easy for others." She smiled again. "We usually know the difference."

"So you've never had a Queen's Wine?" I asked, already thinking how I could help, how my notoriety and the uniqueness of such an offering would work in the business world. The Protocol Specialist Carr part of my brain awakened and stretched.

Brinna's eyes flashed with glee again. "Maybe it's time."

We ate in the shade of a large tree. The pilva bushes stretched into the distance, rising and falling with the gentle hills, perfuming the air with the subtle sweetness of fruit. The breeze was warm and carried the hum of insects. I relaxed on the rug and tried to stay in the here and now of this summer and not ones past. Valemar handed me a glass of wine, pale and golden and sweet.

"Is this from fruit grown here?" I asked.

Valemar shook his head. "Those bushes —" He gestured toward them with his glass. "— produce the red wine you like so well. The

skins and flesh are darker. I'll go inspect the fields this wine came from tomorrow."

"Brinna told me the story about your ancestor," I said.

"I was surprised she hadn't heard it," Brinna said.

Valemar smiled. "They come up as they need to."

"Yes," I said. "Two thousand years' worth of stories takes time to be told. And heard."

"How about you?" Brinna asked. "Would you share some stories of the moon with us?"

Valemar's sharp glance pinned me to the spot. I'd been evasive the few times he'd asked me about the moon.

"It's not so different from here," I said, and watched as Valemar's eyes narrowed. "On a fine summer day, people picnic on the grass, eat good food, drink good wine, enjoy the company of others."

"Wine made from … grapes?" Brinna asked.

I laughed. "You've got a good memory." Valemar gave me a quizzical look. "When Brinna told me about the King's Wine, I got mixed up and called the pilva 'grapes.' On the moon, we make wine mainly from grapes. They grow in clusters on vines. The fruits are smaller, fingernail-sized. It sounds like the process is the same though."

"And do your kings make wine?" Valemar asked. I caught the thread of something there. Instinct told me he was probing. Perhaps, for the first time, wondering just who I did come from.

"No," I said. "Kings drink lots of wine. They do not help in the making of it. There are a few who oversee agriculture, but for the most part —"

I stopped. How could I explain that the few kings and queens left on Earth were governed rather than ruled? They were important as the line that connected the past to the present, both symbols and

divining rods, yet held no true power. "For the most part, they are like the King's Wine. They do what they can to help their people."

"And your family?" As Valemar drank, his eyes met mine. A seed of doubt glowed in them as he looked at me over his glass.

The base of my skull buzzed and indignation filled my veins. I sat up taller. "My ancestors were warrior kings. Not so different from you — tall, blond, blue-eyed, and good with a blade. They traveled the world in sailing ships with dragon prows and sails of red. But every warrior eventually longs for peace. Every man wants his sons around him."

Valemar's eyes flashed. I recognized my mistake too late. I held back a gulp and plowed on.

"So they turned their attention away from their neighbors' lands and focused on their own. The urge to travel never settled, though. We still travel, seek new experiences, new places."

"Is that what brought you here?" Brinna asked.

Is it? Valemar asked with his eyes, hiding again behind his glass.

"It is," I said. And then the image of Viktor, missing half his face and most of the skin on his arms swam before me. My ears filled with the echo of Doc's last rasping breaths as he died in my arms. My hands twitched, covering body after body with white shrouds, folding the cranes, and programming the journey to the sun.

I set my wine aside as the twitching grew in strength and clasped my hands together to hide their shaking. Jaros, Brinna, and Valemar shifted uncomfortably. I tried to force a smile onto my face. They deserved an explanation for my reaction to Brinna's simple question.

"I was traveling … and there was an accident. I —" But my lips wouldn't form the words. My throat constricted, adding its voice to the *Don't say it! Don't say it!* that filled my head. I took a deep breath and changed my answer, kept the full horror to myself. "I managed to reach the emergency ship, and it brought me here."

"You can travel beyond the moon?" Jaros asked, his voice husky with wonder.

"Yes." I looked over at Valemar. His hand covered his mouth. His eyes were now unreadable. "But I've no way back."

"If your people travel," Jaros asked, "won't they come looking for you?"

"I've no way to contact them."

"But surely ..." Brinna said, though that was as far as she got before her awe silenced her.

"They don't know I'm here. They're sure to think I perished in the accident." Practice enabled me to say it calmly, for I'd thought it a thousand times.

"Won't they come looking?" Jaros asked again.

"It is forbidden," Valemar said. All eyes, including mine, turned to him. "It is forbidden to come here."

"But the —" Jaros started then stopped.

He knows about the strangers trading with the Cordair, I realized.

"She's under our protection now." Valemar sat up and handed me my wine. I sipped it thankfully. "Are the sulee doing as well as these?" he asked Jaros.

"The variety we're drinking," Brinna softly said to me when I frowned. "The pilva in this field are known as pinwah."

Thank you, I mouthed at her, and let the men's discussion slowly erase the cloud that had settled.

I lay on Valemar's chest, slowly tracing the outline of the barat leaves. His strong arms drew me closer to him. "Tell me about the

accident," he said. "When you mentioned it before, I didn't realize …" I pushed away, but his arms tightened and held me fast. "I should have asked you about it earlier, why you came here."

My heart pounded, trapped between Valemar's embrace and the memories that stalked me. I couldn't do it, relive it yet again. And I knew once I did tell Valemar, he'd know the Mödatal had been wrong. He'd realize that I wasn't the Moon Princess. Everything would change.

And I didn't want it to.

Tears slipped down my face, forming small puddles on Valemar's chest. His arms loosened their grip. His hands began to stroke my back, my hair. And still I stayed silent. He wouldn't comfort me if he knew who I really was.

Valemar sighed. "I wish you would, but I can see you're not ready."

I brushed my lips against his chest and wiped away the tears with my hand. Then I burrowed into his embrace and hid, from the past, from the future. Valemar continued to caress me, as if to reassure me that all would be fine. But it wouldn't. There would come a time when I'd have to tell him. And it was a tale that had the power to destroy us both.

CHAPTER 17

Valemar held my hand the next day when we toured the fields of pilva that produced the white wine and personally explained how the pressing process worked. He inspected the new kegs in the winery that were being prepared to replace the old ones. The Alfari, too, used a special wood to impart tannins and flavor into the wine.

None of the wine-sales I'd negotiated had afforded me a first-hand tour of how it was made. Or provided me with such an attentive host. The only thing missing from the experience was an actual harvest and press. Something that would be rectified when we returned in a month or so.

"The queen wondered yesterday, since there is a King's Wine, whether there was a Queen's Wine, as well," Brinna told Valemar as we toured the racks of wine aging in their casks.

I blushed. "I wasn't sure what the tradition was."

"We could do a Queen's Wine," Valemar said. "Preferably with the sulee. I wouldn't want your beautiful feet stained," he said with a smolder.

"Do you press the pinwah?" I asked.

"I do. And will have red feet as a result."

"I would love to help," I said. Valemar read the unspoken, *Since I can't help you with the outsiders.*

He took my hand and drew me forward and kissed the top of my head. "I would expect nothing less from a queen who believes that nothing is beneath her."

My head snapped up, nearly hitting him in the nose. "What?"

Valemar eyed Brinna and Jaros. Someone had been gossiping, telling tales that had traveled to Valemar's ears. He just wasn't sure they'd heard the story as well.

His eyes returned to my face, and he stroked my cheek. "My queen believes that she needs to serve and shelter others. Since the king does that through the King's Wine, then my servant queen should have a Queen's Wine." His eyes told me he'd heard the rest of my speech to Laera and the others.

Valemar looked over at Jaros. "Could you secure the arrangements?"

"Absolutely, my king." Jaros grinned broadly. Such a unique opportunity would be a boon to Torfin, and Jaros was already counting the profits.

I was pretty sure the source of the story from the solar could be traced back to one person. Laera and the others wouldn't want to make me look good. But someone else would.

"How did Valemar know about my little speech to Laera?" I demanded from Daria when she arrived to dress me for dinner.

She blanched. "It wasn't me. I wouldn't tell tales about you to anyone."

I sat down hard on the dressing table chair. "I'm sorry. Valemar quoted it back to me this afternoon, practically word for word."

Daria gave me a sad smile and picked up the hair brush. She opened her mouth and then closed it.

"Go on. Say it," I told her as she began her brushing.

Daria lifted a section of my hair and held it tight by my scalp as she eased out the snarls. She kept her eyes on her work. "It's not my place."

"Do I have to command you?" I asked, half in jest.

She met my eyes in the mirror. "You know what they say about asking questions."

I did. But I said, "Go ahead and tell me."

"While you meant it in earnest, and I'm sure the king quoted it back to you as a compliment, there are others that would have … taken it as a rebuke. And quoted it. Where other ears then heard it."

"And reported it to the king." It stung, knowing they'd made fun of me. But it did make Valemar's desire to get me away from Aedenfal more clear.

"I'm sorry," I said again to Daria.

She held the brush in both hands. "I'd do anything for you. When I worked in Reina's household, I was really just another face." She smiled. "But you treat me as a friend."

"You are a friend," I said. "And I thought moon children were treated as equals."

Daria picked up another section. "Not equals. We are important, and we could even be the children of kings or princes or steward's daughters, but my role is to serve."

"As Heymond's or Orin's is to protect."

"Yes."

"And you have served me. You are doing so now. I *can* brush my own hair," I said.

"But you are weary. You've done your own work."

I snorted. "Tell that to the farm wife with four young children.

She needs your service more than I do." But my words hurt Daria again. She dipped her head. Her lashes fluttered as she blinked.

"What I mean is that I don't work nearly as hard as she does. And she has no help. You say that I treat you as a friend, and that is true, for I do not feel worthy of your waiting on me. And yet, you do."

"But how would you get dressed on your own?" Daria asked.

"I would need gowns that don't lace up the back. But then I would miss out on spending time with the person who's encouraged me the most since I came to Crenfor. You've stood by me through everything. And for that, I shall be eternally grateful. You are my friend."

Daria sniffed and blinked again. "And I shall always stand by you, my queen."

My heart swelled. With her by my side, maybe I could become a true queen.

The next day, Valemar took me out to see the Dunna River. The road there was well traveled with people and goods moving between the small town of Piltur and the city of Torfin. Nestled on the east bank of the river just above Taspar's Bridge, Piltuir served as a way station. Torfin was situated central to the fields of pilva, but, as with most pre-mechanized places, the river made transportation of goods easier so the majority of its wine flowed down the Dunna to be dispersed throughout Bánalfar, or beyond from the port in Vanerife.

The Leisna River that ran by Aedenfal was small, more like a canal compared to the Dunna. Here, I was reminded of the Thames that runs through the city of London on Earth: boats coming and going, traffic moving, goods and people being loaded and unloaded along the banks. The Dunna was not as large a river as the Forma on

Hautel Seven or the Mississippi on Earth or the Alfari would have had to cross it by ferry instead of the bridge, the expanse being too great to build one with their technology. And, like the Thames, the banks of the Dunna were pleasant once you left the bustle of town behind.

"You're smiling," Valemar said to me as we walked along.

"This reminds me of home." I traveled so much that even though I had a room at Finn's in Edinburgh and I loved the time I spent with my family, I was more at peace in London with all its parks. It was the only city I'd found on Earth that had managed to retain a village atmosphere, even with all the high-rises that ringed its ancient core. I tried to spend a few weeks there each year — the weary voyager returning to her roots.

"What was your home like?" Valemar asked.

I snapped off a flower from the grass along the bank and twirled it. "In truth, the interior of a ship most of the time." Valemar's face fell. He knew the interior of my ship was nothing like the ones passing by us on the Dunna. "But when I was home, when I wasn't on a ship, I liked to spend my days in a town that has a river like this."

"What did you do when you traveled?"

"I worked as an emissary, though my title was 'Protocol Specialist.'"

"And what did that entail?"

I gave Valemar a sidelong glance. It was clear he was leading me not only down the path along the river but to some other agenda. "I studied the customs and business practices of different peoples." I gestured to one of the larger ships being rowed up the river. "I would have been aboard one of those, traveling with wine or anapali cloth, or with the men — and women — who brokered the deals. Instead of sewing with Cadalin, I would have traveled with her husband."

"I see." Valemar was silent for a moment. "So, you don't sew. You don't ride."

"Didn't."

"Do you fight?"

I stopped in my tracks. My heart took the opportunity to jump into my throat. *Let's get the Moon Princess nice and comfortable and then put a blade in her hand.* He may not have said it, but I had the feeling that was exactly what he was thinking.

"No, I was just the emissary. Not even that. The assistant to the emissary." I sought wildly for a comparison. "I'm more like Padrid. Does Padrid fight?" I asked. And then sincerely hoped the answer was "no." The Alfari seemed to be the prepared type.

"Are you protected?" Valemar asked.

I tried to swallow down my heart. If it rose any farther, it would fly right out of my mouth. I knew exactly where this was going. And, sure enough, that was where it went.

"If you are protected, should you not be willing to protect? If the need arose," Valemar asked, using my own words against me.

"Yes," I whispered. I stared hard at the flower in my hands and tried hard not to think about the result of any encounter. We wouldn't be just scaring people away.

Valemar caressed my cheek then lifted my face until my eyes met his. "There is going to be danger out there. I would feel better if you learned how to use a blade. To move silently. I would not have you be the knife that stands between death and destruction. But I would have you learn to protect yourself. Just in case."

His eyes held a fear that had not been there before. Reports passed in and out of his hands all the time. Was there some threat to me that he hadn't shared?

Valemar's hands encircled my hips. His thumbs lightly pressed against my belly. I closed my eyes so he wouldn't see the answer in them that it was empty.

He wanted a wife who could protect herself and his future child. I couldn't give him the latter, but I could give him the former.

"What would you have me do?"

Daria dressed me in a short tunic and hose and braided my hair into a plait that hung down my back. Valemar took me to the large chamber he used in Torfin to practice jaldun. He drew out one of the short, curved swords from the belt at his waist. I tried to catch the precise movements as he quickly ran the handle through his fingers before the hilt came to rest in his hand.

"A sword or knife is an extension of your hand." His knees bent, his leg shifted, and his arm extended. "You learn to dance with the blade, to move like the breeze, bend like the river, and slice —"

"Like Death himself," I said.

His smile turned dangerous and his eyes gleamed. "Exactly. Men train from early boyhood to move in such a way."

"And I am neither a child nor a boy."

Valemar's eyes danced. "For which I am extremely grateful."

"So why introduce me to jaldun?"

The sword hissed — steel against steel — as Valemar slid it back into its sheath. "I want you to be able to wield a knife, should you need to. I want you able to move silent and swift as the wind should you need to fly."

"What aren't you telling me?"

"Just a precaution." His eyes said otherwise, but I could tell that was as much explanation as I was going to get. Valemar drew a knife

from his belt and held it out to me hilt first, his fingers wrapped around the end of the blade. I took it from him.

The knife had the weight of a tablet but fit into my hand like it was part of me. I swallowed. "You'd have me kill someone with this?"

"I'd have you save yourself with this."

I tested my thumb against the edge. I didn't even need to apply pressure to tell that it was sharp enough to cut straight through to the bone. And maybe even through that.

"Yes, it's sharp," Valemar said. "You wouldn't need much skill, but I would have you learn what someone could try to do to you."

"*The ability to anticipate is the ability to succeed,*" I said, quoting one of my protocol professors.

Valemar gave me a satisfied smile. "Exactly." His eyes turned to the knife in my hand. "A perfect fit, and you're holding it well. It is an extension of your hand, an extension of your will. Fists can pummel and nails can scratch —"

"But the blade will slice and tear."

"Be it man or beast."

"Those things aren't mutually exclusive," I said.

"No. They're not."

I swung the knife about, testing its balance. Valemar laughed.

"I know. I'm rubbish," I said.

"Rubbish?"

I winced and tried to think of a definition. "It means 'garbage' in the sense that I'm something you'd sweep up and take out rather than keep."

"Rubbish. Interesting." Valemar came to stand behind me. "Unpracticed is a better observation. One that will change if we don't sweep you up and take you away with the garbage."

Valemar matched his arms up with mine and curled his hands around my hands. "Do you stand so close to the children you train?" I asked.

"No," he said. His lips tickled my ear. "But there has to be some advantage to teaching my wife." He began to slowly move my arms in graceful yet deadly arcs. "The wind brushes everything, curling and twisting. It is here and then it is gone. The river, too, bends and twists. Calm on the surface, swift and dangerous underneath. Both cut and carve. Both are the essence of life — the air we inhale and exhale, the blood that flows through the rivers of our veins. So, too, must you flow if it comes to kill or be killed."

"*Not today*," I whispered, thinking of the ancient greeting one gave to Death.

"Hmm?" Valemar's question buzzed in my ear.

"One says, 'Not today,' when one meets Death," I said.

Valemar chuckled. "Until it is, 'You are welcome, my friend.'"

"I suppose." I couldn't see Death as a friend.

"My father said, 'Not today,' until the pain became so great that it became, 'I am ready.' So it was, 'You are welcome, my friend,' when he passed into the next life."

Pain blossomed in my heart. "I can see how Death could be a friend in that way."

"Yes," Valemar agreed. "But for you —" He continued to move my arms, gently pushing and pulling so that they not only moved but the rest of me, too, shifting my weight from one foot to the next. "— I want you to tell him, 'Not today,' for many years to come."

I lost track of what I was doing. All I was conscious of was how the husband I hadn't wanted was wrapped around me.

"Astrid." Valemar's voice tickled in my ear again.

171

"Hmm?" I blinked back my emotion. How had I ended up so blessed?

"Where did you drift to?"

My arms felt empty without him in them. I caught his hands with my pinky fingers and wrapped our arms about me, taking care to keep the blade from drifting too close.

"When I abandoned my ship and set out for Crenfor, I never thought I'd find anyone like you."

Valemar's lips brushed my ear. "And I'd been waiting for you for a long time."

But he hadn't been waiting for *me*.

I squeezed Valemar's hands and extended my arms again. He wanted the Moon Princess to be prepared. I still wouldn't be her, but I could make the last part true.

CHAPTER 18

My days in Torfin lost their lazy, summer feel. Valemar turned my training over to Heymond and a young King's Guard who went by the nickname The Shadow. In both cases, Valemar chose wisely. The body that stood behind me, directing my movements in jaldun, was one I'd been plastered against for hours on my first day on Crenfor. As if it remembered the journey, I found it easier to follow Heymond's movements, limb against limb, than I had with Valemar. There was no anticipation of further joining, only dedication of purpose.

At mid-morning I became The Shadow's pupil. Erris had the ability to move silently through building or field with little more than a hint of darkness to give away his presence. Even that he taught me to conceal. *Ball ... heel ... ball ... heel.* We crept through the passageways of High Torfin, the fields of pilva, and the sheltering groves. He set up watches of the King's Guard and had me attempt to elude them. I was usually unsuccessful, but my skills improved.

Afternoons I spent with Brinna, a respite from the rigors of training. In a few short months, I'd gone from reading files and negotiating contracts, to negotiating hallways and learning "women's ways," to a ghost who wielded a blade and crept through the shadows, if somewhat clumsily. Afternoons with Brinna, lounging in the solar or outside in the shade of the trees, became my refuge from the world of men. With my every hour accounted for, Daria became merely my dresser, for which I was sorry. Valemar still lavished his attention on me at dinner and in the quiet dark of our bedroom. I no longer saw him during the day, but there were times I could sense he was watching me, judging my progress from just out of sight.

The karawack grew old enough that they were caged up and sent off to Glábac (the gateway city to Gladama), Aedenfal, Vanerife, and Lendurig. Only one remained in Torfin so that I could receive messages from there once I left. Ean was already planning the next clutch for me. Valemar had hundreds of birds scattered all across Bánalfar. I only had five. I didn't know how he did it, for each bird seemed to have taken a piece of my soul. It was as if I was sending five children out into the world. Ean had chuckled but agreed when I made the observation.

"It is very like," he said. "For that is how they find you." He secured the cage on the last former chick, now a full-fledged bird, and crossed to its mother. "But you've six. Sari has adopted you." He stroked her cream-colored head. "She would find you, if we sent her."

My thoughts were still on my birds while I trained with Heymond. Though he instructed me in jaldun with two blades, today we were sparring with dull knives — him two blades, me one.

Heymond's knife connected with my empty left hand. I hissed in pain and tried to shake off the sting. "Why do I only get one?" I asked.

"That would have been your hand," Heymond said as I checked my palm.

"Yes, well it's used to moving in the flow of jaldun." I took up my stance again.

Heymond didn't. "You need to be aware, my queen. We may fight with two blades, but you will most likely have only one. You are not a warrior."

I rose out of the pose. "Then why train me? Why would Valemar have me learn jaldun but give me only one blade?"

Heymond's cheek twitched. "You are the Moon Princess. There are those who would stop you."

I swallowed hard. "Have you … Valemar … received a credible threat?"

Heymond's eyes gave nothing away. "It is not my place to say. But you should be able to defend yourself."

"With one blade?"

Heymond sank back. "With whatever is at hand."

I shifted, lowering my center of gravity, and watched for the smallest flicker of movement, the slightest hint as to his intention. Heymond's blades twirled in his hands. An action, he'd told me, designed to distract an opponent.

"Remember, my queen, your left hand is empty. Use it for balance only."

"Unless I pick something up," I muttered.

A smile lifted one corner of his mouth. "Exactly."

The knives twirled again and then Heymond lunged. I twisted to the side. His knives sliced at where I'd been, snagging against my clothing instead of stopping against me. In an unconscious flash, my blade traveled from my right hand to my left and jabbed backward. Heymond grunted as the dull steel dug into his kidney.

"Nice, my queen. Unexpected." He rubbed at his back. "That is one advantage of having a single blade."

Heymond eyed my shaking hand. "Would that blow have killed you?" I asked.

"No. But it would have slowed me down." Heymond took both his blades in one hand. "Go find the Shadow. He's stationed by the High gate," Heymond added when I grinned. "I'll retrieve you in an hour."

Erris peeled off from his place against the wall when I approached. His eyes gleamed merrily. "I'll be back," he called out to the guard standing opposite him. "In — how long?" he asked me.

"Heymond said an hour."

"An hour then," he added joyfully.

The other guard bowed lightly. "My queen."

We headed off. Erris bounced alongside me like a puppy. "I think we should practice moving through the countryside," he said, then eyed my clothing. "Though we should practice in town sometime when you're in your regular dress. No need to advertise what we're doing, but you should still learn how to disappear into a crowd."

I forced a smile onto my face. Why did Erris — and Valemar and Heymond by extension — now think this was something I needed to do? "Why did you learn to disappear and move like a shadow?" I asked him.

"I like sweets," Erris said with a big grin. "Moving quickly and quietly allowed me to sneak them from the kitchen."

"Ah." I smiled. "Instead of Shadow, I could call you Knave of Hearts."

"Knave?"

"It's an old term in my native language for 'sneaky young man.'"

Erris frowned. "Sneaky young man of hearts?"

"It's from an old rhyme based on an even older game," I said. "On the moon we play a game that uses cards illustrated with hearts, diamonds, shovels, and a leaf. The rhyme, though I'm not sure it will rhyme in Alfari, goes:

The Queen of Hearts
She made some tarts,
All on a summer's day,
The Knave of Hearts
He stole those tarts,
And took them clean away.
The King of Hearts
Called for the tarts
And beat the Knave full sore,
The Knave of Hearts
Brought back the tarts,
And vowed he'd steal no more."

"Did he?" Erris looked thoughtful. "I don't know if I could keep that vow if they were lian tarts. Might have to make an exception for that in my vow."

I laughed. "They are good." I didn't get them near as often as I would have liked.

We walked out through the gate and into the countryside that surrounded Torfin. "How old are you?" I asked.

"I just turned sixteen." He grinned. "I know. I'm young for the King's Guard. But they didn't pick me for my fighting prowess."

He put a hand out to stop me. As I fell behind him, I spotted the retreating form of Heymond not too far ahead of us.

Erris gave me a sly smile. "Feel like spying on our esteemed Captain of the Guard today?"

"Why not?" I said.

Erris melted into the shrubbery that lay a few feet from the path. *Toe — heel. Toe — heel.* We crept along, keeping Heymond in sight.

Heymond continued down the path then followed a smaller one that split off on the left. Here we hung back. The path ran through fields until it reached a farmhouse. Erris and I got down low and crept along, trying to keep Heymond in sight.

Heymond shouted a greeting as he neared the house. We watched as a woman came out and spoke to Heymond, then pointed behind the house.

"*Kwarg!* Oh — beggin' your pardon, my queen," Erris said, apologizing for his use of one of the more colorful Alfari swear words, which loosely translated as "pig fucker". "We can try to circle 'round, but if he doubles back before we can get there, we'll lose him."

"What do you think he's doing?" I asked, keeping my voice low.

Erris shook his head. "No idea. If it was food he wanted, he'd go to the kitchen. If it was men, he'd have no need to see a farmer."

"Can we head back to the trees and see if he comes back this way?"

"Sure."

Erris stayed low to the ground, keeping an eye to the farmhouse, and backed slowly toward the trees. Knowing he was watching our flank, I turned and crept toward the trees, scanning for signs of movement.

We found a good-sized tree and crouched beside it. We didn't have long to wait. A few minutes later, Heymond returned carrying something that resembled a cross between a watermelon and a pumpkin.

"Oh," Erris said. The blade of grass he'd been playing with snapped in two.

"What?"

Erris winced. He attempted to give me a smile but his pained expression merely twisted. "It looks like you're moving on to stabbing."

Erris and I snuck back to the High, through the kitchens to snag him some of the sticky pilva-filled buns the cook had cooling, and then into the shadows of the lowest level. His heart wasn't really in the game, and neither was mine, but at least Erris had an easier time seeing in the dark than I did.

"You really can't see that?" he asked me after I'd tripped over a barrel.

"No." I rubbed my aching knee, which I'd apparently skinned. Moisture of some kind clotted on my hand. "My moon is white, so it's easier to see at night," I groused as the throbbing pain spread.

"The moon has a moon? Why can't we see it?"

My heart dropped into the depths of my stomach. Before I could formulate any kind of answer, decide to tell the truth or weave an elaborate lie, Heymond appeared at the head of the passageway with a torch. His face held no expression. I couldn't tell if he'd heard our exchange.

"I have a new task set up for you, my queen." He nodded to Erris. "Back to your post."

I limped over to Heymond, shaking my leg to keep it from stiffening up. He glanced at the damp patch on my leggings. In the torchlight, I could see it was wet with clear lymph fluid and not blood.

"You were easy to follow from the sounds," Heymond said.

"Well, apparently your eyes work better in the dark than mine," I grumbled.

A smile flickered on Heymond's face. "Good to know. We should work on that handicap. But not today. I have a new project set up for you in the yard."

"And why would I work on stabbing?"

There was no trace of surprise on Heymond's face as I asked about a task I shouldn't have known about. "Because that is the purpose of a blade."

The melon had been erected on a stool in the side yard where the knights usually practiced their swordplay. The yard was empty except for the melon, Heymond, and me. "We will begin to work off the surprise that comes from actually using a blade," Heymond said.

"I've used a blade. I've cooked. I can chop a mean salad."

Heymond's eyebrows wrinkled, but he didn't comment. He held a honed jaldun knife out to me, hilt first, his fingers wrapped around the blade. "The kinwah is somewhat like a body — squishy outside, hard surprise at the core."

"Squishy? That outside doesn't look squishy." Any more than the rind of a pumpkin looked squishy.

Heymond rolled his eyes. "Imagine it's a leather-clad person.

"Oh. I get it. Leather then flesh then …" I broke off, imagining hitting —

"Bone. Yes. And your blade can stick to bone." I swallowed heavily as my task suddenly became real. "One blow generally won't save your life. The hesitation that results from surprise can be your death. We'd like to keep you alive."

"There must be some threat," I said. "All this training. You — Valemar — must have received some news of a threat."

Heymond was as impassive as always. "You'll need to ask him about that." He nodded toward the stool. "Take your place in front of the kinwah."

I gripped my knife and walked over, my right knee protesting with every step. "It's not going to fight back," I said as I took my place. The kinwah sat there like a large, dark green watermelon. *Hiyah!* Yeah, right. This was going to be stupid.

"Who says it's not going to fight back?" There was laughter in Heymond's voice, and I heard his footsteps behind me. He moved behind the kinwah with a blunted blade in his hand.

"*You're* going to be the melon?' An expert, sword-wielding melon that was sure to leave me bruised.

"Melon? If you mean 'opponent,' then yes." There was a satisfied smile on Heymond's face.

"Great," I muttered.

"Your opponent will most likely be armed with a sword. Your job is to get underneath and stab him."

I heard a barking laugh and then realized it was me. "Get underneath *your* sword. Me?"

"Will the Cordair send a less qualified man?"

"Aha!" I pointed my knife at him. "So you have received threats from the Cordair."

Heymond twirled his sword. "You have known that they want you since that first day. It's why you agreed to marry Valemar. That information is nothing new."

"Then why act like it is?"

Heymond kept his eyes on my knife and continued to twirl his sword. "Are you willing to save your life, my queen?"

I sighed. "Yes." But I didn't know how much bruising it would take.

Quite a lot, it turned out. Even though I could feel Heymond pull back at the last second and even though he was hampered by the stool and the kinwah target it held, I still felt the sting of Heymond's blade *a lot*. Out of sheer frustration, I began to whack at anything I could reach — Heymond's arms, the legs of the stool.

"Better, my queen. Work your way to the flesh," Heymond told me after I'd dived under his arm and swung at the legs of the stool. "A leg injury will slow down an opponent, but you need to follow it up with a mortal wound."

"Right," I grumbled, and shook out my stiffening limbs. If Heymond wanted follow up, I was going to give it to him this time.

I shifted the blade to my left hand. Heymond's eyebrows rose. I sank down into my stance and watched him.

"What do you think you're going to do?" he said, taunting me. "Use your left hand? You're just making it easier for me."

"Try me," I said, my voice barely even a whisper.

Heymond smirked. "Come and get me, little girl."

I darted toward him. Heymond's blade came down toward me, but I turned, narrowing my profile, and put all my force into my shoulder. Had I a steel glove, I would have grabbed his blade. I rolled, smacking into the legs of the stool, then launched myself upward. Heymond uttered an "oof" as the stool, the kinwah, and I landed on top of him. My right arm came up under his, blocking his sword. With the left, I plunged the knife deep into the kinwah. Firm then squish then jarring halt as the blade sank into the stone at the center of the massive fruit. The knife hilt slammed into the bones of my hand, sending rivers of shooting pain through it.

"Don't let go," Heymond wheezed from underneath me as I made incoherent noises of pain. "Whatever you do, don't let go. Pull it out and ready for another strike."

I did as I was told though very inch of me now ached. "Are you okay?" I asked. "You didn't break a rib or anything?"

Heymond gave me a lopsided smile. "No. I'm sure to feel it tomorrow, but I did ask for it."

I scrambled to my feet. Heymond pushed the stool and the melon aside. "Now you know the knife is going to stick, especially if you hit bone. Don't trust a single thrust. Yank it out and stab again." He got to his feet, his sword ringing as it slid against the cobblestones of the yard. "And don't forget to listen. An assassin often works alone, but not always."

"Assassin?" My knees sagged.

"Assassin. Invading army. Should you be confronted by someone wishing to do you harm, you need to be prepared to fight and flee. Not necessarily in that order."

Heymond nodded toward the castle. "That's enough for today. You did well, my queen. You're sure to be sore, but you did well."

I held my knife out to Heymond, hilt first. "Thank you." It was an automatic response, for my mind was stuck in a loop, playing Heymond's words over and over. *An assassin often works alone.* I swallowed heavily. They must have received news of a credible threat to my life.

Heymond certainly wasn't going to tell me. I was going to have to ask the one person who possibly would.

CHAPTER 19

Daria had a bath waiting when I returned to my room. I moaned when she had me raise my arms so she could pull the tunic over my head. Her eyes widened as it came off. Red patches that were already turning black and blue colored my arms like spots on a Dalmatian. Even my ribs had blossoming patches of blue. She gently pulled at the crusted patch on my knee, but I still hissed as the thick leggings came away, taking the start of the scab with them.

"We'll get you into the water, and I'll go for some salve," Daria said. "The massage and ointment will help the bruises heal faster."

I nodded and held onto the rim of the tub as Daria helped guide me in. I sank down into the warm water and rested my head against the back, only moving to allow her to undo the braid against my scalp. She let the ends of my hair drop into the water and massaged the back of my head.

"Just rest. I'll be back soon." Daria swirled a cupful of bath salts into the water and then left me. I closed my eyes and drifted. A few minutes later, the door opened. But the footfall was heavier than Daria's.

With Heymond's warning still fresh in my mind, I sat up, splashing water over the rim as I prepared to flee. But it was only Valemar. In his hands was a jar of salve.

"I thought I'd come inspect the damage."

I eased my grip on the edge of the tub and sank back again. "Well, it was done on your instructions," I said, and closed my eyes. I placed my arms along the rim, the better for Valemar to see the bruises.

He sat down on the stool next to the tub and placed the jar at his feet. Gently, he lifted one arm, raised it high, slowly turned it, fingered a spot here then there, then placed it back on the rim before repeating the process with the other arm. I kept my eyes closed while Valemar worked at his task, shutting out, at least for a little while, the marks and the reason they were there. Once he was done, Valemar held my hand, running his thumb along the back of it.

"You would have lost your arms."

I snorted. "That would have been the least of my worries. Or rather, the last of them. I would have bled out and then there'd have been nothing to worry about." I cracked an eye open. "So why the training? All that time in Aedenfal, just hours away from Rock Dorach, and nothing. Yet now that I'm days beyond the reach of the Cordair, you decide that I need to know how to defend myself."

"Let's get you out," Valemar said. "I'll dress your bruises."

Valemar took the towel from its place by the tub and held it open for me. I stood up, waited for the water to stop cascading from my body, then used Valemar's arm to steady myself as I stepped out. Valemar came around behind me and wrapped the towel around me. He lingered a moment, then bent and picked up the salve and drew me over to the bed.

Valemar took the lid off the pot. A flowery, herbal smell drifted up from the creamy white ointment. I sat down on the edge of the bed and held out an arm. Valemar smeared a dollop on the first bruise and began massaging it in.

"Why now?" I repeated.

Valemar briefly met my eyes. "They think there's something you can do — the Cordair and the strangers." Valemar looked up again. "*She has power she knows not*, Shale has told me."

I mentally cursed the Mödatal. "So the Cordair believe the prophecy?"

Valemar shook his head. "No, it's more that you make the strangers nervous."

"Well, they're not supposed to be here."

It could be that the Cordair had told them about the prophecy. *Stupid Mödatal.* She really would be the death of me.

"And they fear you," Valemar said.

"It doesn't help that everyone thinks I'm the answer to driving them away."

Valemar dipped his finger into the pot again and started work on another bruise. "And you still believe you can't?" His fingers were gentle but the spots still smarted under his ministrations. "No," I whispered.

"And you don't trust the Mödatal?"

"I don't believe in prophecies."

"Even though we found you exactly where she said you'd be?"

I shivered. That was the piece that bothered me the most. How had she known? "I don't know how it could be true."

Valemar's fingers ran up and down my arm. A trail of goosebumps rose in their wake. "You do not know what you can do." He stared at my bruises. Valemar turned my arm over. His gaze

traveled up the inside of my arm, almost as if he were counting the number of times I'd blocked the blows.

"Would you have thought you could wield a knife?" His eyes met mine.

"No," I whispered.

"Yet you defended yourself today."

I gave a small laugh. "You said I would have lost my arms."

"At first." Valemar paused. "And then you nearly took out Heymond." Pride shone in his eyes. Valemar dipped into the pot again and started on a new bruise. "You do not yet know what you are capable of."

He meant it as a compliment, but instead of filling me with hope, Valemar's words filled me with dread.

The next day, Valemar appeared in our room just as Daria finished braiding my hair. He, too, was dressed in the leather tunic and thick hose used for training.

"You're joining me?" I asked.

"You might say that," he said. "I thought I'd supervise today."

My mouth went dry. "Supervise or take me on?" I had no desire to fight for my life with Valemar. I had the feeling Heymond would go easier on me.

"Supervise."

But there was something about the way he held himself, something in the tone of his voice, that told me today would be different.

I wiped my now sweaty palms against my legs. "Thank you, Daria." I tried to lift a smile but it kept sliding from my face. Daria's eyes were as wide as my own.

"I'll have the water waiting for a bath when you return," she said. Then she dipped her head and slipped from the room.

I followed Valemar through the castle and out the back gate into the fields beyond. No one joined us. In a small clearing screened by a row of trees stood a pen that had to measure no more than six feet by six feet. An anapali traversed the small confines, anxiously peering through the rails.

My feet became too heavy to move. "No." Surely he couldn't mean me to do what I feared he intended.

Valemar took a blade from his belt. "There's a natural reluctance to killing. Unless something or someone is twisted. Or a natural predator. You are neither of those things."

My weight shifted back, moving me away from the pen. Valemar took my arm.

"Astrid, look at me." But I couldn't. My eyes wouldn't leave the anapali pacing the pen, its ears flickering, knowing something was wrong. "It's one thing to stab a kinwah, or even a carcass, but taking the life of a living thing … it's hard at first."

I knew Valemar was right. My father had often taken me fishing as a girl. Not one time had I been able to take the fishhook out, let alone beat its head against a stone or the dock.

The anapali bleated.

"You need to do this," Valemar said. "I can't risk you hesitating."

My feet took two steps back. Valemar's hand increased its grip on my arm.

"Astrid." Valemar drew me toward him. "Astrid." Still I wouldn't look at him.

Valemar re-sheathed the knife and took my other arm. "Astrid." He took my face in his hands and held it, waited until I finally met his eyes. "I would die if something happened to you. Do you hear me?" His face was filled with a fear I'd never seen before. "I can't have you hesitate. I can't have you wait. You need to do this."

"Fine." I looked away, not wanting to see the relief that would fill him. "Fine."

Valemar drew the knife again and placed it in my hand. Somehow, I managed to make it to the pen. As I touched the rails, the anapali's eyes widened in fear. It began to dance about, desperately seeking a way to escape.

I climbed up and dropped inside. "You'll need to chase it down," Valemar said.

I whirled around. "What?"

"Chase it down."

My jaw dropped. "I thought you just wanted me to defend myself."

"I do. But if you're running from Raislos or someone else, you'll be tired. You need to be able to do this no matter how you shake, no matter how your heart hammers or your lungs won't fill. You need to be able to take a life with your last bit of strength."

The back of my mind registered the logic behind his words, but it only added to my anger.

"Fine!"

I turned and faced the anapali. Built more like an alpaca though the size of a sheep, I knew I could take it down. If I could catch it.

Around and around we went. It darted here. It darted there. It scrambled off the rails and kicked me in the chest. My breath came short and fast, just as Valemar said it would.

He leaned against the rails and didn't say a word. But I could hear him in my head. *Take it down, Astrid. Finish him off, Astrid.*

I lunged at the animal and slashed at it with my knife. It screamed as the blade connected. The anapali darted away, blood flowing from the wound. Again, I danced toward it, arms wide, and attempted to

crowd it into a corner. Terrified, it leapt back, hit the rails, and tried to jump over me.

I threw my arms around it, and we both fell to the ground. Its screaming bleats filled the air as I stabbed at it again and again. "Cut its throat," Valemar shouted. "It can get away, it can hurt you, until you cut its throat. Heymond injured you yesterday and your rage allowed you to take him down. Don't give that advantage to an opponent."

Finish it off, Astrid.

I moved the knife to my left hand, grabbed the anapali's head with my right, ignored the hooves that pummeled me, attempting to throw me off and right itself, and sliced at its throat with the knife. Blood spurted from the severed artery, hitting me in the face, temporarily blinding me. I shook my head and blinked, trying to clear my vision.

The anapali gasped, its tongue hanging out, and I watched its eyes go glassy as life left it. I wiped my face with the hook of my arm, pushed myself off the carcass, and crawled back over the rails. I dropped the knife at Valemar's feet and walked back to the castle. He may have spoken to me, but I never heard him. All I could hear were the ringing, echoing screams of the anapali.

I must have been a sight — covered in dirt and blood — but no one stopped me, and I didn't look close enough to see their faces. Once I was through my bedroom, my knees gave out. Huge shuddering gasps tore at my lungs. I heard the door fly open and Daria run in. She dropped down and took my arms, her face a mask of horror.

"Get it off me!" I screamed at her and grabbed the edge of my tunic. "Get it off me!"

"Okay, okay." Her voice was soothing, like a mother's. Gently, she lifted the tunic over my head as I collapsed into a weeping

puddle. Daria carefully pulled off my hose and then covered me with a towel. The sound of water began to echo in the room.

She must have made several trips, filling the bath, but I lost track of time, rocking back and forth on the floor, clutching the towel to me.

"Let's get you into the water."

Her hands raised me until I could crawl into the tub. I sat down, curled my body around my knees, and continued to rock back and forth.

"I'm just going to wash your hair."

The pitcher dipped into the water. Warm rivulets ran down my head and back and splashed red, coloring the water where I gazed. Again, the pitcher dipped. Again, the water ran red.

A cloth splashed, unfurling in the water, and Daria took my face. I closed my eyes as she scrubbed, not wanting to see her expression or the blood growing darker on the cloth. She rinsed it out, washed my face again, and then tenderly bathed the rest of me. I kept my eyes closed. I didn't want the image of me sitting in a pool of blood added to the others burned into my brain.

"Up you go."

I stood and let her wrap a towel around me. Daria helped me from the tub and sat me down. She poured a large glass of wine and handed it to me. "Drink that while I get you a nightgown."

I gulped it down, draining the glass, hardly stopping to breathe. Daria took the empty glass from me then pulled a nightgown over my head. A blue one, not white. We looked at each other, both knowing the color would better hide any blood that the bath had missed, but didn't say anything.

"Let's get you to bed."

Daria drew back the covers and I crawled in. "Make my excuses," I croaked at her. "And if it's anapali —" My voice strangled in my throat, but I pushed it out. "— I'll skip dinner!"

Daria pulled the covers up and stroked my hair. "I'll bring you some bread and cheese later. You've nowhere to be." Her hand rested on my shoulder for a moment. Then she picked up the clothes and slipped from the room, quietly closing the door behind her.

The shadows were long in the room when I awoke. "My queen," Daria called softly. "I've brought your dinner."

Every part of me ached. Every muscle. Every inch of skin. Even my soul.

True to her word, Daria had brought bread, cheese, some fruit, and a glass of white wine. I took that first and drained half of it before I nestled against the pillows Daria placed behind my back. She set the tray on my lap, but I could only stare at it. I held the wine glass close, fingers curled, the glass clutched to my chest. My eyes pricked as an old image settled itself over the new one — eight-year-old Astrid sitting in bed after Mum had told me Grandma Sarah was dead, holding Emerson, my stuffed bear, in just the same way. As if filling my heart with him could make her death not true.

I looked down at the wine and set it aside. It would numb me, take away the aching edge of pain, but I had killed and nothing could erase the truth.

I handed Daria the tray. "Not now. Maybe later." She set it on the table near the window. With a soft breath, she opened then closed her mouth.

"Do you want me to stay?" she finally asked.

"No." I tried to lift a smile. "I'm just going to rest."

The shadows gradually darkened until night filled the room. I heard a click as the handle turned, and the door swung open. I could tell, just from the change in energy, that it was Valemar. I kept my back to him.

The mattress shifted as he sat down beside me. He began to gently stroke my hair. "You did what needed to be done," he said. My eyes began to burn, heavy with hot tears I refused to let fall. "You did what needed to be done."

Valemar lay down next to me. He matched the curl of my back, fitted his legs behind my knees. His arm came around me and drew me closer.

It should have been comforting, as Valemar intended it, but, instead, it filled me with anger. He would have had no need to coddle me if he hadn't pushed me to kill. And I fell asleep, hating him for it.

When I awoke, the sun was shining, and the bed behind me was cold. I heard Valemar's voice, low at the door, and then the door softly closed. I didn't stir, but somehow he knew I was awake.

"Breakfast," he said, and placed the tray on the table. I didn't move. His footsteps crossed back over and he came around the bed to face me. I closed my eyes as he reached out and lightly stroked my face. "Astrid." I turned my face into the pillow. There was the whisper of fabric against fabric as Valemar's hand snapped back.

"Very well. Your breakfast is waiting. You need to eat something." My stomach grumbled at his words. "I'll be back in fifteen minutes."

My eyes snapped open though all I could see was the dark depths of the pillow. I lifted my head as Valemar marched to the door, opened, and then closed it. The little hairs on my arms rose.

"I think you're right," I said to them. "I think we're in trouble."

True to his word, Valemar was back in fifteen minutes. Bearing my cleaned training leathers. I jumped up from my breakfast and moved

behind the chair, holding it between me and my approaching husband.

"Put them on," Valemar said.

"No." I shifted my weight to the balls of my feet and bent my knees.

"I will chase you down and dress you," Valemar said. "Or, barring that, throw you over my shoulder, carry you out in your nightgown, and put you in the pen." His eyebrows rose. "Actually, that's an idea. You're more likely to come under attack dressed like that."

I gripped the top of the chair and calculated a way out the door.

One side of Valemar's mouth curled up. "Go ahead and try."

I swallowed, flicked my eyes to the door, then darted in the other direction. My feint fooled Valemar for only the briefest moment. His hand came around my wrist. I dropped and became dead weight, nearly pulling him down on me.

Valemar managed to catch his balance. His feet straddled my prostrate form, hand still wrapped around my wrist. "This is why you need to do it again. You can't hesitate from shock if you need to —" He stopped before he said the word. "If you need to save yourself from more than one."

And with that, I knew he'd fight me until I did what he wanted. I glared at Valemar. He released my hand and stepped back. I yanked the nightgown over my head, grabbed the hose and jammed my legs into them.

"You're not going to have Daria dress you?"

I snapped the tunic, grabbed the end, and jammed my head through the hole. "No. I've dressed myself for twenty-nine years just fine, thank you." There was enough venom in my voice to kill a snake.

"Twenty-nine years?"

It hit me then that Valemar had never asked me how old I was. There were a lot of questions he'd never asked. A lot of assumptions

195

he'd made. I'd been grateful, for it allowed me to hide behind who he thought I was.

I shoved on my shoes, stood, and then marched out the door.

I didn't stop until I reached the pen. The anapali pacing back and forth was nearly white. *Kind of Valemar to give me a dark one the first time,* I thought sarcastically. This one would surely show the blood.

I looked at Valemar's feet and held out my hand. "Knife."

I hate you.

My eyes met his when I took it from him. For a brief moment, I considered stabbing him. His eyes clouded as he read my thoughts, and I looked away.

The anapali panicked as I turned toward the pen, darting back and forth, bleating. I clenched my jaw and climbed over the rails.

This time, I wanted it over quickly, no chasing around the pen. I held my arms out, lowered my weight, and shifted from side to side. The anapali stamped the ground as I blocked it. It backed up, its eyes wide, searching for a way around me while keeping me in sight. I slowly kept at it, shifting my weight, watching its eyes, reading its moves. Back it went. Back some more.

Until it hit the corner of the pen. The anapali gave a startled and panicked leap that I read correctly. I launched myself at it, hands grasping for its neck, my hip angled forward with all the power I could muster behind it. We both went down.

I managed to get one leg over its chest and planted my foot onto the ground. Sunlight flashed on the knife as I bent the anapali's head back and cut its throat, angling my body away from the gush of blood. One gurgling breath. Two. Air rasped from the gash. I pushed

myself off before it took its last breath, wiped the knife on the soft wool, and climbed back over the rails.

I dropped to the ground. Instead of handing over the knife, I gripped it tighter and stared at Valemar's feet. "Don't you *dare* come to my room tonight," I said, my voice as sharp at the weapon in my hand.

He didn't.

We left for Gladama the next morning. I'd lost track of the days with all the training, so I was unsure if we were on schedule or if Valemar wanted to put distance between me and yet another city I found unpleasant.

I hung Loenir back as we traveled, maintaining at least two lengths between me and Valemar. Daria rode at my side. She alternated between telling me interesting facts about the places on our route and silence, letting our journey be filled with the sound of the animals' hooves, bird song, and the hum of insects. The Mödatal rode along the rear. I hadn't seen her since we'd arrived in Torfin.

We stopped at an inn for the night. I was thankful I wouldn't have a host or hostess for whom I'd have to put on an act. I followed the innkeeper to my room, the largest and finest the inn had to offer. The small town of Riorgin lay on the pilgrimage route to Gladama and attracted many wealthy visitors with its fine inns.

I stripped off my riding gloves and sat on the bed. The large, double bed. Valemar opened the door moments later. I jumped to my feet. "No."

"Astrid —"

"No. I am not sharing a room with you."

I backed up as Valemar took two steps toward me. "Astrid." My feet continued their journey. My head moved from side to side, echoing my words.

"No."

But Valemar continued his slow advance, keeping his body between me and the door.

"No." My throat began to constrict.

"Astrid." Valemar's hand reached for me. I knocked it away and clenched my fists. My foot reached back again. With a jarring *thump*, I hit the wall. "Astrid."

"No."

Valemar reached again. There were now only inches between us, and I was left with nowhere to go.

"No." I struck out with my fists, pummeling his chest with blow after blow. Valemar's hands gently closed around my arms. My anger ebbed away in his sure and stead grip.

"No." The word was little but air.

Valemar pulled me to him. "No what?" he softly asked into my hair.

My legs gave way. Valemar slowly eased us to the ground. I sucked back the sobs gathering in my chest. "No what, Astrid?"

I wanted to hate him at that moment, hate him for asking me, for making me unpack the box I'd been shoving things into ever since Bari had told us to stay put. Ever since the explosion that had —

I flinched and skittered away from the memories. Only to have a new one rise up to take their place — the hanging tongue of the dead anapali.

My head moved back and forth. *No more glassy eyes staring at me. No more living things with the life sucked out of them.* "Death," I whispered. "No more death."

Valemar stroked my hair. "Who died?"

I heard a whine and realized it was me. "The accident?" Valemar asked.

But I couldn't do it. I couldn't say it. I couldn't make it real.

I began to shake. "Okay," Valemar whispered. "It's okay. You're here now. No more death."

Valemar held me all night as I struggled to put the horror back in the box I'd constructed for it, both of us silent. The soft, rhythmic sweeping of his hand along my back, even after we'd traded the floor for the bed, eventually lulled me to sleep. He was still at it when I awoke the next morning.

I mentally shoved the box away, unfinished. I had a job to do. I was Astrid Carbrev, Queen of Bánalfar, and this man's wife. There was no time for me to wade in woe or pull him down with me.

The corners of my mouth curled up. We had places to go. People to see.

"Better?" Valemar asked. I nodded. He lifted my chin and looked into my eyes. Under his scrutiny, tears gathered in my eyes but I blinked them away.

"Ready."

Valemar gently frowned, then leaned forward and kissed me.

I had a new life. The past didn't matter.

CHAPTER 20

The trees of Gladama took my breath away when I first spied them. They rose like the highest skyscrapers, visible even two days from Glábac. The giant sequoia that grow in the forests of central California on Earth were mere twigs by comparison.

"*Yggdrasil*," I said under my breath, for they looked like the immense Tree of Life from Norse mythology. Trees whose roots stretch into other worlds while the branches hold up the heavens.

The impression only strengthened the closer we got. I could well imagine the three Norns living there, the goddesses of fate — Urd, the past, Verdani, the present, and Skuld, the future. Here they would spin the threads of life, every twist and turn of the journey decided.

The trees were so large, dwellings could have been constructed among the branches. Instead, the Alfari had erected the city of Glábac — Barrier to the Glade — just before them.

"The Cordair cut down these trees?" I asked Daria as we rode up to the gates of Glábac. The air was filled with the sound of the barat leaves rustling in the late summer breeze.

"And would do so again if given the chance." Valemar's angry voice sounded from behind us.

I watched the sunlight catch and twist on the leaves. Something, almost like electricity, pressed against my skin. *What sort of people would cut these down?* I knew, but it still amazed me, and it made me glad that Valemar's ancestors had come down from the north and driven them out.

And yet, the Cordair still lurked along the Fairfada. Aided now by the Hormani. I could see why Valemar and the rest of the Alfari put so much stock in the prophecy. Their world teetered on the brink of war. The Hormani traders could undo two thousand years of relative peace. The Moon Princess was all that stood between the Cordair and destruction of Bánalfar.

And they thought that person was me.

Shale rode by me, dressed in green. She was still the Mödatal, but the green robes and green ribbon braided into her hair removed the mystery that surrounded her with the red, made it easier for me to think of her by her name and not her title.

There was no Cair in Glábac. The trees, the glade itself, were the church. No Mother Moon. No Father Sea. Just the barat trees with their life and their sheltering protection.

The town of Glábac was an overflowing mix of pilgrims, inns, and armed soldiers. Half the buildings seemed to be inns, all bustling with people coming and going. Every block had four or five soldiers standing at attention, scanning the crowds. They were unlike any others I'd seen in Bánalfar. Small barat leaves, like green tear drops, had been tattooed below each eye.

"They are the Baraáda," Valemar said when he saw me staring. "More deadly than Heymond." He met my eye. "More deadly than me. They have pledged to give their lives for the trees. They have not been needed in nearly two millennia, but still they stand. Still they train. Still they watch."

Valemar turned in the saddle and looked back the way we'd come, to the east. It was nearly a fourteen-day ride to Rock Dorach, but even I knew that was nothing to a determined army.

Valemar shifted his gaze back to the trees. Awe filled his eyes as he scanned the wide branches gently swaying with the wind. Awe and something I couldn't quite put my finger on. Hope? Longing? Neither word was right, but they were still there, one element in something that was entirely different.

I felt it, too. A charge that rippled under my skin. Life and change and eternity. Possibility and endlessness. They were all here, in those trees. Urd, Verdani, and Skuld twisting the past, the present, and the future into a rope that colored our lives, brought us together, tore us apart. Determined who we were.

I had not come on pilgrimage, but I was becoming a pilgrim.

We stayed in the castle first built by Antilli Carbrev, Valemar's ancestor who had driven out the Cordair. The castle backed onto the grove itself, standing as a sentry while the town of Glábac spread out in front of it like pawns on a chessboard, ready to protect the protectors.

Daria helped me change into a dress of green and gold then took out one of the padded boxes that contained the royal jewels. She removed the small crown of gold barat leaves and peridot and placed it on my head.

"Who are we receiving?" I asked her.

Daria stepped back to survey her work. My appearance met with her approval and she smiled. "You are being received. Valemar will be here momentarily to take you to the glade."

Before I had a chance to ask any questions, Valemar opened the door to my room. "Thank you, Daria," he said. She bowed her head and left us. Valemar stepped around me and checked my appearance as well. Then he smiled and held out a hand. "Are you ready?"

Down we went, through hallways that led to the back door, without the twists and turns that I had grown accustomed to. Valemar pushed the door open, and I stopped in surprise. The grove spread out before us, fifteen feet away, but the massive, open space beneath the green, leafy canopy was empty, despite the crush of pilgrims in Glábac. Valemar and I were alone with the trees. Their ancient, heavy branches bathed the forest in shade. Patches of gray sky poked through. Valemar led me down an unseen path that wove its way through the gnarled, ancient roots that anchored the trees. There was no birdsong, just the creaking and groaning of the trees and the rustle of leaves as a light wind passed through them, carrying with it the smell of impending rain.

"Where is everyone?" I whispered to Valemar, for I had the same feeling as when I walked into a church — that hush of respect that made you lower your voice because you sensed you were in the presence of something greater than yourself.

"Letting us pay our respects in private."

"And how do we do that?"

Valemar didn't answer me. I trotted alongside him, the difference in our heights much more noticeable due to the lengths of our strides.

We wound our way through the trees. Eventually, I could see the meadow between them, the glade that had given the forest its name. A basket sat nestled by a root. I giggled when I saw the bottles of wine it contained.

Valemar stopped. "What?"

"Well, I'd been thinking that this place reminded me of a myth of my ancestors," I said.

"They may have come here."

Not likely, I thought. "Though this is a grove with many trees, they are much like what I imagined Yggdrasil, the Tree of Life, looked like. There are three goddesses there — the past, the present, and the future. Every day they draw water and pour it on the tree so that its branches do not rot."

"Ah." Valemar smiled. "And we are to pour wine on the trees."

He wrapped his arms around me and pressed his lips to my hair. I held him close, my nose buried deep in the fabric of his robes. As if he knew I wanted to linger there, Valemar kissed the top of my head and took my hand again.

Valemar removed the stopper from one of the four bottles and handed it to me. "Just pour a little on the roots of one tree and move your offering to the next."

I held the bottle to my chest. "Do I say anything?"

Valemar smiled. "Only in your heart."

"And what do you say?"

He uncorked his bottle. "It is said that we came from the sea but Gladama sheltered us, protected us until we were strong enough to go out into the world. We offer thanks for the life it's given us. We —"

But he didn't continue. "I'll meet you in the middle, on the far side," he said, then he stepped left and poured a small measure onto the roots of the tree.

I thought I saw his lips move, then I stepped right and poured my offering. *Thank you for the life I have here.* I reached out and touched the tree. My hand snapped back almost as soon as it brushed the bark. I curled my fingers together to stop their shaking and brought my hand back to my side as I swallowed. Surely, I had been mistaken.

I walked twenty or thirty feet to the next tree and poured the wine. *Thank you for my husband.* I cautiously held my hand out this time and placed it against the knobby, gray bark. It was probably only the wind, moving the branches, moving the tree, but it felt like a heartbeat. Which only added to the sense that the trees were somehow more than alive.

Slowly, I lifted my palm and moved down to the next one that ringed the glade. Life. These trees were life. And then I knew what Valemar's prayers were. I didn't turn my head, didn't turn around to watch him at his task, but I knew.

I poured wine on the roots of the next, unable to form any words or thoughts of thankfulness. My fingers brushed the tree. *I wish …*

But there was no point in wishing. I stepped to the next. *Thank you for my life here. Thank you for my husband. Protect him. Protect us all.*

My prayer was different when I poured the last of the wine from my second bottle on the last of my trees, Valemar doing the same thing twenty feet from me. *Show me how to help him for I do not know how.* I laid my hand against the tree. *For you are threatened again, and I am no savior.*

There was the faintest of whispering in my ears. I looked up and searched the tree, ready at that moment to believe in dryads. And then the leaves rippled in the breeze, louder than they had been before.

"It will rain tonight," Valemar said, joining me.

"Um," I hummed in agreement, still beyond words.

Valemar embraced me from behind and pressed a kiss to my head. "We should go. Let the others into the glade before the weather changes."

I leaned into the protective circle of his arms. "Why was it just us?"

"Antilli Slácran Carbrev pledged his life and the lives of his people to these trees. Every generation since has come to offer up their lives in service. It is a sacred vow. The Alfari know we stand first, and while they come to offer their thanks to the trees, they stand behind us. So, they wait for us to finish our offering and our pledge."

I folded my arms over Valemar's. Two thousand years of prayers. Two thousand years of service. My eyes began to sting.

Valemar kissed the top of my head again. "We should go." I nodded.

Two thousand years, and it would all end because of me.

The rain broke about dinner time. Dinners at Aedenfal had been noisy, crowded affairs where I was grudgingly welcome. Dinners at Torfin and been smaller, quieter, but filled with Brinna's sparkling personality. Dinners on the road had been even smaller, mainly just our party at a table in the public dining room, but the Alfari let their king eat in peace. Dinner at Glábac reflected its setting — quiet and reverent, with each person treated more or less as equal.

The crowns we'd worn to the glade were put away, and our green and gold robes exchanged for plainer ones of a medium green. We ate at long wooden tables set with long wooden benches. After dinner, a minstrel perched by the fire and sang the ballad of Antilli Slácran.

Valemar sat with his arm around me, his fingers gently tracing the curve of my shoulder. I laid my head against him and watched the musician and the flames, though in my mind Antilli rode down from the north, leading his army. He destroyed the forges, burned down the mills, and drove the Cordair before him, all the way to the

Archjarn — the Iron Hills. The land was green and peaceful then. The song reminded us that the Alfari were still called to watch, to prepare, and to give thanks for the trees.

Valemar and I went up to bed shortly after the minstrel had finished. Daria put me into a cream colored nightgown.

"I'll have a hot bath waiting for you when you get back," she said.

"Get back?" I asked. But she slipped from the room before I could ask, *"From where?"*

Valemar came in a short time later dressed in a loose fitting tunic and trousers. He held out his hand. "Come."

"Where are we going?" I asked, but he didn't answer.

We followed the same route from the afternoon, down to the door that opened onto the grove. Valemar pushed it wide. Rain pelted, splashing the threshold. The night was inky dark beyond.

"I can't see in the dark like you can," I said, knowing he was going to take me into the trees.

"You'll be fine. I'll keep you out of the way of the roots." He squeezed my hand and drew me out.

The rain was warm but soon left me sopping wet. Rivulets ran down my face and snaked through my hair before draining onto the increasingly wet nightgown that clung to my skin. It was dryer under the canopy, but the leaves collected and passed on the water which then fell in marble-sized drops. Daria was correct in her prediction that I'd need a bath after tonight's foray. I just wondered what it was for. What was required besides the prayers and the wine?

I could tell when we reached the glade. Mud turned to springy grass beneath my feet. The electric current that seemed to connect the trees changed, and the rain became steady. Even in the dark,

there was the sense that this place was sacred. Sacred and protected and life-giving.

Valemar stopped. I held out my hands, searching for him. His came around mine and placed my hands on his chest. He released them and took my face. Valemar traced the line of my jaw, gently brushed my mouth with his thumb, then lifted my chin and kissed me. His kiss was hungry but not demanding. And I realized why he'd brought me here.

I kissed him back, willing to try, but my heart grew as heavy as the clouds, their tears running down my face, for I knew the effort would only lead to more disappointment.

Valemar pressed me against him and kissed me until I became breathless. Then he pulled the nightgown over my head and dropped it onto the grass. His tunic soon followed. He stepped out of his trousers and lowered me to the ground.

I brushed his long hair from our faces and prayed he couldn't see the sadness that filled my eyes. In one smooth motion, he was inside me, and I could feel his prayer with every stroke. *Please. Please let there be a child this time. Please.*

I offered up my own as I opened myself further, spread my legs wider and lifted my hips, allowing Valemar to drive even deeper. I held him to me, tears rising in my eyes, knowing that in a matter of days, his heart would break again. Valemar Dönal, heir of Antilli Tree Savior and the last of his line, would have no child with me.

His thrusts drove me into the ground, and I took them, crying out when he climaxed and reached so far inside me he could have planted himself in my womb.

Valemar shifted his weight and caressed my face. "I didn't hurt you?"

I shook my head. "No. You didn't." His lips came down on mine. He kissed me gently this time. I wished I could see him in the dark, see his face. And then I realized — he could see mine.

I lifted a smile into place and reached out a hand, searching for his face. Valemar kissed me again and flexed inside me. I twitched and felt him go hard.

"Again?" I asked.

"Again," he said. "This time for you. Let me show you how much I love you."

I didn't bother to fight back my tears. Then Valemar started to make love to every inch of me and they were washed away.

As the days slipped by, I spent increasing amounts of time among the trees, often curled up against the roots, my back to the ancient trunks, seeking my own shelter. Here in the Glade of Time, mine was running out.

Valemar was with me when I got out of bed one morning to discover my period had arrived. The devastation on his face killed me.

"We can try again," he said. "You've been drinking the Mödatal's tea, haven't you?"

I closed my eyes and clenched my teeth. *I should have known.* "Yes, of course. It's …" I trailed off. It was time to tell him. "Let me just change first."

I pulled off the nightgown, put on a clean one, then wiped down my thighs and inserted a cloth tampon. I washed my hands and padded back to the bed. "I …" My lips trembled so badly, it was difficult to speak.

"Astrid." Valemar scooted over and took my hand. "Astrid, what is it?"

I wanted to snap my hand away. How could he comfort me when I was about to destroy his world? "There won't be any children," I whispered.

"Why do you say that? We can try again."

I shook my head. "It won't work."

"What makes you think that?"

"Because you and I are as different as … an anapali and a darana! They can't have young together."

Valemar's hand slipped from mine. "Why would you think that? You're —" But he stopped. Just how foreign I was finally hit him.

"I'm not of this world. I am as different from you —"

"As an anapali from a darana." I heard the first vestiges of anger in his voice. "Is it really so different on the moon?"

I'm not from the moon, I said, but only my mouth moved. I'd not been able to put any air behind the words.

"Astrid!"

"I'm not from the moon," I said, forcing the words out.

"What do you mean you're 'not from the moon'?" The anger was unmistakable now in Valemar's voice. The mattress shifted as he stood up.

"Just that — *I'm not from the moon.* I'm … I'm from a planet that circles a distant star."

Valemar stumbled. His hand reached out for the wall, and he braced himself against it. "That's madness."

"Is it? You've seen my ship. Well, it's not even my ship. It was the escape pod. My ship was huge. About the size of this castle —" I broke off as Valemar turned and stared at me in horror. "That's why it is forbidden," I said, desperately grasping at something to make this better.

"But … but you're the Moon Princess."

I smiled weakly. "No. That's what you called me."

Valemar's head moved from side to side as he stared at the floor, unseeing. I shrank back as he changed, as rage filled and twisted his face. "You said you were the daughter of kings!"

"I am. I mean, I was. Astrid was. I am named after Astrid, Trygve's daughter. King Trygve Olavson of Viken. I carry the blood of three hundred years of Viking kings, but my family hasn't ruled anything in nearly as long as yours has ruled Bánalfar."

"You LIED to me!" Valemar roared. His eyes turned dangerous. I shrank back further, afraid that I'd just released the lethal warrior inside him.

"I didn't correct your assumptions." My words were little more than a whimper.

The man I loved disappeared before my eyes. "You utter *ombrác*!" The word translated, and its vulgar meaning sliced at my heart.

Valemar clenched his hands and roared his frustration at the ceiling. The eyes he turned to me were full of hatred. I tucked my feet under me, ready to spring away, even though I knew it would be useless. Valemar was too tall, too quick, and he could snap my neck before I ever saw it coming.

My fear only made him roar again. I scrambled away when he moved, but a nearby chest of drawers fell victim to his rage. He grabbed it, taking it with such force that I expected the wood to splinter. Then the chest rose into the air, and he tossed it. Shards flew when it hit the floor. Without looking at the damage or at me, Valemar stomped to the door and flung it open. It banged against the wall and swung shut behind him.

Fifteen minutes later, a terrified Daria found me cowering in bed.

"Hurry, my queen," she said, raising me with shaking hands. "We have to pack."

"Pack?"

"We leave in an hour."

Valemar was casting me out. "Where are we to go?" I asked. Daria was already pulling things out of drawers.

"Vanerife. Valemar is sending you to his mother."

CHAPTER 21

The Mödatal waited in the yard, already astride a darana, and dressed in her usual red. She shrugged. "I, too, am no longer welcome."

"You got us into this mess," I muttered. I turned my stirrup and shoved my foot in. Keyan, Heymond's lieutenant, rushed up to help me, his eyes averted. I wanted to snap at him, but Vanerife was hundreds of miles away. It would be a long journey if I alienated him now. "How far do we ride?" I asked him.

"To Piltuir. We'll take the royal barge from there."

I hummed an acknowledgement that was more of a grunt and jumped, pressing my weight into the stirrup. Keyan caught my right foot and boosted me over Loenir's rump. I found my seat and looked around. We were a small party — three women, five men, and one pack animal. No Heymond to guard me this time.

Keyan mounted up and clicked to his darana. I didn't look behind me as we rode out of the castle gates and onto the cobblestone streets of Glábac. I had the feeling that Valemar was watching me, and I didn't want to see his face. Anger, indifference, or happiness, I didn't want that image seared into my memory.

We made good time and stopped in the late afternoon at an inn to spend the night. I managed to stay upright until the innkeeper's wife closed the door to my room then my legs gave out. I bit back my sobs, but couldn't hold back the tears that flowed down my face. Daria found me like that a few minutes later.

"Oh, my queen!" She sank down next to me and put a hand on my back. "What happened?"

But I couldn't answer. Daria sighed and began to rub my back, her hand moving in small circles. Even sitting upright became too difficult. I tipped over. My head came to rest in Daria's lap. And still she kept at it, rubbing my back, stroking my hair.

The shadows lengthened. The sounds of laughter and tankards pounding against wooden tables drifted up to the room.

"I can't go down to dinner." My voice was hardly more than a whisper.

"Why is that?"

"She'll be down there."

"Who?" Daria asked.

"The Mödatal. It's all her fault."

"Why is that?"

I swallowed, trying to find my voice through the sobs that filled my throat. "She filled Valemar's head with that ridiculous prophecy."

Daria's hand stopped a moment then began to stroke me again. "I see. And what's ridiculous about it?"

"That I'm a savior." I closed my eyes, shutting out the images of my dead comrades that rose up. "I can't save anybody."

"Why do you think that?"

I hadn't been able to tell Valemar, but something about the way Daria held me and protected me allowed me to whisper, "Because they're all dead."

"Who's dead, my Astrid?" Her hand continued its soothing strokes.

"The people I was traveling with."

"All of them?" Her voice was gentle but I could hear the horror in it. I nodded. "I see." Moments ticked by in silence before she spoke again. "Well, that would make you a survivor."

"I hid," I whispered. "The plasma leaked and they tried to stop it and I sat in my room and hid."

Daria absorbed the information for a moment. "Was it your job?" she asked. "To help them?"

"No."

"What was your job?"

To do what I had been doing, to study the files. As my mind lingered on the now useless details of that file, Daria continued. "If it wasn't your job, how could it be your fault?"

But it was. It had to be. My place had been to join them on the journey to the sun, and I had cheated. I had cheated, broken the rules, and then lied. I had cheated Valemar and all of Bánalfar.

"I deserve to die," I whispered.

"Hush. No one deserves to die, least of all you."

"But I lied. Valemar's right, I lied. I'm not the Moon Princess."

Daria's hand stilled again. "Who are you then?"

"Protocol Specialist Astrid Carr. An outlaw."

I heard Daria swallow. "What makes you an outlaw?"

"I'm not supposed to be here."

"Here, in Bánalfar?" she asked.

"Here, on this planet. It is forbidden."

"Then why did you come?"

"I didn't want to die."

Daria laughed lightly. "That's understandable. None of us wants to die. So, being here makes you an outlaw?"

I nodded. "Yes."

Daria laughed and began to stroke me again. "Oh, my queen. You are here because you are supposed to be. If that makes you an outlaw … well, then I'm glad I serve an outlaw."

She didn't understand. She didn't understand at all. But I let her pet me until I fell asleep.

I roused briefly at the sensation of strong arms lifting me up and placing me in bed. The covers were drawn over me. I kept my eyes closed and ignored the grumbling hunger that churned in my belly. I wanted no food. I wanted no company. This bed would be empty of the one thing I now found important, and no food could fill that void.

When my eyes opened in the morning, I added a new rule to my list, the list I'd neglected to follow or even think about for weeks:

Rule thirty-seven — Don't fall in love.

I allowed Daria to dress me, picked at the bread and cheese offered for breakfast but didn't eat it, ignored the fruit, drank water instead of wine. I longed to dull the ache that had settled into my body and every corner of my soul, but I deserved the pain. When the others had eaten, I had Keyan help lift me into my saddle. I was too weak to pull myself up.

I saw Daria and the Mödatal exchange a glance, but they said nothing to me, only clucked to their mounts and followed the lead rider out onto the Eastern Road.

Another day in the saddle. Another inn. Again, I picked at the food Daria brought me in my room and refused the wine.

"You'll lose your strength," Daria said. "Lose your strength and fall from the saddle."

"I don't care."

Daria took my hands. "Yes, you do. You care so much that it's paralyzing you." She sat down on the bed and put an arm around me. "You love so much that you're lost without them. All of them." I blinked as tears welled in my eyes. "You chose to come here, to break the rules and come here. The reason for that may be hidden from you right now, but I don't believe for a moment that it was selfishness. You're going to have to trust — trust me, trust the Mödatal. And trust that Valemar's anger will wane and he'll forgive you." She sucked in an irritated breath. "He was looking for the Moon Princess and he found you. Right where he was told to look."

"But I'm not her! I'm not her, and I should have told him that."

Daria squeezed my hand and bent her head until she could peer into my downcast eyes. "What did I say about trust? You don't know why you're here. And things played out the way they did for a reason." She patted my hand and bit back a smile. "There are worse places than Vanerife to be exiled to."

I moaned. She was right. I was being sent into exile.

"Sun. Sea. Unlimited lian tarts." Daria rubbed my shoulder. "Just get yourself there. Which will be hard to do if you're falling out of the saddle." She handed me my plate.

I took it from her and set it in my lap. "You don't care?" I asked. "You don't care that I'm not the Moon Princess?"

Her eyes closed and I saw her give the smallest shake of her head. "You are my Astrid, and that is enough."

Just who was I? The question played in my head until I fell asleep. In my dreams, I wandered through the grove at Gladama, never reaching the glade, following a voice that sounded like my own but I could never catch up to.

When my eyes opened, I realized I'd been trying to find Protocol Specialist Carr. I'd lost her somewhere along the way and had become merely Astrid. At this point, I didn't know what about her — Astrid — was real and what was a lie. As much as I wanted to fade away, it wouldn't solve any of my problems. It was time to wade through the lies and figure out how to go on.

I was the sole survivor. *Truth.* I was an outlaw. *Truth.* I was the daughter-in-law of my future host. *Truth.* Welcome or unwelcome? I'd have to ask Daria. I knew little about Valemar's mother other than her name was Reina and she was from Capalnoc, the country to the west on the Aelon Sea. But based on the fact that Valemar's father had decided to share the steppe with the Cordair, my guess was that the son took after the mother. The answer to the question was probably, *Unwelcome.*

What would Protocol Specialist Carr have done about that? Current Astrid was terrified by the prospect of showing up in disgrace. I mentally ran through my list of rules.

Collect allies. Probably my best bet, though breaking rule number eighteen — *Never drink wine with a Yüzü diplomat* — sounded good about now. I already had an ally in Daria. The Mödatal probably counted as another, but I viewed her more as an adversary than an asset. Without her ridiculous assertions, I would have never married, and would have had a much easier job blending into life on Teridun … Crenfor … when I arrived.

Always know whom you're dealing with. That was my next step. Since Daria had been a member of Reina's household until Valemar came south in search of the Moon Princess, she could help me. But I'd wait until we'd boarded the royal barge two days from now. We wouldn't have much privacy on the barge, but more than we currently did — out in the open, mere feet away from six other riders.

I ate my breakfast, had Keyan lift me onto Loenir, and continued down the road with more resolve than I'd had the previous days. My goal when I'd left the *Palmas Cove* had been to survive. Today, I would work at stripping away the lies, find me, and figure out what to do next. It would be PS Carr who met Reina, not Valemar's disgraced wife.

I pushed away my heartache at the thought of Valemar. I needed to look forward, not back. That was one advantage of having been sent away — I didn't have to see the disappointment, or hate, on his face day after day.

Daria and Shale began to relax as I started to eat again. Shale kept her distance, usually riding alongside and chatting with the rear guard, but the air of mystery around her gradually waned. We'd ridden together from Aedenfal to Torfin, and Torfin to Gladama, but I'd never spent much time in her presence. Shale — the seer and priestess, the Mödatal — began to evolve into Shale, the woman. I still didn't trust her. She had her own agenda, her own plans for me. Valemar had stopped listening to her. I wondered what Reina would make of her.

We boarded the *Ruthion*, the royal barge, four days after we'd set out from Gladama. I had Daria move her things in with mine. There was room for her to have her own cabin, but I didn't want to be alone. And my cabin offered more privacy for whispered conversations.

On deck, we sat on cushions laid out under the large striped awning and watched the ropes being untied and tossed aboard, the men running back and forth. Oars pushed us away from the pier and then took up a steady rhythm, speeding us downstream faster than the current itself.

"Moon children?" I asked Daria with a nod toward the oars.

"Yes."

"They used slaves on my planet." Daria's eyes widened. "They still do some places."

"Planet?" she repeated, and I remembered it was Valemar I'd confessed to.

I glanced at the men, making sure their minds and their ears were focused on their tasks. "I'm not from the moon," I whispered.

Confusion clouded Daria's face. "But the —"

"Prophecy? It's not about me."

Shale appeared, as if summoned, from around back of the state house. "Where did you fall from?" A look of triumph filled her face. "A satellite?"

If I had not already been sitting, I would have dropped to the floor. The *Palmas Cove* had been a satellite around Teridun Four for nearly two weeks. A man-made moon.

"The Çölka keep slaves," Shale said. "Taluendi whispers on their desert winds. Father Sea is lost to the sands and Mother Moon bleached by the sun. They've lost the dance of life and stand on death instead." She leaned against an awning post. "These are free men and volunteer their service."

I glanced around me. I was the only marriage-born person on the ship.

"It's a matter of pride," Daria said. "Being chosen for the royal barge. They love to race." A dreamy look entered her eyes. "Especially in Vanerife. All the men lined up, rowing."

"Shirtless," Shale said with a smirk.

I held back one of my own. "I see." Daria smiled at me. She could eventually marry, as long as her mate wasn't clergy or active military. Soldiers could only marry once they'd retired from service, when their reflexes had slowed and their eyesight grown weak. I wanted that for her — a husband, children she could keep. She'd make a wonderful mother.

We watched the men work, watched the countryside slip by, fields of pilva soon ready for harvest.

Valemar wouldn't be too far behind me on the road. Returning to Torfin to observe the harvest. Make the King's Wine. There'd be no Queen's Wine, I realized with regret. One thing I could have actually done for these people — gone.

"This year," Shale said, as if she could hear my thoughts. She looked over her shoulder and met my eyes. Hers were filled with certainty.

I would have asked her what she knew, how she could be so certain. But Daria was there, so I just turned my attention to the landscape moving swiftly by us. The rowers on the deck below us broke out in a song:

"Oh, my love's hair is a red cascade
As bright as the moon.
So pull on lads, pull on boys
Get me to her soon."

"Blood Moon tonight," Shale said. My heart swooped and banged against my chest before it shot up to my throat. Its pulse throbbed in my neck. "Poor lads," she said. "It will be the draught for them tonight." The glint in her eye told me she wouldn't be taking it. I wondered if she had someone picked out. Keyan, maybe?

Daria blushed. She, too, must have someone in mind. I would have gladly gotten drunk and spent the evening in oblivion if I hadn't needed to make sure I slept alone. My bed would be empty.

I wasn't so sure that Valemar's would be the same.

We didn't stop in Lendurig, the great town that sprawled near the convergence of the Dunna and Leisna rivers, deep within the flat plains and rolling hills of the Red Valley — so named for the amber-

red grain that was grown there. I sat under the awning and studied the curved roofs of the buildings. People came out and waved as we glided by, in increasing groups as word spread that the royal barge was passing. Here, at least, I was welcome.

We were now three days out from Vanerife. I tried to think of how far we'd come. Five days on the road at about forty miles a day. Two and a half days by river at about sixty miles a day since we traveled day and night. Vanerife was probably six hundred miles from Gladama. The karawack from Valemar to his mother would have already arrived.

"What is Reina going to think of me?" I asked Daria that night.

Daria hung up the dress I'd worn that day. She moved slowly, deliberately.

"She's very astute. She wants the truth spoken at all times, no games." Daria turned. "Though, should you play them, she will outplay you. Tell her the truth, all of it. Don't give her your interpretation unless she asks for it." Daria picked up the hairbrush and began to brush my hair. "They say the Capalnoc people are much like their darana — proud and fiery. I can't say for I've only ever met Reina and her brother, Rákal." Her hand lingered on my head. The pressure of it was like an embrace. "Valemar is much like his mother."

"I am an unwanted wife who can bear my husband no children."

"What?" Daria bent around me to look in my eyes. Hers were large. "But the prophecy!"

"What about the prophecy?"

Daria swallowed and returned to her task, her face now out of sight behind me. "I asked Shale about it, after I couldn't remember it that time. She —" Daria stopped, but the brushstrokes continued.

"She ..." I prompted.

"She was hesitant to recite it to me, and it didn't sound right when she did."

"Whatever for?"

"I'm not sure. The ending didn't sound right. The last line was, *And she shall save us all.*"

The line that Valemar had quoted. I closed my eyes. The one he'd spoken over Shale and received the strange look when she'd recited the prophecy to me. "Did she change it? Did you ask her about it?"

"She did. When I said I remembered something about life being the last line."

I gripped my hands in my lap. "What was it?"

"*And create new life for all.*"

Of course. Valemar had interpreted it as creating a child. "If I remember correctly, the Moon Princess is supposed to drive away the outsiders. That would create new life for those in Bánalfar."

"That's true."

I relaxed into Daria's ministrations though I could tell her thoughts were churning. The brush strokes stopped. "But that's not how Valemar interpreted it, is it? And you told him."

"The last of his line," I whispered.

We both remained motionless for several heartbeats. The huge finality of that statement and all its implications hung in the air like a death sentence. For it was a death. The death of a dynasty.

Daria's hands shook when they began again.

"So you see why I'm wondering about my reception," I said.

"You're sure?" Daria asked. "That you can't have children?"

"I'm not from this world. Valemar and I are as different as an anapali and a darana."

"Where are you from? You keep saying you can't be the Moon Princess."

"From beyond the farthest stars."

The brush clattered to the floor. "Truly?"

"Truly." I laughed. "*That* was not spoken of in your prophecies."

Daria knelt down to retrieve the brush. Her eyes were wide with fear when she looked up. "The outsiders. The ones trading with the Cordair. They're from beyond the stars, too. Aren't they?"

I instantly regretted confiding in Daria. The Shororato hid information about the developed galaxy from unprepared worlds to stop this kind of panic from occurring. I dropped to my knees beside her and took Daria's shoulders. "Yes, but you can't tell anyone. There's a reason contact with your planet it forbidden. You're not ready. There's so much I could tell you, but it would only frighten you. And if the —" I broke off. There was no reason to go there. No one would know. I changed course. "If you looked at me in fear, I don't think I could bear it."

"I'm not afraid of *you*!" Daria placed her hands on my arms. "But ... but if they arm the Cordair. If they can travel here ..."

I nodded. "I know. But I don't think they will risk it. The ore they are trading for is tremendously valuable. Leaving a mark on a planet, evidence that they were here is a risk. Places like this do get checked on from time to time."

My words didn't relieve her. "But *you're* not supposed to be here, either!"

"There's no one to know," I reassured her. I bit my lip when her expression didn't change. "There's no evidence," I whispered, forcing my mouth to form the word, forcing the breath to leave my lungs. "I ... sent them into the sun."

Daria's eyes widened. "Oh, my poor queen!" She drew me to her. For a moment I relaxed into her embrace. Then her arms tightened. "But your ship? The one you came here in."

"It's okay," I told her, whispered into her ear. "No one knows I'm here."

We knelt there on the floor, holding each other. I rested my head on her shoulder and returned to my original question. "So you see, I can't tell Reina the truth, not all of it. Valemar doesn't even know as much as you." Maybe he did. I could no longer remember how much I'd revealed during that fateful conversation.

Daria began to stroke my back. "I wouldn't tell her all of it. She's going to think you came from the moon. Who would —" I felt her shake her head. "There's no need to tell her otherwise. But don't tell her you're not the Moon Princess." Daria fell silent. Her hand continued in rhythmic, absent minded fashion as she wrestled with this new reality. "We don't know," she said when she spoke again. "We don't know what's meant to be."

CHAPTER 22

Vanerife – The Golden City. I actually "oohed" when we came around a bend in the river and I caught my first glimpse of the beige-gold buildings sparkling under the ever-present sun. The glittering spectacle was made possible by tiny flecks of mica within the local stone. The roofs of the Low had been tiled in sheets of mica to better to reflect the sun and help keep them cool. But my eye was drawn to Vanerife High. Perched on a hill, it loomed above them, a white, marble giant among the more common golden stone.

"The marble is cooler but rarer," Daria explained.

"A pearl among the sand," I said.

"A pearl?"

"There's an animal that lives in the sea … on the moon," I said, looking around, aware of the listening ears. "It creates a shell like a stone. The inside is creamy white, yet iridescent, almost like a gresán. When a grain of sand gets in and the creature can't get it out, it coats the sand with the nacre, layers and layers, until a pebble forms that we call a pearl."

"Sounds beautiful."

"It is." I thought of my own moon, a pearl in the sky, not the cabochon ruby that hung overhead every night.

The barge picked up speed. I gripped the railing and stared at the castle that loomed before me.

"Nothing to be afraid of," Shale said.

"Are you staying with us or the Cair?" I asked.

"The Cair. It is my place."

"And what do you foresee?"

Shale gave me a wry smile. "It doesn't work like that."

"Then how can you be certain things will be fine?"

"Your story does not end there," she said with a nod toward the castle. "That I do know."

I laughed. "How can you possibly know that?"

Shale leaned against the rail and looked at the city slowly growing before us. "Can you feel your mother?"

I recoiled as her words hit me. "What?"

"Can you feel your mother? Can you reach through space and time and feel her presence?"

Daria turned her head away from us. "I ..." But words failed me.

"I know you try." Shale's eyes met mine. "Can you?" My jaw clenched as the emotional box began to rattle. Shale adjusted her shawl and looked back at Vanerife. "Some things you just know. Some things are whispered to you if you pause to listen. Some people hear them. Others don't. Even to those who listen not all things are whispered. Your story, though, it does not end here. So there is no need to worry."

But I did worry. My mother-in-law was a tightrope that I was afraid to walk.

We were escorted from the barge through the city, into the castle, and up to one of the most splendid bedrooms I'd ever been in. More the feel and size of a living room but with a bed on one end. Waist-high windows lined the length to catch breeze that drifted in from the Aelon Sea. Snowy white, sheer curtains hung in the empty, open spaces of the windows for privacy, though we were up so high that all I could see out of them were the turquoise blue waters of the sea and the green dots of the Lian Isles in the distance.

I'd seen something like it on the big ad screens that graced the sides of buildings in every major city, but they didn't fully convey the warmth in the air, the mix of salt and fruit and perfume on the breeze, the damp moisture of the humidity.

"Yes," Daria said, as I looked around in wonder. "Better Vanerife than Snow Reach." She crossed to one of the wardrobes and began sorting through it. "Red?" she asked, pulling out a dress. "Or do you think blue?"

"Not red. Let's not bring the moon into this." All the dresses hanging in the wardrobe were someone else's. "You don't happen to have my dress, do you? The one I was wearing when Heymond found me?"

Daria hung the red dress back up. "I think it's in one of the trunks. But it's heavy. You'll be hot in it."

"But it's mine. I want to stand before Reina as I am."

Daria opened her mouth then closed it. She gave me a sad smile. "I'll go check on our luggage."

The dress had been squashed in a trunk. After days of travel and damp, heavy creases had set in. Daria sent it out to be quickly ironed. "You're sure you don't want to appear before her as queen?" she asked. I shook my head. I was starting over. Valemar and I had

had such a rushed introduction, a mere dance of a game. I wanted to back up and do it differently this time.

Daria had barely finished helping me into the dress when the summons came. "As much truth as possible," she reminded me. "Reina will know if you're hiding anything. She's a master at reading people."

I nodded then followed the escort through the passageways. My mind went back to that first to and fro that Valemar and I had done. He'd had his agenda. I'd had mine. He'd wanted the Moon Princess. I'd wanted life. I didn't know what goal Reina might have now. For me, I just wanted me back.

I was shown into a presence room. Reina sat behind a desk in a tall, almost throne-like chair. She herself was tall with long, golden-blond hair. Valemar's mother must have been absolutely stunning in her youth for she was still amazingly beautiful, with the same undercurrent of "lethal" as her son.

"So you are my new daughter." Her voice was steel sheathed in velvet.

I lowered my eyes. "Yes, my queen."

Reina tapped a small scroll of paper twice on the table then threw it aside. A karawack message. "My son says that you have lied to him."

I kept my head down. "Mainly by omission."

She laughed, a light, dangerous laugh. "And what have you omitted?"

I swallowed. "He was expecting someone. When I arrived, he told me that I would need to marry him or be handed over to the Cordair."

Reina made a sound between a hum and a growl. "Did he ask if you were who he thought you were?"

I raised my eyes. "Not exactly. He asked if I was the daughter of kings."

She flashed her dangerous smile again. "And what did you say?"

I wet my lips. "I said 'yes.'"

"And are you?"

"I am named after Astrid, a king's daughter. My grandmother of seventeen hundred years ago. I carry the blood of generations of fierce warrior kings who sailed the seas. I claim their blood, but I am no princess."

Reina laughed. "I think I like your ancestors. You do have fire." She leaned across the table, resting before me on her arms. "So what is the truth, Astrid?"

I glanced down, stared at the floor, then forced my eyes up. "I mean no disrespect, my queen, but I have broken laws in coming here. Would you have me break more by speaking of things that are forbidden to be told?"

An icy gleam entered Reina's eyes. "And who has forbidden this?"

"You know I'm not from here, from Crenfor." Reina nodded. "To tell you the truth, all of it, would change you forever. Not even the Cordair know the truth of who they trade with." Her eyes narrowed. "They would become more greedy if they did." Reina's eyes widened and she sat back in the chair. "I could tell you. I could break the law and tell you, but you know what is said about truth ..."

"It can't be unheard once heard."

"Do you want that?" I asked. "Do you want me to tell you things you shouldn't know? Things that can't be unheard once spoken?" I knew the answer before I asked the question, and it saddened me. I saw it form, though Reina wrestled with it. "My world thought they were ready for those things," I whispered and Reina's eyes latched

onto mine, an edge of panic in them. "But they weren't. They adjusted. They eventually thrived. But they were never the same."

Reina clenched and unclenched her hands. As they stilled, she squared her shoulders and lifted her chin. "Tell me."

"My name is — was — Astrid Gabriella Carr, and I was the protocol specialist aboard the starship *Palmas Cove* …"

I told her all of it. The problem that caused us to put into orbit around Teridun Four. How I was in my cabin. How no help came. How everyone died but me. I told her about my decision to break the law, to save myself. And how I agreed to marry Valemar to save myself again. My confession to Daria had drawn off some of the pain, so even though the words often caught in my throat, I was able to do it, to actually get through it.

Reina was silent when I finished. Her questions had been few.

"Would your son have wanted to hear that?" I asked. Grief filled my voice — the loss of my comrades, the loss of my husband, the loss of my world. Reina gave a tight shake of her head. "So how could I tell him?" My voice broke on the last word.

"I don't know," she whispered.

I looked at the wall and slammed the box's lid shut in my mind. I'd opened it long enough to share the story with Reina, but its power lurked, waiting for the right opportunity to consume me. "What now?"

Reina sucked in a breath and sat up straighter in the throne-like chair. "You are his wife. You —" She caught my gaze. "You're sure you can't have children? With my son?"

I wanted to say, *It would take a miracle*, but simply answered, "I am sure."

Reina nodded thoughtfully. "Well, you are still his wife. He has given you his protection. This is your home. Daria is familiar with the rhythm of life in Vanerife." Reina gave me a wry smile. "Vanerife is not like Aedenfal. I hope you find it more to your liking."

She pushed back her chair and came around the table, took my hands and kissed my cheek. "My daughter. I would be happy to have you dine with me tonight."

"Thank you," I said. Reina released my hands. I bowed my head and turned for the door, slowly releasing a breath I'd held from the time I'd entered. I had survived my first encounter.

They say that confession is good for the soul. That may be true. I had confessed who I was to Reina not only to unburden my soul from the lies I had been telling but to re-find Astrid. But I didn't like what it had revealed.

As Protocol Specialist Carr, I had been a master at my job. I always knew how to read a situation, how to work out the correct move. I had been a master chess player, so to speak. However, as I walked back to my room in Vanerife, the illusion of my "mastery" fell away — I was only as good as the file.

I stumbled into the wall as the truth hit me. I had successfully negotiated more contracts than I could count, had been able to create my list of rules *because I'd always had a file to read.*

I braced a hand against the wall, blind to everything but the racing thoughts in my head. When had I done it on my own? When had I dealt with the unexpected?

Never.

I felt my way to an alcove and sank down onto the bench. All this time I'd thought the Moon Princess had been the lie. It turned

out the lie was me. I had no file on Crenfor, no information to help me other than: *Medieval level planet. Do not contact.* I was useless.

I pushed myself up and managed to find my way back to my room. "What did she say?" Daria's voice was all horror when I entered. She was across the room in an instant, gripping my arms.

"I'm a total failure." I couldn't even meet Daria's eyes.

"What! What does that mean? Is she sending you away?"

"She should."

Daria guided me to a seat. "Tell me, my queen, how have you failed?"

I stared at the floor. "I was only good at my job because I could study. I had information on every culture I worked with. Here, on Crenfor, I'm not prepared. I don't know how to make the next move."

"The next move?"

"It's a phrase from a war game played with pieces on a board."

"Oh!" Daria exclaimed. "Carbonay."

I lifted my head. "Carbonay?"

"The men play it in their free time in Vanerife. You'll see them in cafés and down by the docks with their boards and their pieces, each trying to successfully invade and take the queen."

"The queen?" In chess, you want to capture the king. In tahtasi, the high priest.

Daria goggled at me as though I'd lost my mind. "Of course, the queen. With the queen captured, the king must do as her captors command."

"Won't they kill her?"

"No!" Daria said. "Then the king would just remarry. You take the young queen before —" She broke off abruptly.

"Before?" I prompted.

Daria's head bowed. "Before she has children."

"Ah." Before she can supply him with heirs. The whole future of the kingdom would be in question.

"A queen's ransom," I said. Daria looked up at me. I smiled. "The saying on my planet is, *A king's ransom.* You'd want to capture the king."

"Huh," Daria said. "I guess that would work, too. They say that carbonay has been played for more than three thousand years. A prince from Çölka swept down from the deserts of Siak Kumlar and captured King Baram of R'Kesh's bride. Baram eventually offered his sister in exchange. What happened to her, no one knows, but Baram got his bride back. They're crazy, the Çölkans. Taluendi speaks to them on the wind."

My eyes grew large as Daria spoke. Not from the tale she told. Daria's words sounded like the dulcet tones of one of my files. I took her hands. "Would you teach me? Tell me what I need to know to survive?"

"Survive?"

I was being too dramatic. I had known the character I would need to create to survive on Teridun Four wouldn't be PS Carr. So far, I hadn't even been able to pull off Eleanor of Aquitaine. *Except for marrying Valemar.* I pushed the thought aside.

"I don't feel safe," I told Daria. "Valemar doesn't want me. Shouldn't want me since I mean an end to his line. Now I'm here with his mother, in a place I don't know, with few friends or allies. You know Vanerife. Can you help me navigate it in every sense of the word?"

Daria squeezed my hands and smiled. "We'll start at the beginning."

Daria meant "the beginning" quite literally. After squeezing my hands, Daria lifted me to my feet. She opened one of the wardrobes and handed me a dark blue tunic with short sleeves and a pair of leggings that reached to mid-calf. She took a second set for herself.

"We are going down to the beach, and I'll begin there."

We followed a winding staircase built into the rocks on which Vanerife High was perched down to a golden beach. The sand glittered with flecks of mica and tiny rainbow-colored grains, little bits of tourmaline often found in mica deposits. Instead of palm trees shading the back of the beach, the trees reminded me of the umbrella trees still found in protected areas of the Serengeti plains of Africa. Wide crowns created a leafy green awning over the dry end of the beach.

Daria waded ankle-deep into the surf and sat down. Two guards took up post a discreet distance away. Farther down the beach, children played in the water, their delighted laughter audible over the rumble and hiss of the waves. Old men sat at tables under the shade of the trees, playing carbonay.

I dropped down next to Daria into the warm water and leaned back as she had, resting on my elbows, knees up, as the waves tickled back and forth around us.

"They say that life began here," Daria said, staring at the green rise of the Lian Isles visible beyond the bay. "Father Sea met Mother Moon on these shores and they joined, creating life." Daria cracked a saucy smile and flashed her eyebrows. "He's still at it. Thrusting like a devoted lover."

It did feel like that, the pressure of the waves as they broke against my thighs and traveled over my belly. "Certainly not one

caught in Blood Moon fever," I said. Daria giggled before she sobered.

"No, then he rages and claims the land, pulling it down into his depths." Her eyes scanned the horizon. "Thousands and thousands of years passed. We emerged from the sea to live on the land. Built shelters and eventually left our Father behind.

"The trees protected us. Gave us shade to shield us from the burning sun. Gave us wood to keep us warm and fashion homes and tools."

"Gladama," I said. Daria nodded.

"When we moved south, the barat trees were there, reaching for the sky."

"Do the Cordair have the same story?" I asked.

Daria shook her head. "No. Their life began in the south, back when Snow Reach was green and the lands to the north even hotter than they are now. At least, that is the story they now tell."

"Oluendi?" I asked.

"Yes. Oluendi carved them out of rock and breathed life into them. *All you see is yours*, he told them. Still tells them," she said with disgust.

I let the waves wash over me a few times. "So the Alfari wouldn't marry a Cordair."

Daria huffed. "No. But that's never stopped them from carrying off our women against their will."

"And have such unions produced children?" Sometimes you got more than one humanoid race on a planet. Like the Neanderthals that eventually interbred with humans on Earth.

Daria shook her head. "I don't know. Valemar might. Reina might, for that matter. They haven't done it in recent years. At least, not that I've heard."

I watched the waves swell, grow taller and foamy as they neared the shore before breaking over me and rippling their way onto the sand with a hush. The sea inhaled and drew them back again. Life had started here. Maybe mine could, too.

"Who do I need to be?" I asked Daria. "Other than the Moon Princess?"

"That's a strange question."

"Maybe to you, but that's who I've been, someone who is different depending on the situation."

"So why not the Moon Princess?" Daria asked.

I sat up and put my arms around my knees. "She's a savior. I'm not a savior."

"I see." Daria sat up, too, but splayed her hands, letting the waves run through her fingers. "What does Astrid want? Not the Astrid who became 'someone different' for every job, but the beginning Astrid."

I swallowed. "She wanted adventure."

Daria slowly nodded. "And now?"

My lips trembled. I wanted Edinburgh. I wanted Finn's house and the room he kept for me. I wanted to hide under the bed there and never leave. "Home," I whispered. The waves hushed at that moment and my voice carried. "She wants home."

CHAPTER 23

W e sat in the surf, Daria with her arm around me, and didn't speak. The task was monumental. I couldn't leave, and my place on Crenfor was uncertain. Our hands and feet had pruned by the time Daria lifted me out of the surf.

"Time to wash the salt off and dress you for dinner," she said. My face betrayed my anxiety for Daria added, "Start at the beginning."

I nodded. I was a surprise bride. Reina had surely known Valemar's plans, but none of them knew what he was actually getting. *My daughter.* Reina had accepted me.

I gave myself a shake. No time for Astrid Carr. She was currently a mess. Eleanor. How would Eleanor have met her mother-in-law?

I thought about that during the long climb back up the stairs to the High, thought about it while Daria bathed me and washed the salt from my hair with perfumed soap.

I was a supplicant and she was my queen. I was her son's wife. The next move was not mine to make but hers.

I could do that. I could sit back and wait and make my counter-move.

In Vanerife, Reina didn't dine in the banqueting room. Dinner was to be just the two of us. She usually dined alone. A small round table had been arranged with platters of roasted meats, dishes of salads and fruits, and a tray of sweets. Reina smiled when I entered and gestured for me to take the seat across from her.

"How was the water?" she asked, and poured me a glass of wine.

"Refreshing," I said.

"That is one of the blessings of living in Vanerife. We are connected to Father Sea and his breath renews us." Reina picked up her glass and sat back, scrutinizing me. "I've been in counsel all day about you."

I bowed my head. "And what advice have you been given?"

"Raislos would love an excuse to get his hands on you."

I shivered at the thought of being turned over to the Cordair leader. "I see."

"Neither of us wants that," Reina said.

"Not if the tales Valemar told me are true."

"He means to retake Bánalfar, and your Hormani traders have given him the courage to dream."

Raislos could dream but the Hormani knew where to draw the line. "They'd never truly arm the Cordair."

"And risk drawing attention to themselves."

"Exactly," I said.

"But they've made themselves invaluable."

"They have," I agreed.

"And you make the Hormani nervous," Reina said.

I swallowed. "Yes. Valemar had me learn to protect myself."

"So you can't afford to appear weak."

The full implication of my actions slammed home. I'd been nothing but weak since I'd left Gladama.

"You mourn the loss of the child you carried. I, too, struggled to conceive and so Valemar has sent you here to receive my sympathy and my guidance." Reina's eyes pinned me, making sure I understood the importance of the story she was spinning to explain my sudden departure from Glábac. "You will rest. You will pray. And, when the time is right, you will be reunited with your husband."

I started to open my mouth, to ask what would happen when nothing came of the fertility treatments, but Reina silenced me with a look. Her eyebrows rose as if to say, *No other thoughts are permitted,* and brought to mind rule number nine — *Have nothing but confidence in your meetings.*

"Did you ever wonder if you were barren?" I asked.

Reina stared into her wineglass and sagged against the hard wood of her chair. "No." Her voice was low, hardly more than a whisper. "I'd had a moon child. A son." A ghost of a smile twitched on her lips. "Part of the reason Enartin chose me. That and the ten Capalian darana that were part of my dowry."

I filed away the fact that Valemar had a half-brother. "How many generations?" I asked, trying to remember everything I'd read in Valemar's genealogy.

"Four," Reina said. "Four generations of a single son. That's partly why Enartin gave Fairfada to the Cordair. He wanted peace. He wanted his only son to avoid the peril and burden of war."

And yet it loomed. "Were there any moon children?"

Reina gave her head a shake. "More than three thousand years of kings. Two thousand since they took the title of Carbrev — Tree Guardian. And it could all end with my son."

Will end, I thought. *With me as his wife.* "I assume I will be on a steady diet of the Mödatal's tea."

"Iced, in this climate," Reina said. "Daily bathing. You will offer gifts to the Father and the Mother. Be pampered." She pushed the tray of sweets toward me. "Daria said the lian tarts were your favorite."

I pasted a smile in place as I tried to think when Daria could have shared that information. "They remind me of the lemons at home. The flavor anyway."

"Any other comforts you desire?" I shook my head. "You are not what I would have chosen for my son. But I have been reminded today that our paths are not always clear. Sometimes it is veiled in mist and you must trust that the way will be shown."

"How long?" I asked. "How long did you wait for a child?"

"Five years," Reina said. "Five years before we were blessed with Valemar. We'd hoped ..." A grim smile flashed across her face before it fell. Reina picked up her wine and drowned the unspoken words. Her tongue ran across her teeth as she set the glass back down.

I don't have five years. I wondered how many days or months I would.

"We have ... I have Valemar. He is everything his father and I hoped he'd be." The eyes Reina turned upon me were sad. An attempt to smile merely twitched her lips. "Do what you can. Do what you can to make him happy."

Thus began my "transformation" in Vanerife. I was bathed in and drank copious amounts of braghar milk (and peed a lot due to my tea intake as well). I offered blood to Mother Moon and braided flowers interwoven with my own hair to Father Sea. Twice a day I walked the stairs to the beach, clothed only in a dark blue tunic that came to my knees, and sat in the surf, letting the waves wash over my lady parts. I left

Daria home after the first session for we'd spent the entire time giggling. The hope was that Father Sea indeed would get me pregnant.

The Blood Moon came and I barred myself in my room. The treatments had worked in that my breasts and genitals swelled, eager for the caress of a lover. I buried my head under my pillow to block out the sounds of sex that drifted in through my open windows and increased the ache of unmet desire between my legs.

Had Valemar taken the draught? Or had he found comfort elsewhere? It would make sense if he had — trying to father a moon child while his wife underwent treatment for her barren womb.

I nearly sat up when I realized that his partner wouldn't be Zhanet. She, too, had not been able to give him a child. If she had, I would have heard about it.

I changed my prayers the next day. I'd always believed in God. I'd seen too many unexplainable things not to. I changed my empty, roll-playing prayer from *Give me a child* to *Give him a child*.

Something had gone wrong genetically for the Carbrev men. It broke my heart to think that this line of warriors who had protected the trees and watched over their people for two thousand years would end. Their world would never be the same. War would come when the old regime fell and alliances shifted. I'd read about it. I'd seen it too many times all over the galaxy.

"You are wise." Shale's voice startled me.

"Why do you say that?" I asked, still on my knees in front of the side chapel's altar.

"Because you, too, can look into the future."

"I am no seer," I said.

"You may not have the gift of second sight, but you do have the gift of foresight. You recognize patterns when you see them. You know that Bánalfar is on the brink of being forever changed."

"All things change," I said. "Change is the one true constant in the universe."

"True," Shale said. "But how long has our star burned? How long has it bathed Crenfor in its warming light?"

"Millions of years."

Shale smirked. "An eternity, unchanging. *The sun rises in the east —*"

"*And sets in the west,*" I finished.

"The greatest truth we have. Should we focus on its end?"

I shook my head. "No."

"Should we let Crenfor descend into chaos?"

"There is a whole planet," I said. "We're only in one small part."

Shale rolled her head and her eyes. "Should we allow chaos to reign in any part of it?"

"No," I answered glumly.

She reached down, took my hand, and raised me to my feet. "Come."

Though she was dressed in her red robes and we were in the Cair, she was Shale today, to me, and not the Mödatal. I followed her through the open sanctuary, past the people knelt in prayer, to the door at its side. My guard left his place along the wall and followed us.

Shale's rooms in Vanerife were nearly identical to those in Aedenfal — dark, windowless. There was even an empty fireplace, which surprised me given the warm climate. A pile of ashes said that she actually used it.

"The flames allow my mind to drift and my inner eye to see," she said in response to my scrutiny of it.

I turned. "Even desert cultures appreciate a good fire." I joined Shale at the dark, wooden table. "There was something you wanted to show me?"

Shale set a bowl in the center. "You are familiar with many kinds of magic?"

I eyed her warily. "Yes."

"And you believe you cannot bear Valemar a child because of this magic."

"It's called DNA — deoxyribonucleic acid. It's the recipe that exists inside every … bit of every living thing. It determines species and sex and hair color and height. It tells your body to give you five fingers and five toes and whether your eyes will be blue or green or gray. It's not magic. It's science."

"Oh, we have philosophers of our own that ask questions of the universe. Seek to find answers to the 'why' and the 'how.' And then there are things that defy explanation. Like how I can see that which is to come." She shrugged. "Science may one day answer that question but, until then, it is magic." She stepped around me, whispering as she passed. "Just like it is magic to travel the stars." Her head came close, her lips nearly brushing my ear. "Do you believe in magic, Astrid?"

The little hairs on the back of my neck stood up. "No, not really." My eyes followed her as she stepped away.

Shale brought over a stoppered bottle of green glass. "Father Sea," she said and uncorked it. I bent my head and sniffed. The briny scent of the ocean filled my nose. Shale poured it into the basin. The hairs on my arms lifted.

From a pouch at her waist, Shale withdrew a small vial. She held it up between her forefinger and her thumb. "A gift to the Mother. From a man desperate for children." She closed it in her hand.

My perception of her wavered. No longer Shale, not even the Mödatal, the woman before me took on the presence of a witch. "If I pour the blood into the water, what should happen, my queen?"

I wet my lips. "It will drop and swirl, blossoming like a flower before it colors the water red."

"And if I add your blood?"

My heart gave a giant leap toward the door. I stood my ground even as it continued to thrash against my ribs. "The same."

"And if it didn't?"

"I'd say that you doctored the water or the supposed blood."

She grinned. "Wise answer. Wise, but wrong." She held the vial up again. "Curious?"

I was, despite myself. Despite the smoke and mirrors and elaborate stagecraft. "You'll only show me what you want me to see. You've some conclusion you want me to reach, and you're hoping this elaborate charade will make the point."

"Charade?"

I rolled my eyes. "Game."

She smiled. "A bit of a game. But an illustration of the truth."

I crossed my arms. "What truth is that?"

"That you're here for a reason."

"Fine. I'm here for a reason. What's your point?" I held up a hand. "And don't say I'm the Moon Princess because you and I both know I didn't come from the moon."

"Not Crenfor's moon," Shale said. "But you did come from our orbit." Every hair on my body stood up. "Do you want to see my point, Astrid?"

I slowly uncrossed my arms. *Rule twenty-six — Find out what they truly want.* I thought I knew what that was — to convince me that I was the prophesized savior. That had always been her goal as she'd circled me like a predator, looking for a weakness. But she'd never been malevolent. Only unwelcome. Had she been a true threat, I would have felt it. My gut was never wrong, which was why it was rule thirteen. Right now, it was saying I wouldn't like what I saw if I gave her my blood and let her pour it into the bowl with what she claimed was Valemar's.

"It's a trick," I said. "Something to make me moldable."

"It could be. But it's not."

At that moment, I wanted the lie-detecting eye sensor more than anything I'd ever wanted — more than my crew alive, more than me home, more than my own life. None of those things mattered because I knew what she would show me would change my world. If only I could be certain that what it revealed would be true.

"Reina survived your telling," Shale said. "You talked of magic and she believed you without proof. So why are you afraid of this?"

Of course, Reina would have turned to her after my bombshell. My story had irrevocably altered her, brought danger and uncertainty into her world. This was the least I deserved. I held out my hand. "Fine."

I'd offered blood on five occasions as part of my treatment. My hand was almost used to the light sting of the blade. A vial pressed against my thumb and then Shale pinched the wound closed and elevated my hand. After a minute, she released it and nodded once to remind me to continue the pressure.

"What does the blood do?" she asked again.

"What blood does. It matters not the species, it will begin to mix with the water."

Watch, she said with her eyes. Shale removed the stopper from the first vial with her thumb. My eyes followed the cork to the floor before the movement of Shale's hand drew my gaze back to her. The contents flowed darkly into the bowl and then swirled. Moments later my blood was added.

A strange thing began to happen. The swirls of Valemar's blood reversed direction, retreating from its journey around the bowl and began to inch toward my blood.

"It's a trick," I said, unable to tear my eyes away from the sight of the blood reaching for mine, blending together until they were one.

"No trick," Shale said.

"I …" But words failed me. The blood pooled together, forming a mass that undulated in the water. "It's a clot," I said. Blood clotted, especially blood exposed to an incompatible type. There was the proof that Valemar and I, too, were incompatible.

"Touch it." Shale's face held a hint of smugness. I huffed, reached out a finger, and brought it down into the middle of the blob.

Only it was no blob. My finger moved through it as easily as if it had been cream. The motion stirred the water, pushing at the mass, straining its bonds. But the connection held.

"It's a trick," I said again. "It didn't do that at our wedding."

"Did you love him then?" Shale asked. The question was like an arrow to my heart.

"No."

"And he wanted you, but he didn't love you."

"He doesn't love me now," I said, and pushed at the pain the words brought. But my eyes were captured by the sight of Valemar's blood swirling around mine, refusing to be parted.

"He mourns," Shale said. "You have wounded him and he mourns."

I blinked and looked away from the bowl. "Why show this to me?"

"Because the time is coming when you will need to know that you are loved. Because you pray for him and not yourself. Dark

forces are gathering, my queen, and you are lost. This is a reminder that things we don't understand can still be the truth. And it's one you needed to hear."

I recoiled as the words hit me. *I needed to hear?* A tidal wave of anger surged. I had needed to hear I was some savior in order to keep my place? I had needed to pretend to pray for a child to cover up Valemar's actions? Where was "the truth" in any of that?

I turned on my heel and marched across the room. I threw the door open, startling the guard both with my sudden appearance and my thunderous expression. I stomped down the hall and flung open the door that led to the sanctuary. Men and women jumped, rising from their prayers. I tromped across the floor inlaid with the mosaic of a red-haired woman reaching for a white-haired man, and shoved the outer door, coming to a standstill as the bright sunlight temporarily blinded me after the dark of the Mödatal's rooms.

I was done. I was done with the fertility charade. I was done with the Mödatal. *Damn them all to hell.* Even Reina. Goosebumps rose on my arms as I thought about facing down Reina's potential wrath, then I set my jaw and pounded down the stairs.

I was done, and there wasn't anything they could do about it.

CHAPTER 24

Despite the fact I knew that Daria would be the one to clean up the mess, I returned to my room and hurled piece after piece of fruit against the wall. Their weight filled my hand then splattered across the plaster with a gush I found immensely satisfying. *Almost like smashing the heads of my enemies*, I thought with a savage glee. The Viking blood in me flamed to life.

Daria rushed in through the door just in time to see another fruit smear its pulp across my wall and get caught in the back splatter. "What!?"

I hefted another fruit like a baseball. "Fucking charlatan!" I wound up and hurled the fruit. Daria closed the door behind her. I picked up another. She edged her way toward me along the wall. "Thinks she can trick me!" There was another resounding splat as I aimed for where the Mödatal's head would have been if she'd been standing there.

"What happened?"

I ground my teeth. I couldn't say it. I couldn't say it out loud and have somebody, anybody, think that it had been real.

"They're manipulating me." I picked up the last fruit. "I'm just a pawn."

The fruit was soft in my hand, pliable. I brought my other hand up and cradled the plump yellow orb. Rage washed over me again, and I squeezed, watching as the pulp oozed between my fingers.

"Astrid, what happened? I know you went to pray."

Pray. I hurled the remains at the wall. With its protective cover torn, the flesh fell in clumps, splattering along the floor. Juice dripped from my hands, pooling by my shoes, as I stared at the mess I'd created.

Daria left the safety of the wall and placed the back of her hand on my forehead. "Just checking," she said. "Southerners can get sunstroke here fairly easily." My eyes wouldn't meet hers.

Daria retrieved a towel from the bathroom and began to wipe my hands. "I'm sorry," I said, and took the towel from her. I knelt down and began to wipe the juice from the floor and wall.

"That's my job," Daria said.

"It would have been my job at home. You make a mess. You clean it up."

Daria got another towel and joined me. Together we scrubbed the wall and gathered up the sticky remains, working silently as I waded through the cocktail of emotions coursing through me and tried to find my footing.

"Feeling lost?" Daria asked when I finally rocked back on my knees.

"I'm just a pawn," I said again, my arms as limp as the towel in my hand. "I have no power."

Daria scoffed. "Of course you have power. You're the queen."

My eyes widened. I *was* the queen. Reina was the Queen Mother. I outranked her. I got to decide what my life looked like.

"I'm going to take a bath," I told Daria, as the calculations began to spin in my head. "And then I want you to show me the library." This queen was going to study.

Vanerife High was home to more than two thousand years of books and scrolls. The most recent and frequently consulted were housed on two floors in the southwest tower, the rest in three levels of basement rooms that were temperature and moisture controlled in a way I didn't understand.

I'd studied the basics with Padrid in Aedenfal — geography, climate, key products. I wanted to pick up where I'd left off and read the file, become an expert at this perilous world I now found myself in. The intrigue wasn't going away. The time had arrived for me to learn to play my part, to truly become the queen, and I was now determined to do whatever it took to be prepared.

Harrig, the librarian, nearly had heart failure when I gathered up *Two Hundred Years of Cordair Intrusions*, written at the end of Valemar's grandfather's reign, and *The Art of Diplomacy* by a R'Keshan prince and studied by every noble son along the Aelon Sea.

"You're taking them out of the library?" Spit flew from his mouth and his jowls wobbled.

"They were mine to borrow in Aedenfal. Are you trying to tell me the queen isn't allowed use of the books?" I arched my eyebrows and waited.

"No, it's just … they're precious. There are so few copies."

I nearly laughed. The books cradled in my arm were far more hefty than fragile.

"I see. So you have Valemar read here —" I gestured around. "— when he's here."

Harrig drew himself up. "He is the King!"

"Exactly. And I am his wife. I require these books and eventually many more, and I will read them where I like."

"Where you like!" He turned a startling shade of purple and his eyes bugged out of their sockets, almost as if he was choking.

"Down at the beach in the morning, I think. I find the sound of the sea enables the mind to relax and focus."

I turned my back on him and strutted out, the books clasped to my chest, waiting for the sound of a body hitting the floor. It didn't come, and I bit back a giggle. Once things settled down with Valemar, I'd have to see about getting Padrid installed up here. He, at least, didn't fight me about my reading material.

I actually did take the books to the beach in the morning. I had padded chairs with footstools set in the shade of the trees. Between them was a pitcher of fruited wine and a plate of pastries that wouldn't sticky my fingers and, therefore, the pages. Daria brought with her a basket that held a bolster-like pillow studded with pins. Slim, wooden bobbins hung from one side and several inches of airy, shimmery lace draped from the other.

"What is this made from?" I asked her.

"The beards of the fegog," she said. "A creature that lives in the sea. It uses these long, fine fibers to snare its food."

I ran my finger along the nearly weightless lace. "They used to do something similar … on the moon," I said, aware that voices carried along the water, even with the waves. "They called it 'sea silk.' Egyptian princesses would have gowns made of the soft, gold fabric. It was said that a pair of ladies' gloves could fit into half a walnut shell." I put my forefinger and thumb together as a reference.

"This … this is beautiful."

Daria blushed. "We call it 'sea foam.' It was one of my first tasks as a girl. A child's fingers are much more nimble. I was very good at weaving it and eventually came to live at the High. Richeza, Valemar's grandmother, liked pretty things. She used to like to watch me weave and eventually had me help dress her." Daria ran her fingers over the bobbins. "I like to weave when I get the chance. Especially here."

"Of course!" I said. "I'm going to be sitting here reading. And since I do want your company, I'm glad you have a task as well."

Two Hundred Years turned out to be the kind of book best read by the calming presence of the sea. It graphically accounted the harassment the Alfari endured along the western edges of the steppe. Fairfada itself had been a battleground of sorts. Shepherds trained in jaldun. They were warriors who watched over flocks of anapali. When the death toll rose, the Laocotan — the common army — would move into the western slopes of the Archjarn, slashing and burning everything, forcing the Cordair farther east, rather than create fortifications that would intrude on the precious grass. The descriptions were vivid, and I lost all interest in the food and drink beside me. I began to see Harrig's hesitation in letting me leave with the book.

After about fifty pages, I switched to *Diplomacy* instead. "Have you heard of Adzil Jaharan?" I asked Daria.

"Isn't he that R'Keshan prince?" she asked.

I hoisted the book. "He wrote this."

"I think he's the one who married the last Alfari princess. The R'Keshans are famous for their metal work, especially their swords. They'd need to be, wouldn't they? Living so close to the Çölka," she said. The desert people who worshiped Taluendi.

I placed the book on my lap. "Tell me what you know about the countries along the Aelon Sea."

Daria's hands moved the bobbins, weaving the lace while she thought. "Well, the Archjarn mountains run down until they meet the sea, and with them the Cordair, in the east. I'm not sure what's beyond Cordair lands. R'Kesh is north, across the Aelon Sea. They've a neighbor to the east. West and north of them are the deserts of Siak Kamlar and the Çölka. You won't find the Çölkans in town trading, even if their lands are rich with diamonds. We have the Lian Isles. To the west of Bánalfar is Capalnoc. Reina's brother rules there. To their west is Zagré. South of Capalnoc is Tuljerd. To the south beyond the Scangorn mountains and Snow Reach are the Darland. Their lands are cold most of the year. They keep herds of renar and don't travel or trade much beyond their own lands. Sometimes to Verlun, the Cordair's southernmost city, for they have no metal of their own and the Cordair do like warm furs."

"Any politics I should know about before I dive in?" I asked.

"The R'Keshans are peacemakers in that they want to get along with everybody. And when you have the best swords, people tend to listen to you. You don't need my opinion of the Cordair." Daria's eyes fell to the other book sitting on the table. "Enartin wrote about the treaty. It's somewhere in the library. Not that it's done much good," she added under her breath before continuing.

"Reina is truly Capali. You'd have no trouble spotting them down at the docks — proud, fearless. They are the best riders with the best darana. Muirbrook was Valemar's king gift from his uncle. They'd back us in a fight, but only so far." The look in her eyes told me she knew why I asked. "The Tuljerd remember Gladama before the Cordair came. They still consider the land tainted so they've never returned, even after Antilli drove the Cordair out. They keep to themselves.

"Adzil will tell you how the R'Keshans think. I know it's required reading. I remember when Valemar read it. But every prince, every king filters it through the values of their own land."

"You certainly are more than you seem," I said.

"I ... I don't understand."

"You appear to be a servant, but you are very knowledgeable and very wise. I'd have hired you to assist me, had we met elsewhere. Though you could have eventually run your own company."

Daria frowned. "How is that different from what I do now? Though I don't think I'd want to command people."

I smiled. "Maybe it's not. Maybe it's just my perception clouded by my history. We have no moon children where I'm from."

"I think I'd find it very strange where you come from," Daria said.

"You would," I agreed. "You'd find it very strange indeed."

"Has Harrig recovered from my trip to the library?" I asked Reina at dinner.

She smirked. "I don't think anyone's stood up to him before."

"He'd grown quite purple before I turned my back on him. I thought I'd hear him drop dead from a heart attack before I left the room."

Reina's eyes danced with admiration. "So, my daughter, what are you doing with Jaharan and *Two Hundred Years?*"

"What I would have done before — study the file."

Reina bit into a fruit, using the time it took to suck the juice and chew to watch and consider me. "And what have you learned?" she asked when she'd swallowed.

"That this deadly dance with the Cordair has gone on for two thousand years. That Enartin's plan has not worked, though I'd like to read the treatise he wrote on it."

"That can be arranged." She hadn't flinched when I'd mentioned Valemar's father, so maybe she agreed with me. "What else?"

"That the Hormani do not know the history. They don't care, usually. They only care about profit. They prefer to work with the 'disenfranchised' as it were, for those groups are usually less concerned with right and wrong, feeling wronged themselves."

"But?"

"But I think the Hormani have bitten off more than they can chew this time. The Awrakian armor has emboldened the Cordair. They will wheedle the Hormani right along the knife's edge until the Hormani do more than they should. With otherworldly weapons and armor, the Cordair will march west and take back everything they can."

"Explain 'more than they should.'"

"At some point, someone is going to check in … here," I said, changing the word at the last moment, remembering there was the possibility I could be overheard. We were not in Reina's presence room. There was usually someone listening for the next part of the meal to be needed. "A few suits of armor won't leave a trace —"

"But an army would," Reina finished.

"An army that suddenly begins to overpower everyone it encounters will draw attention. Then the armor will get noticed."

"And then your friends will know."

I ground my teeth. "They're not my friends."

"But the enforcers would know?" Reina asked.

"Yes."

"And?"

"And they'd make contact. Centuries before your … world is ready."

"What would they do about the Cordair?"

"Arrest their progress."

Reina's face hardened. "Not undo?"

I shook my head. "No. They'd leave it as is."

"And the Hormani technology?"

"That would depend. They would take back a few suits of armor, but they might leave an entire army's worth alone. They'd want to create as small a footprint as possible." It would take an army of their own to line up the Cordair and confiscate scores of suits.

Reina ran her thumbnail along her lower lip. "So, we'd need to stop them before too long." She looked at me, and I knew what was in her eyes. But she didn't say it out loud. She just let Protocol Specialist Carr continue.

"You're going to need help," I said.

Reina snorted. "And what do I tell them? The truth?"

"No." She couldn't tell them about the Hormani. "But you could say that Raislos yearns to make another attempt to reclaim the lost lands. That is the truth. Word of the armor will eventually get out. Bánalfar's lands are vast, but you do have neighbors. They remember the tales of why Antilli rode down from Vanerife. Do they want to risk the poison spreading?"

"Only if Gladama falls."

"Would they really wait so long?"

"War taps a country's resources. What happens in Bánalfar doesn't affect them and sending help could leave their back door open, make them vulnerable to others." Reina tapped her thumb on her mouth. "You really know nothing that works against that armor?"

I thought back to the group in the throne room, closed my eyes so I could better focus on the memory. *Body armor.* Five had worn Awrakian body armor. Including that smug son of a bitch trader.

But no helmets.

"A direct blow to the head. Or arrow. Fire won't harm the suits —" Reina groaned. "— or their wearer, but they didn't have the helmets, so you could burn the heads. You don't have fire-breathing dragons on this planet, do you?" I couldn't resist throwing in the joke, even though Reina goggled at me. "Sorry, creatures of legend … on the moon. Flying beasts that —"

"Breathe fire," Reina finished, not amused. "Just the sort of creature the Cordair would love." She gave me a sharp look. "They *are* legend? Not something that could be imported?"

I pushed my plate aside and leaned across the table. Reina's eyes widened. "The beasts — no," I whispered, so low my words were barely even air. "But do you want the truth?"

Reina's eyes widened even farther. Her head slowly shook from side to side, as if the motion could push my words away. One hand rose to cover her mouth. "They wouldn't?" she said from behind it.

I gave my head a shake. "No, for if the Shororato found out, there would be no more Hormani traders anywhere." The color drained from Reina's face. "No star would be safe for them."

Slowly, she lowered her hand, her eyes as round as saucers. "Just who are you, Astrid?"

I laid my hand on the table before her, palm up. "Exactly who I told you I was."

Reina gripped my fingers, tears in her eyes. This strong, proud woman had finally realized how much danger her world was in, and it killed me to know that I'd been the one to forever change her.

I walked down to the beach after dinner, lifted the hem of my dress and let the surf swirl around my ankles. Sunset was not far off. The water was already coming alive with the gleam of phosphorescent creatures. Teridun Six winked in the east, the evening star already rising. I missed my moon and its soft glow. A lamp that lit the night with magic.

The waning blood-red moon of Crenfor was rising somewhere behind me. Dark. Like so much of my life was dark now.

I turned my head at the sound of footsteps on the sand. Daria.

"I could hold your dress if you want to go swimming," she said.

I shook my head. "No. I just wanted the sea to wash away my thoughts."

"Is it working?" she asked. I shrugged. There wasn't much that could wash away what was going on. The Shororato, if the Hormani hadn't blocked our distress calls as I suspected they had.

I stumbled and dropped the edge of my dress, nearly bowled over as what the Hormani had truly done sank in.

"Astrid!" Daria grabbed for me as I blindly scrambled for my footing in the shifting waters, my mind still reeling. "What is it?" she asked, taking my arms.

"They let them die." My words were little more than gasps. "They blocked our transmissions and let them die."

"Who?"

"The —" My knees gave out and I landed butt-first in the surf. A tiny part of my brain worried about the state of my dress; the rest whirled as my trip in the escape pod played again and again in my head. "They tried to kill me," I croaked. Things were fine. The panel beeped. The thud. My desperate praying.

The Hormani had fired on my pod. They had tried to blow me out of the sky but I'd survived. I'd survived and the Alfari had found me. Not the Hormani. Not the Cordair. The Alfari.

All because of the Mödatal.

"Oh, dear Lord."

Daria's arms went around me. "What is it?"

"I think I may be the Moon Princess."

CHAPTER 25

I sat in the surf, Daria's arms around me, while day slipped into night. Light flickered behind us as the guards lit torches. And still I sat.

It's not an easy thing to realize you're the answer to a centuries-old prayer. Especially when you have no clue what you're supposed to do. At least God had talked to Moses and Jesus and Paul. I only had the Mödatal, and I knew she wasn't God.

Daria asked, "What are you going to do?" and fell silent after receiving my vacant head shake.

What was there could I do? I had found some basic instructions and had stripped the pod of everything but the guidance system before I'd left. At the time, I hadn't wanted any technology falling into alien hands. There was no way I could contact the Shororato.

I sat in the surf so long that I half expected Shale to slink up behind us like a red ghost and cart me off to the Cair. Now that I believed it, wouldn't that be where they'd house me — a savior?

"Don't let them," I whispered to Daria. "Don't let them take me to the Cair and become a figurehead. Don't let them use me."

History was full of people held against their will and trotted out to be used as a rallying tool.

She gently laughed. "Reina's not about to allow that."

I gave a bitter huff. "Don't be so sure about that. I scared her. I scared her tonight."

Daria stiffened. "What did you do?"

I rocked back and forth in the surf, let the breath of the sea ease and fill me before I continued. "I gave her a glimpse of the truth." Daria's head bobbed up and down. "Do you have tales of people who look beyond the veil or into the great abyss and are confronted with a truth so strange and terrible that it leaves them blind or forever mad?"

"The mirrored pool at Horcair," Daria said. "It's said to be hidden in the mountains of the Archjarn, far to the south. *Oluendi's mirror.* Part of the reason the Cordair are so crazy. As for Reina —" Daria chuckled. "She will recover. The woman is truly Capali. Once, when she was a girl, riding alone on the plains, a maskpol attacked, killing her darana. Reina survived by using the bridle as a whip, striking out at the beast with the bit and cheek rings until she was able to drive it away. A rescue party found her standing guard over her dead darana. They had to throw her, kicking and screaming, into the saddle with one of the guards. She wouldn't leave. The next day, she went back out, cold and hard as steel, armed with a bow and arrows. Reina hunted down and killed the beast. I'm sure you've seen its skin on her wall."

I gasped. "*She* killed that? I thought it was just decoration."

Daria gave an amused hum. "It's a warning. A reminder of what she can do if you cross her. But you haven't crossed her, my queen. You've opened her eyes. The shock will wear off, and she will be forever grateful."

I shivered. "Time to go in," Daria said. "You're getting cold."

She pulled me to my feet. The sodden fabric clung to my legs. Daria gathered it up and knotted it above my knees. "There. That will make it easier to walk. If you weren't so modest, I'd just strip it off and have you walk back naked to the High."

"If I were a different queen," I said, a grin growing on my face. "I'd have you strip and take your gown."

Daria's hands went to the clasps at her shoulders. "I could do it. Bit of advertising for the next Blood Moon."

I put my hands on top of hers. "Stop. I was joking." This style of gown made it far too easy to get naked, which was probably the intent. "We may need to save that trick for a time when we truly need a distraction."

Daria slipped her hands from her shoulders. "Very true." Her eyes flashed with glee. "You're always getting into trouble of some sort.

We met no trouble on our way back up the stairs or down the halls to my room. Daria rinsed the salt off me with a quick, scented bath.

"Do you want a sleeping draught?" she asked as I put on my nightgown.

I wavered then decided I did. Otherwise, I'd be up all night, playing with the implications in my head, rehashing everything that had happened in the two weeks leading up to my —

I blinked and swallowed as the other pain in my heart rose. My wedding. I shuddered. "Yes. That would be lovely."

Daria took a small vial from her kit and let two drops fall into a glass of wine. I drained it down and handed the glass to her before crawling between the sheets. The curtains fluttered in the windows with the night breeze. Daria dowsed all the lights, save one.

"Good night, my queen." She hesitated in the doorway. "And, Astrid? Nothing's changed, you know. What is — is. Maybe Oluendi's mirror came before your face tonight, as it did Reina's, but what was true before the telling is still true."

Daria gently closed the door behind her. *Gods,* I thought. *How did I get so lucky to get her in Aedenfal?* Or maybe Shale had placed her. I rolled over to face the windows.

Daria was right. Reina's impression of the world had been changed, but not her actual world. Did it matter if I was the Moon Princess or not? *Maybe.*

Way back in the outer reaches of my mind, I had the feeling there was something — *something* — I could do. I just couldn't reach it.

As my mind became fuzzy, I let it slip away. Maybe it would be revealed to me in my dreams.

I didn't dream. I awoke to the tickle of the breeze and the gentle hush of the waves upon the shore far below. The breakfast tray rattled, sliding across the table, and I realized that Daria's movements must have been what had awakened me.

"Please tell me that's not the Mödatal's tea," I said when I heard liquid being poured.

"Would it be so bad if it was?" Daria asked.

I sat up and took the offered cup. "I suppose not." I patted the bed beside me. "Pour yourself one and come join me." Daria filled a cup and sat down on the edge of the bed. "If you were me, what would you do next?"

She sipped as she considered. "Does the prophecy matter to you?" she asked. "You've spent months thinking it didn't. If you were right or if you were wrong, does it really matter?"

I frowned. "I suppose not."

"So, let's say last night was an episode of moon madness. The stress you've been under has been unrelenting. Put away yesterday evening and what would Astrid Carr do today?" I noticed she used my maiden name.

"Astrid *Carr*," I said, raising my eyebrows. "Would read the file."

Daria smirked. "Then isn't that what Astrid Carbrev should do?"

She had me there. "What file would you suggest she read?"

"Enartin Carbrev's treatise explaining his reasons for the agreement with the Cordair. The son is like his mother, but he respects his father. You should know what he struggles with upholding."

I held back a grin that threatened to split from ear to ear. "I do love you," I said.

Daria spluttered on her tea. She jumped up, torn between staining the covers and staining her dress. Holding the teacup out with one hand, she wiped her mouth with the other.

"Not that way," I said with a laugh, and watched her blush. "Though if I had to choose a woman as a mate, it would be you."

"Thank you?" she said.

"I meant that I love how you're always the voice of reason. You're always there for me. I don't know if you were another of Shale's manipulations. And frankly, I don't care. You are the best thing that's happened to me since I stepped aboard the *Palmas Cove* —" My mouth hung open, waiting to add the months, but I couldn't recall how long it had been. I knew it had been months, but there'd been no easy way to track time. There'd been, what? Four Blood Moons? Five?

Daria sat again. "I'm sorry. You just startled me."

"No need to apologize." I took her hand. "I just don't know what I'd do without you."

Daria embraced me. "I will always be there for you. And no, the Mödatal did not direct me to you. It was Reina who suggested that I be among those that Valemar took when he rode south to look for you."

I leaned my chin on Daria's shoulder and sighed. "I should be thankful that Shale's vision was accurate. I'd be dead otherwise."

Daria pulled back and searched my face. "I know that's what everyone suspects, but you sound so sure."

"The outsiders tried to kill me when I fell from the moon. Actually, earlier than that. I'm sure they blocked out our distress calls, so everyone —" I swallowed. "Died. I sent one last message before I left, saying that I, too, was dying and was sending my ship into the sun."

Daria's eyes widened. "And then you didn't. You came here."

"I'm sure they fired on my escape craft."

"And then Heymond found you."

"Right where the Mödatal said I'd be."

We both stared at each other, our eyes wide with shock. "I know you don't like to hear it," Daria said.

"I know," I agreed, both of us leaving it unspoken, the thing that still terrified me.

Daria gave a firm nod. "Then you're going to need Enartin's treatise." She stood up. A crafty smile began to creep up her face. "And Harrig is going to have to hand it over whether he likes it or not."

I covered a smile with my hand as Daria sauntered out. I didn't know who was rubbing off on whom. But I liked it.

Years of struggle and pain on both sides can be summed up by the word 'uncompromising.' Change can only come with willingness to change. What is right is often hard. But only the hard things are truly worth doing.

I had begun to picture Valemar's father as weak. Maybe because Reina was so strong. Maybe because the treaty hadn't worked. But Enartin's treatise on his agreement with the Cordair revealed him to have been a thoughtful, risk-taking visionary. He hadn't given the Cordair an inch. He'd given them a proverbial half mile in hopes that it would keep them from trying to take the full mile. And it had worked, in that sense. Things were better than they had been.

Enartin had also backed up his plan with additional training for troops stationed along the border. Aedenfal, Snow Reach, and even Lendurig had quietly been fortified and improved.

And I discovered that I had the only copy in my hands, the ink put there by Enartin himself, a visionary's gift to his future generations. And the single copy meant that the Cordair didn't know everything that Enartin had done. Observation would have told them many things, just not all of them.

I ran my fingers over the ink. What a loss it was to have lived in a time and place where a tablet was the norm. Or implanted in the eye so a person only needed to blink the information. Or speak it and have a computer answer. Information so far removed from the creator that it became like a cloud in the sky or a drop of water in the ocean.

But Valemar's father had touched these pages. My fingertips caressed the lines. It was almost as if I could reach through time and space and brush his hand. There were theories that we could do just that. We know that energy never truly goes away. That it only changes.

I closed the book and pushed it away before I could slide any further down the rabbit hole. Mysticism wouldn't help me.

There was a plate of pastries and two different drinks — wine and a type of lemonade — on the table in my room. I uncurled from

my chair and went over. Daria had brought lian tarts, a pilva pastry, and cookies made from nuts that were rich and sweet like chestnuts. I ate one of the lian tarts and poured myself a glass of wine. I began to pace the room, the wineglass curled in my palms.

It should have worked — Enartin's treaty. *How much of the current unrest was a result of the Cordair ethos and how much was due to the interference of the Hormani?* I tapped a finger on my glass as I thought. *When had they arrived?* Valemar might know. *How much information did he have about the Cordair and the workings of their lands?*

I brought the glass to my lips and drank, savoring the burn in my stomach as the alcohol hit it. Maybe Reina would know. I swallowed back the rest and went to find my mother-in-law.

Why is it that we feel so deeply with our hearts and not our brains? Is it because the heart is responsible for our survival, more necessary to engage in fight or flight than our brain? Why else would our emotions be housed there — love, hope, fear, longing? Our brains don't feel these things. Our hearts do.

My brain filled with endless scenarios as I walked down the corridors toward Reina's rooms, and every shift in thought changed the adrenaline, changed how my heart responded. *How long had the Hormani been here? A year? A decade?*

A decade — then things with the Cordair probably wouldn't escalate very fast. A year — then warfare was potentially very close.

My mother-in-law. I hated how my heart always sped up with that one. We'd come to cordial working relationship. In many ways, Reina was just another client. But she wasn't.

I pushed aside the pang and made myself follow the next thought. *Would Valemar accept my analysis?* I needed — we needed —

to establish how extensive the Hormani infiltration was into Cordair society. Did they live openly? Did they have separate outposts? If so, how many?

Thump thump. Thump thump. My whole life was encapsulated in that one muscle that speeded up, slowed down, clenched to aching, or floated free of my body depending on the situation.

My brain wanted to build a new life. *You could live happily in Vanerife*, it told me. *You can read the files. You can fit in here. This city sits at the crossroads of multiple civilizations that no one has yet explored. No one, other than those native to Crenfor.*

But my heart. My stupid, aching, yearning heart beating out a rhythm I could feel as I walked down the halls. It wanted things that I couldn't have.

I sighed. Life would be so much better if hearts came with an off switch.

Reina was in her presence room. I knocked and waited for her to call, "Enter."

"Astrid," she said, putting aside a dispatch that she'd been reading. "What can I do for you?"

She gestured for me to sit. I did and leaned across the table. "How much do we … you … Valemar know about the —" I changed the word in case anyone was listening. "Strangers trading with the Cordair?"

Reina leaned back and tossed down her pen. "I assume you don't mean 'where they're from?'"

"How integrated are they into Cordair society?" I asked.

Reina drummed her fingers on the arm of her chair. "I don't know." Her eyes flashed to mine. "Does it matter?"

"It would give us an idea how long they've been there. Does anyone know?"

Reina's lips thinned. "I will ask. Should we be worried if they've begun living with the Cordair?"

"No," I said. "You should be worried if they have not."

CHAPTER 26

Reina sent a karawack to Valemar with my inquiries. A karawack could only travel about a hundred miles a day, so it would be six or seven days, at the earliest, before we would hear back. I had a feeling that Valemar had returned to Aedenfal. Vanerife might be the capital and Bánalfar's most ancient city, but Aedenfal was its heartbeat.

I wondered if that would have been true if a different people lived in the Archjarn. Glábac and Torfin were important. Even Lendurig. But they all stood in the center of peaceful activity. The Fairfada — the Golden Steppe — had been anything but peaceful for hundreds of years. And so Aedenfal pulsed, always on the brink of rising to defense, much like a heart.

I spent chunks of time in the library, Harrig and I having come to a grudging truce. I read, mainly skimmed, books about the Cordair, the R'Keshans, the Capali, and the Tuljerd. Harrig must have told Reina about my activities, for four days after she sent the karawack to Valemar, she asked for my presence at a dinner with the R'Keshan ambassador. It was time to put my big girl pants on, so to speak. Which, in reality, was a flimsy dress.

This would be my first real activity as queen without Valemar by my side. And while I outranked Reina, I was more than willing to let her take the lead.

Daria and I chose a dress of bright blue that represented the Lian Isles and the light circlet of gold barat leaves. Around my neck, she fastened a necklace that held only a single stone — a teardrop about the size of my thumb, in a color that was neither sapphire nor blue topaz, which fell to nestle just between my breasts.

"Are you sure I should wear this?" My eyes kept being drawn down to the stone sitting seductively like a blue fruit between two pillows on my chest. "Do we want to draw attention to my cleavage? My husband isn't at home."

"The R'Keshans like a good bosom, and their women would be wearing even less. It's much warmer there." Daria stepped around to my front and surveyed me. "We want Sapir Ilahni to appreciate Bánalfar's queen."

"More like my bosom," I muttered.

"Which is part of its queen." Daria smiled at me. "Dazzle him with your bosom then impress him with your mind." She fiddled with the fit of my dress. "You can't tell me Protocol Specialist Carr never did the same."

I had actually.

"Fine," I said, giving in. "The necklace stays. Any suggestions on how to dazzle him with my mind?"

Daria grinned, a mischievous smile as if she had a secret she couldn't wait to share. "Would he expect the Moon Princess to have read Adzil?"

My mouth curled up to match hers. "No," I said. "No, he wouldn't."

I had read many treatises on diplomacy when I was at the academy — Machiavelli, Henwick the Wise, and even Bedan Fortaire's famous work from Guigel Ten. But my favorite quote came from twentieth century Earth and Winston Churchill.

Diplomacy is the art of telling people to go to hell in such a way that they ask for directions.

Churchill's sentiments would have resonated with Adzil, though he would have found them too blunt. But the R'Keshan prince had said, *All diplomacy is better with a knife at your back.* Which actually translated as "in your belt," according to my chip (the original had been there in R'Keshan). I took Adzil as meaning, *Be prepared for anything.*

I certainly didn't feel like I was, but then rule number eleven was: *Never enter a negotiating room stressed.* Whomever you were meeting with would smell your fear, sometimes literally. Things never went well when you became prey.

I sent Daria away so I could visualize and put on the mental armor of PS Carr. She would have seen tonight as a challenge. Astrid Carbrev needed to stop viewing everything as a life or death situation.

I shook the tension out of my hands. Goal — *Prove that I was a wife worthy of Valemar.* I was educated, exotic, and had a gift for languages. I looked down at my chest and mentally thanked Daria. And I had a good bosom. That, at least, would keep the Sapir occupied until my other assets became noticeable.

Knives. Courtly manners. Everything done with a smile. These were things that, thanks to Adzil, I knew R'Keshans valued. Astrid Carr would have entered with a smile. Astrid Carr knew how to put everyone at ease. Astrid Carbrev knew how to wield a knife. But I was going to keep that particular talent hidden tonight.

Right. I straightened my head. Time to go meet another ambassador.

Reina was adorned in a brilliant yellow dress that highlighted her still golden hair and showed none of her cleavage. Her crown of barat leaves was more substantial than mine, which did make me wonder at my status, but didn't actually bother me. Crowns were heavy, as I'd discovered, and I didn't relish having my small one on all evening. Neither Reina's head nor neck showed any strain from the weight. Of course, hers was less bulky than the Imperial State Crown of Great Britain or the lavishly adorned hairstyles of the Ztemyatans.

The Sapir was dressed in a tunic and trousers of bright green, heavily embroidered in gold. His skin was lightly tan, more sun-kissed than the bronze of the Cordair. His hair was chestnut, just a few shades paler than mine. The sides had been pulled back into a braid that hung down his back and was tied off with a large peridot carved to resemble some insect. Of approximately middle age, he had a smile that could have melted chocolate and dazzling green eyes that had probably melted the clothing off of countless women. His eyes went from my face to the jewel nestled on the tops of my breasts, to my ears (hidden by my hair), then back to my face.

"Honored queen," he said, bowing low.

"Sapir Tanic Ilahani. I am honored to make your acquaintance." I smiled and inclined my head while I brought my hand to my chest, covering my heart and the jewel with the formal greeting. I was tempted to leave my arm there but forced it back to my side.

"Shall we?" Reina asked, and gestured to the table. An assortment of sliced meats and breads, cheeses, nuts, fruits, and refreshing salads had been set out. The Sapir poured wine for Reina and myself then filled his glass and set the decanter aside. He drank, both the wine and the view of my chest. My eyes flicked to Reina's in silent question as to why I was here for the energy in the room told me that this dinner was not just a simple introduction to Valemar's wife.

"Tanic," Reina said with a purr in her voice. "I'm having trouble securing the best price and delivery dates on our latest order."

The ambassador's eyes moved away from me. "There are others with requests ahead of yours, Reina."

A contract. A switch flicked on inside me. This dinner was another contract negotiation. This was something I could do in my sleep, even with a scant file.

I leaned across the table toward the ambassador, the jewel rising as my breasts tilted toward him. "But my honored Sapir, it is not Bánalfar's Queen Mother that asks you. It is the Moon Princess's representative." I offered up a quick prayer that Reina wouldn't take that as an insult. "I would see my people protected and your R'Keshans make the best steel." I leaned back and jutted my lower lip out in a small pout. "Unless you are telling my honored mother that we need to look elsewhere?"

The Sapir's eyebrows rose, a small flag of panic though his eyes barely widened. His hand came to his chest. "My dear Princess, my honored Queen, I had no idea the order was for you."

I placed a hand on Reina's arm. "My mother has been taking care of details while I better acquaint myself with Vanerife and my husband is attending to business in the south." Reina smiled at me and took my hand. "I do not like the whispers that have reached me. Dangerous men trade with the Cordair. Dangerous men who would do anything to ensure their supply of ore." There was the faintest click of apprehension in the Sapir's eyes. He, too, had heard the whispers.

"The days are coming when your steel will be tested in ways it hasn't been before. You could have us try … or wait until you can do so on your own shores." I smiled sweetly but made sure he read the

threat in my eyes. "All diplomacy is better with a knife at your back. I would prefer a R'Keshan knife but —"

"Perhaps the Zagré steel, instead?" Reina asked. I nodded my agreement.

The Sapir laughed and clapped his hands. "Is this what the prophecy meant by 'a new life for all?'"

"Life comes in many forms," I said, letting his reference to my barrenness slide. "Fulfillment can take many forms. I, myself, would like to see fulfillment in the form of our order in —" I turned to Reina.

"Thirty days?" she said.

"*Simek!* Thirty days!" The Sapir threw himself back in his chair.

I hummed. "One and a half moons?" I returned my gaze to Reina. "Would that be fair?"

Her eyes danced with glee before she put on a mask of suffering. "I suppose. Would that be possible, esteemed Sapir?"

I put my hands under my chin and leaned forward, resting on my elbows, a look of hopeful expectation on my face. The jewel left my chest and swung gently before my breasts. The Sapir's gaze swung back and forth, following its path. I sighed.

"I understand your hesitation, honored ambassador, for the R'Keshans are a peaceful people. Our Mödatal may be a seer, but I, too, have a gift." His eyes finally traveled up to my face. "I know, without the benefit of any seer, only of my own discernment, that the day is soon coming when all the old will stand on a knife's edge. The blade may cut and take the old with it, or the blade may rise and block the old from harm." His eyes widened slightly. "Which way would you have the knife move, esteemed Sapir? Where would you see R'Kesh? An old and glorious country, still whole, or the subject of a regime you cannot possibly understand?"

The color drained from the Sapir's face. "What do you bring with you?" he whispered.

"It is not me that you need to worry about," I said. "It is the Cordair who have unleashed the devil. Oluendi grows tired of living in the mines." Sweat appeared on the Sapir's brow. "The Alfari are willing to make a stand, as they have always done. Is R'Kesh willing to stand with us? Or will you take your chances with the devil?"

The Sapir refilled his wineglass then drained it. His eyes filled with a mixture of resignation and horror. "By the Father and Mother and Turend himself, I will find a way to get you what you need."

"I never doubted it," Reina said, the purr returning to her voice. "And now let's leave business behind. I didn't ask you here to talk business. I asked you here to meet my new daughter."

"*Alahanue,*" I said.

The Sapir's eyebrows shot up. "You speak R'Keshan?"

"A bit." I smiled. "I've been reading Prince Adzil's fascinating book, and I do have a gift for picking things up."

The Sapir poured himself more wine, this time with a smile on his face. "Valemar has found himself a fine wife, my Reina."

"Would you have expected him to do anything else?"

We talked of *The Art of Diplomacy*, the lands of R'Kesh, of its proud people, full of life. He asked me for tales of the moon. I brushed his request away with, "It's more different than you could ever understand. I'd rather not talk of it." Being from a more courtly society, the Sapir merely smiled through his disappointment and changed the subject.

He looked pleased when he departed, full of wine and food, sweet tea and pastries. He bowed low over my hand and kissed it. It was only after the door closed behind him that I rounded on Reina.

"What was that?"

"Dinner with a dignitary. You did superbly well."

"For someone with no warning as to its true purpose," I retorted. Reina raised one eyebrow. "I told you, this —" I waved my hands in emphasis. "— is what I used to do for a living. But did you let me read the file? No. Had I read the contract? No. I didn't even know there was one. I'm *guessing* we were on the same page goal-wise because you went along with everything I said. What was this? Some kind of test?"

Even as the words left my mouth, I knew the answer, knew it before the faint bit of color appeared on Reina's cheeks. "Why?" I asked.

Reina turned and walked to the table. She tapped one hand on it, but didn't seem able to answer.

"Because you were looking for me to have *some* value?" I asked. I blinked away a sting that rose in my eyes.

"Because I needed to know how you'd manage against our neighbors." Reina faced me. "Because your looks would have enchanted Tanic enough that I could have gotten the answers myself, had I needed to."

I gritted my teeth, biting back the words I wanted to hurl at her. "*Never* do that to me again." Then I turned on my heel and marched out before I did something I'd later regret.

I didn't go back to my rooms. I clenched my jaw and headed down the long stairway to the beach. I needed to move.

I peeled off my dress once I'd reached the sand, not caring if there were guards to see, and left it on a chair with my shoes and the crown. The sea sparkled with the glowing phosphorescent creatures, and I waded out into the surf to join them. Once the water was waist high, I dove under, wetting my hair and pushing myself out into deeper water.

I would have done anything for her. I would have done anything if she'd asked.

I broke the surface and treaded water. As my hands swept back and forth before me, I was struck by the fact that I'd been treading water for months. That was why tonight stung. I had finally been able to combine the old me with the new, and it had all been a test.

With a real client.

I flicked my head to shake off a trickle dripping from my hair into my eyes. *The contract had been real.*

My hands and feet moved on their own as my mind went into analysis mode.

With or without me, Reina would have met with the Sapir. She would have pushed for better terms. She'd dressed me up, shoved me in there, and sat back to see what would happen.

I blew out a slow breath.

And PS Carr and Astrid Carbrev had come together. Hell, I'd even put on the mantle of the Moon Princess.

I closed my eyes. She still should have told me it was more than a simple dinner, asked for my help. I desperately needed someone I could trust. And while my head said that I could trust Reina, my heart wasn't sure she wouldn't find some way to break it.

I swam away my tension. When I turned for shore, I noticed that Daria stood by the water's edge. I walked out of the waves and into her waiting towel.

"Was it bad?" she asked, wrapping it around me.

"No," I said, and leaned my head against her shoulder. "It was a test."

"Ah."

"It went really well," I said. "Other than I got mad at Reina at the end because it was a test."

"I see."

"Then I marched off before I did something really stupid. So I came for a swim."

Daria guided me back to the chair and dried me off before helping me back into my gown. Her quiet presence promised me that everything would be okay. That I would be okay. I'd shown Reina tonight that I did have value. I might not be able to produce children, but tonight I had produced results.

CHAPTER 27

The next morning, I "picked up the file" and continued on. R'Kesh was one neighbor. I would eventually need to meet with the others.

Reina found me in the library. "I do apologize," she said. Her hands were grasped in front of her, and I was surprised to see a look of contrition on her face. "You are right. I should have told you what was at stake."

I closed the book I'd been reading. "Yes, you should have. I understand why you didn't, but you should have."

Reina glanced around. Harrig was nowhere to be seen. For all intents and purposes, we were alone. She took a chair across from me. "There is one thing," she whispered. My heart gave a thump. Reina reached out and took my hand. "You can't let anyone know. You can't let anyone know … you're barren." She lifted her head, and I was shocked to see tears in her eyes. "The succession is difficult. Enartin and I despaired about it until we were blessed with Valemar."

"Daria said that Adzil Jaharan married the last Carbrev princess." Reina nodded. "Which was when?"

"She was Enartin's great aunt. Ötten's sister."

"Are there any moon children?" I asked. "Could a moon child inherit?"

"There has been no precedent because they enter service."

"Ruling a country is service," I said.

Reina smiled. "It is. But removing someone from service has never been done before."

"Ah. And to change a system that works —"

"Is to invite potential chaos," she finished. "Yes, we'd thought about that."

"Where is the line now? It's been four? Five? Generations since there were two princes?"

"Valemar's great-great-grandfather was one of three brothers and a sister."

"And where are their offspring now?"

"Toren, the youngest brother, moved to Snow Reach and married a Darland princess. Carwyn, the middle brother, died defending Aedenfal during an attack."

I gasped. "But no one talks of it. The Cordair?"

Reina gave a tight nod. "It was a long time ago now. A spare uncle. It is said that Toren fought fiercely." My eyes widened. Reina nodded. "Yes, he was there, too. There wasn't much left of the Cordair army by the time the Alfari drove them back to the gates of Rock Dorach. Some say it was only a karawack from Dönal that kept Toren from burning the city.

"Toren turned his back on Bánalfar after that. Went south and found comfort in the arms of the Darland princess. Said Aedenfal would always be colored by his brother's blood and he'd no wish to see it ever again."

"So his line would inherit," I said.

Reina's expression became pained. "No. Technically a daughter could inherit."

I groaned. "So, because Adzil married Lareen, the R'Keshans …"

"Yes, could be next in line."

Reina rubbed my hand, still in her grip. "You are a woman worthy of my son. Is there no …?" She swallowed. "Your gods must be different."

"Yes and no," I said.

"Do you pray to them?"

I shook my head. "Not as often as I should."

Her eyes found mine and pled with me. "Do they grant miracles? Are there miracles in your travels? Do your people ever conceive with others?"

I hadn't been able to tell her the first time, but this time it slipped out on its own. "Yes," I said. And then I couldn't pull it back. I prayed it wouldn't give her false hope.

Reina bent forward and kissed my head. "Then I shall ask the Mother and the Father." She cupped my face with her free hand. "It took me five years, and then I got my miracle." Her thumb rubbed my cheek. "And there was no prophecy about me."

I decided my next step would be to meet with the Capali ambassador. Reina had set up the last meeting, and she could set this one up, as well. But it would be of my choosing, and we would strategize together first.

"If R'Kesh is going to provide us with steel, is your brother going to provide us with darana?" I asked Reina at dinner.

Reina finished chewing her bite of stewed meat. "I've put out feelers."

"And since you thought it was so important that I meet the R'Keshan ambassador, shouldn't I meet the Capali?"

Her eyebrows raised then lowered. "I suppose you should."

I smoothed the folds of my dress as Daria hooked the necklace around my neck. The silky drapes were a deep, grassy green. "Like the fields in Capalnoc," she had said.

The dress was more substantial, and so was the necklace, than the ones I'd worn for dinner with the Sapir. "I take it that I'm not supposed to impress Aren with my bosom," I said.

"Ha! Reina would not thank you for that." Daria stepped back and looked me over. "Unlike the R'Keshans, Capali women don't go flaunting their sexuality. Remember, they've bred the sort of woman who could kill a maskpol."

"Great," I said, and moaned. "You do know I'm considered a klutz."

Daria's brow furrowed. "Klutz?"

"Awkward. The kind of person who'd trip over their own feet."

"You are not awkward," Daria said. "You ride well." Her face colored, and she lowered her eyes. "You're good with a blade."

My face flamed as I recognized the double entendre that had colored her cheeks. "Yes," I whispered, acknowledging her last statement. "I guess I am." *How had that happened?*

"Those are traits that the Capali admire. Be you." Daria took my hand. "I know you feel like you are walking blind, but you need to let that fear go. You do know how to do this."

If it had been another other place, any other client, I would have agreed with her. It had taken me so long to get to the where I accepted that I might be the answer to a prophecy, and yet … I felt like if I embraced it fully, was arrogant enough to truly believe, then

the gods would laugh and say, *Nope! Not you!* and things would be worse than if I'd never come at all.

One more meeting, one more piece set in motion, and it could all come crashing down.

Just like my marriage.

"What if I'm wrong? What if I'm not ..." I whispered.

"I believe," Daria said. "I've always believed. From the moment I walked into your room at Aedenfal and saw how different you were, experienced how kind you are." She reached out a hand and touched my face. "The gods sent you to us, Astrid. Your ship was doomed, and you along with it. But it brought you here, just as foretold, and you were saved. You will save us all."

I squeezed her hand and nodded.

"And tonight I will save you from yourself. What do the Capali revere?" Daria asked. My brain whirred.

"Strength," I answered automatically, and the mental file flicked open. "Respect. Independence." It was what made them such excellent horsemen.

Knowledge began to curl in my heart, driving out the fear. Rákal's king's gift to Valemar had been Muirbrook — a war animal. The king of Capalnoc had already begun to arm his nephew.

My spine lengthened. Daria smiled at me and nodded once, an action I repeated. I blew out my breath.

Time to go do this.

Aren Loör, cousin to Reina, was a striking man. Long golden-blond hair, just a shade lighter than Reina's, framed a face that could only be described as rakish. Modeling agencies on half the worlds in the galaxy would have fought over him if given a chance. Added to

that, the toned, muscular body visible even with the green tunic and slacks he wore, and I was glad I had not dressed the same way I had for the Sapir. Married or not, I was half-tempted to throw myself at him, even with my mother-in-law watching. Especially with the appreciative once over he gave me.

"Cousin." Reina's voice interrupted Aren's inspection of me. "I'd like you to meet my daughter-in-law, Astrid. Astrid, this is Kyvet Aren Loör, the ambassador from Capalnoc."

"Kyvet," I said, inclining my head.

"*Kira* Astrid." Parts of me quivered in response to Aren's husky voice. A voice that soothed yet demanded attention. I could well imagine him draped across his darana, whispering commands in its ear.

Reina gestured to the table. "Shall we?"

"I hear this is a working dinner," Aren said once we were seated.

I shook out my napkin and placed it in my lap. "It is."

Aren's gaze slid over to Reina. "Since you've already met with Tanic Ilahni to secure his steel, I would guess you'd like me to secure Capalnoc's darana."

"Very astute," I said. Of course gossip about my action would have spread. "On the other hand, as queen it is my duty to meet with all of Bánalfar's neighbors."

"And how did you find Raislos?" Aren asked with a roguish grin.

"Aren!" Reina reddened visibly.

"Dangerously confident," I said, smiling my challenge. "Dangerously armed."

The playfulness melted from Aren's face, and he looked at Reina. "What does she mean?"

"I mean," I said, answering for myself, "that their new friends are supplying them with armor that no blade can pierce. There are no weak points within it. No plates to sneak a knife between. No special arrow

bolts you could even begin to imagine that could pierce the material."

Aren paled so much that he turned nearly white. "That can't possibly be true," he whispered.

"It's true." Reina darted a glance at me before returning it to her cousin. "We've had … skirmishes the last couple of months." I gave Reina a startled look. This was the first I'd heard of it.

Reina felt my gaze but kept hers on Aren. "Arrows bounce right off. *Agillian* arrows." She emphasized the word but it was meaningless to me. Something else I'd need to study up on. "We've had some luck with flaming arrows — *saigbreaos*." Aren nodded. "But the fuel needs to spread to the head to be effective. Otherwise, the Cordair do not appear to feel the heat."

"I bet their darana can't say the same thing."

Aren was right. A flaming rider was probably the last thing any creature wanted on its back. Other than maybe a maskpol — all teeth and claws.

He slowly shook his head. "Not good. How is this possible? Who are these strangers that they have such armor?"

Reina and I shared a glance. I hooked an eyebrow in question, but Reina gave her head a tight shake. "I would rather tell that to Rákal myself," I said. "I mean no offense, Kyvet, but this is not information to be shared with a subordinate first."

"By the sea and the moon, Reina!" Aren exclaimed, nearly jumping out of his seat. "What is going on in Bánalfar?"

Reina gave me a sad look before answering her cousin. "The fulfillment of a prophecy."

It was, after that revelation, a sober dinner. None of the charm and flirting that had gone on with the Sapir occurred. Aren's astonishing

good looks did keep me from drifting too much into melancholy. How could one be morose when confronted with such beauty?

I worried, though, the next day. Would the darana be enough? Would the R'Keshan swords be enough? Would any of it be enough if the Hormani fully armed the Cordair? What if they just attacked us with lasers instead? What if, instead of saving these people, I was leading them to slaughter?

Daria brought a tray of lian tarts and iced tea to cheer me up, but I was in no mood to enjoy it. "Eat them yourself," I said with a wave of my hand. "I'm not sure I could keep them down."

I could hear Daria gently sigh as I looked back out the window and watched the rhythmic surge of the waves, hoping they'd help calm my turbulent thoughts. So far, it wasn't working.

A strangled noise from Daria made me turn. Her eyes bulged. A tart dropped from one hand as the other flew to her throat. I stood in shock, unable to believe what I was seeing. It was only when her knees buckled that I raced across the room.

"What is it?" I asked, holding her up. Daria gasped for air. "Are you choking?" I could grab her from behind and force the piece out.

She shook her head. Her weight became too much for me, and I eased us to the floor. Her mouth began to move, trying to form words as her wide eyes filled with fear. Foam appeared on her lips, and I knew that she wasn't choking

I screamed, calling out for the guards, and cradled her to me, rocking us back and forth. Daria's hand searched for mine, and I grasped it tightly. "You're going to be fine," I said to her. "The guards are coming and you'll be fine." I expected her to nod, but Daria's eyes filled with tears. It was a look I'd seen too many times before — the beginning of a goodbye.

"No!" I shouted. "You are not going to give up. Help is coming.

Don't you dare leave me. Do you hear me? You are not going to leave me."

Daria's lips began a frantic struggle. Her lungs shuddered as she fought for air. Then her free hand fumbled and pulled me close.

"Bet … ter … meee"

The words were nothing but breath. My ear barely caught them. I opened my mouth to argue and watched as she slipped from this life, leaving me staring into yet another pair of beautiful but empty blue eyes.

CHAPTER 28

B*eep. Beep. Beep. Beep. Beep. Beep. Beep. Beep.*

The world around me spun. I held on. *There's a crash coming. Get ready for the crash.*

Beep. Beep. Beep. Beep. Beep. Beep. Beep. Beep.

"Harry, there's something wrong with the —" But my mind was focused on the sales figures in the file, so I didn't catch what exactly it was. "Take us out of hyperspace in the nearest star system." That sounded bad though, and I clutched my tablet to my chest.

Kaboom! Beep. Beep. Beep. Beep. Beep. Beep. Beep. Beep.

The ship rocked. The lights went out. People screamed. I clutched my tablet. Whatever had been bad had gone intensely worse. My teeth began to chatter. Space travel was dangerous. If the Earth were a grain of sand and Pluto was the next sun, we'd need to move Pluto light years away to represent the distance between us and the nearest star.

"Plasma leak, stay where you are," Bari broadcast moments later. Things were bad. Definitely bad.

Beep, beep … Beep, beep … Beep, beep.

"Hello?" My mother answered the phone. "Yes, this is she." The color drained from her face. Mum put her hand over the speaker. "Go to bed, Astrid. I'll be up in a few minutes."

I slid off the chair and went to my room. I crawled into bed and pulled Emerson onto my lap. I knew from the look on my mother's face that it was about Grandma Sarah. I knew that she was gone.

It's not Grandma Sarah, a voice in the back of my head said.

"No," I whispered, fighting against the scream that filled my throat. And then my ears were filled with it, a keening cry like the death wail of a banshee.

Crash!

I flinched and held Emerson closer.

It's not Emerson, the voice in my head whispered.

Someone tried to pull Emerson out of my arms.

"No," I said, holding on tighter. I couldn't do it. I couldn't do any of it without Emerson.

Without Daria.

"No," I whispered. My arms began to shake and my teeth to chatter. "Don't leave me. You can't leave me. I can't do this without you." They were all gone. Grandma Sarah and Mum and Finn and Zhou and Doc. And Daria.

Better me.

"Don't leave me. You can't leave me. I can't do this without you." I held her tighter. "It can't be you. It's not better that it's you." Tears poured down my face. I fought for breath. "It should have been me."

It was supposed to have been you, Death whispered in my ear. *You've cheated me again.*

He was right. I had cheated. I'd hidden in my cabin when everyone else was trying to save us. I'd cheated when I sent out that

transmission — broken my word, broken the law. I was nothing but a coward and a cheat.

That's why Valemar left you.

Death was right. I'd told Valemar the truth, and he'd recognized what I was and sent me away.

Where I'd caused more death.

Death pulled at me again. "Astrid, you need to let go." His voice was louder this time. And different. It sounded more like a woman's voice.

Death tugged on my arms again, stronger than before. "You can't do anything for her." He was right. I couldn't save her. I had killed her. "You need to let go." *You need to come to me.*

I loosened my grip and gave myself over to the darkness that waited for me. Anything, other than feel Daria leave me again.

CHAPTER 29

Death was ranting and raving when I floated back to consciousness. His anger called me back, required my presence. "In my own house!"

Not Death. Reina.

A knife cut into my chest, scooping out my heart with fire. I longed to return to the peaceful embrace of Death and the oblivion he offered. Anything to make that agony in my heart stop.

"How could this happen in *my* house!"

A tear slid down my cheek. "Take me, too," I whispered to Death. I reached for darkness and pulled it around me like a blanket. Reina's angry words faded away.

Strong arms lifted me up. My head thumped against a man's chest. "How long has she been like this?" a voice asked. It was strangely familiar.

"Almost seven days. Ever since …"

"By the sea and moon!"

My head rose, searching for the source.

"*Dia du, mo banorisa.*" Hello, my princess.

Heymond.

Safety.

Death couldn't reach me in Heymond's arms. But he paraded his other conquests by. A wail rose up from my throat as they marched before me. Heymond's arm came up, and he cradled my head against him. "Hush now. You're safe. I've come to take you home."

I was in no condition to ride. After so many days with no food but the broth they'd poured down my semi-conscious throat, it was all I could do to raise my head. They placed me in a wagon lined with cushions to ease the jolts, hoping the air and scenery would revive me.

Something inside me had broken. Some essential part of me had vanished with the light in Daria's eyes. I tried not to think about it. Every time I did, a whooshing pull grabbed me just behind my navel and my breath caught in my throat as if it were the last I'd take.

Only Heymond helped. I don't know why. Maybe a link had formed between us when he'd pulled me away from the Cordair. Maybe part of me thought that since he'd rescued me once, he'd rescue me again.

But then I'd remember why I had needed rescuing. Both times. And down I'd go again.

Slowly, the ache became bearable. I knew without asking that we rode south, for Aedenfal. By the fourth day, I was strong enough to get on the back of a darana. Of course, that was when I discovered that Shale rode with us. I actually turned the reins, pointed my mount's head away — not back to Vanerife, not south toward Aedenfal, just away from her and toward anything else. Heymond reached out and grabbed my darana's bridle.

"She says it's important that she's with us."

Right. Just like it had been important to perform that trick with the blood.

Because the time is coming —

I squeezed my eyes shut. "She rides at the back."

With a squeak of leather and the shuffle of hooves, Shale obeyed my command and joined the riders at the rear. I opened my eyes. Heymond nodded his head toward the empty road before us, and I turned my mount to follow.

More than thirty riders ensured our safety, the most I'd ever traveled with. Of course, an attempt had just been made on the life of Bánalfar's queen. Part of me wondered why they bothered protecting me. With me gone, Valemar would be free to marry someone who could give him children. Was my role as Moon Princess really so much more important than the succession?

We skirted Lendurig and its masses and camped along the Leisna where it became its own river and hadn't yet been swallowed up by the Dunna. It then that the time frame filtered into my mind.

"Where were you?" I asked Heymond, frowning as I warmed my hands with a mug of glow wine. Everything felt cold after the warmth of Vanerife. "You're no karawack. How did you get to Vanerife so quickly?"

"I'd been in Lendurig," Heymond said. "Valemar —" Heymond winced when I cringed. "— wanted me to personally interview some farmers. There'd been reports of Cordair this far north and west."

For the first time, I wondered who had tried to kill me. But then Daria's face swam before me, and I pushed my questions away.

"They're getting bolder," I said. A statement, not a question.

Heymond sighed. "Yes. There are problems almost daily. For about the last month." Ever since I started meeting with ambassadors. "It will soon be open warfare."

"Is there more armor?" I asked.

"I don't know," Heymond answered. "Valemar sent scouts out to try and get a count. That's part of the reason he stayed behind."

"Smart move," I said. "Kill off his wife. Draw him out of Aedenfal." I laughed. An achy laugh, full of irony, that tore at the ragged remains of my heart. "Too bad it didn't work out for them."

Two days later we rode into familiar territory. I pulled my darana to a standstill when the walls of Aedenfal appeared through the trees.

"I can't." I couldn't ride in. Couldn't risk seeing their animosity and knowing they whispered about my disgrace.

Heymond took one look at my face and knew what I meant. He sent a rider ahead to let the High know of our change of plans. Shale left with him, traveling directly to the Cair. We hadn't spoken the whole trip.

Her eyes met mine before she turned up the road. There was kindness in them, which only made me feel guilty. But I couldn't forgive her for not warning me. Not yet.

And so, I entered Aedenfal the way I first had — by boat. Only this time, much to my surprise, Valemar waited on the watergate's steps to greet me.

"Thank the Mother and the Father," he said, and pulled me out of the boat and into his arms.

I'd thought I'd been fine. I'd thought I'd put the worst of the horror behind me. But there, in Valemar's arms, I trembled.

Valemar tightened his grip, ever so slightly, then extended a hand to Heymond who was just climbing out. "Thank you, my friend." A

look passed between them that told me Valemar knew the state I'd been in before Heymond arrived.

"King's Guard. Queen's Guard. Seems to be my job to bring her to you." Heymond clapped Valemar on the arm before he climbed the steps and disappeared through the door.

"Can you walk?" Valemar murmured in my ear. I nodded. Valemar's hand closed around mine.

He led me through the warren of passageways, matching his gait with mine, but when I realized that Valemar meant to take me back to my old rooms, I planted my feet and refused to go any farther.

"I can't," I said for the second time that day. Not when Daria wouldn't be there. Not when Daria would be the only thing I'd see everywhere I looked.

Valemar met my tear-filled eyes and nodded. He changed direction and led me to a room that was clearly his. The place he must have retreated to when I'd kept him from my bed.

And I wondered, for the first time in ages, if Zhanet had been warming his bed while I was in Vanerife.

I faltered and Valemar, thinking that my legs had given way, scooped me up and sat in a chair, cradling me in his lap. "I so nearly lost you," he whispered, and I didn't know what to say. He was the one who'd sent me away.

An insidious little voice in my head started to whisper that if he hadn't, Daria would still be alive. But it was my fault. I'd made myself a target — meeting with ambassadors, helping Reina arm Bánalfar. If I had stayed quietly in the background, Daria would still be alive.

I leaned my head into his chest. It would have been easier if Valemar was still angry with me. I'd have had a reason to crawl away and hide, a reason to build walls. Sitting there on his lap, with his heart beating against my ear, his fingers trailing gently up and down

my arm, the glue began to lift from the shattered bits that had been my soul. Once that glue was gone, I'd break completely. Again. And I didn't know how I'd survive it this time.

Heymond had been my protector, and the little fragments of normalcy he'd given me had patched me up well enough to travel. But Valemar and I had unfinished business, and I could feel it bubbling up between the cracks. Especially with his own grief and horror washing over me. And so, my tongue tied, not wanting to start any of it.

"Do you want to rest?" Valemar asked. I nodded and slipped from his lap before he could carry me to the bed. Ghost images of him and Zhanet rose up as I approached it, but I blinked them away. I was tired. My soul was too tired to care.

I slipped between the sheets. The pillow smelled of him. A scent that was comforting and painful at the same time. Valemar's hand ruffled my hair, then he bent and kissed my cheek. Before I knew it, I'd slipped away into sleep.

I awoke to the dark and a body curled around mine. The rhythmic breathing told me that Valemar was asleep. I should have felt better — my husband was happy at my return. But Aedenfal oozed poisonous little tendrils that wormed their way into my heart, as if this place was kryptonite and I Superman from the old Earth myth. All my powers seemed to fade. Why couldn't Valemar have been in Torfin or Lendurig or even Snow Reach? Anywhere but here.

Piece by little piece, jagged glasslike shards ripped from my soul, cutting through my heart, revealing a bloody mess that in no way resembled flesh. Nothing remained of the strong, confident person

I'd been once upon a time, back when the *Palmas Cove* still had an engine. It would have been better if it had been me.

I must have stirred for Valemar woke. "What is it, my love?" he whispered.

Covered by the blanket of darkness, I spoke the words I had so often thought. "It should have been me."

"No!" Valemar shifted and laid his cheek on top of mine. "But it shouldn't have been Daria, either."

Tears flowed, wetting my face. Valemar lifted his and sat up. He patiently, gently wiped my tears, his hand tracing across my face as each one was erased, only to be replaced by another. When the last had dried, I turned and looked at him.

Valemar smiled and bent down to kiss me. It was little more than a feather's brush, but the kiss ignited a fire that burned through my veins. After so long with nothing but pain pumping through my body, I reached up and pulled him to me. I wanted to burn. Maybe … if I was lucky … the fire would finally consume me.

CHAPTER 30

I awoke the next morning, still breathing, the in and out of my lungs matched by the rise and fall of Valemar's chest — my pillow. I'd survived. I'd poured out all my pain, used our lovemaking as a crucible, sure that I was nothing but slag to be burned away. But somehow, I still existed.

I ran my lips across Valemar's chest, ready to try again. Surely this time I would disappear. Valemar's arms tightened around me, and he rolled us over. But instead of kissing me, instead of starting again, he simply brushed the hair out of my face. I would have brought his lips to mine, but the discerning look on his face stopped me.

"Will nothing make it better?" he asked, searching my face.

"This will," I said, pulling his hips closer.

Valemar chuckled. "As nice as that would be, it would only be a temporary fix."

I curled my legs around his. "Temporary is fine with me."

Valemar groaned as I pressed myself against him. "What do you need, Astrid?" he asked, his voice husky, his eyes half-closed.

"This."

Valemar's lips brushed mine. My eyes rolled into the back of my head. "And then what?"

"Life," I said, without thinking. "I need there to be life."

Valemar answered by drawing back his hips. A moment later, he was inside me, filling me. *Life,* I thought, hanging onto him as if I might drown. *All I need is life.* And then I lost myself in the dance that created it.

I lay on him after, as close to content as I'd been in an age. Ever since Glábac. "I'm sorry I sent you away," Valemar said, his fingers tracing patterns on my back. "I hated you for a long time." And like that, the darkness opened up again.

Valemar brushed his lips against my hair. "But when I thought you were gone, I realized I couldn't live without you. You are my heart."

"I'm sorry I lied." Valemar stiffened. "I let you believe I could have children. I didn't … I didn't know how to tell you without crushing your dreams. And inflicting the horror that would follow when I told you why."

"We're so vulnerable," Valemar whispered, and I knew that Reina must have passed along the details.

"That's why contact is forbidden. Your world isn't ready." I lifted my head. "And I ruined that. I ignored the rules and saved myself."

Valemar brushed back my hair and tucked it behind my ear. His finger traced the flat curve of it. "Shale would say that you were listening to a call you didn't know you heard."

"I don't know how do this." My voice was barely more than a whisper. "And people are already dying."

Valemar curled a lock of my hair around his finger. "They were dying long before you arrived. You can't blame Daria's death on

yourself. You make the strangers nervous. They tried to eliminate you."

A lump rose in my throat. I'd never asked. I hadn't wanted to confirm that it was all my fault.

I swallowed. "Reina found the culprit?"

Valemar nodded. "The kitchen girl had talked to a 'stranger' who said he was like you — from the moon. He convinced her that you pined for it, that you missed the taste and spices of your own world. He gave her a bag to add to your favorite lian tarts, but warned her that you would know if any of it was missing so not to taste it." I closed my eyes. *Foolish girl.* "She made the tarts."

"Only Daria ate them instead of me." I settled my head back on his chest. "She ... she said ... *Better me.* Her dying words were, *Better me.*"

Valemar's hugged me closer. I hadn't told anybody. Not only would it have made it real, but they might have agreed with me. *It should have been me.*

"What happened to the girl?" I asked.

Valemar sighed, and I knew with the sound that I wouldn't like the answer. "Reina had her hands cut off." My stomach rolled and I tasted bile. "And then she had her disemboweled as a warning to others." My eyes closed against the images that rose up, the violence. But I wasn't really surprised. This was the woman who'd hunted down the maskpol that had killed her horse. "I think I would have killed her on the spot," Valemar said.

His anger would have given the girl a quick death. Quicker than Daria's. I could kind of see Reina's wanting her to suffer, to think about what she'd done. True, it was Daria the girl had killed. Unintentionally, on all counts. But it had very nearly been Bánalfar's queen.

"Did they catch him?" I asked. With their shorter stature and pug-like nose, a Hormani would have stuck out as much as I did.

"No."

"So we know he wasn't a Cordair?"

"The girl said his ears were flat like yours. That's why she believed him."

"And do we know if he acted alone or with Cordair help?"

"We don't. But Vanerife is a long way from Rock Dorach. He would have needed assistance getting there."

Maybe, I thought. There were ways of getting close without Cordair help, though the risk would be greater that their craft would be spotted. The Archjarn were much more sparsely populated than most of Bánalfar. "How much did your mother tell you?" I raised my head, not wanting to hide from him if I had to do it all again — frighten someone to the core by revealing they were just an insignificant bug in the universe.

"That you're from the stars." Valemar smiled. "You told me that when you gave me the spyglass. The stars — not the moon. You told me that, but I just assumed ..." He closed his eyes and lightly shook his head. "Even the moon is far."

"About two hundred fifty thousand miles. More than three hundred fifty round trips from here to Vanerife."

Valemar's eyes grew large. "Mother and Father," he whispered. "You're ... you're from even farther?"

"We measured distance by the speed of light. You know how quickly a lantern illuminates a room once its shield is removed." Valemar slowly nodded — a look of utter awe frozen on his face. "We can move thousands of times faster than that. I am from a place about twenty thousand light years away. Meaning that today's light from your sun will reach my planet in twenty thousand years."

Something akin to horror crossed Valemar's face. "How is that even possible?"

"I don't know exactly. I'm dismal with mechanics. That's why I was in my room —" I broke off.

"Oh, Astrid," Valemar whispered. Concern replaced the shock.

"But I do know that the thing necessary to drive the engines — like water to a waterwheel, rowers to a barge, or wind to a sail — the fuel for those engines is being mined in the Archjarn. The Hormani will never give that up unless the Shororato —"

"The Shororato?" Valemar asked.

"The enforcers of law in the galaxy — all the stars you see and even the ones you can't." A new look of fear entered Valemar's eyes as he stared at me. "They would stop the Hormani. They would punish the Hormani, but —" I rubbed my fingertips on his chest. "— my guess is that the trade could continue in some fashion. The chalcopyrite olivine is too precious a substance to just leave behind, and contact has already occurred."

"Would they continue to arm the Cordair?" Valemar asked.

"No. And they'd take back the Awrakian armor. But trade would continue with the Cordair. That is why contact is forbidden. Your planet isn't ready to explore. You have no way to leave your world. Your technologies are primitive compared to what's out there."

"Besides being able to travel to the moon and beyond?"

"Part of the reason I refused medicine my first night here was that I'd already injected tiny things into me that would repair the damage and help stop any allergic reactions. I wanted them to do their job without interference."

"*She already has help.*" Valemar closed his eyes. "Shale knew it when she checked you." I shivered, and Valemar chuckled.

"She still scares me," I said.

"But you believe her now?"

I gave Valemar a wobbling head nod. "I have accepted that I may be the Moon Princess." My lower lip began to tremble. "But that's what got Daria killed." Valemar stroked my face. "And I still don't know what I'm supposed to do."

Valemar leaned forward and kissed me. "Then it isn't yet time."

"But things are getting worse. And what if they try again?" What if they killed Valemar instead? With the line of succession not settled …

Valemar placed his lips on mine again. "Hush, my *grabeg.*" His words buzzed on my mouth. "You are safe here."

I snorted. "Right. I was so welcome the first time I was here." And now I didn't have Daria as my shield. My face fell. Who *would* dress me?

My jaw trembled. Valemar gathered me into his arms. "Maybe they need to see a queen who can wield a blade. Maybe we should continue the training you began in Torfin." I stiffened. "Mainly jaldun. I know you need life around you." A breath I didn't know I'd been holding rushed out. "And Erris is here. We can continue that. We don't yet know what you are to do, but we should be prepared for anything."

I prepared myself for the arrival of my new dresser. A seldom used study attached to Valemar's rooms had been cleared out to make space for my new dressing room. Valemar seemed as reluctant to see me housed elsewhere as I was.

Part of me marveled at the change. My husband who had sent me hundreds of miles away now kept me closer than ever. It was as if he knew part of me just wanted to walk into the Leisna and let the water claim me. I had broken — had utterly shattered — and the prospect of putting myself back together overwhelmed me. The fulfillment of the prophecy hanging over me was like facing down a tidal wave, and I stood alone against it.

At least I had a familiar and welcome face to dress me. Brinna sent her servant, Iree, to me. Iree stood a good six or seven inches taller than me. She had beautiful flaxen hair and a kind face. In some ways, our roles had reversed from Torfin. This time, she was the stranger and I was the one who knew their way around.

"There you go," she said, tying off my braid.

I again gave thanks to Brinna. Iree had been used to my training in Torfin. I felt the back of my hair and checked my reflection. "Thank you," I said. "Daria —" I sucked in a breath and focused instead on the request. "Can you have a bath waiting for me when I return?" I gave her an apologetic smile. "I usually come back rather messy."

"Not to worry, my queen. I remember." Compassion filled her eyes.

I squeezed her hand and made my way down to the jaldun practice room. Valemar was already there, flowing in the deadly dance that made my heart beat faster simply viewing him. So strong. So powerful. So graceful.

So mine.

The ancient, instinctive part of my brain always sent out *breed now* messages whenever I watched him flow through the graceful, deadly moves. The lower parts of me quivered, remembering how I'd had him inside of me that morning.

As if he could sense my thoughts, Valemar gave a small chuckle and relaxed his grip his blades. "You don't need to stand in the doorway," he said.

I stepped in and clasped my hands in front of me so that I wouldn't be tempted to stroke him. "Sometimes, I just like to watch you."

Valemar put his blades together. "Observation is part of learning."

"Um hmm." I tightened my grip.

Valemar re-sheathed his knife and sword. He crossed to the small rack of spare blades and picked out a set for me. I walked to the center of the room and blew out a breath, then I spread my feet and bent my knees, lowering my center of gravity, and grounded my body and mind.

Valemar came behind me and slipped the knives into my hands. Unconsciously, I leaned back, pressing myself into his embrace. Valemar bent his head and nuzzled my ear. "You need to focus."

"Focus. Right," I said. His hands curled mine around the knives.

"Become one with the blades, with the ground. You are the blades. You are the force. Defend."

And then he slipped back to stand against the wall.

I am the blades. I moved into the first position then shifted my weight to begin the next. *Defend.*

Attack.

In a heartbeat, my vision clouded with an image of a smiling Hormani trader. *I killed her,* his smug smile seemed to say. My blades moved, I moved, to protect Daria. I was vaguely aware of the sound of Valemar shifting behind me. I kept my mind's eye on my invisible opponent and ran through the deadly choreography as if I were the only thing that stood between him and Daria.

Over and over, set after set, it didn't matter. This could have been real. It might one day be real.

"Astrid —" I sliced out, fighting off the attacker, as a hand touched my shoulder. Valemar's I realized a moment too late.

"Don't —" I panted as relief flooded by body. Valemar stood, unharmed, a couple of feet away. "Don't ever do that again." I wasn't sure how close I'd come to gutting him. Probably not very, but it still scared me.

Valemar closed the space he'd created to avoid my knife. "You don't need to kill them all today, my love." He lifted my chin and stroked my jaw. "Besides, you still need some energy for The Shadow. Erris will not be happy if you're panting along behind him."

That was true. He always hated when my heavy breathing gave him away. "Where I'm from, our soldiers train to the point of fatigue so that their endurance is increased."

"As do we. But one day at a time. It's been awhile since you trained like this."

I lowered my eyes as the reason for that reared its ugly head. But Valemar still caught it. "I am sorry," he said, drawing me to him.

"I'm sorry, too." I rested my head against his chest for a moment. "Would you have done it?" I asked. "Would you have married me if you had known that doing so would end your line?" Valemar's arms trembled as I spoke aloud the ugly truth.

"I don't know," he said, his voice a ragged whisper. "Perhaps that is why we aren't meant to see the future." I laughed. "What?"

"Says the man who married me because he thought he'd seen the future."

"I guess all we can do then is trust."

Erris decided the first thing I needed to learn was how to quickly and quietly exit a boat. We went out the watergate and were rowed to shore. Erris sprang from the boat into the weeds silently, smoothly,

and without causing a ripple in the water.

"Frick," I muttered.

"What was that?" he asked.

"Nothing," I said as the boatman chuckled, having guessed that I'd uttered a curse of some sort. I stood on the small board in the bow and stared at the grass that bent over the bank into the water. I'd always had someone to help pull me out before. I could see me sliding right down the grass and into the water.

"Looking at it's not going to make it easier," Erris said as I continued to calculate and visualize all the things that could go wrong. *I could end up doing the splits and fall in.* "Come on. Failure builds success."

I'd hated those words every time I'd heard them uttered by every coach I'd ever had. *Make a fool of yourself, Astrid. It's only by landing on your face you learn not to break your nose.*

I leaped, immediately knowing I'd put too much force onto my left foot while my right sprang for the bank. The boat shot back a good half meter as my right foot landed in then slid down the weeds. I grabbed handfuls as my momentum propelled me toward the dank, smelly edge. Erris managed to grab the back of my tunic and slam me against the bank before I could topple in. Thank God, though he was small for an Alfari, he was still larger than me.

"All right," he said as I gasped for air. "What did you do wrong?"

"Too much force," I panted as the boat bumped into the bank behind me.

"You pushed with your whole foot. You only want your toe. It's your center of gravity you move."

Now you tell me.

Over and over, Erris had me leap from the boat, correcting

my movements, never ceasing to amaze me with how he moved so much like a deer. It was only after we'd begun to attract attention — certainly not because my limbs were shaking — that we headed off into the trees and continued the work we'd begun in Torfin.

CHAPTER 31

I whimpered as I lowered myself into the water. Climbing the stairs to the beach had not kept me in good enough shape to keep up with The Shadow. Iree added an oil to the bath. It smelled like a cross between lavender and mint, and I recognized it as a muscle relaxant.

"I might stay here all evening," I said to her. "Just so you know." I didn't relish the communal meals in Aedenfal. Showing my face. Having them judge me.

Iree came around behind me and massaged my shoulders. I moaned and slid a little deeper into the water. Her hands worked along the length of my neck and started on my brow. She gently rubbed the center of my forehead and then brushed out across to my temples. I closed my eyes in bliss. "Some cultures believe that opens the third eye," I said.

"Third eye?" she asked, never stopping her ministrations.

"Our two physical eyes see the world around us. But the third eye is hidden, right in the middle of our forehead. With it open, you become more like the Mödatal."

"Do you wish to see, my queen?"

"No," I said. "For I fear what the future holds and don't want to observe any closer than it is now. A blind man might fear a maskpol but will pass by it unafraid since he does not see it."

"Unless it eats him."

"By the time you see a maskpol, it's already too late if it wants to eat you."

Iree hummed. "Very true."

She moved to the other end of the tub and started on my feet. My conscious mind began to make a comparison, chalk up the differences between how I was served before and now, but I pushed it away.

"Which dress for dinner?" Iree asked, shifting her attention to the knots in my aching calves.

"The red, I think." As I said it, I had a vision of me standing there, proud and terrible — well, as terrible as I could be at five foot four and a good six to eight inches shorter than everyone else — dressed as the Moon Princess. They'd cheered for me at my wedding. Maybe now that I had begun to believe it, they would, too.

I still shook as I entered on Valemar's arm, but my mantra of, *I'm the Moon Princess. I'm the Moon Princess. I'm the Moon Princess,* allowed me to hold my head high. And I had my warrior husband at my side.

I scanned the crowd and smiled. Padrid would be on my right, as per usual. Garris was seated at Valemar's left and Laera on her husband's other side. I detected Niah and Vienne at a table toward the center of the room. And the young man sitting with them was probably Reez. Though there were other red-heads in the room, I didn't see Zhanet. I wondered if Valemar had sent her away.

"Oh, my dear!" Padrid took my hand when I sat. "I hear you've been continuing your studies in Vanerife."

Loss washed over me, but I wasn't going to let this wonderful man know that his words had caused me pain. "*Two Hundred Years and Adzil Jaharan* —" Valemar's eyes flicked our way. "— and Enartin Carbrev's treatise on the treaty."

"You've read my father's work?" Valemar asked, abandoning his conversation with Garris.

"*Change can only come with a willingness to change.*" I said the words to my plate, unable to lift my eyes to meet Valemar's. Would he consider this an insult or a compliment? Would it pain him to think of his father and the mess the son now cleaned up?

"You're one of only —"

"Seven," I said. "As Harrig scolded me when I returned it."

"Returned it?" Valemar smiled. "He wasn't grumbling when he handed it over?"

My lip began to wobble but I forced it still. "Daria fetched it for me. She thought I needed to be prepared."

Valemar smiled gently. "She was right."

Padrid clapped his hands in glee. "Then we can discuss it!"

"He's one of the seven," Valemar said unnecessarily.

"So I see." *Only the hard things are those worth doing.*

Cracks traced their way along my heart, but I couldn't figure out if it was breaking or healing. Sometimes, with a wound, it was hard to tell.

"What did you think of my father's work?" Valemar asked me as we lay together hours later. I didn't want to answer. I didn't want to break the spell that our lovemaking had created: that somehow, draped together, our hearts beating as one, chest to chest, skin to skin, I was no longer me but a welcomed piece of the universe. To answer, I needed to become Astrid again.

I ran my lips gently across Valemar's chest, tracing the outline of the tattooed barat leaf near my chin as I thought. Then I raised my head and met his gaze. "I wondered if he'd been weak." Valemar flinched, and I laid a hand on his chest. "Because his actions hadn't solved the problem and he'd given away Bánalfar's lands."

A sad smile filled Valemar's face. "That is true."

"But he was quite the visionary. Quite the thoughtful visionary." I gave a small laugh. "Your parents' marriage must have been interesting."

Valemar smiled — a deep, yearning, yet tender smile. "He used to call her 'maskpol' —" Which I'd begun to translate as "hellcat." "— and she is much like one. He was always much more the philosopher. I think he'd probably read every one of the books in the tower library in Vanerife at least once." I smiled. That explained Harrig's possessiveness of the library a bit. "But he was a warrior, too. He's the one who taught me jaldun. He let Reina have her head but was quietly more than a match for her. She was a maskpol, is a maskpol, but he was an agré."

"That's a bird, right?"

"Yes. They're found in the mountains. Slightly smaller than you, they hunt animals. They have been known to take a maskpol or two."

"Remind me to stay out of the mountains," I said. Valemar laughed. "You must miss him very much."

"I do." Valemar ran his fingers through my hair. "Were both of your parents living when you left?" The look in his eye told me he wanted to know how much I had lost when I came here, how much pain was old, how much was new. My chin wobbled as I nodded, and I laid my cheek against his chest again. "Oh my, *grabeg*. I am sorry."

For now, I had lost both of mine, while he still had Reina.

"What does 'grabeg' mean?" I asked. "That's the second or third time you've called me that in the past couple of days, and it's not translating."

Valemar chuckled. "It's old Alfari. 'Gra' means 'little' and 'beg' means love." He gave me a squeeze. "You are certainly both."

I snorted even as my heart crunched. An insult and a compliment rolled into one. "Not my fault I landed on a planet of giants."

"So are you tall for … your people?"

"We call ourselves 'humans' or 'Earthlings,' for our planet is known to us as 'Earth.'"

"Like the ground?" Valemar asked.

Stupid chip. I must have used the Alfari word. "Yes, like the ground. But in our language, my language — for there are many — it is 'Earth.'"

"Ur – th," Valemar said, trying it out on his tongue. "And are you a giant among Earth people?"

"No." I sighed. "I'm on the short side, even there. But here I'm a dwarf. Do you have dwarves?" I asked. "People who never grow beyond the height of a child?"

Valemar chuckled and kissed the top of my head. "Yes, and you are taller than them. We don't get many, but we do have some. They are generally viewed with suspicion. Why would the Father and Mother have denied them height?"

The strikes against me kept adding up — hair color, ear shape, and now height. "How will they ever accept me?"

Valemar raised my chin. "They will believe it if you believe it. You wore the red dress to dinner tonight, proclaimed yourself to be the Moon Princess. What do you need to truly accept it?"

"To not feel like a fraud." I bit my lip then raised my head to

look in his eyes. "I'm not a savior. Everyone on the *Palmas Cove*, my ship, died. All of them but me. My last distress call, I lied. I said I was going with my ship to the sun —"

"*Vashedna!*" Valemar exclaimed. "You planned to burn?"

"No," I reminded him. "I lied. I should have been on it." I managed a weak smile. "I gave them the funeral of my ancestors who buried their dead by turning a boat into a funeral pyre on a lake or in the sea. And sending my ship into the sun left no trace that we'd been in your system. Nothing for you or the Shororato to find later.

"But I cheated. I cheated death, I abandoned my comrades, I broke the law, I lied by omission to you. I have done nothing honorable since I arrived in your star system, so why should your people accept me as a savior? Why should you?"

Valemar rolled us, coming to rest on top of me. "You have loved," he said. "You have loved so much that it has broken you."

I realized then that Valemar had changed position because he knew I would have run. There was no way I could push him off of me. I was trapped.

"I don't want to love."

"Maybe," Valemar said. "But you do. You loved Daria. You loved your crew. You've sought to protect all of Crenfor from the knowledge you carry with you. I even think that you love me." Valemar ran his fingers through my hair. "I don't think it was penance that caused you to deny yourself food those first days on the road to Vanerife. Initially, I thought it was your guilt at having lied to me. But now, after Daria …"

Valemar tightened his grip around me. "No more wanting to die, Astrid. You are alive for a reason. You —" He broke off and kissed me deeply. "You have become my heart," he said when he finally released me and I was breathless, without the capability of speech.

"You are mine," he said, and entered me with a thrust so great that I gasped. His fingers wound into my hair. "You are mine, and I forbid you to leave me."

His lovemaking was fierce, demanding. I hung on as he sought to possess every bit of me. When his ardor slowed, he looked down at me and kissed me. "You are mine," he said, gently this time. "You are my heart, you are my blood, you are my bone. Let me fill you so that you know you are loved."

It hurt. His words ripped the protective cover off my shattered heart and began to glue the pieces back together. Valemar continued to love me — softly, tenderly — as I lay in his arms, tears running down my face. Our lovemaking became a crucible, but one that burned off the sludge from my shattered life and slowly started to fuse it together into something new.

CHAPTER 32

The Mödatal's trick had become the truth. My blood and Valemar's blood were now bound, seeking the other out, longing for connection. I thought about that as I lay spent and trembling on Valemar's chest while he slept, worn out from the frantic activity and now reassured that I was indeed his.

I also thought about her words: *The time is coming when you will need to know that you are loved.* Had she foreseen Daria's death?

A wave of hate washed through me. How could she have seen Daria's death and not told me? How could she have let it happen?

Valemar stirred, and I forced myself back to calm. He didn't need to deal with this as well.

As Valemar settled back into sleep, I returned to my assessment. She'd followed me. Shale had followed me from Aedenfal to Torfin to Glábac to Vanerife and back. Wherever I'd gone, she'd gone. It was time for us to have another talk.

"Jaldun?" Valemar asked me when we rose in the morning.

"Later," I said, and kissed him. "I have something I need to do first."

After much debate on my part, I had Iree lace me into the sky blue gown. "Do you want me to go with you?" she asked when I drew out the red veil.

"No," I said and smiled at her before drawing the lace over me. "I know the way. And I'm not sure how long I'll be."

Four guards peeled off to accompany me when I walked out the gate of the High. Not the usual two. I received stares from the people I encountered along the way to the Cair and turned my thoughts inward. I had four shadows to deal with any unrest and, after last night, I knew that Valemar's anger should anything happen to me would be completely without mercy. He had, indeed, instilled a measure of confidence in me.

I knelt and prayed at the altar, offered up thanks for the husband I hadn't wanted, offered thanks for the friend who had loved and supported me and, in the end, given her life for me. I prayed for guidance, that I would be shown why I was here, what I was supposed to do.

I made the sign of the cross when I finished praying. It had always made me feel like I was drawing God into my heart and mind and lifting the burdens from my shoulders. And then I rose and walked through the door and down to Shale's room.

"Come in, Astrid," she called when I lifted my hand to knock. I rolled my eyes and opened the door.

Shale sat curled in a chair, drinking a cup of tea. A pot and an additional cup sat on the table before her. "Are you trying to get pregnant?" I asked before I closed the door behind me and removed my veil.

"A child would be a nice gift to the Mother and Father." A smile lifted the corners of her mouth. Shale's face became serene.

"Hmm." I sat down in the chair across from her and leaned back.

"Yes, I knew that Daria would die. No, I wasn't sure how." Her words were like blows, and I gasped as they hit me. "That is why you came to see me?"

"Warning would have been nice," I said, still grasping for equilibrium.

"Then or now?" she asked, then added, "No. Both."

I pressed a hand to my heart and continued to force myself to exhale. "You know that's one of the reasons I don't like you. Can't you be normal for once?"

"This is my normal," she said simply.

"It's not good for people. They need warning."

"Do they?"

"Yes!" I said emphatically. "They can't make good decisions when they don't have time to prepare."

Shale hooked an eyebrow. "So I should have told you not to get too attached to Daria since she was destined to die in your stead?"

"I —" But my jaw just dropped and refused to close.

"I should have told you that no matter how much you tried to shield him, that your truth would cause Valemar to send you away?"

"My truth?"

"Do you really want me to tell you what you are going to do next? Do you really want to know the consequences of your actions?" *Do you want to know the future, Astrid?* There was a weariness in her voice that hadn't been there before.

"What's it like?" I asked instead. "What's it like to see the future?"

Shale absentmindedly ran her finger along the rim of her cup. "Like looking at a tapestry. So many threads woven, yet moving."

"With one certain future? One certain path?"

"No. But the thickest one is usually the true one." She shivered. "It's why I so rarely speak it. Things can change the future." She

looked at me. "Telling you Daria was to die could have changed it. There was one where you sent her away, ate the tarts, and our land descended into chaos."

"So you let her die."

"I let *you* live."

I tucked my feet up under me and fell silent.

"I let you live and showed you that your husband loves you. I showed you that you love him. And it still nearly wasn't enough to save your life."

"You could see that I wanted to die?" I asked.

"I could see you fading away. I hoped to provide you with an anchor."

"I thought it was a trick."

Shale smiled. "I know."

"Was it a trick?" I asked. But she only gave me a silent, cat-like grin in return. I sighed and then poured a cup of the tea. What was the harm?

We sat silently, sipping tea for a while. Shale refilled her cup. Her eyes focused on the stream of amber liquid as it poured. "Ask," she said.

"Am I going to know what to do?"

She smiled and tucked her bare feet under her again. "You will." Tears filled my eyes. "Yes, it will be painful, but you will know what to do."

A lump caught in my throat as she answered my unvoiced question. Had she saved me from one death only to lead me to another? "How can you stand it?" I asked. "Knowing the future?"

Shale shrugged. "I am the Mödatal. That is my blessing and my curse." She sipped her tea. "I suppose it is better that I am here where my gift can be used. And I am glad it is me who got to see you. So many have looked for so long without answer."

I stared down into the tea that remained in my cup. "I guess I owe you my life. You seem to have saved it several times over the last few months." I wondered again if I was a lamb saved only to be led to the slaughter.

"Your life is not mine. It is Valemar's. Your blood was joined in this very Cair."

"But it was your vision that brought me to him."

"And then he stood and offered you his protection."

"Because you told him that I was the Moon Princess."

"He didn't have to believe me," Shale said. "And you didn't have to agree. You freely accepted the protection that he freely offered."

"Because I didn't want to die and it was clearly pointed out to me that I would."

"But the choice was still yours." I growled in frustration, and Shale continued. "And the choice was still his. He'd been looking for you ever since his father signed that treaty when Valemar was a boy. Long before the outsiders came. He has been drawn to you ever since he first heard the tale."

"Oh, it's a tale now, is it?" I muttered.

Shale shrugged. "A prophecy is just that — a tale. Until it becomes true."

So Valemar had spent years imagining what I would be. "He certainly didn't know what he'd be getting with me."

Shale gently laughed. "No, he didn't. But is it the myth or the woman he loves now?"

It was me. Something that still astounded me. "I wish …"

Shale brought her cup to her lips and glanced down at the floor, hiding her eyes. Hiding any answer that might be lurking in them. I sighed.

"Are you satisfied, my queen?" she asked.

Yes. I'd done what I needed to do. "Thank you for the tea."

"Any time," Shale said. "My door is always open for you."

It was a statement that earlier would have raised my hackles. But, somehow, this time it filled me with comfort.

After lunch, I had Iree braid my hair. Valemar came to collect me, but instead of taking me to practice jaldun, we headed for the watergate. My steps slowed and my heart pounded, remembering all too well what had happened the last time he'd taken over my practice.

Valemar reached back and took my hand. "We're just going to run in the woods."

And my body responded to his touch. It wanted to follow him anywhere. Even when a caged mouse part of my brain squeaked, *You can't trust him.* Because my heart did. It needed to trust that I had found a home here: with him, with these people. My brain would catch up in time.

My practice with Erris the previous day allowed me to jump out of the boat without making a fool of myself. It wasn't graceful, it was barely even pretty, but it was efficient. Valemar leapt out, landing by my side, and then, with a sly smile, he took off for the woods.

On Earth, children still play hide-n-seek. My favorite way to play the game had been outside in the woods with a base that hiders could return to, adding the additional element of eluding the seeker if we wanted. Inside, I liked the challenge of finding one place and staying hidden, curled up someplace where no one could find you. But outside … outside I liked knowing I could reach safety if I needed to.

It is a simple game. A throwback to when such things could actually be done, before thermal scans and chip-trackers. There are still ways of melting into a crowd, and most places rely on visual imaging. A few planets I've been to require you to provide DNA upon entry, and I still wonder if there are cloned copies of me out there in the galaxy. But overall, things haven't changed much. People have always been pursued and seek to hide.

So following my husband through the woods brought out the little girl in me. The giddy *"Ha! Ha! You can't find me!"* little girl. A glow ignited in my chest, and a melting sensation as little shards of me fused back together. Yes, I'd follow this man anywhere.

We walked and ran for miles, skirting around farms, though sometimes Valemar would whisper, "Go count their anapali," or "Go count their bohar." And I would sneak in and try and do it, conscious all the time that if I was spotted, everyone would know it was Bánalfar's queen skulking around their farm.

"Even it if were Erris or Heymond, the farmer would still know they didn't belong," Valemar told me when I apologized for my latest incomplete count. An odd glint entered his eye, though. Like he had a puzzle piece that I'd been searching for hidden in his pocket. And I knew, just like with killing the anapali, that this was a test.

"You are going to tell me someday," I asked. "Why you're having me do this?"

He drew me to him and kissed me, then traced a finger along my ear. "The Moon Princess should be prepared for anything," Valemar said.

I grasped his hips and pressed him against me. "Including having her husband take her in a field?" I asked.

"This is not Gladama," he said, even as he went hard.

"Don't want to get caught with your pants down?" I stroked his buttocks.

"Wife!" Valemar reached behind him and took my hands. "There will be enough time for that later."

"Promise?"

Valemar laced his fingers through mine and kissed me again. "Promise," he said, his lips still against mine.

I kissed him once more. "Then where to?"

Valemar kept hold of my left hand and led me back to the tree line. "I want you to open the next farmhouse door."

And suddenly, it wasn't a game anymore.

"I need you to sit Laera next to me tonight," I told Valemar on the way back to Aedenfal. If I'd been able to sneak into a farmhouse and leave a coin on the table without being discovered then I should be able to confront my true fears.

Valemar drew to a standstill. "But she doesn't like you."

It was hard to hear him confirm it. "And that is why. She is the steward's wife. Technically, beside me is her place."

"Technically, the queen gets to choose whomever she damn well pleases."

"And it will please the queen to have Laera tonight."

"Why, Astrid?" Valemar stroked my face.

"Because I need to make inroads, and I won't be sitting in the solar sewing." I brushed my fingers along the curve of Valemar's jaw. "Besides, dinner is only an hour or so, and the solar would be all afternoon."

Valemar squeezed my hand. "Then I will have Laera seated next to you tonight."

It was easy to say, harder to do. Bathed, dressed in my favorite gown of green, and with the gold circlet of barat leaves glittering on my head, I entered into dinner on my husband's arm. Laera's face bore a strange mixture of satisfaction and distaste on her face when she rose at our arrival.

"Thank you for the honor," Laera said as I sat.

I smiled. "My education has come far enough now that I don't need a tutor at my right hand."

Her eyes widened as if I'd surprised her with the reason she'd been kept away. She struggled to put a smile on her face. "Then I am glad your education has been so successful, my queen."

"A woman should have someone next to her with whom she can simply chat, don't you think?"

"Yes, my queen."

I took a drink of my wine. "I see Niah is sitting with a young man. Is that Reez?"

Laera looked over to their table. "It is."

"Have they married yet?"

"No, my queen. It is planned for next month's Blood Moon."

Just over a month from today. "I'll have to make sure I send them something. I'm afraid the king has me training —" I sensed Valemar's eyes on the back of my head. Laera switched her gaze to him. "— so my days aren't free."

"And what do you train for, my queen?"

"War," Valemar stated simply. "The queen trains for war."

Laera's face turned sickly pale. "You can't mean —"

"The signs are all there, my dear," Garris said from Valemar's other side. "And our queen knows these outsiders that are supplying the Cordair." Laera wasn't able to keep the disgust from showing on her face. I'd just managed to drop even further in her estimate of me.

"It's my job to drive them away," I said. "They've already attempted to kill me once." Laera muttered something I didn't catch, but Valemar put a hand on my shoulder.

"Would you perhaps like to go to Lendurig, *Grada* Laera?" Valemar asked. Conversation ceased. Quiet rippled through the

room as one table then the next fell silent. "If being in the company of the Moon Princess causes you so much distress then perhaps you should leave Aedenfal."

Laera lowered her eyes which were full of hate. "How do you know she's the one?" she asked, her voice laced with venom. "She's nothing like the moon. She's nothing like us."

Valemar's fingers bit into my shoulder. "Because I say she is. Because the Mödatal says she is. Because she was exactly where the Mödatal said she'd be."

"Because the Hormani tried to kill me." A puzzled look entered Laera's eyes, and I realized that I'd named the outsiders. "Would the outsiders, would the Cordair, send someone to Vanerife to kill me if I wasn't the key to their undoing?"

Whispers traveled through the hall. "Garris," Valemar said. "You may remain in Aedenfal if you choose, but your wife leaves for Lendurig tomorrow."

"You can't —" Laera said, half rising.

"I what?" The cold steel of Valemar's voice rang through the quiet hall like a sword unsheathed.

No one moved. No one breathed. Not even Laera who, too late, realized her mistake. "You ... you can't separate me from my family and friends." Her hushed voice was choked with sobs.

"You're lucky," I said to her. "Had you insulted Reina, she'd likely have had your life."

Laera blanched further and began to weep openly. "I am only sending you to Lendurig," Valemar said. "And the queen is right. The queen mother would be much less forgiving."

Garris bowed his head and stared at the table. His grim expression looked like he faced the axe himself. "If you want me to resign my king —" he said, and Laera began to wail. Garris winced and continued. "I will willingly do so."

Valemar's jaw clenched. His eyes closed as he slowly drew a breath. "Do you feel incapable of doing your job?"

"N-no, my king. But my disgrace —"

"At having a silly, small-minded wife? Does *she* do your job for you?" Snorts and chuckles echoed around the hall.

"N-n-no, my king."

"Would Aedenfal be better served by someone else?"

"I'm not sure," Garris whispered.

Valemar's jaw tightened again, and he slowly exhaled. "Bring me a list in the morning. The reasons why you should stay, and who might better serve me during the dark times to come."

Garris bobbed his head in agreement and rose from the table. He took Laera by an arm, hauled her up, and dragged her away, still crying. The room fell silent again.

"Anyone else feel like they can't live with the Moon Princess? Are there more of you who are willing to let the Cordair do as they please?" Valemar's icy glare roamed over each table.

"No, my king," the crowd muttered.

"This will serve as your warning. The Cordair seek to reclaim these lands, and they have finally found allies who may assist them in doing so. If you do not support the Moon Princess, then you do not support me. Treason will be dealt with as it always has."

Valemar rose and extended his hand. "Time to let them digest their meal," he said to me, and we walked from the room.

Valemar poured me a glass of wine as we waited for food to be brought to his study.

"You know the Hormani assassin only came to Vanerife after I

began meeting with the ambassadors," I said.

Valemar smiled. "No, he finally caught up to you in Vanerife. It's such a crossroads of people that it made it easier for him to slip in." He handed me the wine. "Do I need to remind you that I taught you to kill in Torfin?"

I blanched. "No."

"They'd been looking for a way to get to you for a while." Valemar's fingers tightened around his glass. "And it's my fault you were sent into danger."

"I'm sorry," I said again.

"I don't blame you for your deception," Valemar said. "Now. I certainly did then. But now that I've heard it all —" He turned to me. "I have heard it all, haven't I?"

I closed my eyes, trying to remember what I'd told him at this point. "I'm from the stars. I don't know how to save anyone. The Hormani aren't supposed to be here and neither am I. We're too different to have children together." I opened my eyes. Pain etched Valemar's face, and I knew there was one thing I hadn't told him. I set my glass down and went to him, wrapped my arms around him. "And I love you." I felt him melt. "I love you and would do anything for you. If you need to set me aside to save your line, I will go."

"Astrid." Valemar placed a hand over my mouth. "Don't you dare. Don't you dare even suggest such a thing."

I bent my head, and Valemar removed his hand. "I can't bear to have it all end with me," I said.

Valemar lifted my chin. There was an argument on his lips, but he didn't speak it. He simply kissed me. "We have other things to accomplish before we worry about that."

"Like what the hell I can do that would stop the Hormani," I said. Valemar burst out, laughing. "What?"

"It just surprises me when you curse," he said.

"Why?"

"Well, you're so small."

"I called the Mödatal a 'fucking charlatan.'"

"Fuck-king?"

I smiled. "It's a not very nice word that means what we do every night."

"Ah. A *kwarging* charlatan," Valemar said.

"Yes," I said. Though the "pig" part didn't really fit.

"What had she done this time?"

I buried my head against Valemar's chest. "Showed me a trick."

Valemar stroked my hair. "Are you going to tell me about it?" I shook my head. Even though I now believed it, there was something mystical about it. To speak of it might break the spell. And it was the one thing that now held me together.

A knock sounded at the door. Valemar and I drew apart as dinner was delivered. I sat and picked at my food. "Do you think Garris will leave?" I asked.

Valemar brought the bottle of wine over to the table and took a seat next to me. "I don't know."

"What will you do if he does?" I hadn't paid enough attention to the hierarchy at Aedenfal. I didn't know how everyone fit into the picture.

Valemar carefully cut into his meat and lifted the piece to his mouth. He chewed slowly. "I'll have to see what — or who — is on his list."

I put my hands in my lap. "I'm sorry."

Valemar reached over and grasped them. "It's not you, Astrid. By the Father! These people have been living too close to the Cordair for too long. Resentment has crept into their souls."

"A similar poison that the Cordair have."

"True." He squeezed my hand and went back to his dinner. "You're sure there's no way for you to contact the Shororato?"

"There's no way for me —" The words died in my throat. "There's ..."

"Astrid?"

I could feel my jaw working, but my mind skittered horribly away from the thought and tried to hide it from me. *"There's —"* My mouth moved, but there was no sound, not even air, to go with it. I vaguely saw, felt, Valemar put his hand on my arm. Then my hands rose on their own and covered my mouth, trying to stop me from speaking the words that could change everything.

"Astrid, what is it?"

If there was a way, I might be able to do it. I could call the Shororato. But it would change everything. *Everything.*

And I wasn't sure that was a price I was willing to pay.

CHAPTER 33

I sat frozen in my chair. Valemar called first for Ferrick who checked my pulse and looked into my eyes as I sat in a semi-catatonic state.

"Medically, she's fine."

"She's not fine!" Valemar thundered. "Look at her!"

"It's shock," Ferrick said. "I can't do anything for that. Her body has entered a protective state. If I drug her or bleed her or do anything to disrupt that after Vanerife …"

Valemar dismissed him with a grunt and a wave. He knelt by my chair and took my hand. "You can tell me. I will understand."

But he wouldn't. I knew he wouldn't. And so, I sat there in silence and tried to work out the thing on Earth they call a "catch-22."

I was not surprised when Shale arrived next. Valemar placed a chair for her in front of me, and she, too, took my hand.

"You can tell him."

I looked up, tears gathering in my eyes.

"You can tell him. This is why you're here."

A ripping sensation tore through my heart, lifting the glue from its shattered pieces.

"This is where you need to be strong, Astrid. This is where you need to trust. But Astrid —"

My eyes found hers again. True warning showed in her eyes.

"Only what you can do. Nothing more."

I felt my brow furrow.

"What comes after isn't clear." Though my eyes were on Shale's, it was as if she slipped behind a mask. A little tic in my brain that felt like the orange falsehood light of the ocular implant flashed a warning. Part of what she said was a lie. And she knew that I knew it. "Don't change the future. Follow the thickest cord. Tell him what you can do."

With Shale holding my hand, I spoke my words to the floor. "If you can get me onto a Hormani ship, I can contact the Shororato."

Shale embraced and kissed me then slipped from the room.

"Why does this frighten you so?" Valemar asked, taking her place.

"It's sure to be the last thing I do," I said, my voice as dead as I now felt. "And I'm a coward."

"How can you think that being frightened of this would make you a coward? Astrid —" Valemar wanted me to look at him, but I wouldn't. Couldn't. "It frightens me as well. The idea of you going into Cordair territory … onto a stranger's ship … what if you were caught?"

"I'd be dead," I said simply. They wouldn't bother to hand me over to Oluendi. The Hormani would have their fun with me and then they'd kill me. And then Bánalfar would suffer.

"I'm not losing you," Valemar said. "You can teach someone else how to do it."

I laughed. "Could you send a blind and deaf man out into the forest to hunt? Could he actually catch anything? Because you have

no idea — none! — what our technology is like."

"Your ship. The one you came on. Someone could practice on that."

Wild, hysterical laughter bent me double. "Nothing works! And even if it did, my ship is more like an outhouse compared to what we'd be facing. Useful if you want to take a crap but not much good for anything else."

My laughter gave way to tears. I pressed my eyes into my knees and let it take over.

"Hush." Valemar knelt beside me, stroked my hair, then pulled me to him. I went limp. I was safe here in his arms. Valemar rocked me back and forth and whispered words of comfort to me, like a child being soothed after a nightmare.

Which it was.

Shale was right. This was why I was here. Only I could contact the Shororato.

But we were all going to pay the price when I did.

Valemar carried me to bed. I knew gossip would fly like arrows through the High, but I couldn't get my legs to hold me. If they did, I'd be one step closer to being a savior. I didn't want to be a savior. I wanted to hide in my room and let the danger pass and then deal with the aftermath. I truly was a coward.

Valemar lay down next to me. "What scares you about this? Having you attempt this is a theory, just a theory. I'll not risk you for a theory."

"But it needs to be considered." I sighed. "In theory, it should work. Get me aboard a Hormani ship and I can use the comm program —"

"Comm program?"

"Communications program on the —" He was never going to understand. "It would be like me going to the Cair and asking Shale to use her Mödatal abilities to send a message to Reina. Another seer would receive it and tell her." *This is going to be a longshot since they can't actually do it.* But it was the best comparison I could think of.

Valemar's brow wrinkled. "So you'd talk to Shale?"

"Yes."

"And she'd send a thought or some kind of invisible karawack to another seer?"

"Yes."

"Okay." A glimmer of understanding shone in Valemar's eyes. "So you send the message, and then?"

"The Shororato come."

"And make the Hormani leave."

I sat up. "If by some freaking miracle I'm able to send a message, the Hormani will probably leave as soon as they realize what I've done."

"That would be a good thing."

"That would," I said, making myself agree with him.

"And this frightens you, why?"

I laced my fingers together to stop their trembling. "Because the Shororato will inspect your planet. They will need to assess what the Hormani have done."

"And they will stay, yes? You said something about chalk?"

"Chalcopyrite. Yes, the Shororato will stay. And your people will never be the same."

Stopping there kept my promise to Shale, but I wanted Valemar to understand how much things would change. "My people, my planet, had found ways to travel to our moon and our neighbors

in the solar system — the other planets. We had colonies on worlds that had never seen life before." Valemar sucked in a breath and then slowly exhaled. "And we still weren't prepared to meet people who could travel between the stars. My planet had spent hundreds of years searching for those … unseen signals in space. Proof that there was other life out there. And then one day, they heard it." I took a deep breath. "And a few days later, the Shororato showed up.

"If my arrival had been different, if I had killed everyone who attacked me, with weapons or methods you couldn't understand, what would you have done?"

Valemar went pale. "Fought."

"The Cordair are not going to be happy when the Shororato arrive. They seem to be a 'shoot first, ask questions later —'" Valemar's eyebrows inched together creating a furrow on his brow. "Old Earth expression. Someone surprises you —"

"Got it. You fire your arrow before you ask what they're doing."

I laughed at his simplistic, yet accurate, interpretation. "Yes." Then I sobered. "These people here, your Alfari, can't imagine traveling to the moon. They don't like that I am different. What are they going to do when the Shororato appear in ships that can fly? There was mass panic on my planet when they showed up on mine, and we had *thought* we were ready for it."

Valemar stroked my face with a finger. "I begin to see your pain. You would not change my people — our people. But the Cordair …" Valemar gave a heavy sigh.

I put a hand on his arm. "I know."

Garris stayed. Laera departed for Lendurig at first light. She was not the only one. By noon, a small but steady trickle left Aedenfal

headed either north or west, people who had heard that the king claimed war was coming. That the Cordair had friends who would help them reclaim the lost lands.

I remained inside the High, afraid for my life. Valemar and I had lit a match, hoping to create a backfire, but I was now afraid of the wind. It wouldn't take much to send that fire racing back toward us instead of creating a protective swath.

I dressed on my own. Braided my hair on my own. Lost in my thoughts, I dismissed Iree as soon as she'd brought my breakfast. I walked down to the jaldun practice room, selected my blades, and went through the movements on muscle memory alone. In my head, I ran through what it would take for me to even get to a comm panel should we ever find a Hormani ship.

Valemar was out, doubling the efforts to find one. Based on the information Reina had sent him from Vanerife, he'd had time to ascertain that they weren't living openly with the Cordair. They'd probably been on the planet less than one Earth year.

I switched into the next kata and let myself mull over the concept of time. Days were longer on Crenfor. I wasn't sure by how much, but at least two, maybe as much as four, hours. Blood Moons came every thirty days, almost the same timing as full moons on Earth. I had no idea how long a year was. They did have four seasons, and we were now into autumn. I'd never asked how far north the snows came in winter. Not that I'd get to see winter. Unless we couldn't find a ship before snow came to the Archjarn. Then footprints would give us away no matter our stealth. I wondered if our enemies would let me live to see the spring.

I felt more than heard a brush of movement on the stones behind me. I turned, blades raised defensively, to find Valemar standing there. "Aedenfal is losing citizens," I said.

Valemar walked over to the rack and armed himself with a sword and a knife. "Others will come to replace them. The Alfari do not want to see Aedenfal fall."

My mouth turned up into something resembling a smile. "A rhyme." Valemar came to stand behind me. "What does 'Aedenfal' mean?"

"The town is older than the Alfari — here, anyway. It means 'fire fall.'" A shiver marched across my skin. "I suppose that's why the High has the 'rabbit warren,' as you like to call it, of defense. The skies used to burn here."

"Mother and Father that they won't again," I said.

I had expected Valemar to lay his arms over mine and teach me a new form, but instead he pressed his back to mine. "Today we work on defense. I want you to learn what it feels like to have someone on your flank, someone you can count on to defend that side. Your muscles, your nerves will be heightened in a fight and learning to trust someone else's movements at your back can be difficult. It can be the difference between knowing you're protected and knowing you're in danger."

I swallowed. "I could never keep up with you. And if I'm — we're — fighting on two sides, wouldn't the situation be … bad?" I wanted to say "hopeless" but that was too depressing, even for me.

"You train —"

"Yeah, yeah. So your body learns what to do and your mind can focus on other things." I blew out a breath. "Fine. Let's do this." I raised my blades. Then furrowed my brow. "How are we going to do this?"

Valemar chuckled. "Imagine someone standing between you and Daria again. You get him while I watch your back."

"Right." This was never going to work. Valemar would never watch my back. He'd take the front.

But I could watch *his* back.

I bent my knees and became one with the ground. Our blades began to twirl, and I imagined Valemar trying to get us out of here while I gave him time to do so.

"Astrid. You're defending."

"Of course, I'm defending," I snapped. "Do I really think you'd let *me* take point?"

Valemar grunted. "No, I suppose not. Unless you saw the smug Hormani *kwarg* who poisoned Daria."

"True," I said, saving my breath. "But I'm not sure which one it was."

"Does it matter?" Valemar asked. I was both pleased and irritated that his breathing hadn't changed at all.

"Can't kill them all."

"Well, you could try."

I rolled my eyes and concentrated on the parries and thrusts of my knives. At first, I was distracted by Valemar's movements behind me, and mine, though rote, were slow, sluggish. But as my back got used to the feel of him there, I began to develop a sense of when he'd press or retreat, and the two of us began to move as one.

"Tomorrow we'll add Orin and one of the others," Valemar said when we finished. "Use blunted spears and truly spar."

I could feel the bruises already.

I dressed in red again for dinner. I wore the crown with the cabochon rubies that I'd married in. And I left the place next to me empty. Who would sit at my right hand was a question I wanted Aedenfal to ask themselves. I sat at Valemar's right, Garris at his left,

but who would take the place of honor at the Moon Princess's —
Bánalfar's queen's — side?

Had we been in Torfin, it would have been Brinna. There were
several I wanted — Heymond, Orin, Erris, even Shale. Any of them I
would have welcomed, but instinct told me that an empty place would
make those who remained squirm. Who would rise to help me?

I had braced myself to see resentment on the faces that greeted
me, but there wasn't any. Padrid even glowed with pride, as if he
was responsible for my transformation. For I did feel transformed.
The Astrid who had first sat at this table had been in survival mode.
Frankly, she'd just hoped to survive her head injury. And then her
wedding night.

I now felt as if a sword hung at my throat, and the moments were
rare that I didn't feel its pinch, didn't know what the end result would
be. And yet, I was so much more than I had been. I was still PS Carr
at my core, but I had grown into Astrid Carbrev. It was the name I
wanted on my memory stone, though my title wouldn't be there.

In reality, my name would probably be on a plaque at Agçay
headquarters on Earth, listed with the rest of the crew of the *Palmas
Cove*. Once the Shororato arrived — if I was successful — then they
would write their own version of history. And I was slowly making
myself okay with that. These people needed me.

It generally wasn't good business to come down on a side of
right or wrong. Those ideas were usually just a matter of vantage
point. Were the Alfari wrong for keeping the Cordair from their
former lands for two thousand years? The Cordair would say, "Yes."
Having been to Gladama, I would say, "Show me I can trust you."
But then, Enartin had done that and the Cordair had broken his trust.
No, the trees and the land needed to be protected. Off-worlders had
disturbed the balance, and it was up to me to put it right.

I sighed and made sure my smile was still in place. I knew so few of the people in the hall. Just the weaver's family really. And they were still there. But then, their livelihood was tied up in anapali wool.

I had one of the servers ask Vienne if she wanted to join me. Heads turned and followed my finger as I pointed her out to him. Even from here, I could see her face turn red.

"Is that Arken's wife you're sending for?" Valemar asked me. The eyes in the room followed the server's progress.

"Is he the weaver?" I asked, as the server bent and whispered the invitation to Vienne.

"Yes."

"Then, yes. I am."

Valemar washed down the piece of meat he'd been chewing. "What do you think you are doing?" he asked as a grave-faced Vienne now made her way to the high table.

"Making sure a wedding goes through." I lifted a smile in place as Vienne joined us and gestured for her to take a seat. The server poured her some wine and passed a plate of meat to her.

"My queen," she said, her eyes fixed on the table. "To what do I owe —" She swallowed. "Owe the honor?"

I realized she was afraid that she, too, would be sent from Aedenfal. She hadn't been any more welcoming that Laera. "I was glad to see that you and your family are still in Aedenfal. I wanted to see if the plans were still going ahead with Reez and Niah's wedding."

"Nothing has changed, my queen," Vienne whispered.

"That is good because so much else has. Please let me know if there is anything that you, or they, need. Aedenfal needs a celebration." I looked at Niah and Reez, their faces full of worry, and smiled at them. "We need life to go forward. If the worst comes, then they can cling to each other as husband and wife." There would be no "best" for them. They faced either the Cordair or the Shororato. "Let me make sure that there is at least some joy in Aedenfal."

The next night I had Cadalin seated beside me, though I knew the sight of her belly pained Valemar. We talked of babies, of cloth, of my time in Vanerife. "I pray that you, too, have a child," she said, and rubbed a place on her stomach that had bounced from a kick from within.

"That has got to hurt," I said.

"Sometimes," Cadalin said, and pressed her fingers against the spot, moving the offending foot. "And it's not much fun when they kick your bladder. But mostly it's just such a miracle, knowing there's another life inside you."

"Do you have everything you need?" I asked. "Is there anything at all that I could help you with?"

Cadalin's gaze swung to Valemar then fell. "My husband no longer wishes to travel," she said in a small voice. "It's not just the baby. He fears being away from me and ..."

"Having you here alone if something happens," I finished when she didn't.

"But if he can't sell the cloth ..." Cadalin wrapped her arms protectively around her belly. Unconsciously, I thought, for her eyes were blank as she stared at the table.

"Is there an apprentice or journeyman who can travel for him?" Valemar asked from over my shoulder.

"None he'd trust with so great a task, my king."

I bent my head and whispered in Valemar's ear. "I know you would find this difficult, but couldn't we have her move in here? Surely it would put her husband at ease, knowing that she and the child are protected. And trade must continue."

I hated the pain that entered Valemar's eyes. He'd hear a child crying, all the while his own cradle would remain empty. And yet —

"The queen and I would like to offer you our hospitality *Grada* Cadalin," Valemar said. I took his hand under the table. "Bánalfar needs your husband's trade. Perhaps he will rest easier with the assurance that you and his child are guarded well."

Cadalin's eyes grew round and her mouth dropped open. "Someone should be using the solar since I don't have much time to sew these days," I said.

"Thank you, my queen. You are too kind."

"Are you going to invite them all here?" Valemar asked me later that evening.

"In case you haven't noticed," I said, "I don't have many friends. Many women friends. Cadalin and Niah were the closest thing I had here. Even with Laera glowering at me and Daria the whole time."

Valemar ran a hand through my hair. "I hadn't really paid much attention."

"Men don't," I replied. I kissed his chest. "Is it going to bother you horribly, having a child within these walls?"

Valemar rolled us over. "Yes," he said. "I can't imagine what my father went through, knowing my mother had been able to give birth and then nothing."

"Do you know what became of your brother?" Valemar's eyes widened. "Did you not know?" I asked.

Valemar slowly shook his head. "Brother. I had a brother." He rolled off of me. "Such a different concept than 'child.'" Valemar blinked then rubbed my arm. "No, I don't know what became of Reina's child. Moon children are given to the Cair when they're fifteen days old. Time enough for mothers to pass along their strength and then given to other Moon Mothers to nurse."

"Such a different concept," I said.

"Why?" Valemar asked. "What do you do with your moon children?"

"Well, as I told you, we don't have Blood Moons. In this time period in my planet's history, a man's sons were everything. Children born outside of marriage were considered scum, their mothers even worse."

"Their mothers?"

"Well, yes. She'd let someone who wasn't her husband bed her. And if she bedded someone else's husband, well — she was the one leading the poor man astray. Muddying the lines of succession."

"So men were weak on your planet?"

"No. They were like rutting animals, trying to produce as many children as possible."

A puzzled frown grew on Valemar's face. "But it takes two people to produce a child. So why wouldn't they want the child? Why would the woman be looked down on?"

I sighed. "In your mother's case, your father would have never chosen her. She'd have already proven that she'd take someone else to bed. How could he be certain that you were actually his?" Understanding grew in Valemar's eyes. "And your brother wouldn't have disappeared into anonymity. Someone would still have known he was there. Even though it was through your mother, he would have been steps away from the throne, the only brother of the king."

"Is that why you asked?" Valemar said. "Are you worried about the succession?"

"Yes," I answered.

"I don't think I like your Earth," Valemar said.

"Why is that?"

"They seem cruel. Greedy."

"That was hundreds of years ago," I told him. "Now we don't care who marries whom or if they even marry. We don't care where children come from, only that they're loved. Our kings are few, and even then, they have little power."

"What? How does that work?"

"The people rule themselves by elected committee."

"How do people learn to lead? How do they learn what is needed to keep a country together?"

"They do it by committee," I said.

Valemar snorted. "How foolish." He looked at me with suspicion. "Do you think committees are better than kings?"

"I think a good committee is better than a bad king and that even a good king needs to listen to the advice of others."

Valemar's mouth thinned. I couldn't tell if he was happy with my answer or not. "Good answer, wife," he finally said. But he didn't smile. Valemar caressed my face with the back of his hand, a frown growing.

"What is it?" I asked.

Valemar blinked and his hand cupped my face. The corners of his mouth turned up briefly before they fell again. "You've got me to wondering about the succession."

"Do you have any moon children?" I asked. Valemar shook his head. "I'm sorry."

"So even if it weren't you … our incompatibility … I …" He stopped. Valemar picked up and kissed my hand. "That's why I wanted you. Her. *Create new life.*" He smiled "I'd hoped the Moon Princess would give me children. That this curse hanging over my family would finally be lifted. Orbach Carbrev had three sons and a daughter."

"Yareena," I said.

"You've been studying my family tree."

"It's come up."

"So you know that Dönal only had Ötten and Lareen —"

"Who married Adzil."

"And Ötten only had Caparen, and Caparen only had Enartin, my father, and my father only had me."

"One hundred … one hundred fifty years of loneliness," I said.

Valemar sighed. "I think that's why my father gave the land to the Cordair despite what he says in the treatise. He feared our line dying out and what the Cordair would do then."

"Surely one of your grandfathers had a plan. What about Toren's children?"

Valemar frowned. "An heir would probably need to come from there. I doubt the Alfari would accept a R'Keshan king."

I opened my arms and drew Valemar to me. "I'm sorry I brought it up."

Valemar stroked my face. "Why do you look so sad Astrid? It's not your fault."

"No," I said. "It's not."

But I could only think of one way to fix the problem, and it was all tied up with the rest.

CHAPTER 34

I visited the Cair and offered blood with my prayers. Before Crenfor, I'd found the idea somewhat abhorrent. But now I understood. Words were easy: things tossed out. A hope. A wish. A prayer. All fleeting moments. But allowing yourself to be cut took courage. Giving away part of yourself made it more meaningful. Blood spilled made something more valuable.

Just like the marriage mark on my finger. A ring was easily slipped off. Part of the reason some cultures tattooed theirs on. I'd been told tattooing was painful. But my cut with its butterfly-like scar …

I'd offered myself. Opened up myself. And mingled my blood with my husband's. Everything marriage was — is — was represented in that scar. No taking it off. It would always be with me. It couldn't be erased, just like time couldn't be erased.

Four guards escorted me to the Cair. Four guards escorted me back. I'd feared what people in the Low might think of me, but any haters appeared to have left. The people I encountered wore serious expressions, but I didn't see suspicion in their eyes or the smoldering resentment I'd feared.

I changed into my practice clothes, had Iree braid my hair, and went to join Valemar for jaldun.

"We may have a lead on where the Hormani are staying," Valemar told me when I arrived.

My stomach dropped. I went over to the rack to select my blades. "In town or on their own?"

"On their own."

I nodded and wrapped my hand around a knife. "Astrid." Valemar laid a hand on my shoulder. "Tell me what you're going to need to do. We need to prepare you."

I reluctantly removed my hand from the knife. I was stronger with them in my hands, but I wouldn't — couldn't — be carrying them with me when I did this. "I need to get onboard their ship. Hopefully it is a ship. Finding a comm panel could prove difficult."

Valemar rubbed my shoulders. "And then?"

I sighed. How I'd ever accomplish the next part without being discovered, I didn't know. "There are a couple of places a comm panel would be. The bridge. The sick bay. And the captain's quarters."

"So you're going to need to move through the ship? It wouldn't be something just inside a door?"

I looked over my shoulder and smiled at him. "'Yes' to your first question and 'no' to your second."

I had expected the impossibility of my task would frightened him, but Valemar just nodded thoughtfully. "Then we should have you practice moving quietly," he said. As if that were my only problem in the scenario. He patted my shoulders twice then gripped them. "Come. You won't need your blades. Let's find you someplace to rehearse."

Rehearse what? I wondered.

I stared at the shields laid out on the floor. "This isn't exactly what I meant," I said to Valemar.

"You said the floor was metal."

"Of a sort. It has a composite on it that keeps you from slipping." With my leather soled shoes, the "floor" before me was basically a skating rink.

"Then you'll be overprepared," Valemar said practically.

"Ballet dancers at least get rosin," I muttered.

"What was that?"

I raised my voice. "Graceful dancers on Earth get to put dried tree sap on the bottom of their shoes so they don't slip when they're on stage."

"You're not going to be dancing," Valemar said.

"No, I'm going to be doing the splits," I said under my breath. Handle side down, every shield was a curved tray. Valemar was right about one thing. If I could silently and efficiently traverse a room of these, getting down the hallway of a Hormani ship would be easy. Except for the part of being seen.

I tiptoed out and cautiously put one foot then the other onto a shield. The jaldun practice had helped my center of gravity. My knees bent. The muscles of my core engaged. From the corner of my eye, I saw Valemar lean back against the wall and cross his arms. I reached out a foot for the next shield.

Thunk ... thunk, thunk, thunk. A ringing clang filled the room as I swiftly moved one foot then the next, racing to keep my balance as the shields rocked under me. "The floor of the Hormani ship will be stable," I said. My arms windmilled, and I heard Valemar chuckle.

"Overprepared," he said.

I carefully turned. "You may not have noticed this about me, but

I have been known to trip over my own feet."

Valemar's eyebrows rose. "You're joking."

"No, I'm not."

Valemar frowned in concentration. "Must be an Earth or space thing. You've been fine here."

I sighed and turned back around. "When I fall and break my nose, at least you've been warned."

But I didn't fall. The exercise was much like jumping out of the boat. There were moving parts and my balance to get right. After the first five minutes, I gave up trying to be quiet and just went for being efficient. I didn't trip. I didn't fall. And eventually my hammering, elephant-loud feet became just a patter.

Valemar took my arm and pulled me off when my limbs began to shake. He brushed the flyaway ends of my hair from my flushed and sweaty face and kissed me. "See. Nose still intact." I didn't have the breath to argue with him.

Niah and Reez were married the morning of the Blood Moon. Valemar and I attended dressed in our full regalia. When the Möd cut Niah's finger, Valemar's hand found mine and held it tight. I winced with Niah, remembering the pain, but the joy on her face when Reez joined his hand with hers and they moved forward to offer their mingled blood to Father Sea made my heart swell. I'd been so frightened, so in over my head and just hoping to survive at my own wedding.

I leaned against Valemar and squeezed his hand. Now I would willingly go through it all again. My vows would be real and not just words.

I had been very lucky. Valemar had always respected me. I was sure that was what had made the difference. He could have used

me poorly. Married me and then imprisoned me. Kept me as a plaything. Or sent me somewhere to languish in neglect while he claimed the title of Consort to the Moon Princess. I would like to think I would have sensed those intentions. Just like I had known from the moment I saw him that Raislos wanted me dead. But instead, I had a husband who loved me. And in return, I would do anything for him.

The wedding feast was a wedding luncheon. In different times, it would have been a wedding dinner with all the guests drifting away to mate. But a cloud of fear hung over Aedenfal. Many of the inhabitants had asked for the draught, wanting their wits about them when darkness fell, just in case the Cordair chose to attack.

Valemar and I ate dinner in our rooms, and I brought my husband to bed as evening fell, before the full flush of moon lust was upon him. The moon came out as he climaxed, leaving him shuddering in my arms but quickly recovering. He kissed me, slipped from bed to dress, and went to join the patrols.

I lay on my back after he'd departed, and a half-forgotten conversation with Amy, my sister-in-law, brushed at the edges of my mind.

My doctor says to cross my ankles, bring my knees to my chest, and try and keep Finn's seed inside me as long as possible.

Finn and Amy had spent more than a year trying to get pregnant. Even though science could tell a woman when she was ovulating, fertility could still be a problem. Amy had done everything to avoid the hormone injections and mood swings that would follow. And something eventually worked, for the next time I saw them Amy had been expecting Henry.

What the hell. I crossed my ankles, brought my knees to my chest, and tipped my hips. I'd made my own pledge at the wedding. And

while Valemar's dream was impossible and nothing would come of
the attempt, I owed it to my husband to at least try.

Seven days after Reez and Niah's wedding Valemar led me
through the dark recesses of Aedenfal's basement levels, deeper than
the karawack nursery, to a locked door that stood at the end of a
passageway. The hairs on the back of my neck prickled. Everything
about it said, *Dungeon.* My limbs began to shake as Valemar took out
a heavy key and unlocked the door.

"Do not speak to anyone of what you see down here," he said
to me.

I managed an "okay" and followed him past the threshold onto
a small landing at the top of a dark, narrow staircase. Valemar locked
the door behind us and led the way down. A low-ceilinged passageway
extended about forty feet from the last step to another heavy door. A
substantial lock sat beneath the handle of this one as well.

But it wasn't locked. Valemar pushed the door open and stood
aside. A large room lay beyond it. Empty wooden cages sat in stacks
four-high around most of the room. I walked in, and the hairs on my
arms joined those on the back of my neck. A humming noise filled
the air, almost like electricity. Two men seated at a table at the far end
of the room rose at our entrance. One was a member of the King's
Guard. The other I'd never seen before.

The table before them was piled with tubing and needles. But
there was no antiseptic smell of medicine here. My nose caught the
crisp smell of leaves and something sweet. An odor that reminded
me of animal sweat. Like horses, but not.

Valemar placed a hand on my shoulder. "There are few who
know about this place, and the information needs to stay that way.

If you can't —" Valemar's voice trembled, and he broke off. "If you can't handle the secret it contains, you will be drugged and sent back to Reina."

Involuntarily, I took a step back and bumped into him. "You can do this, Astrid. But this secret is worth your life."

"What is here?" I asked. *Medical experiments*, my mind screamed. *And you're next!*

"The secret that has allowed us to find the Hormani ship."

"What?" I looked over my shoulder. Pride glowed in Valemar's eyes.

He took my hand. "Look around. What do you see?"

"Cages," I said. "Lots of cages. And tables of medical instruments. Chairs. That cushioned bench. Boxes of what smell like leaves. Those two gentlemen."

"And what do you sense?"

I removed my hand from Valemar's and locked my fingers together to stop their shaking. I slowly surveyed the room. The humming noise lifted and vibrated along every hair on my arms. I had the sense I was being watched. I had the sense of fear.

"We're not alone," I whispered.

"No. We're not."

"What's here?" My eyes darted around the room. Something, no *somethings* were hiding here. *In the corners?* The dark recesses were empty. Everywhere I looked was empty. But there was a presence, the humming noise, and a palpable sense of fear in the room.

"Something we'd wondered about for hundreds of years."

The gentleman who wasn't with the King's Guard picked up a pail from underneath the table, set it on top, and took off the lid. It was full of a substance that looked like milk or white paint. He pulled on a pair of heavy leather gloves and walked over to one of

the cages. The humming noise increased. The man reached in and a frightened squeak filled the room as straw went flying.

I gave a startled gasp. "There's something in there!"

The man returned to the table, his hand clamped around nothing but air. The squeaking continued.

"Oh, my God," I said, and looked around the room. Even before he dipped his free glove into the paint and started to wipe it onto the nothingness in his other hand, I knew that there was some kind of creature there. That none of the hundred or so cages were actually empty. My hands covered my mouth. All the cages contained something that was the best chameleon I'd ever seen.

"We call them *heichdar*," Valemar said.

I watched in mingled horror and amazement as a small, furry creature began to appear beneath the paint. Perfect cloaking technology existed but was illegal for use by everyone except the Shororato. This animal had some way of making itself as invisible as the best of their technology. *The secret that has allowed us to find the Hormani ship.*

"I need to sit down." I took a seat as far away from the table and the crying animal as I could. "What is he painting on the heichdar?"

"Liquid chalk," Valemar said. "He needs to be able to see the animal to insert the needle."

"Needle?" My stomach rolled, and my mouth filled with the sour taste of bile.

"There's something in their blood that makes them invisible," Valemar said.

I clenched my jaw and willed my stomach contents to stay put. "So … this King's Guard …"

"Alill," Valemar said.

"Is going to have to drink the blood?"

"Directly from the animal."

Sweat broke out on my forehead and I felt somewhat faint, but I forced myself to watch. Valemar didn't say it, but I knew where this was going.

The wrangler picked up a tube, a needle already attached to one end, bent the open end over his fingers, and found a vein or artery in the animal's hind section with practiced ease. Alill took the end of the tube from the wrangler's fingers and drank when the blood began to flow. He shuddered slightly as he swallowed. Just a few times, and then the wrangler removed the tube and replaced the animal.

Alill took a seat on the cushioned bench and closed his eyes. He slowly breathed in and out but I could hear a rattle to it. The wrangler removed another animal and the process began again.

"It generally takes three animals before the body begins to produce the wax that hides them," Valemar said.

Alill drank again. His breathing became labored and his body began to shake. "Alill doesn't have fur. How will he hide his clothing, his hair?" I asked. I sincerely hoped he wouldn't strip. Even though I wouldn't be able to see him, I still didn't want him naked in front of me.

"He drank heavily before he came down. He'll use the wax in his saliva to comb though his hair. When he's had enough of the blood, his body should produce enough of the wax to work it into the light fabric of his clothing. His boots he will cover with saliva as well."

Alill groaned and sat down again on the bench as the second animal was returned and a third brought out. His teeth chattered as he rose and went to stand again at the table. Every swallow became obviously difficult. The wrangler removed the needle. Valemar moved forward and took the tube, held it between two of his fingers and forced the last of the blood down it and into Alill's mouth.

Valemar held Alill's chin up as he swallowed one last time, then held Alill's arm as he sank to the ground shuddering.

And suddenly, pieces of him weren't visible anymore. Skin first, then parts of his clothing rippled away like a growing puddle. Slowly, Alill's breathing returned to normal. Shortly after that, patches of his braid began to disappear and, lastly, his shoes. "Did I get all my hair?" he asked.

"Yes, I can't see any of you," Valemar said.

The wrangler went to one of the boxes, took off the lid, and placed a handful of leaves in each of the three crates of the heichdar that had been bled. "Let's get him up," Valemar said to me.

It was a strange journey. Valemar and I reversed our trip from the dungeon-like room, though he frequently delayed, giving Alill time to move with us. I never saw Alill. I never heard him. All the way up to the courtyard we went.

Conmel, one of the guards who'd been with Heymond when he brought me back from Vanerife, sat on a darana next to a mounting block. Valemar took the animal's bridle as it began to shuffle its feet nervously.

"Same report from the steppe, Conmel," Valemar said to him. "Remain vigilant." Valemar released the darana's bridle. Conmel gave a nod and turned his mount's head for the gate. Valemar tucked my hand around his arm, and we strolled inside.

We didn't speak until we were back in his study. I sank down onto one of the chairs in front of his desk. "You've found the Hormani ship," I said.

"Yes."

"Using your invisible scouts."

"Yes."

I swallowed heavily. "How does it work?" I asked, both curious

and wanting to delay where I knew the conversation would go next.

"Through experimentation over the last four years, we've found how to harness the heichdar — the 'forest whispers' as they were called of old — we've found out how to harness their camouflage ability." Valemar sat next to me. "For thousands of years, people heard whispers in the canopy of the trees. Occasionally, they'd find a dead animal. But a living one was never seen. Then a boy, climbing in the canopy, happened to put his bag on a nest. He brought the creature home. His father contacted a King's Guard —"

"How will you keep the boy from talking?" Children, in my experience, had a hard time keeping secrets. I looked at Valemar's face and lurched to my feet, barely making it to a corner before my stomach emptied. Valemar held my hair as I wiped my mouth on the back of my hand and moved away from the smell.

"You killed the rest of his family, too, I suppose."

"Astrid, can you imagine if anyone else found out about this? No one would be safe. The Cordair, the Hormani … they wouldn't need poison. They'd just creep in at night and slit all our throats."

"That's why the Shororato have made cloaking illegal." I sank into my chair. I wished I had a handkerchief or something to breathe through to filter the sour smell that followed me.

"We only use it for reconnaissance. Nothing else. Nothing that could give away the secret." And then he said the thing I'd been afraid he'd say ever since I realized what was going on in that room. "This is what will allow you to sneak aboard the Hormani ship." And then, even though I covered my mouth, I threw up in my lap.

Iree cleaned me up, bathed me, and tucked me in bed where I sat, leaning against the headboard. She left me with a basin and

departed. Valemar climbed up next to me. I hugged the bowl tighter to my chest. He brushed the hair from my face and ignored the angry tears rolled down and dripped into the basin. I understood why he'd had the family killed. I understood, but it didn't make it right.

Lethal. That had been my first impression of him. I'd forgotten that in the intervening months since Glábac, but it was true.

"If you know where the ship is, why did you send Alill out cloaked?"

"Cloaked. Hmm. Interesting description."

I ignored the sweat that broke out on my brow and concentrated on keeping what little was left of my stomach contents. "Earth had legends of cloaks of invisibility. You throw a cloak over something to hide it." I closed my eyes and swallowed.

Valemar took a cloth and wiped my brow. "We know where it is. We're watching their movements. It's difficult since the cloaking effect lasts less than a day. By morning, Alill will be completely visible again and very thirsty. Any dilution of the blood, any food or water, and the effect goes away. If the heichdar have a predator, that keeps them from becoming invisible as well."

"And I'm going to have to do this," I said.

"Not *have* to, Astrid. I would think you'd want to. This will allow you to call the Shororato. This will allow you to save us all."

"I need to think about it," I said to Valemar. My eyes stung. I handed him the basin and laid down, turning my back on him.

I faked sleep. Eventually Valemar got up from the bed and left me alone. It was all coming crashing down on me, and I didn't want to go there.

My eyes flew open. I'd had the same thought months ago when I'd stared out the window at the planet that was then Teridun Four to me. I hadn't wanted to come. I hadn't wanted to change. Back then, I hadn't wanted to change me. Now, I didn't want to change everything.

Really? a small voice in the back of my mind asked. *Are sure that it's not* you *that you don't want to change?*

We were both right. It was my everything that I didn't want to change.

CHAPTER 35

My stomach still churned in the morning, but I'd begun to come to grips with what I needed to do. I looked at Valemar's arm draped over me, at the circle of barat leaves that wrapped around his forearm, and came to a decision that would prove to myself that I could do anything and, like the cut on my finger, give me something that would stay with me always.

I brought his arm to my lips and kissed the tattoo. Valemar groaned as he awakened.

"Good morning," he said and kissed my ear.

"Good morning." I ran my fingers along the barat leaves. "This tattoo is a sign of protection, if I remember correctly."

"It is."

I rolled over and traced the chain along his chest. "Was it painful?"

"Very," Valemar answered. "Why?"

I laced my fingers through his and raised his arm. "Because I want these. The arm ones." Valemar sucked in a breath. "If I am going to do this, if I am going to walk into the enemy camp and change your whole world, then I want Bánalfar's protection to go with me."

I looked at Valemar's horrified face and kissed him. "Don't worry. I'm not asking for the one that goes around my neck and chest. As much as I would like to protect my heart, I'll settle for quick, sure hands."

"Why?" A mask of confusion contorted his features. "Why would you want to put yourself through that kind of pain?"

I looked down. My hair fell, hiding my face. "You've been training me as a warrior. I would like to be marked as one."

"Is it really that important to you?" Valemar brushed back the curtain of hair and tucked it behind my ear.

"It is," I said, keeping my eyes averted.

Valemar ran his fingers through my hair and slowly inhaled. "I suppose you'd want to do it as soon as possible."

My head snapped up. "Yes, please." My fingers traced the leaves on his chest. "I'm sure it won't be many more days before —" The word caught in my throat. "Before you know the Hormani schedule, before you send me out. I should have as much time as possible for them to heal."

Valemar stroked my face. "I do not think you a coward, you know."

"I know," I whispered. "But I am. I want the barat leaves so they may provide me with strength." I would need every bit I could find to actually do this.

"Very well." Valemar rolled us over. "Then I want your arms around me while they can still grasp something."

I blinked and smiled up at him. "That I can do."

I had one more request that angered him so much, I feared he would change his mind. "I think I should have both arms done at the

same time. Two artists working at once."

"What!" he roared and jumped up from the bench where he'd been pulling on his boots.

"If it's as painful as you said, I can get them done in half the time. Twice the pain but shorter session. Or is there only one guy who does them?"

Valemar closed his eyes and muttered something. Then he sat down, pulled on his other boot, and stood again. "I'll check." Valemar opened his mouth, closed it, and then left the room without giving me a kiss.

Iree dressed me in a short sleeved tunic and pants. She kept my hair simple, just caught it with a tie at the nape of my neck. No braid to press against my head while I laid and got my arms tattooed. I spent the next couple of hours distracting myself with a book on the raising and care of darana.

Valemar arrived well before lunch with a plate of food and a large glass of fruit juice. "You're sure you still want to do this?"

I slipped a bookmark into place. "Yes."

"Then you'll need to eat. It will take several hours, even with two artists working on you."

"No wine?" I asked, taking a seat at the table.

"You'll bleed more if you have alcohol."

"Okay, then." I hoisted up a smile. "Fruit juice it is."

Valemar didn't join me in the meal. He sat and silently waited while I ate. And I pretended that things were fine. I had to. If I told him the real reason I wanted the tattoos, he'd stop me. He'd stop so many of the things that I needed to do that I paid the price of his silent disapproval.

When I finally wiped my mouth on the napkin, he rose. "You're still sure?"

"Still sure," I said, not meeting his gaze.

"Very well, then. Follow me."

We went up a floor to a room that overlooked the river. Large windows filled the space with light. A rectangular table had been spread with blankets. Two smaller tables had been set against it at right angles, forming a large cross. Two men were organizing supplies on a small table near the top.

"My queen," the older of the two men said and inclined his head. He gestured for me to take a seat on the table.

"May I?" the younger asked, motioning to my arm. I sat and extended it to him. "Her arms are so small," he said to the older man. "Can we get three on here?"

I held the other one out to the older artist. He turned it back and forth, looked from my inner arm to my outer and back again, measured a distance on it using his index finger and thumb. "Just two would be silly." He picked up a thin black crayon made from tallow and began sketching a good six inches up from my wrist. The younger man watched the pattern evolve.

Valemar stood near the table, arms crossed, as the two artists created a template first on my left arm and then a matching one on my right.

"Do you want us to start on the outside of your arm or the inside, my queen?" the older asked when he and his partner were satisfied with the pattern.

"Does it matter?" I asked.

"Inside will hurt more," the younger said.

"What does it feel like?" I asked.

He held up one of the tools. Rows of needles had been wrapped around the end of a stick. It looked more like a prickly knife edge than anything else. "Ever get a needle scratch?" he asked.

"Yep," I said, thinking of all the times I'd poked myself with the needle while sewing with Daria.

"It won't hurt as bad as poking your finger. Not as many nerve endings and we won't be going that deep. But it is going to hurt. More like a burn."

I'd burned the tops of my feet in Vanerife my first day out by the Aelon Sea, and the pain had stayed with me for days. This wasn't going to be fun. But then I needed it not to be. I needed to prove to myself that I could do the painful things. "Let's start with the inner arm."

They had me lay down on my back. I placed one arm on the adjoining table and then stretched out the second. It was then that the idiocy of doing both arms at once became apparent. Open, exposed, no arm to curl protectively over my chest or drape across my eyes. I closed my eyes, took a deep breath, and tried not to flinch when the tool began to cut into my skin. Valemar would suffer soon enough. He didn't need to be tortured, watching me wrestle with the pain.

My arms tensed, straining to fight off the needles. The artists tightened their grip. Then, after a few minutes, after poke after poke after poke, my body began to relax. The pain was still there. The burn was still there. But my body didn't fight it anymore, accepted this as the new normal, and it gave me hope.

I don't know how long they worked before they had me flip onto my stomach. Each artist now had the opposite arm than they'd started with. The back of my arms was less painful than the inner had been. I drifted. The movement of the needles became like a painful metronome — *tick, tick, tick, tick, tick*. Then the outline was finished and a whole new pain began.

I'd been able to trace the outline of the barat leaves, follow the curve as the tattoo knife worked, but now it traveled over entire

sections of my skin. I was glad I was still lying on my stomach, the blankets pressing into my heart. I set my jaw as the knife punched away, burning the leaves onto me. The sensation was a reminder that if I didn't succeed, if I failed in my quest, it wouldn't just be my arms that burned. It would be the barat trees.

A hand gently touched my shoulder. "Time to turn over, my queen."

There was respect in the eyes of both the young artist and the old when I sat up and turned over. Valemar still stood by the head of my table, but I didn't look at him. I laid down, offered up my inner arms, and closed my eyes. Valemar gasped through his nose when I winced.

"You don't have to stay, you know," I said to him.

"Yes, I do." he retorted, his voice choked. "I promised to shelter you."

I gave a small laugh. "You are. You are providing me with the protection of the barat trees."

His hand hesitantly touched my head. "If this is too much …" And I knew he didn't mean the needles.

It *was* distracting, an extra thing for my brain to process, but I merely swallowed. "I'll let you know if you need to move it."

Valemar drew up a stool and sat behind me. I seared the moment into my memory — my husband's hand on my head in blessing while the protection of Bánalfar was being driven into my skin. No matter what came later, I would be at peace.

Again, I drifted, letting the pain wash over me. But unlike all the pain I'd suffered since I'd arrived in the Teridun system, this pain was welcome. *Much as a mother must suffer with labor pains.* It was fitting. This was the birth of a new Astrid — an Astrid who was willing to be the Moon Princess.

"We're done, my queen."

The voice lifted me from the fog I'd been floating in. Cream of

some kind was rubbed into my arms. "Do you want to look before we wrap them?"

I nodded and sat up. My bands were not as spectacular as Valemar's. Just one barat leaf was visible at a time, with the top of one leaf and the tail of another framing the one. Still …

"They're beautiful. Thank you," I said. The young artist smiled and wound a cloth around the one on his side.

The older artist tied off his bandage and handed a pot of salve to Valemar. "You know how this works," he said to Valemar who nodded. The artist then turned to me. "The bandages come off later today. They're only there to absorb the weeping. Scabs may form. Don't pick at them. Your tattoos should be completely healed in seven days. Until then, mind what they come into contact with so they don't get infected."

"Thank you," I said again. Valemar took my hand and helped me from the table.

The artists began cleaning their things up and putting them away. "The honor was all ours," the older one said with a smile.

Valemar led me to one of the smaller rooms he used as a dining room, not far from the place I'd been tattooed. Lunch, or a meal at any rate, had been left for us. "You can have that wine now," Valemar said. "Do you need anything for the pain?"

My arms burned, but I shook my head. "Wine should be fine." My stomach protested at the sight of the food. I'd spent too long processing the pain.

I accepted a glass from Valemar who handed it to me with a frown and sat down. He had no trouble pulling over a plate and digging in. Just the smell was enough to turn my stomach.

I sipped on the wine. "If that's what you're like when I get tattooed, what are you going to be like when I actually go out?" I asked.

Valemar shot me a single glance before returning his focus to his food. A scowl twisted his features. "I'll be sitting in a room with a karawack by my side."

I arched my eyebrows. "Won't that give away the fact that I'm gone and you're worried about me?" Valemar's chewing slowed but he didn't raise his eyes from his plate. "Everyone knows I've been training. That hasn't been kept a secret."

"Then I'll have the bird brought up now," he said. "And we'll start sending you out with Erris for longer periods of time." Valemar raised his eyes and they were filled with fear. "I knew something had happened — well, we knew — in Vanerife, when Daria died. Your birds went crazy. We knew you hadn't died, but that some kind of trauma had occurred." Valemar set his fork down. "It was agony, waiting for the karawack from my mother."

"I'm sure I'd do the same thing if you were out on campaign," I said.

Valemar reached out and cupped my face with his hand. "In all my training, I never thought what it must be like to be the one left behind."

I smiled. "It took men on Earth a long time to get used to dealing with that. They find it easier to do the leaving. Women often get viewed as the weaker sex, but look at what we go through. And childbirth." A sad look crossed Valemar's face. "I'm sorry, my love," I said.

Cadalin was due any day. It wouldn't be long before the High was filled with the sounds of crying.

"It's not your fault," he said. "I was the one who interpreted 'new life' to mean a child ... that you'd be the one to break the curse that has settled on my family. That this 'new life' will be a world connected to the stars and the Cordair reined in, that's enough. And I will have you." I forced a smile onto my face. "Please come back, Astrid. You have to come back."

My heart broke. A thousand little spider webs shot through the pieces. I took his hand. "I'll do my best."

Cadalin's son arrived before Valemar decided they knew the Hormani schedule well enough to send me out. Erris and I had slowly lengthened the amount of time we spent away from Aedenfal, and Valemar now spent his days in the company of one of my imprinted karawack. I ran through what I'd need to do to reach a comm panel every time Erris and I went out. Since there were no layouts to memorize, no file full of schematics, I'd just have to do my best.

My last bit of preparation was to write Valemar a letter. There was still one, well two, major things that needed to happen if I was successful in contacting the Shororato. Only one if I was successful but didn't return. So I put it into a letter to Valemar. I poured out my love and my thankfulness, told him what needed to be done, and left it with Iree.

"Only if I don't come back," I told her. "You need to swear to me that you won't read it, to give it to Valemar if I'm captured, and to return it — unopened and unread — if I do."

Her eyes went large but she swore to follow my instructions and to hide it well.

My tattoos healed nicely. I loved tracing the pattern of my permanent green bracelets. Valemar fingered them often enough that I teased him.

"I'm not getting the necklace," I told him one night as we lay spooned together and his fingers traced the path it would have taken on me.

"You don't need it," he whispered in my ear. "And the necklace was much more painful than the arms."

"Hmm. Pain *and* spoilage of the bosom that made the Sapir hand over R'Kesh's steel."

"What!" Valemar's arms tightened around me.

"Didn't Reina tell you? Daria made sure my assets were on view for the dinner with Tanic Ilahni. She told me the R'Keshans enjoy a good bosom."

"Your bosom is mine, wife!"

I leaned my head against him. "Are you saying you wouldn't have had me distract him if you'd been there?"

Valemar growled, then turned me around and proved that I was his. It was the last bit of play we had. With the reports that came in the next morning, plans were made for Heymond and me to attempt contact the following night.

The Hormani ship was in a valley a three hour ride southwest of Rock Dorach. Scouts usually had only two to three hours of observation time before the heichdar blood wore off. That they were even able to slip into the camp and observe astounded me. That meant the Hormani weren't using thermal scans, which gave the crazy plan at least somewhat of a chance. At least in contacting the Shororato. Those scans would no doubt change once my transmission was detected.

"Are you sure you want to send Heymond with me?" I asked Valemar. "Are you prepared to lose us both?"

He grimaced and pulled me to him. "There's no one else I'd trust with you," he said. So I let it go. And truth be told, I knew Heymond would be the one who would do everything to ensure that I made it back from the Hormani ship.

It was still hard, and my stomach stayed twisted in knots. I forced myself to eat, knowing that the next day, after drinking the heichdar blood, I wouldn't be able to. Erris and I went out as usual, but I

couldn't play the game. My limbs shook and my stomach churned, so we found a quiet, out of the way spot and spent the day with our backs against a tree, swapping stories. He was fascinated by mine, and it comforted me that he, at least, knew what was coming and was excited by the idea of being visited by people from beyond the stars.

"It doesn't frighten you?" I asked.

Genuine shock appeared on his face. "Why would it? *You're* not frightening," he said, which made me laugh. And his simple stories of growing up in Bánalfar reminded me why I was doing this. To keep the peace. To keep the moon children from marching off to war. I had thought it would be hard to grow up without a mother or father, but as a moon child, everyone had been mother and father to Erris. He was valuable. He was a gift from *the* Mother and Father, and so he was loved. And respected.

"Who would have taught you them things if I hadn't been?" Erris asked. "I'd have been stuck learning a trade."

"You do realize," I said, "that soldiering is a trade."

"Best one there is," he said. "And only moon children get to do it. Well, and the king. We're what enables the rest of them to have a life. It doesn't get any more important than that."

"No," I agreed. "It doesn't."

That night I took Valemar into my arms and poured out all my love. Filled myself with the feel and touch and smell of him. It could very well be the last time I'd hold my husband, and I wanted the night to be able to sustain me for a lifetime.

"Astrid," Valemar said when I began yet again. "You have a job to do tomorrow. You need sleep." And I couldn't tell him of my fears, so I resigned myself to simply laying spooned with him the rest of the night. And some time later, with my husband's breath warm on the back of my neck, I fell asleep.

CHAPTER 36

The hydrating began at dawn. "You do realize that at this rate I'll be peeing the entire way to the encampment," I warned Valemar.

"Not if you produce enough spit first," he replied, which reminded me that I'd need to, like a cat, lick my palms and cover my braid and my boots.

I dressed in a tight, long-sleeved tunic that hit the tops of my hips and a pair of trousers that were more like leggings. Butter-soft boots skimmed the tops of my calves.

"Why not ankle boots?" I asked Valemar. "There'd be less to cover." The wax produced by my skin would soak through light fabric but heavier material, such as the boots, would need to be covered by hand.

"They're high to offer protection from the grasses of Fairfada and the rocks of the Archjarn," he explained, and so I acquiesced. Valemar checked me over, caressed my face, kissed me, and then accompanied me down to the dungeon.

My nerves skittered with both fear and excitement as he removed the heavy key from his pocket and unlocked the door that led to the heichdar lab. Alill and Heymond were already there when Valemar and I entered. For one brief moment, I wondered if there was a second key, but then things got down to business.

"Heymond will start first, Astrid, and then you," Valemar said. "You'll trade off drinking."

"Why is Alill here?" I asked.

"So he can help Heymond with the final animal while I see to you."

My stomach flipped. "Okay."

The wrangler put on the leather gloves and retrieved the first animal. He painted it, inserted the needle, and gave the end to Heymond. I watched as Heymond shuddered with every swallow. The needle was removed, and Heymond slowly made his way over to the cushioned bench. Then it was my turn.

My heart and stomach both began to hop inside me as I watched the wrangler retrieve the animal. It still looked like his hand closed around nothing. "How will I see Heymond if we're both invisible?" I asked.

"You'll appear as a gray mist to each other." Valemar put a hand on my shoulder as the wrangler approached.

"Please don't," I said. I hadn't even begun to drink the blood and I was already shaking. "I'm going to need to concentrate."

Valemar removed his hand. I didn't look to see if I'd hurt his feelings for the wrangler was already painting the heichdar with chalk. All too soon the needle was inserted and the end of the tube handed to me. I put it between my lips, braced my stomach and mind, and sucked.

It didn't taste like blood. It tasted like fire. Not the fire of the curries I'd had on Jauzara Four that hit your tongue and threatened to boil off its skin. This was more like strong a smoked chili sauce on a shredded pork or goat tilla. Rich, salty, yet with fingers of flame that first moved across the roof of my mouth, then my tongue, then down my throat as I swallowed. I shuddered as the feeling spread, then swallowed again. And again. And again.

Fingers pried the tube from my hand and led me over to the bench. It shifted as Heymond rose to take his turn. "Astrid?" Valemar's voice asked, but I merely shook my head. I couldn't speak. My mind scrambled to process the changes that rippled through my body. Tears welled up in my eyes. Heavy tears that I thought would glue my eyes shut if they were shed. My lungs began to shake as fluid traced its way through them and I concentrated on breathing, fighting off the terrible sensation that I could drown.

And then Valemar took my hand and pulled me off the bench. I sensed more than saw when Heymond and I passed each other, trading places again. My fingers were curled around the tube and, again, I drank. Every swallow filled my limbs with fluid. Every mouthful added weight to my lungs. It became difficult to breathe. The heavy, waxy tears slipped down my face. I let them fall, vaguely aware that they would help my camouflage.

My hand shook as the tube was taken from it. Valemar half carried me back to the bench. My teeth began to chatter. Goosebumps rose on my arms and legs as cold began to curl across my skin and sink into my muscles. I heard Heymond moan and then the sound of a body being dragged across the floor.

"Last one, Astrid." Valemar raised me up and moved me over to the table. I whimpered as the tube was put into my mouth. "Swallow." I did, knowing that Valemar would just force the blood into my mouth and then make me swallow. I only managed two before I began to truly cry.

Something was wrong. Something was wrong with my body. Then the fire filled my mouth again. My chin was tipped back and a

hand stroked my throat. I gagged and gravity took the blood down. My knees gave way but Valemar got under me before I hit the floor. I sagged across him, and the fire filled my mouth again. "Two more," he whispered in my ear.

But I didn't want two more. I wanted the cold comfort of the flagstone floor. I wanted to lay my cheek against the stone and die. And then my chin was raised and another swallow forced upon me.

"How's she doing?" Heymond's voice asked. At least he sounded normal. At least he'd survived.

"She's already turning," Valemar replied as yet another dose filled my mouth. I whimpered. I was human. My chemistry different from the Alfari. What if the heichdar blood killed me instead?

There was a gurgle as I choked on the last one. "All finished," Valemar said, and lowered me the short remaining distance to the floor. My muscles started to spasm. I flopped against the flagstones like a fish out of water.

"Did I get all of my hair?" Heymond asked.

"You still need … there," Alill said.

Alill was going to need to be the one to go with Heymond for I was going to die. But Alill couldn't read Hormani. There was no way for him to send the transmission.

"Astrid?"

The soft patter of boots approached me. A hand took mine. "Let it do its work, my queen. Don't fight it."

I gave up then, gave myself over to the fire and cold that licked at my body, to the hot fluid that filled my veins and my lungs. Someone took my shoulders and raised me to sitting. A hand began to sweep across my face, collecting the tears and wiping them into my hair.

Somehow, I didn't die. "I'm never doing that again," I weakly told the room and watched the gray blur of a hand approach my

face. It was Heymond I was braced against and who was helping to conceal me. It was a good thing that he was invisible, for Valemar would have hated to see how I was nestled against him.

I brought a shaking hand to my mouth, licked it, and started in on my boots. "How are you feeling, Astrid?" Valemar asked.

"Like Muirbrook has walked all over me," I said. Laughter filled the room.

"She's not recovering like the others," Valemar said to the wrangler.

The wrangler shrugged. "She's not Alfari. At least she's invisible."

Heymond took my hand. "You still need here," he said, placing it on the back of my head, under my braid. I licked it and rubbed in the saliva.

"I've been reduced to a cat," I muttered.

"What's a cat?" asked more than one voice.

"I'll tell you later."

Slowly, I began to feel that I could at least function. I did one last check of my boots and Heymond helped me to my feet. "Here we go."

Alill and Valemar led the way out of the room. Their heads bent in whispered discussion all the way through the belly of the High, up and out into the courtyard. Heymond lifted me up and placed me behind the saddle of a darana that Orin stood by, holding the bridle. The darana shifted nervously as my weight settled on its rump. Orin spoke to it in soothing tones as Heymond climbed up the mounting block and took a seat behind Conmel on another darana. Heymond's arms went around him.

Alill took the reins from Orin mounted up. I placed my arms around him. "Until tomorrow," Valemar said.

As Alill turned his mount's head toward the open gate, I saw Erris melt into the shadows, and then my concentration became

engrossed in the task of simply hanging on. Both men urged their darana through the Low at a quick trot then broke into a run once they were clear of Aedenfal's main gates.

"It's eighteen hours from here to the camp," Alill said to me as we flew down the road. "We'll collect fresh mounts in four hours at the edge of Fairfada, so just try to hold on until then."

We never traveled slower than a trot. Aedenfal was usually a six-hour ride from the grassy sea, but I had never made the journey at that leisurely a pace. My thighs burned and my bum ached. I was sure my bruises had bruises. And I had to stop so I could pee.

Alill reined in when I told him, and I slipped from the darana and wandered away from the road. Heymond lifted me back on, mounted Conmel's darana, then slid to the back so Conmel could remount. Our carriers clucked to their mounts, and we raced down the road again, making up the time I'd lost them. But with all the fluid Valemar had had me drink first thing this morning, my bladder couldn't take being both overfull and pounded.

We changed animals at a small paddock not far off the road from the edge of the grassy sea. They say the plains on Earth were once like this — the American prairie, the African Serengeti, and the Russian steppes. Only Mongolia still has the open grasslands, where tourists go to travel with the nomads, stay in yurts, and learn the horsemanship that spread across the planet thousands of years ago.

Here on Crenfor, it was wide and open, free of permanent settlements. Only shepherds and their flocks of anapali lived there. It would take us twelve hours to cross it. Twelve hours before the Archjarn rose and the land became rocky and barren for hundreds of miles to the north and south, all the way from the Aelon Sea until the mountains met up with the Skargorn range that held Snow Reach and Verlun.

Heymond and I sat away from Alill and Conmel in an attempt to at least try to keep our stomachs from rumbling while they rapidly ate their lunch. It was the thirst that bothered me the most. My throat was parched and burning, but it would be hours until I could have anything to drink. Not until my task was done and we'd made our way back to the drop off point. At least I was thinking "when" and not "if." There was every possibility that I'd already taken my last drink. And that had been of blood.

We bumped along on the backs of the darana, all day long and into the night. I began to think I should have spent more time teaching my legs to dangle and my thighs to accept the pounding of something other than my husband. My arms grew tired and I wondered how I'd ever manage two hours walking through the mountains to the camp.

The moon was high overhead when Conmel and Alill reined in. Heymond slipped from his darana and came around to catch me as I more or less fell off. The two King's Guard clucked to their mounts and turned south — appearing to be a border patrol, nothing more. Heymond took my hand and we moved off into the night.

CHAPTER 37

My eyes were really not made to see at night. Especially semi mountain climbing at night with only a faint red glow from the moon to illuminate the nonexistent path. After about half an hour of my stumbling along behind him making all the noise in the world, Heymond gave up and carried me piggyback for the next hour and a half.

My fingers twitched and sometimes even tapped out on Heymond's chest the message I'd been practicing now for days (possibly even weeks), building muscle memory so that I could get in and get out as fast as possible, no matter what happened.

I'd spent much of the day in thought. Hours of it, as my needed silence eliminated conversation. Mine and Heymond's at least, though Conmel and Alill had been fairly silent, too. And I had come to the decision that I needed to survive this for I needed to make sure Heymond returned to Valemar. With what was coming, Valemar was going to need the support of his closest friend. I needed to do this job as fast as possible and get Heymond and myself the hell away from there.

When I wasn't tapping out the message on Heymond's chest, my eyes were drawn to the blanket of stars above. Crenfor had its own Milky Way, its own view of the center of the galaxy. Somewhere out there were Finn and Amy and my Mum and Dad. At this point, they would have determined that something had happened and decided that I'd perished. Agçay would have dispatched another ship. The Rovar silk would have been purchased. Even the Addunka tin that had kept me in my room when the plasma leaked would have been negotiated for, delivered, and sold. And in just a few days, ships carrying the Shororato would travel through those stars, land, and change this world.

Heymond would give my legs a squeeze, as if he knew I'd fallen pensive, and I'd go back to running the scenarios and ignore the way the mountains framed the stars.

I knew we were close when Heymond set me down. Then even I could see the dim glow of the red lights of the Hormani ship in night mode. As we got closer, I could make it out — a class D intersystem mini-freighter. Small for a freighter, which meant there was probably a mother ship in orbit. Or at least a C-size ship.

Crew of five, my mental file pulled up.

At this time of night, four of them should be asleep. Unless they were total idiots, and I was counting on them not to be. Four would be asleep and one would be on watch. If they were total idiots, five would be asleep and the door would be locked.

Then I saw a faint orange glow like a solitary firefly. It moved upward, brightened, then lowered again. One guard on the perimeter, smoking.

I tapped Heymond on the shoulder and gestured for him to carry me to the edge of the ship. We didn't need me tripping and alerting the guard that something was out there. Even though he would probably think it was an animal, he'd be on heightened alert and more likely to notice the door opening.

Heymond put me down by the nose of the ship. I mentally counted to ten then cautiously picked my way to the door. The latch button glowed red. *Red for danger.* Though I knew that wasn't the case. I said a little prayer — both to the God I'd grown up with and to the Mother and Father — and pushed the button.

Would the inside lights have been dimmed to night mode or would the door fly open, bathing the area in light, and inform the guard that a much smarter thing than an animal was out there?

I closed my eyes and waited.

The door whispered open. Black continued to register behind my eyelids. I breathed a shallow sigh of relief. I opened my eyes and stepped in, just catching the blur of Heymond over my shoulder as he inched closer to watch the door. It slid shut behind me.

I'd been on mini-freighters like this one a few times. The safest panel location would be back by the hold. It wasn't the closest, but should someone be up and happen to notice that a comm link had been opened, a cargo check, even in the middle of the night, wouldn't be out of the ordinary.

The training I'd done with Erris and Valemar allowed me to silently slip down the hallways. The comm panel was easy to find — its white light illuminating the door to the cargo hold. For the first time, I wondered if I'd cast a shadow standing there in front of all that light.

No. The sun had been out both when Alill had left and during the long ride here. None of us had cast a telltale shadow on the ground, just a darana and a single rider.

I breathed out a slow breath and crossed to the panel. I exhaled slowly again and wiggled my fingers. As I sucked air back into my lungs, I let my fingers fly.

On. Comm out. Open line. Destination – Shororato HQ Krajiny system. Message: Hormani on Teridun 4 trading chalcopyrite. Signed – PS Astrid Carr. Close line.

My body turned and I had shifted my weight to my toes before I even swiped the panel closed. I'd begun to hurtle down the passageway toward the door when the beeping began.

"What the fuck?!" *Captain's quarters*, my inner file supplied. "What the hell?!"

Doors swished open as the crew, having been alerted to the transmission, tumbled out to find me.

"That bitch is here!"

I was four feet from the door. Three. It slid open, and I threw myself against the wall as the guard raced in. As soon as he was past, I dashed out the door. It brushed my heel as it closed behind me. Heymond scooped me up, flung me on his back, and ran off into the night.

For the first ten minutes, my nerves prickled on heightened alert, fully anticipating that we'd get shot. That the thermals would get turned on, making Heymond and me easy to spot. Easy to kill. Retribution for what I'd done.

When the ship blasted off, I was certain it had targeted us. But once it had lifted into the sky, it just kept going.

When I realized that it really, truly wasn't coming for us, my stomach decided it had enough. I motioned for Heymond to put me down. I bent over double, and dry heaved for about a minute as my stomach purged itself of all my pent-up emotion.

Heymond rubbed my back and spoke for the first time since the dungeon. "It's okay, my princess. Everything will be okay."

I wanted to shout, *'No, it's not!'* But I kept silent and let him comfort me.

After about ten minutes, he spoke the words that spurred my body back into action. "We need to keep moving so that we can meet up with Alill and Conmel. They'll have food and water for us. And Valemar will be waiting for your return. The karawack will let him know that things went fine, but wouldn't you rather tell him yourself?"

I nodded and straightened up. Heymond put me onto his back and we set out into the dark again.

The sun was just beginning to glow behind the peaks of the Archjarn when the rocky hills finally gave way to the grass of Fairfada. Another bout of nausea hit me, and I brought up bile. It was actually more comfortable than the empty heaves of earlier.

"It's the lack of food and water," Heymond told me. "Your body is rebelling."

"Yeah, it couldn't be that I've had nothing but blo—" I said and puked again. As I bent over, hands on my knees, I noticed that I had a shadow. I wiped my mouth on the edge of my tunic and stood up. Heymond glimmered into view. His gray, shadowy form slowly saturated then developed color. Early holo transmissions had done the same sort of thing — gray fuzziness filling out, taking shape, and, suddenly, a perfect image.

I moved away from the sick and sat down. I tried not to think about water and the sour taste in my mouth. "How long?" I asked.

Heymond sat down next to me. "How long, what?"

"Before Alill and Conmel get here?"

Heymond looked back over his shoulder at the edge of blue peeking through the mountains. "Any time. We haven't come out

exactly where we went in. I wasn't —" He broke off and whistled. "I knew that thing could fly, but …"

"Yeah. And that's a small ship."

Heymond jerked. "I thought your ship …"

"Escape pod. Meant for two people. And only to get from where you are in orbit onto the planet you're above."

"If the ship that just left is small, what's large?"

I put my hand on his arm and held it as I crushed his world. "There are ships as big as Aedenfal. The High *with* the Low."

"Oh, dear Father." Heymond's voice went weak. "And that's what you just called? That's what's coming?"

"Probably not. But ships larger than the one that just left. And other assorted sizes. The Shororato will bring with them enough weaponry to take down an entrenched mining operation as well as smaller ships to scan for alien technology."

"Like your ship?"

"Like my ship," I confirmed, and mentally wrapped a hand around my heart so I didn't wince. "It will need to be taken someplace easy for the Shororato to collect it. I'll let Valemar know."

Heymond sat there absorbing the beginnings of this new reality. "I can see why you didn't want to be the Moon Princess," he said after several minutes of silence.

"You expected a savior."

"Which you are. But you're also —"

"A destroyer."

It took a while before Alill and Conmel found us. Heymond and I ate breakfast, had our first food and water in a day. Another long day stretched before us. Twelve hours to cross the Fairfada. Four to

six hours to Aedenfal from there. This time, I sat in front of Alill instead of behind so he could hold onto me. It had been twenty-four hours since I'd slept, and I would have fallen off once the motion of the darana lulled me to sleep.

The darana coming to a standstill woke me up hours later. We were still in the midst of Fairfada — I opened my eyes to see bending grass all around us. Before I could ask why we'd stopped, I noticed a black dot in the sky. A karawack. It glided to us and landed on Heymond's shoulder. He lifted it down and took the message from its leg before returning it to his shoulder. We'd be less conspicuous if it rode there and didn't follow us overhead.

"It's from Valemar," he said as he unrolled it. "He's going to meet us at the switching post."

My heart beat faster. Six hours sooner. I was going to get to see him six hours sooner.

"How long was I asleep?" I asked Alill.

"About four hours."

Every bit of me was bone tired and sore. "How are you even upright?" I asked him.

"Practice. And Conmel and I took turns sleeping last night. I've had a couple of hours."

"Has Heymond slept?"

Alill shook his head. "No. And I don't think he will until he's handed you over to Valemar."

We stopped for lunch about noon. Climbing down from the darana made me wonder how I'd ever manage to get back on. Parts of me just wouldn't unbend.

The food was among the best I'd ever tasted. Just bread, cheese, and a dried fruit bar washed down with water, but my belly had been so achy and empty for so long that I could have been eating Iberico

pork and washing it down with Cambari wine.

Heymond had to lift me into the saddle, and we set off again. Another six hours before we reached the trees and fields of Bánalfar and the switching post.

I wanted to cry when it came into view. Cry from exhaustion. Cry from relief. My heart leapt when our approach was noted and Valemar came out to greet us. Alill helped me lift my leg over the saddle and I slipped into Valemar's waiting arms.

"I don't think I can walk," I said as my feet hit the ground and my legs buckled. How had I ever ridden halfway across Bánalfar and back?

Valemar scooped me up. "You've had a long journey with little food. We'll take a wagon back."

Valemar carried me inside the post. I hadn't seen the interior before since Heymond and I had needed to keep our presence unknown the previous day. The post was outfitted like an inn. Trestle tables lined the front room. The smell of food drifted in from the kitchen. A set of stairs led to bedrooms above.

We ate a meal while the wagon was arranged. Valemar took reports from Conmel and Alill, and asked Heymond if we'd had any trouble.

"No trouble," he replied, but his face reflected the fear of having seen the ship take flight, of the knowledge of what was coming.

Valemar's eyes narrowed, but he didn't ask further, didn't ask me if I'd been successful. And I decided we could wait until we were back in Aedenfal to tell him what needed to happen next.

The sun had begun to set by the time we left. Conmel and Alill were going to rest overnight at the post. Our new King's Guard rode with a remarkably alert Heymond. Valemar settled himself into the back of the wagon and opened his arms for me. Curled in the warm embrace of my husband and with the rhythmic rocking of the wagon, it wasn't long before I was fast asleep.

CHAPTER 38

I barely stirred when we arrived at the High. Valemar carried me to our room, stripped off my sweaty, dirty clothes, and put me to bed. I pulled his arm closer around me and fell back asleep. I had at least a couple of days before the Shororato would arrive.

I awoke in the morning with two thoughts: I desperately needed a bath, and I didn't want to move. But there were things that needed to be said, preparations that needed to be made, so I rolled over and stared at the fierce, beautiful face of my husband.

My movement woke Valemar. He smiled. "Good morning, wife."

"Good morning, husband." Pain flooded my body. Job done, I could no longer hide the cost. Tears crept down my face.

Valemar frowned and reached up a hand to brush them away. "What is wrong, Astrid?"

I smiled. I'd done it. I'd fulfilled my role. I'd fulfilled the prophecy. The Moon Princess had driven away the outsiders. There would be a new life for Bánalfar.

"The Shororato will be here in two or three days." I bit my lips as a sob rose up my throat. "You need to move my ship into an open clearing, somewhere away from people."

Valemar's frown turned into a scowl. "Okay."

"And I —" But I couldn't make the words come. "The Shororato will scan the planet for alien technology, so I —"

Pieces of my heart began to break off and slip away, a growing cascade of shattered glass that slipped through my mental fingers, taking the little that remained of my courage with them.

But I had to tell Valemar. The last piece of the mission still needed to be completed. The piece that I had kept hidden from him — that I needed to be there with my ship. I blinked back tears and forced the words out.

"The chip … in my head."

Valemar's eyes flew wide. He gasped. "No!"

"I don't belong here," I whispered as my soul began to burn, slowly turning into ash.

"Mother and Father, Astrid! What have you done?"

I tried to smile, but my lips simply trembled. "I've saved you all."

CHAPTER 39

Valemar flat out refused. I was his. He had claimed me. He was not going to leave me by my ship. He was not going to hand me over.

"It's not a death sentence," I told him. "It's simply prison."

"For how long?" Valemar asked. I could see the calculations spinning behind his eyes.

"Life," I whispered, and he erupted into a rage again. "If you do this, if you keep me from them, they will come into the High to get me."

"Fine," Valemar snarled, every bit the lethal warrior. "My planet. My rules."

I sighed and sat down. "Raislos is going to have the same reaction over the armor. I don't see him giving it back without a fight."

Valemar scoffed and continued pacing our room. "Technology is one thing. A person is another." He stopped mid-stride and turned around. "Could Ferrick remove this chip?"

"It's too deeply embedded," I said. "And even if he could, I'd lose my knowledge of your language. We'd no longer be able to speak to each other."

"We wouldn't need words," Valemar said. "We'd still know that we love each other."

And then my fierce, proud husband broke down.

In the end, there was nothing I could say or do to sway him. He called the people of Aedenfal to the Cair and told them what we'd done. He told them that the outsiders were from farther away than the moon, as was I. He told them that we'd called an enforcement brigade to remove the outsiders, and that those people would be entering Aedenfal to talk to me. He told them that if they were afraid of strange people or ships that flew in the sky they were free to leave the city, but that these things would now be part of life in Bánalfar, part of life on Crenfor.

I had expected the people to panic, but the prophecy had done its work. For hundreds of years they had looked for people to journey from the moon. Now, it had simply happened. Earth had worried about alien invaders and hadn't trusted the outsiders when they had finally appeared. Bánalfar and Crenfor had anticipated a savior. That others would follow and help the Moon Princess was simply to be expected.

At first, Valemar had feared I'd run. But why would I? If I was going to spend the rest of my life without my husband, then I wanted every moment with him that I could get.

"That's why you got the tattoos," he said at the end of that very long day after I'd broken the news. "You wanted to take part of Bánalfar with you."

"There was just so much staring at my marriage mark that I could contemplate," I said. "Where these are simply beautiful."

Valemar took my hand and ran his lips long the barat leaves

on my arm. "They are symbols of protection, and they will protect you now," he said with utter surety. "You may have been an outsider when you came, but you were in need and we protected you. You did not need to call the Shororato, but you did." His fingers tightened on mine. "I made a vow to shield you from cold and sun and harm. I will not let these people take you. If they insist, it will be war."

I cupped his face and kissed him. "No," I said. "There will be no talk of war. If that occurs, then I will not have been a savior, I will have been a destroyer, and I will not let that happen."

Valemar couldn't speak. Tears flowed down his face. His hands, his jaw began to tremble. He reached out and touched me. His hands drifted from my arms to my face to my side. Nothing brought him comfort.

I opened my arms and gathered him to me. "Hush, my love. Everything will be fine." I gently rocked him back and forth as he cried, whispering words of comfort even as my own tears ran down to join the ones already dampening my chest. He had a future without me, and somehow, I needed to make it all right.

The High and the Low fell into a state of anticipation. My escape pod was transferred to an open field and four guards set by it to keep the curious away. We received reports that Raislos was furious. The Hormani pullout had been abrupt, leaving him with no explanation. He could scarcely credit that Bánalfar's queen had summoned help, that she had friends powerful enough to frighten off his well-paying customers. Yet, raiding ceased on the Fairfada. The Cordair soldiers with their Awrakian armor were recalled to Rock Dorach to defend it in case of attack.

Valemar and I spent our days in the solar, just holding each other. Our nights were spent in tender, gentle lovemaking, as if the other would break and fade away if we asked for too much.

A buzz awakened me the third night, the chip in my head vibrating from the scan. Valemar woke when I trembled. "They're here," I said.

Valemar held me fast against him. "You'll not disappear? Be taken right out of my arms?"

"No," I said. "They'll know you're with me. But we can expect visitors at the High in the morning."

We received a report at first light that my ship had gone. The four seasoned King's Guard had thrown themselves to the ground and prayed for the Mother to spare them when the escape pod rose into the air, all on its own, the leader among them had been ashamed to report.

"Very understandable, under the circumstances," I told him. "I myself have seen things that have defied explanation, and they are frequently terrifying."

The guards dismissed, Valemar and I entered the throne room to await the Shororato. A karawack arrived with a report that a flying ship had landed not far outside of Aedenfal and that men dressed in white armor and carrying black boxes had disembarked from it. Valemar sent word that they were not to be disturbed and to be shown the way in, if at all possible.

"Will they be able to speak Alfari?" Valemar asked me.

"I don't know," I said. "It took several hours for my chip to assimilate your language. They might have set up listening posts last night and have already collected it, but it is possible that I will be the only one able to understand them."

We sat and waited. Shale ghosted in through the side door and stayed near it, refusing to meet my eyes when I glanced her way. Twenty minutes after her, whispers announced the arrival of the Shororato before Orin led them in. I'd spent the day before teaching him how to say, "This way. Our queen is expecting you," in Karjiny.

My heart still fell at the sight of a full general and his four soldiers. They hadn't worn their helmets — a good sign — but if the Alfari had thought my appearance strange, the cat-like Kalunka and fish-like Inet among them said that these people were not of this world.

The general, at least, was humanoid. "Protocol Specialist Carr, you are in violation of Supreme Order four six nine — contact with an off-limit planet. I am going to have to ask you to come with me."

Valemar smiled. That dangerous, indulgent smile. "There is no Protocol Specialist Carr here," he said, and I realized that the general had spoken Alfari. Valemar's eyes flicked over the man.

"General," I said, realizing Valemar was trying to figure out what to call him.

"General." Valemar flashed his dangerous smile again. "The woman before you is Queen Astrid Carbrev, my wife."

The general's eyebrows rose, even though he'd known my position from, literally, my position. I was seated on a throne.

"Assimilation does not negate the offense."

"She didn't have to call you," Valemar interjected. "She could have lived out all her days with everyone believing she'd died like her comrades."

"What did happen to the *Palmas Cove*?" the general asked.

"Oh, now you want to know?" Valemar said. "Strange behavior for someone charged with upholding peace. Arrest first, ask questions later. She is guilty in your eyes no matter what has happened."

The general smiled an indulgent smile of his own. "Yes. That's the way it works."

"Strange laws," Valemar said. "Do not contact a planet and interfere with its development, but when circumstances force that law to be broken for self-preservation and a much more serious offense is

discovered —" Valemar's face became a mask of confusion. "Or am I wrong? Illegal trade in chalcopyrite and supply of Awrakian armor on purpose, truly changing a world forever — something you wouldn't have known without her — is a lesser offense than saving your own life?"

"She knew the rules."

"She tried to contact you. Nine days of distress calls blocked by the Hormani mother ship." Valemar drew himself up and sneered down at the general. "You ought to be down on your knees thanking her. Without her, this planet would have been ravaged by war brought about by that illegal armor and our resources plundered. You weren't there to stop them. She was."

"I'm not here to debate you," the general said.

"Ah, but you are. For we disagree on whom you are looking for. And my wife, whom I vowed to protect from cold and sun and harm, is not going to be taken by someone who intends her harm."

The general sighed and turned to me. "Specialist Carr, you know where this is going to go. Don't let it."

"Would you really inflict further harm on these people by taking me away?" I asked. "Think about how my Alfari have worked with you, welcomed you. They ask for just this one thing. Remember what happened on Earth and on Tiniak. That has not been your experience here. These people were looking for a protector to come from the moon. My contacting you has saved them. Would you turn their warm welcome into hate and distrust, all for one person whose choices had been Teridun Four or death?"

The word hung in the air. People began to inch together and away from the Shororato. Hands went to sword hilts among the King's Guard. The general's eyes scanned the room, a new wariness apparent in them.

"Is there nothing that would save her?" Shale's voice sounded loudly from beside us. My head was among those that turned. A sly, cat-like smile lit up her face.

"No," the general said. "The rules are quite clear."

"The rules." Shale nodded. "Like how nothing can be taken off the planet without its citizens' consent."

The general sighed. "Really, Specialist Carr. This charade needs to stop."

The patience of both groups was beginning to wear thin. I nodded and started to stand. Valemar's hand shot out toward mine. "Astrid!"

"She's pregnant!" Shale shouted over the din that erupted.

"Shale, they have ways of checking. They'll know I can't —" I said, even as the general whipped out a scanner and mounted the steps. The sound of steel rang through room as swords were drawn. I rose and held my arms out, difficult to do while I was also attempting to push Valemar back into his seat.

A sudden silence filled the room as the general ran the scanner over my abdomen. Silent enough for the swishing sound of a heartbeat to fill the room.

"Can't take her now," Shale said as I landed hard on the seat of my throne. My legs wouldn't hold me.

"I can't be pregnant," I said, dazed. "It isn't possible."

"We've tried enough," Valemar said.

I looked up at the general. The Shororato were known for their ruthlessness, not their humor, but this had to be some kind of joke. "It isn't possible. My DNA wouldn't be compatible."

He checked the scanner's display again. "Apparently, it is."

"But ... but that's —"

"More than a million odds against it. But you are pregnant." He tucked the scanner back into his belt. "I'm going to need to consult

with the High Justice, but your friend in red is right. Taking an alien child from its world is a much bigger deal than a simple no-contact violation. I'll let you get used to the news and return this evening." The general's serious expression transformed into a wry smile. "And Specialist Carr —"

"Yeah, yeah." I waved my hand absently, my mind still reeling. "Chip. You know where to find me."

The general laughed. "That, too. I was going to say, 'Congratulations.'"

CHAPTER 40

I still couldn't absorb what had happened. There had to be some mistake.

The general and his soldiers left to joyous cheers, for they had brought the news that Bánalfar was expecting an heir. Bemused smiles kept lifting and falling on the faces of all the Shororato. I guessed they weren't used to being greeted with such adoration.

Shale slipped quietly away in the commotion that followed, so it was just Valemar and me who retired to the anteroom. I leaned into him as his hands traced the length of my back. "I can't be pregnant," I said again.

My cheek buzzed against Valemar's chest as he laughed. "What will it take for you to believe it? A swollen belly?"

"Desire alone can cause the swollen belly of a false pregnancy," I said. Mary Tudor of England had suffered two of them.

"The child kicking?"

The child kicking. I pressed a hand against my stomach. If the scan was accurate, there was a little life in there that one day I would feel move.

"Huh." My head bounced with Valemar's huff. "Do Earth women not feel sick with early pregnancy? You've been ill a lot lately"

Ill. "Oh, my God! The blood." My stomach rolled with fear. "I drank the heichdar blood. What if I've harmed the child?"

Valemar's hand embraced my head. "Hush. Did you not hear the heartbeat? Nice and strong."

It had been. And when could you first hear the heartbeat? How far along was I? "When did I last bleed?" I asked Valemar, raising my eyes to his.

"I don't know." His eyes darted from side to side as he thought. "I don't think you have since you've returned."

Then it was possible I could already be two months pregnant. "How did I not notice?"

Valemar kissed the top of my head. "There have been many things to distract you. It wasn't something you were looking for."

Hoped for. I had hoped. And prayed. And offered my blood.

And my prayers had been answered. My fingers traced circles along my abdomen. Pregnant. I was pregnant.

For now.

Valemar felt me tremble. "What new concern steals your strength?"

"What if I lose it?"

Valemar lifted my chin and kissed me. "Then we will try again. But I don't think you need to worry. You fell from the moon. You've driven back the outsiders. And now you have created new life."

"Technically that order is wrong."

"Yes, but had we known you were with child, I'd have never let you call the Shororato."

That was true. I never would have risked Valemar's child. And the attempts on my life would have continued. I hugged my husband

and rubbed my cheek against his chest. "I get to stay. I get to stay and give you a child."

Valemar laughed lightly. "Sometimes prayers do get answered."

General Creskin returned just before dinner though he declined to stay. "The details will be worked out over the next few days, but the High Justice has agreed that, due to the circumstances, you will remain on Teridun Four."

"Crenfor," I corrected. "The inhabitants call this planet Crenfor."

The general chuckled. "Which is why they've recommended that you be appointed the Council ambassador to this planet. Due to the Hormani interference, Teridun … Crenfor is about to take its place within the Astrun Federation. Your experience both as a protocol specialist and as an inhabitant of this planet make you the perfect candidate."

"So she'll be able to communicate with other planets?" Valemar asked. He squeezed my hand hopefully.

"Uh, no." The general didn't meet my gaze. "She will officially be listed as having perished with the crew of the *Palmas Cove*. Your planet is not ready to fully join the Federation and will continue to have protected status. Probably for the next several hundred years. Until you've developed technology on your own that will allow you to travel within space."

I bit my lip. My parents would never know that I had survived. That they had another grandchild. Or that I was married and happy.

Valemar squeezed my hand again.

But this was an outcome I could live with. I had called the Shororato fully expecting to give up everything, taking only my tattoos and my wedding mark with me. And now, I got to stay. I had a new job. And a new life was growing inside me.

The general rose. "I don't understand why you did it … Ambassador Carr."

"Carbrev," I corrected.

"You could have lived here undetected. If not for your miraculous pregnancy, you'd already be on a ship bound for Krajiny Five."

I looked at Valemar and smiled. "Doing nothing was not something that the daughter of kings could have lived with."

The general frowned. "The what?"

"The one who fell from the moon," I said, finally claiming the title that I'd hated. "She had a job to do. And doing the hard thing is always the right thing to do."

Sometimes it just took a while to get there. Especially if it was too fantastic to believe.